NORTH BEACH GIRL

Erin is tired of being an artist's model. She's tired of
working. Jobs are such a drag. The night she quits her latest
modeling gig, she goes back to the pad she shares with her
girlfriend, Bruno, and their roommates, Lilly and Marian,
and starts drinking. They all live in San Francisco's North
Beach, where nights are filled with bar hopping and Beat
poetry. Hanging out. This night she meets Riley. He's
looking for a nude model but Erin turns him down. He
follows her home anyway. Bruno takes an immediate dislike
to Erin's new drinking friend, and threatens him away. But
Erin keeps running into him. And then Erin's rich
grandmother dies, and everything changes. Why is Bruno
now so nice to Riley? What are the secrets that Lilly and
Marian suddenly keep? And what world does Erin really
belong to after all?

SCANDAL ON THE SAND

Hobart can't figure Karen out. The sex was great last night,
so why is she in such a sour mood this morning? All he
wants is a hearty breakfast, but she insists on a walk along
the beach. When they find a live, beached whale on the
shore, all she can think to do is try to save it. The cop who
shows up, Mulford, has got the right idea, according to
Hobart—he wants to kill it and have it towed away. But
before long some onlookers arrive. There's Joe Bonniano, a
hitman waiting for his pickup to arrive and whisk him to
freedom. Fredric Langfield, has-been actor and drug addict,
waiting for his fix. Earle Kavanaugh, nudie photographer,
waiting for his big break, knowing his career is now behind
him. Hobart, waiting for Karen.... And while they wait,
Mulford prepares for the kill.

JOHN TRINIAN BIBLIOGRAPHY
(1933-2008)

The Big Grab (1960; reprinted as Any Number Can Win, 1963)

North Beach Girl (1960; reprinted as Strange Lovers, 1967)

The Savage Breast (1961)

Scratch a Thief (1961; also published as Once a Thief
as by Zekial Marko, 1961)

House of Evil (1962)

A Game of Flesh (1963)

Scandal on the Sand (1964)

North Beach Girl

Scandal on the Sand

Two Novels by

JOHN TRINIAN

STARK
HOUSE

Stark House Press • Eureka California

NORTH BEACH GIRL / SCANDAL ON THE SAND

Published by Stark House Press
1315 H Street
Eureka, CA 95501
griffinskye3@sbcglobal.net
www.starkhousepress.com

ISBN: 1-933586-55-9
ISBN-13: 978-1-933586-55-7

Cover design and layout by Mark Shepard, www.SHEPGRAPHICS.COM
Proofreading by Rick Ollerman

First Stark House Press Edition: May 2014
FIRST EDITION

Contents

Contents

In Pursuit of a Pleasant Oblivion
by Rick Ollerman

In January of 1950, the Fawcett company expanded on their magazine and distributing background and emulated Robert de Graff's Pocket Books line by bringing out (after three non-fiction trial balloon titles), the first paperback original for Gold Medal books. *The Persian Cat* by John Flagg (real name John Gearon) helped set the tone for one of Gold Medal's objectives: to not shy away from more "realistic" genre fiction (or what passed for it at the time). They wanted to publish great stories that didn't hide behind the action. They wanted to show the sex and the vices that readers experienced in real life. Sometimes this included drug use, and it certainly featured booze. Sometimes lots and lots of booze.

One of the most realistic of the Gold Medal writers was John Trinian, who wrote deftly defined characters without shying away from any of the popular sins of the time. His seven books were published from the late fifties through the early sixties and reflected a sort of pre-hippie, Beatnik atmosphere of sex, drugs and alcohol (and jazz). Some of his books take a more traditional storytelling approach, like 1960's *The Big Grab*, a heist novel, but his writing really shines in his Gold Medal offerings where he essentially creates a cast of characters, endows them deeply with individual and non-clichéd attributes, and lets them react against each other in order to advance the story.

Scandal on the Sand (1964), his final Gold Medal novel, is perhaps his definitive work. It shows the interactions of small, disparate groups of people, all empty and searching in their own way, brought together at a point in time by nothing less than a sleeping whale stranded on a beach. The whale's presence is an unanticipated accident, the kind of one in a million lightning strike that takes place every day, only not to you or anyone you know. But it happens somewhere, though, and to someone else. It's not necessarily real, but it's possible. This is the twilight land that Trinian explores.

Though he passed away in 2008, much of who John Trinian was is still unknown to the general public. His books show him as a "literary" writer whose works could stand outside the genre, who could belong to a market beyond that of the PBO landscape. They also give us an authorly stepchild of John O'Hara and Jack Kerouac, a writer who knew what his characters wanted and delighted in showing us how they interacted with each other, their relationships determining their often less-than-happy fates.

The name "John Trinian" was a pseudonym for a man called Zekial Marko. The Marko byline is best known for work on the big and small screens even though the number of "John Trinian" books outnumber actual "Zekial Marko" screenwriting credits. And who was Zekial Marko? Upon his death in 2008 it came to light that his real name, his original name, was Marvin Leroy Schmoker, a man whose pre-Marko years are seemingly obscured by mystery.

In 1961 he published his fifth book (after *A Game of Flesh*, 1959; *The Big Grab*, 1960; *North Beach Girl*, 1960 and *The Savage Breast*, 1961), called *Scratch a Thief*. Said to be based on autobiographical events, it is the story of a one-time thief, now married and trying to go straight. He lets himself get drawn into one last heist by his brother, a career criminal, and the rest of his gang. Were these pages reflections of the exploits of a young Marvin Leroy Schmoker? Were these the actions that led to a change of identity and vocation for the newly named Zekial Marko?

We do not know. Marko published two more books as John Trinian, *House of Evil* (1962) and *Scandal On the Sand*, and then seemingly ended his publishing career.

Although all but *House of Evil* were later reprinted, Marko most likely made more money from Hollywood than he did from the Trinian books. In 1963, his second novel, *The Big Grab*, was filmed as *Any Number Can Win*, starring French actors Alain Delon and Jean Gabin. This is the story of an ex-con, one of the old-school professionals, fresh out of jail and needing one last score so he can take his wife and child and retire once and for all. All he needs for the perfect crime, or so he thinks, is someone he can trust. For this he turns to his old cell mate, a much younger man who, like the veteran thief, believes he just needs a reliable partner.

They have the score, they know the plan, and a last minute impulse has an effect on the final outcome. Or does it? Marko/Trinian leave us with a masterful open ended crime story that manages to satisfy the reader without necessarily connecting all the dots.

Later Marko wrote the screenplay for the 1965 film version of *Scratch a Thief*, retitled *Once a Thief*, and directed by Ralph Nelson. It starred Alain Delon; a young, shrieking Ann-Margret; Jack Palance and Marko himself as Luke, a mumbling, hip-speaking barfly later arrested for murder. His deadpan delivery and thick black mustache seem to belie the elegance of his written words. The film also featured veteran actor Tony Musante, who would continue to cross paths with Marko's Hollywood career.

In 1974, Musante became the star of the televison series *Toma*, based on the real life career of a narcotics cop known for doing whatever it took to take down the bad guys, including dressing up in all manner of disguises. The real David Toma made cameo appearances in each episode. *Toma* only lasted for one season, canceled after Musante wanted the network to change the format to a series of fewer but longer movies-of-the-week. In that one season, though, Marko wrote two episodes: "The Street" and "A Funeral for Max Berlin." After Musante left the show, it was retooled with Robert Blake as the new star (and a cockatoo named Fred). The show was *Baretta*.

That same year, Marko wrote one of the best episodes of another one-season show, the cult classic *Kolchak: The Night Stalker*. The original *Kolchak* movie and its sequel, both written by Richard Matheson, broke viewer records when they first appeared on television. Star Darren McGavin was reluctant to be involved with a weekly version of the show, fearing that there were only so many supernatural mystery stories that could be told week after week. Ultimately, McGavin was proved right, and many of the season's episodes devolved to low-budget special effects shades of those original movies, but a few of the early episodes stand out, chief among them Marko's own "The Zombie," the series' second episode. Truly creepy and suspenseful, it was written with David Chase, future creator of HBO's *The Sopranos*.

Back when Marko was working on *Toma*, a young Stephen J. Cannell wrote an episode with a character he called "Rockford," based on an idea by PBO author and television legend Roy Huggins (creator of classic shows like *Maverick, 77 Sunset Strip, The Bold Ones* and *The Fugitive*). The script was rejected but Cannell and Huggins rewrote it and eventually developed it as *The Rockford Files*, starring James Garner, which went on to air for six seasons, canceled only after an executive change at the top of the network. Both *Rockford* and *Baretta* lived on after their initial runs to great success in syndication.

In 1975, though, Marko wrote his own episode for *The Rockford Files* (from a story by "John Thomas James," a pseudonym for Roy Huggins) and starring guess who? Tony Musante, who played Charlie Harris, a one-time chiseler wanted for possibly murdering his wealthy wife. Did he do it? We don't really know, in another example of Marko/Trinian's willingness to leave the viewer/reader with an ambiguous ending. Marko himself had a role in this episode, playing Dr. "Gabe" Gabriel, complete with deadpan delivery, thick brush mustache and cardigan sweater.

To complete his Hollywood career, Marko appeared in a film produced and written by his artist brother, Kenn Davis, called *Nightmare in Blood* (1977). The film is about a vampire and his cohorts kidnapping guests from a horror convention and the two men and a woman that try to stop him.

Clearly the person behind the "John Trinian" name is a tough one to know from a distance. What is the truth behind the criminal background of Marvin Leroy Schmoker, and what prompted the change to the more exotic-sounding "Zekial Marko"? Other than the Gold Medal reprint of the Ace Double *Scratch a Thief* (reprinted with the same title as the movie version, *Once a Thief*), all of his books appeared under the "John Trinian" name. Once can't help but notice the beginning of "Trinian" is "tri"–deriving from the Greek word for "three," which could easily represent the three names of Schmoker, Marko and Trinian.

In any case, the Trinian books are full of unique style, reflecting a deep observance of the people around the San Francisco scene in the early to mid–sixties. His ability to create characters that personify the vices and lost voices of the time and place them in plots that are more organic than formulaic in nature. They go beyond most PBO and genre fiction. In *North Beach Girl*, Trinian voices the character and attitude of not only his protagonist, but of an entire group of people living in that time:

Why bother with it? What was the sense of it? She only received thirty dollars a week, and the only advantage was that she only had to work eleven hours of the week. But was it worth it? Of course, she had been able to live on that amount, had even been able to put enough aside to live for a while without working. But what was the sense of it all? Who the hell wanted to work? Working got you nowhere. It was just like voting. Your one lousy vote didn't *really* count. The system certainly wouldn't collapse if you voted against it. So why try? Why work?

No matter what job you were performing, the system wouldn't care if you walked out on it. There would always be another sucker to take your place. And Erin had had jobs enough to uphold her way of thinking. Carhop, waitress, usherette, receptionist, cocktail waitress, file clerk, and now artists' model. She had walked out on them all at one time or another. And no one had missed her. Life had been able to stagger on without her shoulder to the wheel. So, all jobs were the same. She hated them. And now she had had her fill of them and she would do absolutely nothing. And perhaps, while her money lasted, she would be able to figure out a way to be done with working for good. She remembered how rotten it had been in Los Angeles after her friend Bunny had left their apartment. She had felt suddenly cut off and alone, the apartment a constant reminder of how life had always been for her. Empty. Life had been an aimless chore for her to face. But in Los Angeles, where she had known only a few people, it had been more unbearable than usual. She had believed that she had returned to her home town, San Francisco, to find a job and settle down to something worthwhile, but now she knew that wasn't true. She had left Los Angeles because she was afraid. And her present situation hadn't settled her at all. She was still bored, and still afraid.

Disillusioned, sexually confused, Erin gets through each day looking forward to the release of booze and different company. Trinian pairs her both with a cynical yet rabidly ambitious lesbian named Bruno as well as the opposite: a free-spirited man known only as Riley, who wants to paint her. This trio sets the stage that serves as more or less a common background in much of Trinian's work: three primary characters, with one at the center and two reflecting in different ways off each other. He never strays far from sex, drugs, music and/or alcohol. The playing off of each character's personality with their addictions and obsessions goes to the core of each book.

Perhaps nowhere is this more apparent than his book *Scandal on the Sand*, quite possibly the only PBO book ever written with passages written from the perspective of a stranded whale who finds himself caught up on shore:

With half a mind he wondered where the rest of the herd had gone. It had been quite a while since he had seen another whale. Somewhere during the night, migrating south along the coast from their last headland guide point, he had become separated. However, he wasn't too concerned. He felt safe. He had traveled the Arctic-Baja run many times before and he knew what landmarks to watch for. So, once again feeling playful, he wallowed and whisked from the surface to the deep, establishing an even four-minute diving rhythm, his huge back glistening as the black-green waters broke and roiled and foamed in his wake.

[..]The whale gave a massive sigh, exhaling loudly, and his flukes wriggled halfheartedly in the sand. His eyes blinked slowly, watching the dawn and the calming waters. One gull settled a few feet from the whale, clacked his orange beak and watched. The whale gave a deep sigh, closed his eyes and slept.

This sets the stage for Trinian's orbiting groups of characters to begin appearing. In this, his final book, Trinian goes beyond his usual group of three main characters and brings us twice as many groups—each small, each containing its own individuals—than his other books. In *Scandal*, he shows his considerable understanding of the natures and cravings and attitudes of different people as they find themselves, for wildly different reasons, sharing common space on a lonely stretch of beach with, of all things, a beached and sleeping marine mammal.

Trinian depicts the uncertainty of youth, the re-birth of a drug-addled mind, the always bored and always seeking dissatisfaction of a second generation born to money, a perpetually lost drifter, a man on the run, and the catalyst for them all: a sociopathic authority figure bent on the destruction of others and the assertion of his own authority. As a novel, this adds up to an intricately plotted character study, littered with equal parts happiness, sorrow and redemption. An ambitious and wholly successful novel, one unlike any other Gold Medal or PBO you're likely to find.

If *Scratch a Thief* was based on an autobiographical story, it's fair to wonder how much some of the common elements in Trinian's work were also based on a kernel of real life. Trinian writes with depth not only about thievery but wanting to get out of it, one way or another; he writes of erotic and homosexual subcultures, the dissatisfaction of the idle rich, and the damning yet unavoidable tightrope of survivalist hard-core drinking. To the extent that any of his work had its basis in his own life, Trinian's had to have been an interesting one, to say the least. Traveling in more than one of these circles would seem daunting and self-destructive to most. Perhaps the truth is Trinian existed himself more as a figure on the periphery of these worlds, more so than as an active participant—we don't really know.

In any case, what's clear in all his work is the deep observance of his fellow man. He writes female characters as well as male, of personality types across the board, but his real specialty is writing of those existing on the fringe. His characters tap dance along the fine line of survival and failure, often driven to do what they do not because they want to, but because they have to. It's simply who they are. These crevices of motivation, spawned by the traps of his characters' own lives, are where the real magic of Trinian's writing takes place.

You may not know these people, but you know of them; you may not see these people, but you suspect their presence. What Trinian does is show you that it's all true, every bit of it: the good and the bad, the happy and the miserable. He works both sides of the street, as well as the up and the down—class and society may confer privilege, but there's always a price, often a tragic one, typically unseen.

There's not one without the other, or, if there is, it doesn't make for a good story, at least not of the sort John Trinian gives us. And for tightly plotted, deeply characterized stories, not many have ever done it better than Trinian.

Whoever he was.

Littleton, NH
November, 2013

North Beach Girl

By John Trinian

CHAPTER ONE

Erin covered herself with the pale green robe and sat on the empty packing crate by the narrow barred window. She cupped her chin in her hand and gloomily watched the summer fog settle intimately in the early night over the San Francisco hills. She was tired. She dragged slowly on her cigarette and shivered.

The storage room where she sat was small and cramped. Rough wood frame bins were fixed against the wall opposite the single window. The bins were carelessly filled with stacks of classified stretcher bars and limp bolts of unfinished linen. Over the curtained doorway an unshaded electric light burned like a glob of orange wax and cast smoky red shadows along the brick walls. Beyond the curtain Erin could hear the low rumble of voices and the grating sounds of approaching footsteps.

It was time. The smoke break was over. She pinched out her cigarette and returned to the other room, hugging the robe about her body, her naked feet padding softly.

It was a dreary room, long, low-ceilinged, and brightly lit with a double row of overhead lamps. Several finished paintings were exhibited on one wall. There was the warm taste of oils and paint thinner in the air. The tall windows were kept closed and tightly shaded. The heating system purred in one corner. The mingled odors of paints and canvas were sickening to Erin and she wrinkled her nose. She turned her back to the room. The artists were hunched over their sketch boards, half hidden behind their guillotine-shaped easels.

"Are we all set now?"

"I'm still stiff," Erin said.

An old man, one of the senior members of the class, pushed out his thin wrist and looked at his watch. "You have only fifteen minutes more to go."

Erin nodded, hardly listening to him. She was bored and restless and her back muscles were still stiff.

The group sat in a rough curve around the brightly lit platform. Erin mounted the platform, squinting under the spotlights, and removed the robe, letting it slip graciously from her bare shoulders. She settled on the couch and watched herself in the grey filmy posing mirror to one side of her, studying her position and moving into the now familiar pose. The lights were hot. The air in the room was stuffy.

Erin was young, and even now, as she studied herself in the mirror, she realized that she was beautiful. Her thick brown hair fell carelessly down to her shoulders, her waist was narrow, the legs were long and perfect. She had misty grey eyes with dark lashes and eyebrows. The expression on her face was one of boredom.

Eyes glanced at her now, studying, critical eyes, without eagerness. She had become used to posing by now. In the beginning there had been a certain amount of embarrassment, but after almost three months of posing, it was a tiresome chore for her to sit for hours before men and old ladies. She had ceased to think of her figure as something to be desired. During the sessions, it was merely an object to be sketched or painted. She obeyed the students' suggestions, lowering her head, moving her legs a shade to the left.

An old woman with popped blue eyes and a flowery smock looked up from her board. "Move your shoulders just a bit more to the left, Miss Howard." She studied the effect for a long moment, closing one blue eye and cocking her head. "And your hand a little more towards the arm. That's it. Thank you."

Under the overhead lights Erin's figure was a dramatic study of shadowing. She held her head lowered and her eyes cast down. The room was overly warm. She resigned herself to another fifteen minutes without movement. She listened to the rough charcoal sticks and the lead pencils scrape on the paper as the artists hurriedly sketched her figure.

Why bother with it? What was the sense of it? She only received thirty dollars a week, and the only advantage was that she only had to work eleven hours of the week. But was it worth it? Of course, she had been able to live on that amount, had even been able to put enough aside to live for a while without working. But what was the sense of it all? Who the hell wanted to work? Working got you nowhere. It was just like voting. Your one lousy vote didn't *really* count. The system certainly wouldn't collapse if you voted against it. So why try? Why work?

No matter what job you were performing, the system wouldn't care if you walked out on it. There would always be another sucker to take your place. And Erin had had jobs enough to uphold her way of thinking. Carhop, waitress, usherette, receptionist, cocktail waitress, file clerk, and now artists' model. She had walked out on them all at one time or another. And no one had missed her. Life had been able to stagger on without her shoulder to the wheel. So, all jobs were the same. She hated them. And now she had had her fill of them and she would do absolutely nothing. And perhaps, while her money lasted, she would be able to figure out a way to be done with working for good. She remembered how rotten it had been in Los Angeles after her friend Bunny had left their apartment. She had felt suddenly cut off and alone, the apartment a constant reminder of how life had always been for her. Empty. Life had been an aimless chore for her to face. But in Los Angeles, where she had known only a few people, it had been more unbearable than usual. She had believed that she had returned to her home town, San Francisco, to find a job and settle down to something worthwhile, but now she knew that wasn't true. She had left Los Angeles because she was afraid. And her present situation hadn't settled her at all. She was still bored, and still afraid.

"Miss Howard?" It was a sickly thin-faced kid with a straggly red beard and broken Mexican sandals. He was looking at her with dead narcotic-like eyes, the lids half closed and unblinking. "Head up a little, man. You got it."

She glowered at him with hate for a moment, then looked back to her hand. Her back was aching and she wished that the period was over. It seemed unusually long tonight. Especially tonight. Tonight was the night that she had decided to quit, to rid herself of the burden of work. She wanted to drift, jobless, contented, to look for something that would satisfy her.

The electric clock on the wall showed ten minutes past nine. She stifled a yawn. She was aware of the students' eyes on her, their hands sketching on their boards. The thought of them made her sick. Bruno was right about them. Bruno had said that they had no *real* talent—and Erin knew that she was right. None of them was worth the oil and canvas they wasted. All except one—Merlin, the old man with the big laugh, and big hands, the drunken painter who had done a huge oil of Erin and had sold it to Bruno two months ago. But Merlin hadn't been a student at the classes. He had dropped in one night to visit with Mr. Richard, the class instructor, and he had hired Erin for private sittings outside the class. The finished painting, titled *Merlin Sees Woman*, was still on display at Bruno's Sedge-Hammer Gallery.

"Time's up. That's all."

The session had finally come to an end, and Erin's arms and neck were tingling. She grabbed her robe and slipped it quickly over her. She returned to the cramped storage room, brusquely ignoring the words of thanks from the students, and lit the stub end of her cigarette. Again she sat on the empty crate. She waited until the building was empty. In the beginning a few of the male students had waited for her in the brick courtyard to ask her out for a drink. It had irritated her to see them there. So she usually waited for ten minutes until she was sure that anyone waiting would be discouraged.

The fog was becoming thicker. The moaning sounds of the foghorns in the bay seemed more muffled. Here and there the misty glow of a light showed through the fog.

She dressed hurriedly, pushing her long, careless mass of hair away from her face and hastily clipping it behind her. Then she pulled her black sweater over her and grabbed her hooded canvas jacket. She left the room, not bothering to screw the orange light out, and walked through the darkened classroom. She stopped at Mr. Richard's cubbyhole office and knocked on the pebbled glass panel.

"Hello, Miss Howard." The old man's smile was pleasant enough, and his false teeth glittered in the office light. He drew a pink slip of paper from a ledger book and held it out to her. "I suppose you'll be wanting your check. It's all made out."

"Thank you," Erin said.

The old man wet his lips and fumbled with his wrinkled hands. "You'll be with us for the next session? It starts two weeks from now...."

"No."

Mr. Richard looked at her for a moment. "Has your work here been unsatisfactory?"

"It's been all right."

"You've been bothered by one of our students?"

"No one's bothered me."

There was a silence.

"Well, we'll certainly miss you. Good models are pretty hard to come by. And you're a very good model. You're popular with the students. They like you."

Erin didn't answer him.

"I see. Well, Miss Howard, any time you need a little money and your nights are free, you just give me a ring. Don't hesitate to call me. I can always find a spot for you. Remember that, won't you?"

"Okay. I'll remember."

"And if I have any reason to get in touch with you...."

"You have my number."

"Then you're still at...."

"I'm living with Bruno Snider."

"Yes... of course...."

It was there, as it always was—old Richard's eyes saddened and he looked disappointed, even hurt. That look was always there whenever Erin mentioned Bruno.

Erin didn't smile. The hell with the old buzzard's disappointment. The hell with everyone. She nodded an abrupt good-bye and left the office, walking down the long tiled hallway to the street.

The brick courtyard was empty. No students were lounging against the wall. She supposed they had all been informed of her special coolness towards them. Across the street a few apartment house lights were lit and she could see shadowy figures moving against the drawn blinds. A man passed by, walking a small dog, the training leash jingling, the pawnails of the dog rattling on the wet pavement. The foghorns were sounding from the bay. The air tasted of wet streets and shrubbery.

Why do they resent Bruno? What was the matter with them all? It was no business of theirs what Bruno did with her life. Why did they have to shove their smug faces into Erin's business?

She began to walk down the steep hill towards North Beach. It was at times like this, when she sensed the righteous resentment of others directed at her, that her otherwise slipping convictions strengthened. It was at times like this that she felt justifiably rebellious, and the more resentment people felt towards her, the more convinced she became that she was right. She certainly didn't want the phony alternatives that others were trying to shove on her.

Erin smiled secretly to herself.

CHAPTER TWO

Erin stepped from the cable car where it turned west from Powell at Jackson Street. She walked the rest of the way. Vortigern's Bar was near the church which was a half-block west of Upper Grant Avenue. The traffic on Columbus Avenue, the main street of the North Beach district, was heavy, practically bumper to bumper, moving slowly in the fog. The shops were still open. The street was well-lighted and the restaurants were full, even though it was far past the usual dinner hour. A sweet and oily smell of cooking came from the open brass doors of the Arabic bar. The coffee houses were open. She heard the irritating sounds of car horns along the Upper Grant Avenue.

At Vortigern's she half hoped to find Marian or Lilly, the roommates who shared the garage with Erin and Bruno. She didn't expect to find Bruno because the Sedge-Hammer Gallery stayed open until eleven. It was only ten.

Vortigern's was packed, as usual, but she didn't see anyone that she knew in the crowd. Tobacco smoke hung in the large gloomy room thicker than the fog outside. A small jazz group was resting in the far corner while the crowds at the tables peered through the bluish haze. There were many bearded faces. There were the rancid odors of cheap wine and damp sawdust. Bizarre paintings were on the walls.

Erin found an empty stool at the far end of the bar, directly in front of the draft handles. She ordered a beer.

Fully awake for the first time since morning, she thought of Bruno Snider. Lately she was aware of an unwanted struggle inside herself, and she was no longer as comfortably self-assured as she felt she ought to be.

Her first date, at the age of fourteen, had been with a boy of sixteen she had met through mutual friends. Foolishly, she had told the boy she was sixteen, and, even at that time, her figure was developed enough for him to believe her. In fact, he had even thought her to be older than sixteen. The boy had been tall and well-muscled for his age and had boasted of a reputation as a tough kid. The night of their one and only time together he had borrowed a friend's car and had taken Erin to a movie in the Marina district, then later to Aquatic Park. She had been curious and even somewhat excited at first. But when she had been pulled roughly to him and kissed in an insistent and obvious manner, she had felt herself freeze, and her first tender stirrings of excitement turned to fear. She had fought him off, had left the car and, full of terror and sudden revulsion, had run down the sandy stretch of beach. There, after straightening her clothes and washing her feverish face with the cold salt water of the bay, she sat alone on the stone walkway and cried.

Perhaps she had been too young and sensitive. At any rate she had intended to forget the incident and pretend nothing had happened. But then, six months later, she had her first experience with her stepfather. She was fifteen at the time and that had been a more nerve-wracking experience than the first, so she had ended it there.

She ordered another dark beer and lit a cigarette, allowing herself to unwind slowly, and she could feel the tension from her working hours peel from her body layer by layer. Even the frenzied babble of Vortigern's Bar was relaxing to her.

"Want a beer, Howard?"

It was the thin-faced kid from the art class, slouching on the damp bar top and looking at her with his sleepy unblinking eyes. When Erin didn't move away or make any sign that she had heard him, he ordered two beers and paid for them. The bartender pushed a dark beer next to Erin's elbow.

"I didn't want one."

The kid shrugged and picked up his glass, turning away from her with a note of complaint in his voice. "Okay man, so drink it anyway. What difference does it make? It's a free beer, isn't it? So don't complain."

"I'm not going to pay for it by talking to you or listening to you, so why don't you shove off and take your beer with you? Go beat your chest somewhere else."

He didn't move away. He had propped his elbows on the bar top and the cheap corduroy jacket was becoming dark from the beer puddles. He didn't seem to notice this. He was busy studying his grey face in the bar mirror behind the draft handles.

"You're not very friendly, Howard."

"That's right, I'm not very friendly."

"Well... I've seen you around."

"I wonder why."

"I've seen you with Bruno Snider," he said slowly.

"Is it any of your business?"

Erin moved her hand to her hair pushing the straying strands away from her face. She turned on her stool and stared angrily at the farthest corner of the bar. Why did she have to go through situations like this? Why come to Vortigern's in the first place? She should have gone straight to the gallery. She might have known that something like this would happen. If she were with Bruno it never would have happened. Bruno had toughness. And so did Marian. But Erin and Lilly didn't seem to have it in them to be as hard and direct as Bruno or Marian were.

She turned again on her stool, forcing herself, and looked directly at the kid. Her face was slightly flushed and her misty grey eyes were glittering as though in a fever. "I told you to shove off. I meant it. You can take your lousy beer with you."

"Don't be a meany," the kid said lightly.

Erin's voice was even and low, but insistent. "If you don't get away from me I'm going to throw this beer into your skinny face."

He nodded, drank the beer in two or three swallows, then left the bar. Erin sat calmly, outwardly undisturbed, but inside she was shaking with fear and anger. She didn't like to act tough. It wasn't typical of her. But she felt she had to prove something, no matter how she felt about it.

It was ten-thirty by the electric clock behind the bar.

She ordered another beer, her third, and lit another cigarette. The bartender thumped the draft handle and pushed the beer in front of her. Erin returned to her thoughts, sipping the beer and waiting for the gallery to close.

Erin had known Bruno Snider for only two days when she was invited to stay at the reconverted garage to save rent costs. But that hadn't been the only reason why she had accepted the offer. She had been attracted to Bruno.

Two months ago the old painter Merlin had brought his painting of Erin to the Sedge-Hammer Gallery. Bruno had bought it, and then had inquired about the model. That had been Erin's first contact with Bruno. There had been a lunch together in a small restaurant on Fisherman's Wharf, then later a pint bottle of Scotch at Bruno's reconverted garage.

Bruno had felt her out to see if she was agreeable, and then she had invited Erin to live at the garage and cut down on her expenses. The rent would be free, and there was plenty of room. Marian and Lilly paid more than enough for food expenses, so Erin's share of food costs would be very small. Erin had accepted the offer on impulse.

Why was she afraid of Bruno? She didn't know. At first she had felt that it was safer and much easier for herself not to question her fears.

Bruno was a violent personality. She acted as if she owned a person. And Erin found herself understanding Bruno less every day.

But now there was the tiresome babble of the voices behind her, and she didn't bother to turn on her stool to see the faces. They would be the same. Ever since she had left Los Angeles, three and a half months ago, she had been living in the neighborhood and drinking in the noisy beat bars, and she knew that for the most part the faces would be tired, hollow, downcast, half-hopeful and watching one another. There was always a dark theatrical note in the air. Everyone seemed to be waiting for something. Erin sat quite still. The jazz group in the far corner stopped drinking and began to play. No one moved or turned their eyes to the direction of the music. It was as if no new sound had been introduced.

Erin left the bar when the clock said eleven o'clock. Despite the heavy fog she could make out the spotlit, simply lettered sign of the Sedge-Hammer Gallery hanging out over the street a block north from Vortigern's doorway. She had to press herself against the building to pass a knot of people who were lounging in front of a coffee house. Arms jostled her. Two men, wearing overcoats and bow ties, were standing in a doorway drinking from a bottle masked with a grocery sack.

"Take it easy, baby."

"She's all right. She's all right by me."

She dodged traffic and stood by the gallery window. Marian appeared alone at her side, weaving drunkenly and not recognizing Erin at first, then stopping and making a half-circling turn. She stared at Erin, then her thick mouth broke into a smile. Her short dark hair was damp from the fog.

"Have you seen Lilly?"

"No."

"I think maybe she passed right along here somewhere," Marian muttered thickly. "At least, I think she did. She didn't pass me going the *other* way."

"This street?"

"Sure. We been sitting in Bruno's car, drinking, goofing around."

"She might get picked up," Erin said. "You'd better find her."

"Oh yeah, I'll find her. I'm not worried. Like a St. Bernard dog with a keg around my neck, I'll find her. Woof woof. Hey, did you just get off work?"

"Yes."

"Well, I'll see you later at the garage."

Marian disappeared down the street, erased by the wall of fog. Erin stood by the window. Across the street, vague and unreal in the fog, she saw a man with a guitar sitting on a motorcycle watching her. He saluted with his free hand and waved to her. Erin turned her back to him and looked through the window.

She saw Bruno standing before a painting, tall, dark haired, dressed in an expensive suit. She wore no lipstick and her dark eyes were naturally accented with black lashes and eyebrows. Her face was strong, but appealing and strangely beautiful. Usually she seemed more cunning and handsome, but when she was at work she acted quite pleasant and seemed to be a shrewd businesswoman rather than a hard and selfish person. To an outsider, Bruno would probably be thought of as a dedicated career woman, sophisticated and aloof, darkly handsome and self-assured.

There were two other people in the shop. One a stout, pigeon-breasted woman with a pillbox hat and sunglasses, and the other a delicate looking young man with thin features and short pale hair. The way he stood and glared obstinately at Bruno showed that he was probably drunk. An empty cigarette holder was stuck defiantly in the corner of his mouth.

When the first customer, the woman, left the shop, Erin entered and nodded to Bruno. Bruno's reply was brief; then she turned her attention to the pale young man, her face suddenly hard and her eyes flat with anger.

"I thought I told you to get the hell out of here."

The pale young man had a cultured voice. "Why don't you throw me out? I'm not doing anything. I came in here to look at paintings, not to be insulted by you."

"Get the hell out of here, you slimy sonofabitch."

"This is a public place.... And I'm public."

"You sure as hell are." Bruno grabbed him by the lapels of his jacket and thrust him through the open door. She slammed the door behind him and locked it. Then she turned calmly and walked to her desk at the rear of the shop. "That bastard gives me a pain. You should have been here when he first came in with his friend. Both of them oohing and ahing and touching the goddam paintings with their goddam fingers." She sat behind the desk, turned on a green-shaded brass lamp, and lit a cigarette. She spoke without looking at Erin. "Did you just get off work? You're late. I expected to see you a half hour ago."

"I stopped for a drink."

"Oh? Where?"

"Vortigern's."

"Don't you like the Mad Mummy?"

"Sure, but Vortigern's was on the way." Erin actually didn't like the Mad

Mummy at all. Vortigern's was more relaxed, more easy to get to, and better lighted. One thing that had always bothered Erin about the Mummy was its dimness. "You don't mind if I go into Vortigern's now and then, do you? I don't think it's so bad a place."

"Me? Why should I mind?" Bruno smiled softly. "I'm not your keeper."

Erin smiled then.

Bruno returned to her desk. She opened a walnut box of index cards and started to pull an occasional card from the file and pile them on the green blotter.

"I quit my job tonight," Erin said after a minute.

Bruno's eyebrows lifted. "Why? Somebody make a hard time for you up there?"

"No."

"Are you planning on cutting out?"

"No. I just don't dig working. I never did."

Bruno nodded, then moved her attention to the piled cards before her. She didn't say anything more, and Erin had the impression that she had been dismissed for the time being. She went to the front window and leaned against a marble shape. Shuffling hunched figures blurred past in the fog. The motorcycle across the street popped and roared, the rider with the guitar gunning it; then it skidded into the street with a sharp yelp of tires and roared out of view. A minute later a pair of policemen stalked past, looking troubled and unsure of themselves.

Erin thought of the delicate-faced man with the cultured voice. She wondered how bothersome he had really been. She moved through the shop, looking at the canvases and the framed drawings. The largest of the canvases was the study of herself, *Merlin Sees Woman*. It was privately lighted and situated near the desk.

"You like that painting, don't you?"

"Yes," Erin said.

Erin smiled and unconsciously touched the ends of her hair at the shoulders. She looked at Bruno, into the dark ambitious eyes, not saying anything. All she saw was amusement.

"Do you want a drink, Erin?"

"Yes."

"We're going to get slightly drunk and stinking high this wet and foggy night. How does that strike you? Are you agreed?"

"Why not?"

Bruno brought out a half-full bottle of bourbon and poured two drinks.

Bruno poured herself another, smacking her lips and raising her glass a second time. She drank half of it, then set the glass aside.

There was a silence.

"Do you think I ought to sell that painting of you?"

"If you want."

They had a few more drinks, talking occasionally, and watched the fog close in on the narrow street. By the time they finished the bottle Erin was beginning to feel a bit drunk. Bruno, however, seemed hardly affected by the liquor. The gallery lights had been turned off. The only light came from the brass lamp on the desk. The paintings showed on the wall only as black shapes in the darkness. Erin moved away, slowly, folding her arms across her chest and biting her underlip.

"What's the matter?"

"Nothing, Bruno." She shook her head. "I don't know."

"Are you coming home?"

"Yes."

"Would you like another drink first?"

"I suppose so."

"Sure, you'll feel better once you get a drink. You're just tired, beat out. I know how you must feel."

"I guess that's it," Erin said.

"I'll close this place in a few minutes. Do you want to meet me at the Mummy?"

"Yes."

"We'll have a mummyburger and get something to drink. You'll be there before me, so you just order whatever you want and tell Jerry to put it on my tab."

Erin nodded and smiled.

Bruno let Erin out into the cold street. Erin pulled her canvas hood over her head and waved through the darkened window. As she started to cross the street, a silver-colored touring bus rumbled slowly by. The tourists were peering from behind the tinted windows; some were looking out with embarrassment and cold half-smiles, others with open hostility and resentment. Erin was forced to let the bus pass and she turned her eyes up to meet those of the tourists. One was pressed close to the glass, a fat smooth head without hair, the little piggish eyes looking directly down at her.

Erin wrinkled her nose and stuck her tongue out at the face.

The piggish-eyed man looked shocked and the others in the bus looked away from her with a superior air. The bus rumbled on.

She smiled to herself and, burying her hands deep in the pockets of her canvas jacket, she crossed the street and headed for the Mad Mummy, the fog seeming to part for her as she walked, then closing gently after her.

CHAPTER THREE

The garage was a small two-story building of fading pink stucco on the corner of Vallejo Street and a slot-like alley. The lower floor had once been the garage and it was now closed off with a fairly new brick wall and double doors with brass sheeting. The interior walls were covered with paintings and small statuary on brackets. Bruno rotated pieces from the garage to the gallery. The upstairs floor was used as the living quarters. There were four bedrooms off a narrow hallway at the top of the stairs, and to the rear there was a large kitchen and a porch. The staircase was a rickety wooden affair leading to the upper floor from the far corner of the garage.

Marian and Lilly were still out. The upstairs hall and rooms were silent and unlighted. There was a mixed odor of fried foods. The stairway creaked under Erin's weight. A dim light burned at the far end of the hallway where the kitchen windows overlooked the alley. The garage seemed gloomy and cold, but that was only an impression; the electric heater fan had been left on and the air was warm, almost stuffy.

Bruno turned on the lamp in her room and gestured for Erin to sit down. An African death mask, grotesque and teeth-bared, grinned down at Erin from the wall above the post. The brass was highly polished. The carpet was thick, maroon and moth yellow, curling against the wall like an ancient parchment scroll where the length overlapped the floor.

The lamp bulb was a sickly blue and the room seemed unreal in the sea-colored light. The shadows cast an atmosphere of loneliness, and Erin felt drunker now, aware of the blue light, and she knew that she would become worse now that she was going to get high. The blue light meant pot, and Erin was too drunk to take it right.

The brass posts glittered a bluish-yellow reflection and the ghastly blotches of paint on the African mask seemed to glow. Erin pulled her legs up under her and held her knees in her hugging arms.

"Feel better?"

"I feel drunk," Erin whispered. "It was the last few drinks that knocked me out. To tell the truth I really don't know how I feel. The blue light always makes everything seem funny. It's weird. It's always that way when you turn on the blue light."

"Just before I met you I had a red light, but I had to get rid of it. It made me sweat. The blue one makes me feel just right, like being in some kind of a grotto under the ocean, with seaweed and shells just outside my door."

Erin smiled and nodded.

Bruno opened a drawer. She drew out a band-aid box and shook out two cigarettes about the size of wooden matchsticks, brown-papered and twisted into tight rolls. Erin watched. Bruno lit a black triangular cake of sandalwood incense and set the brass Buddha burner at the foot of the African mask. The musky blue smoke curled up and a small fit of grey ash formed on the crown of the cake; the scent made the room smell like a Chinatown gift shop. Erin knew that once they lit the cigarettes there would be no telling smell or taste in the air. The incense always killed the trace of pot odor.

They sat in the blue darkness and talked in strained, breath-holding whispers. The smoke seared into Erin's lungs and she held it, absorbing it. Combined with the alcohol, the new narcosis pitted her emotions against one another, and she felt dull, apathetic, as she stared at a certain spot on the floor. She was convinced that she could do this for hours, while her inner conflicts made up their minds. She was content to sit on the sidelines of herself and impartially observe the battle, willing to accept the dictates of the victor.... Then the sensation passed. The spot on the floor lost its interest. She blinked and for the next five minutes they smoked in silence. Erin finished the smoke and roached it on the lip of the incense burner.

The tip of her nose tingled and she felt sluggish and delicate at the same time. She was light on her feet... and yet she wasn't standing. She felt safe and secure. Everything was all right. Bruno and the crazy blue light, all alone in the grotto with the shells outside the door. Hell, why was she always plodding around like a zombie? She should take a greater interest in things. Maybe she should play tennis.... That was a rip. She could see herself out on the courts with a tennis racket and a bronze face, batting the ball around and smiling like the women in the *McCall's* advertisements. She wondered whom she could play with. She was sure that Bruno didn't play tennis. Billiards maybe, but not tennis.

The blue light rested her.

"How do you feel now?"

"Like playing tennis. Do you play billiards?"

"I used to."

"I've never played tennis in my life," Erin answered. "I shouldn't have drunk so goddam much. Maybe it was the mummyburger. I feel goofy as hell and I think I'll go to bed."

"Why? What's the panic? You don't have anything to do tomorrow. You quit your job."

"I have to see someone."

"Who?"

Erin thought a minute. Hadn't she promised her grandmother that she would visit? Yes, of course she had. Old Hibbert, too. Hibbert was the servant who had, for the most part, raised Erin. She had promised to visit them both tomorrow....

"I have to see my grandmother," she said slowly. "Dear old granny-gran."

Erin wanted a cold drink. She forgot about her grandmother and Hibbert and she thought about cool water running over stones, and fizzy iced drinks with mint leaves and frost on the sides of the glasses. She remembered how the garden hose had run along the walkway at her grandmother's house.

Bruno hadn't met Erin's grandmother, who was all the family Erin had. It wasn't that Erin was ashamed of her grandmother, it was the uneasiness she knew she would feel with Bruno at her grandmother's that held her back. For some reason it was important to Erin to maintain a dignity before others, even if it was false. She felt it would make her seem stronger. So, for that reason, she avoided introducing her friends to her family.

She rarely thought of her stepfather or her mother—only when it was necessary for her. Since their death she had refused to think about them. She had felt relieved when her stepfather died suddenly, but for her mother she had felt a terrible sorrow. She hated to dwell on family or emotional responsibility of any sort. She was a frightened little girl, playing a game with herself, peekaboo, hide and seek, always avoiding issues and complications. It was just as easy for her to be a cork on water as it was to be the great anchoring stone that served no other purpose but to be the anchor. At least the cork bobbed around and saw something. The cork was more fun.

Bruno watched her with a curious half-smile on her lips. "You said your grandmother was rich?"

"Did I? Yes, she's rich. At least, I suppose she's rich. I never thought about it." She was thinking again of cool water and wet stones. She lit a cigarette and smoked idly, not tasting it. "Do you know the big grey house on the hill? Straight up from here?"

"No."

"It has an iron fence around it and a big tree in the front yard. It's about four blocks up the hill, overlooking the bay."

"I think I know the one," Bruno said slowly. "Is that your place?"

Erin nodded. "I lived there when I was a little girl." Bruno's dull expression didn't change, but her eyes seemed brighter. "I didn't know that. Come to think of it, I don't really know much about you. You could be a spy, for all I know. You just came here one day to drink Scotch, and you accepted my invitation. I guess we just dig each other; it's as simple as that." She smiled. "You're a funny person."

"I don't mean to be."

"That's why you're funny—because you don't mean to be. Now take Marian—Marian means to be funny sometimes, but it doesn't come off too well. She's funny to me only when I'm good and high... or dead drunk. But you're funny in a different way. Know what I mean?"

Erin didn't, but she nodded anyway. Bruno was probably just grass-talking. Erin had heard her like that before. Pot was a strange kick. Your thoughts magic-lanterned on you and you felt sure you knew exactly what you were thinking of and why you were thinking it. Suddenly Erin thought again of cold drinks, magic-lanterned to ice and frosty glasses, bubbling.... It seemed as if she would never stop thinking of ice-cold drinks. The lakes were full of soda pop and the fog outside was a gin-fizz rain. All you had to do was open your mouth and drink it all in. She stood up, thinking of the fog, and started from the room.

"Where're you going?"

She didn't know, but she nodded dumbly towards the kitchen, figuring that the kitchen was as good a place as any. Bruno followed her. Erin searched the kitchen for something to drink, but found nothing. There weren't even any ice cubes in the refrigerator. She turned on the water tap and filled a measuring cup, drinking eagerly, spilling the water down the front of her sweater.

"I guess you got a big grass thirst."

Erin nodded. "That's what I have."

"I never get it any more. Now I get the chili-bean yen. When I get high I want to eat a carload of chili beans. Sometimes I want limes and sometimes beer, but mostly its chili beans."

"I shouldn't have got drunk first," Erin said. "I'm going to bed."

"That's a good idea."

"I'm not thirsty any more."

"Do you feel like eating? I can hustle you up something. Or we can wait until Marian and Lilly get back. We can send Marian out for some hamburgers."

"No. I'm not hungry. I just want to go to bed."

She walked down the hallway to her room and opened the door. She closed the door after herself. She pulled off her sweater, wriggled slowly out of her skirt, then sat on the bed and looked out the window.

A young couple were standing close to each other by the alley corner. The man was lighting a cigarette for the girl, the light from his cupped hands outlining her profile in yellow. Erin felt like an eavesdropper, watching them from the darkness of her room. Across the street from the couple was a small bar with a red fuzzy beer light in the fog. She could hear the muffled sounds of piano music from the bar. The young couple talked in close whispers for a few minutes, then linked arms and crossed the street to the bar.

There was a knocking on Erin's door.

"Hey, Erin? I want to talk to you." The door opened and Bruno entered the room. "And I don't care how tired you are."

"I'm not tired."

"How do you feel?"

"I'm fine," Erin answered, sliding under the sheets and feeling the room spin when she tried to shut her eyes. Her throat felt like alfalfa and her head was whirling feverishly. "I'll talk to you tomorrow."

"I thought you were going to see your grandmother tomorrow?"

"I am."

"Do you want me to go along with you?"

She answered too quickly, "No." Then, more casually, "I don't think you'd like it very much. My grandmother's blind and she's not much kicks."

"That's okay by me. I dig old ladies. I get along fine with them."

"No."

"I like meeting people," Bruno answered.

Erin didn't say anything. She relaxed. She didn't sleep, but she lost contact with the room. She saw a sad vision of her grandmother....

Erin had only seen her grandmother twice since her return to San Francisco. She knew that the old woman enjoyed her visits and she felt guilty for neglecting her. She had promised to visit tomorrow and she knew of no way out of it. Actually, she liked to see her grandmother, but she didn't like to see Hibbert, the Howard House servant and close friend of her grandmother's for twenty-five years.

Hibbert must be seventy years old now, Erin thought. He was as thin as a rail, bent and wrinkled. His washed-out watery eyes had followed Erin lately, watchful, disapproving. And Erin was afraid of Hibbert as she was afraid of most things that she told herself bored her. She realized that Hibbert was aware of how she was earning her living, but she also knew that he had never informed his mistress of this. It would probably kill the old woman. And Hibbert worshipped Erin's grandmother.

Whenever Erin visited the rich old house on Russian Hill she felt uncomfortable, guilty. This was because of Hibbert, and all the disturbing memories of her childhood and her stepfather....

Her thoughts returned to the bedroom, her eyes focusing on the ceiling, tracing a crack to the window where the gin-fizz fog was pressing into the alleyway, blotting out the red beer sign across the street. Bruno was staring out at the alley and the wet sides of the opposite building. She was smoking another cigarette. Erin was again struck by Bruno's handsomeness, as the light touched her firm mouth and the coal blue of her hair.

"I'd like to meet your grandmother," Bruno was saying. "I have an idea that I'll talk to you about later. And maybe, if you like the deal, she could give us some help."

"For us?"

"Sure."

Erin nodded, couldn't think of anything to say, just stared at her in the darkness.

There were soft chiming doorbell sounds and Erin crawled from the bed, put on her robe, and went out into the hallway. Hibbert had come to the garage once before, but only Bruno had been there. If it were he, then something must have gone wrong at Howard House.... The chimes sounded again. Erin went down to the door and opened it, leaving the safety chain in the brass slot, and peered sleepily out into the fog. The damp odors of night and wet streets came through the crack and the chill ran soothingly on her bare legs.

A tall lean man stood by the doorway, his thick hair uncombed and wild, wearing ragged GI clothes, his thin mouth smiling at her. Erin nodded dumbly at him, sluggish and hungover, half asleep, trying to push the coils of hair away from her face.

"Trick or treat," the man said from the darkness.

"What do you want?"

The man shrugged, hunched in his canvas jacket. He looked as if he didn't care if he talked to her or not. He turned the collar of his jacket up around his neck. "You know Merlin?"

"Yes," Erin answered hesitantly.

"My name's Riley. Merlin told me I could find you here, but I didn't know if you'd be asleep."

"I wasn't really asleep," she said, then bit her underlip as if to stop her words. Why did she lie about it? Why didn't she just tell him to go away? "Well, look... what the hell do you want?"

"I'm a painter. I knew old Merlin in Chicago."

"What's that got to do with me?"

"I don't know."

She felt like slamming the door, but the chill was soothing. The red beer light was still lit in the window across the street, so it wasn't closing hour yet. "You're drunk," she said.

"Yeah, I guess I am," Riley muttered. He shrugged again and then smiled. "Look, I didn't want to bother you, but I thought you'd be up and around. It's still early. It's not even two o'clock yet."

"That's not early," Erin said through the crack.

"I guess not."

"What do you want?"

"Pose."

"What?"

"I want you to pose for me."

"You're out of your mind. I quit posing, anyway. Now go away and quit ringing the chimes."

"I know you quit," Riley said. "I went up to the school and the old cat there said you'd quit."

"Then you should go home and go to bed. I'm not posing. And I'll be damned if I'm going to pose at two o'clock in the morning."

Riley shook his head. "I don't expect you to. You can pose for me later. Merlin said that you would."

"Merlin's not my daddy."

"Merlin's too old to be your daddy."

Erin muttered under her breath and closed the door. She listened, hearing the man, Riley, still outside and singing to himself. She heard footsteps behind her, weight on the rickety stairs. It was Bruno, wearing a robe.

"Who is it?"

"Some guy named Riley," Erin whispered. "He's still out there."

"Who's he want?" Bruno asked, irritation in her voice.

"Me. He wanted me to pose for him."

Bruno stood close to the door and scowled when she heard Riley's singing out in the street.

"Is that him singing?"

Erin nodded. "I guess so."

Bruno swung open the door. It caught at the chain and she slid it free. She looked at Riley, who was standing in the center of the sidewalk, singing softly and looking down at his shoes.

"Get the hell away from here, mac," Bruno said.

Riley looked up. "Howdy."

"I said get the hell away from here."

Erin saw the same look that Bruno had when she had thrown the delicate-faced young man from the gallery. She looked over her shoulder and shook her head "no" at Riley. Riley noticed and grinned.

"I'll see you later," Riley said to Erin.

Erin frowned, stepping away from the door, having no intention of modeling for the man. Riley moved away. Erin saw him go down the hill, still singing softly.

In the pale light of false dawn Erin tossed, the streaks of perspiration sliding free from the tiny hollow of her throat and etching along the flesh to her shoulders, then settling. She turned uncomfortably, her closed eyes squinting and her brow creasing.

Erin rarely dreamed, but she was dreaming now, seeing the pictures through a slow-motion film of gelatin. She saw her step-father, reeling drunkenly, standing maniacally over her. Where was she? She wasn't quite sure. She was aware only of him reaching for her and his crooked teeth grinning down at her. It was strange that she made no sound. She didn't think of this. She cowered, trying to cover herself with her hands, and she felt his cheek brush against hers. It sickened her. She tried to shudder him away, but it was impossible.

Then the scene shifted violently. She was running in terror to her mother down a long dark corridor that passed the big room her grandmother used. Her mother heard Erin sobbing, got up from bed and ran out into the hallway. She screamed for an hour at Erin's stepfather, shouting obscenities at him. Then Erin was safe in her mother's bed, being held by her, caressed by her. *My baby, my baby....* And Erin drifted into an uncomfortable sleep, cradled in her mother's arms....

She woke in panic. The accumulated perspiration ran down her body, raking her stomach and itching from under her arms. She had a terrible weed and liquor hangover and she could still feel the ashes of her dreams glowing through her wakefulness.

It came to her very clearly; that was exactly how it had happened. And one week later her stepfather had died, her mother had had a breakdown. Erin had been left with old Hibbert and her grandmother.

She could smell the mothball odor in the big house, the flowers, the fresh paint along the walkway, the grey felt of the two coffins. She could see the glitter of the chromium runways along the floor of the Cadillac hearse. She could see the bees in the cemetery and the reflection of her face in the hearse chauffeur's sunglasses.

At seventeen Erin had left San Francisco and moved to Los Angeles, where she worked in a succession of odd, low-paying jobs. She met another young girl, Bunny, and they shared an apartment together. At that time they had been close friends, almost fanatically close, both being on their own for the first time, and Erin had selfishly wanted that security to last forever. But after four years Bunny left the apartment to marry a man who worked for the telephone company. Erin had hated him, sight unseen, and had felt bitter towards Bunny. She hadn't attended the wedding. She had sent no word of congratulations. As far as she was concerned the friendship had ended with what she thought of as Bunny's betrayal.

Erin stared gloomily out of the window. The new greyness crept into her room. It would soon be bright, the sun coming up over Oakland and piercing the canyons of the city. Erin turned, burying her face in the warmth of her arms.

CHAPTER FOUR

In the late gold of the afternoon she walked slowly up the hill to Howard House. She stood by the tall spiked gate and looked up at the ancient tree that sagged in the front yard, remembering that once she believed it to be the most beautiful tree in the world, and now seeing it as it actually was: a dying, gasping, rotting, leafless and humorless tree. She had once built a house in its lower arms and the rotted nailed steps were still there, along the house side of the trunk.

The house was a handsome Victorian structure of gingerbread and turnip-shaped turrets, a grand old lace lady of the past, still living, holding its ivy-covered face proudly up to the newer, more modern buildings that surrounded it.

Hibbert answered her ring at the door. He bowed slightly, shut the door with a slow shuffling motion, and stood bent, more so than Erin remembered him. His wrinkled face was unmoving. "Your grandmother is expecting you." Then he added, "I didn't think you'd come today."

Erin tried to smile brightly. "Why not? I said I'd come today. I always do what I say."

Hibbert gave no sign that he had heard her. He mentioned that he had tried to contact her at the art school and Mr. Richard had informed him she had quit her job. "I figured maybe you'd gone back to Los Angeles."

Erin shook her head. "It's just that I didn't like modeling."

He seemed pleased at that. His wrinkled hand touched her arm and for a brief moment Erin felt like a little girl again. Hibbert was, after all, more like an uncle to her than a servant. He had been a part of the family for as long as she could remember.

The old house looked the same. It would always look the same. The chandelier, however, looked thinner, not quite as heavy with crystals as Erin remembered it. The great hallway still seemed haunted, and the grand stairway still looked as if it led you to something much finer than just another floor furnished identically to the ground floor. The carpeting seemed the same, the odor of the house was unchanged; it smelled of dark rich wood and camphor, polished brass and sour velvet trim.

Hibbert followed her gaze as she looked at the house, and when their eyes met they caught and held. Hibbert cleared his throat, seeming hesitant to speak. Then, "I'm... glad you quit your job, honey. To... pose like that isn't right. It's not for you."

Erin said nothing.

Hibbert said, "Your grandmother's resting right now. Have you had lunch yet?"

"No, but don't bother. I can pick up something later." The thought of food turned her stomach. She hadn't eaten yet and she doubted if she could.

Hibbert persisted, saying that it was no bother at all, he already had a shrimp salad prepared. He had been making it for himself and he had used too much shrimp, so there would be plenty left for Erin—no bother at all. Erin sat at the huge table and allowed herself to be bullied into trying a little salad. She ate a few mouthfuls and was surprised to find how hungry she was. Hibbert gave her a second helping. It was pleasant. He didn't have an accusing look about him, as Erin had feared; Hibbert was pretty much the same now as she remembered him from years ago.

Why had she been frightened? After all, he was practically her family. There was no reason to hate or fear him.

"I knew you'd eat, Erin. You looked a little pale. I remember that when you were much younger you liked shrimp. That's why I fixed the salad. It's special."

"I thought you said you didn't think I was coming today."

Hibbert's eyes twinkled. "I guess I was hoping you would."

Erin finished her salad and didn't object when the old man brought her a glass of iced tea. They sat together, drinking tea, and watched the sun on the beds of flowers in the rear garden.

"Do you remember how you used to plant flowers in the garden?"

"But nothing ever grew for me," she answered quietly, remembering. "I'd plant first and pray later. But nothing ever came up. Not even one lousy weed."

Hibbert said nothing to that; he seemed absorbed in something else. "How have you been getting along, honey? How are you living now? Have you another job?"

"No. I only quit last night." She looked down into her glass. "I've been getting along fine."

"Do you have enough money? Are you eating well?"

"Yes."

"I'm worried about you, and your grandmother is too." His hands reached clumsily across the table and covered hers. He didn't notice that Erin pulled slowly away from him. He said, "I know that you know your grandmother isn't too well these days. I think you should see her as often as you can."

"Grandma's healthy. She always has been."

"No." He shook his head. "She's not in the best of health. The doctor has been giving her pills for her heart. The kind you put under your tongue. She's a sick woman, Erin. It's very serious."

"But she always seems so cheerful...."

"Whenever you see her she's cheerful. You do that for her. She talks about you for days after you leave. Then she sits in her bed and waits for your next visit. I could barely get her to take her nap this afternoon. She was very excited."

Erin listened to what Hibbert was saying. The kitchen was warm and the screen door was held open by a brick doorstop. She pictured her grandmother waiting for her. It was a saddening thought. Howard House and the Howard money has been the only things that had helped her in the first lean days in Los Angeles, and she recalled how she hadn't even thought of her grandmother once during those times. She felt remorseful now, small and mean, for being so selfish, for not visiting with her grandmother more often.

A bee hovered near the door and snapped back into the garden. For a brief second Erin remembered the cemetery where her stepfather and her mother were buried....

Hibbert's attitude, his reproachful glances and silences, had kept her away from the house after her last visit. But it wasn't that way now. Hibbert wasn't condemning her. Erin could see only the deep sadness and loss in his face. Hibbert was afraid his mistress would die. Erin wished she could comfort him, but she didn't have it in her. She was still hung over. And with the unexpected news of her grandmother's serious illness, she couldn't go out of her way to comfort anyone. She felt even more lost than before. She hadn't realized how greatly she depended on her grandmother.

"That time I went to see you, Erin. I saw one of those girls in the house. You weren't there, of course, but you were angry about it later."

"I wasn't angry, Hibbert," Erin lied. She remembered how she had felt. She was damned if she was going to let Hibbert pry into her life. "I just wasn't myself that day. I'm sorry if it made you feel uncomfortable."

"I didn't like that girl," Hibbert said.

"She's all right."

"Is she?"

"Of course she is. We only live together to share the rent."

Hibbert patted her shoulder. "I think your grandmother's awake now, Erin. You can go right up."

Erin started for the grand staircase.

"And, Erin?"

She looked back to him.

"I'm still your friend, Erin, still old Hibbert. If you ever want to talk to me—you can. Any time."

"Thank you, Hibbert."

Grandmother Howard was propped up in her bed when Erin entered the room. When she bent to kiss the old woman's cheek she noticed that she looked older, more tired, and pale under the light dusting of face powder. The room had the distinct odor of a sickroom, and there was a small silver tray of medicines on a wheeled stand beside the bed. Erin sensed the atmosphere of death. It was in the room like the odor of flowers. The old lady seemed to know this and she smiled calmly in the face of it, easing Erin's discomfort with her cheerful unspoken bravery.

"I'm glad you came, Erin."

"I'm glad, too."

"Sit here by me. It's all right. It's good to have you near me."

Hibbert came in a few minutes later with more iced tea. Grandmother Howard glowed as she and Erin talked. They chatted for fifteen minutes, touching on pre-Los Angeles memories and old friends of long ago that Erin could barely remember. Erin relaxed and enjoyed herself as much as possible. The old lady merely blinked her sightless eyes, not seeing the expression on Erin's face, and chatted aimlessly but pleasantly on.

After a while she fumbled for a magazine on her lap and asked Erin to read. It was a short story about office love and happiness. The illustration was far superior to the text. The old woman nodded when Erin had finished.

"That was a fine story."

Erin folded the magazine. No, it was a lousy story, pablum, stupidity, a square dream built in a grey flannel ad agency, a lie, a farce for apple-knockers whose lives were as vague as their dreams. She thought this, but she said nothing. Let the old woman see and believe in what she wished. She was blind now, and it was all right to believe in fiction if you were blind to life.

"Happy endings are better," the old woman was saying. "Lately there are so many sad endings. Hibbert reads me stories and I become sad. No one believes in life any more...."

They do, Erin thought. Some people believe in life, but the stories weren't life, so how could they believe in them? There had to be a line drawn somewhere. You couldn't live like a dressed-up pig and claim you were something else. It wasn't right. The stories weren't right.... Erin said nothing.

"When I was a little girl," the old woman said softly.

"When you were a little girl...."

"Is that so difficult to imagine?"

"No."

"It is for me...." She smiled gently and touched Erin's cheek. "It seems so much like a dream that I once had. Only lately I've begun to feel old. Lately I feel very, very old, and I can't believe that I was once a little girl."

"You look fine," Erin said. "You don't look old."

"But I feel it. I can't see myself in the mirror, and maybe that's a lucky thing. Maybe it's good I can't see how old I am. I touch your skin, Erin, and it seems so soft.... I'm glad that you have such soft skin. When I was a girl I had rough skin. Your grandfather said that I had skin like an ink blotter. Can you imagine that? But your grandfather was a very loving man...."

A very loving man. Grandfather.

Hibbert finally came in and reminded them of the time. Erin kissed her grandmother and promised to return soon. The old woman asked if tomorrow would be all right. Would it? Yes, Erin thought she could make it tomorrow.

She left the room.

"She does look sick," Erin said to Hibbert when they were at the front door. "I didn't realize it until you mentioned it. It's her heart? Did the doctor say so?"

"Doctor Hayward said it was." Hibbert looked at Erin with his watery old eyes. "Will you keep your promise and come again tomorrow?"

"Yes."

She leaned forward and impulsively kissed Hibbert's cheek. Hibbert glowed, and Erin walked hurriedly down the path to the gate. She didn't stop walking until she reached Columbus Avenue, far down at the bottom of the hill and directly between Russian and Telegraph Hills. She stood for a while on the corner. The sun was dipping towards the ocean now and casting long blue shadows in the narrow streets. Erin debated, not knowing if she should go to Sedge-Hammer or not. She had made no promise to meet Bruno, but she knew that Bruno expected her. Bruno had asked again if she could accompany Erin to her grandmother's and had seemed irritated when Erin refused.

She didn't want to see Bruno right away.

She wanted to be alone.

She walked to Vortigern's and went inside. She ordered a glass of sherry and a dark beer. The afternoon crowd was pretty much the same as the night before. There was a group out on the sidewalk in front of the bar, standing around a red motor scooter. A young girl, thin and dark-eyed, was standing beside the painter, Merlin. Merlin was wearing a corduroy jacket and Canadian GI trousers. He saw Erin and waved to her. She returned the wave. She finished her drink and ordered another. Merlin left the group and came into the bar, squinting in the cool darkness.

"How do you like my motor scooter?"

She nodded, didn't answer him.

"I understand you quit your gig...."

"Word gets around fast."

Merlin smiled at her, folded his big hands on the bar and ordered two beers. Erin didn't make a protest. She liked Merlin, had liked him when he painted her. She felt good, sitting in the bar; after seeing Hibbert and her grandmother she felt relaxed. The hangover from the night before was gone and she couldn't recall how bad it had been. It would be all right to start all over again and have a few drinks. She felt fine.

"A friend of yours came by the garage last night."

"I heard," Merlin said. "I'm sorry about that. He was pretty drunk last night. He came by my pad and told me about it. He said Snider ran him off. That right?"

"Yes."

"Well, I didn't send Riley up there. It was his own idea. He gets ideas like that now and then, and when they come to him it's hard to persuade him not to follow it through. He's obstinate."

"Is he a friend of yours?"

"I knew him in Chicago. He was under a gallery contract there, turning out potboilers and selling them to credit card holders. Then he got fed up and moved out here."

"He mentioned he knew you in Chicago."

"Have you ever seen his stuff?"

"No."

"He's good. You'd like it. He's a helluva lot better than I am."

"That has to be pretty good," Erin said.

"No it doesn't. I'm a photographic painter. I belong between slick pages. It's a lot of crap. I wouldn't know how to interpret what I saw if my goddam life depended on it. I don't even have dreams at night. When I see something I see it exactly as it is." He waved his hand in disgust. "If I wasn't selling the crap I knock out then I'd get out of the racket and sell cookie cutters or something. But, I sell—so I stick."

"Does Riley sell?"

"No. He's too real to make any money at it yet. But he will, maybe by the time he's thirty."

"He said he wanted me to pose for him. Didn't he expect to pay me for it?"

"Are you going to sit for him?"

"No."

Merlin laughed. "He was going to borrow the money from me. He's staying at my pad with my old lady and me, so I guess he figures it's all right." He pointed to the dark-eyed girl by the red motor scooter. "That's my current old lady."

"Where'd you find her?"

"She came with the scooter."

Erin had finished her fourth sherry and her second beer, and was feeling high again, but not like the night before; a more pleasant, relaxed high.

Merlin continued to talk, swallowing half his words with his drinks, chattering in a rapid-fire code. His current woman had left on the scooter with two bearded characters who had been out on the sidewalk.

"Aren't you worried about her?"

"Hell, no," Merlin said grandly. "Them two guys are too shot out to make a decent try for her. One of them is near dead." He cast a bleary eye at Erin. "Don't you know any of the types around here?"

"Not many. I'm not very sociable."

"Didn't you say you were from LA?"

"I just came back from there."

"That's a stinking town. Place is full of Beatnik clowns."

"Just plain old clowns."

Merlin was weaving on the bar stool now. "This town has always been like this. Most of the types around here have always been here. So now they're called Beatniks. So what? Yesterday they were bums or bohemians, but now they've been streamlined, publicized, and graduated into Beats. Who cares? The hell with it."

"I'm from here originally," Erin said. "I only stayed in LA for four years.

I didn't like it either."

Merlin congratulated her, and they had another drink on that. The jazz group from the night before filed in and sat in the far corner, unwrapping their instruments and staring at the tables. One of them, probably the piano player, was unfolding a stick of chewing gum. He worked it into his mouth and chewed, watching the darkened street and moving his jaws.

When Erin turned on her stool and looked out to the street she saw Riley. He came into the bar, smiled at her, and put his hand on Merlin's shoulder. He stood close to Erin's stool.

"Howdy."

"Hello, Riley," Merlin said.

"How'd you get drunk, Merlin?"

"By sitting here and ordering drinks."

"I just left you."

"That was a long time ago."

"You've been here all this time?"

"Sure."

Riley nodded vaguely. "Hell, I just got up. I got a hangover. My head hurts."

"Have some sherry," Merlin said.

"No. It tastes like iodine."

"Does it taste like iodine?" Merlin asked Erin.

"No. It tastes dandy."

Riley shrugged. "I'll have a glass of sherry," he said to the bartender. He didn't pay for it when the bartender poured it. He merely pointed to Merlin's pile of change. The bartender took the money from Merlin.

"That's what I like about you," Merlin said.

"I'm broke," Riley said.

"I thought you would be. Have one on me."

Riley ordered a beer, then turned to Erin. "Are you going to pose for me?"

"I don't think Merlin can afford it," Erin answered.

Riley laughed. He pulled up a stool and squeezed next to Merlin. He lit a cigarette from Merlin's pack and he looked at his face in the bar mirror.

His hair had been combed but he had probably run his hands through it several times since then and it was hanging over his ears now. His eyes, what Erin could see of them, were dark brown and set deep under his brows. He seemed to be about thirty. His hands were strong, the fingers thick and the nails cut short. The right thumb was twisted and seemed to have been badly broken at one time. He still wore his canvas jacket and

GI trousers. The trousers looked like Merlin's and Erin decided that he was probably wearing his friend's clothes.

"What does your girl friend do?"

Erin didn't like the tone of Riley's voice but she felt too relaxed to start an argument.

"She owns the Sedge-Hammer," Merlin said.

Riley grinned. "Well, there's one gallery I'll have to stay away from. I was in there day before yesterday. I wanted to see Merlin's latest."

Erin asked Riley if he had liked the painting.

"No. I hate Merlin's stuff. I liked the figure, though. I wanted you to pose for me. I asked old Merlin who you were and then I met you and Lepke Buchalter."

"Who's Lepke Buchalter?"

"An exterminator."

Erin said nothing to that. She swallowed from her beer and looked out to the street. People were walking slowly past the bar, a tourist bus rolled by, cars were riding bumper to bumper. She said, "I'm sorry about last night, Riley." She felt drunker.

"So am I."

"Everybody's being sorry," Merlin growled. "I'm not sorry. I don't give a goddam if you know it, Riley. I'm not sorry about anything! Who's sorry? Not me. I'm not sorry."

They continued to drink, Erin enjoying herself for the first time in many months. Riley became amusing now, carrying on a conversation with Merlin. Merlin was too drunk to pay close attention to what Riley was saying, and Riley was too busy drinking to listen to Merlin's answers. Erin held up quite well, drinking steadily, and she was surprised. Usually she was the first to get stinking but now she was riding it with ease. She felt secretly proud of herself. It seemed that no matter how much she drank she couldn't get drunk, and the sensation was new to her; she seemed to blossom with it.

Merlin finally left when his dark-eyed girl returned with the scooter. Leaving his change on the bar for Riley to use up, he staggered out to the scooter. The girl came to Riley and asked him if he was going to eat dinner with them.

"No. I'm going to get a bite later on, Mac."

The young girl, Mac, looked uncertain for a minute. Then she noticed Erin and she frowned. Erin looked away, taking another drink of sherry.

"Don't be too goddam noisy when you come in," Mac said to Riley.

"I'll be quiet, honey," Riley said.

Mac left the bar and propped Merlin on the rear of the scooter. The old man held on to her waist when the scooter pulled away from the curb, half unconscious and grinning in the light from the automobile headlights directly behind him.

Riley bought Erin a drink. They sat and listened to the jazz group. The piano player chewed gum while he played. Erin bought Riley two drinks.

People who knew Riley came in and bought drinks, talking with Riley and ignoring Erin. Riley didn't seem to care either way. He was becoming drunk but not sloppy. He was singing softly to himself when they finally left the bar at ten-thirty. Erin walked at his side. They stopped at a grocery store and bought four pints of beer and a package of cigarettes, then continued up Grant Avenue over the steep north hill and down the slope towards the piers. It was dark and the air was warm, smelling of salt, smelling of sea and night. Riley didn't walk as though he were drunk and Erin wasn't feeling very high by now. She felt good... even in Riley's company. He was an easy guy to relax with. She found that she had no fear of him. She felt that he was an honest person in spite of his appearance, and she felt that he respected her.

They walked out on to the dark and lonely piers and sat on a rusty bollard, listening to the wood creak of the moored boats. Riley opened two beers and they drank in silence, smoking and watching the black oily swell of water slap against the timbers.

"You're not mad?"

Riley looked mildly surprised. He shook his head. "No. Why should I be mad?"

"I shouldn't be with you."

"Probably not. Are you bugged with it?"

"No."

"Well, I'm not bugged with it either, so let's forget it."

"Look, Riley, you're a nice guy. I mean—"

"Forget it, man, you'll just get goofed up and probably want to arm-wrestle me on the bollard."

"You'd win."

"Sure I would. I've got a strong arm."

"Just don't expect anything."

"Not a thing, man—no thing."

Erin accepted another can of beer. Riley threw the other empties far out into the water. They finished the beers and left, walking slowly back towards Columbus Avenue where it trailed off near Bay Street.

"I have to get home, man, it's probably midnight."

"I turn into a white mouse at midnight anyway," Riley said. "But I'll walk you up the hill."

Erin said, "I got a real kick out of knocking around tonight, Riley. But just for the record, it doesn't mean anything. Okay?"

"What's it supposed to mean?"

She paused, feeling uneasy, wishing that she didn't have to feel the need to justify herself. "It's just that I don't want any slimy complications. It's easier, and better for everyone concerned, the way it is. I don't know anything more about it. That's all of it."

"I'll honor that."

"Thanks."

"It's your business."

"That's right—it's my business."

Riley lit a cigarette and watched her for a minute. "Merlin can afford it if you feel like sitting for me.... I was serious about that."

Erin shook her head. "I'm serious too. I quit modeling. It made me sick."

"You won't change your mind?"

"No, I won't change my mind."

She made a move to leave, but Riley didn't turn away.

"If you won't get tanked I'll walk you up to the garage. Maybe you'll change your mind about posing along the way."

"I said I wouldn't change my mind and I won't. But you can walk with me if you think you'll get a kick out of it."

They walked slowly.

"You know, there's no need to come on strong, Erin. You don't have to act the sailor with me. It doesn't prove anything."

"Okay, then I won't."

When they reached the slot-like alleyway, Erin stopped. The garage lights were lit and the front door opened before Erin could grasp the knob. Bruno stood in the doorway, wearing paint-smeared jeans.

"Where've you been?"

"I went to Vortigern's," Erin answered.

"I thought you'd still be at your grandmother's. I went to Vortigern's. I didn't see you. I closed at eleven and went straight there. I didn't see anyone. I even tried the Mummy."

"I left Vortigern's at ten-thirty."

Bruno nodded and turned to Riley. Riley hadn't said anything.

"Look, I told you last night to get the hell away from here, and I meant it."

"He's a friend," Erin put in weakly.

"I'll bet he is!"

"Don't be so touchy, Bruno. All I said was that he's a friend."

Bruno snorted and returned her gaze to Riley. Riley didn't move.

Erin said, "Do we have anything to drink?"

Bruno frowned, nodded.

Erin wasn't sure why she wanted to invite Riley into the garage. Perhaps she felt grateful for having had a nice time with him. Perhaps she knew the hour was late and that Riley was broke, having spent the last of Merlin's bar change for beer at the grocery store, and that it would be difficult for him to cadge drinks at Vortigern's at this hour. Or maybe she just wanted to tease Bruno, to see what would happen. At any rate she asked Bruno if Riley could come in for a drink. "He bought me quite a few, earlier. I ought to pay him back."

"I'll bet he bought you drinks," Bruno sneered.

Erin drew back and her grey eyes looked levelly at Bruno. "Riley's a nice guy, so let's not get sour over it. He's a friend of Merlin's. He bought me drinks and now I want to buy him one in return. There's not a goddam thing wrong with that. No need to be touchy about it or make a federal case...."

Bruno looked at Riley. "Get out of here, mac. You stay around and you might get hurt."

Riley said nothing. He looked amused. It was obvious to Erin that he wanted the free drink, but it also seemed that he stayed to see how far things would go.

Bruno whipped out a button knife and the long gleaming blade snicked open. She held it loosely in her right hand and leveled it at Riley's middle. Riley didn't look very worried. He stepped back a foot.

"Now I'm warning you again, mac...."

Riley grinned. "You come at me with that and I'll shove it into your forehead."

Bruno stepped in cautiously. Riley stepped back again. Bruno swept up with the tip of the blade, carefully, quickly, testing Riley's reaction. It was an unusual one. Riley turned his back to her and started to sing a Western song. Then he moved slowly and deliberately away from her, still singing, keeping his back to Bruno and not turning to look at the knife. Bruno did nothing. She looked somewhat foolish, crouched with the

knife, and Erin felt like giggling. Riley had handled it pretty well, in spite
of the near-comic end. Erin watched Bruno replace the blade into the handle and slip the knife into her jeans pocket. Riley was walking down the
hill, still singing.

"He's just a punk," Bruno explained. "I don't like him. And I don't give
a damn if he is a friend of Merlin's. I don't want to see him around here
again. A punk like that's no damn good."

"Yes," Erin said.

Bruno passed a hand nervously through her hair. "A thing like this up-
sets me, that's all. I felt like kind of foolish holding the knife on him. I don't
think I would've used it."

Erin nodded. But she didn't agree.

"You look kind of frightened, honey. Did the knife spook you?"

"I guess it did. I was afraid for a minute."

"For Riley? Did you think he'd get stuck?"

"No," Erin said. "It wasn't for Riley."

"Who for?"

Erin only smiled. She didn't know the answer to that, so she said nothing.

Bruno had been working with her surplus paintings and statuary. She
returned to her work and Erin sat on the rickety stairs and watched. She
forgot about the incident with Bruno and Riley and she began to daydream,
watching Bruno go over the stock and jot things in her notebook.

When Marian and Lilly returned from drinking in the bars they moved
to the upstairs and sat in the kitchen. Marian and Lilly seemed in a sour
mood and they said very little to Erin and Bruno. Bruno scrambled eggs
and opened cans of beer. Marian was pretty drunk and she finished two
cans of beer before she started on her eggs. Lilly sat by Erin and Bruno
stood at the sink. It was silent. Erin could feel the tension between the two
and she wondered if there would be an explosion.

Lilly was slim, a natural blonde. She had a tiny sad mouth and her eyes
were usually dull and colorless. Still, she was an attractive girl, about
twenty-five, with good features and physical grace.

Marian was the exact opposite. Her dark thick hair was cut short and
flecked with grey. Her mouth was thick, and her heavy-lidded eyes were
a solemn brown. She wore a crucifix on a heavy silver chain around her
throat and she smoked Philippine cigarettes in a silver holder.

"The downstairs is a gawdamn mess," Marian finally muttered to Bruno.

"I'm cleaning up, thinking of moving a lot of that junk out of here."

"Where you going to put it? There's no room at Sedge-Hammer."

Bruno shrugged and smiled secretly.

Lilly pushed her plate aside and lit one of Erin's cigarettes. Her eggs were hardly touched. She muttered that she wasn't very hungry.

Marian scooped the eggs from Lilly's plate and started to eat them. Erin sipped from her beer and avoided looking at either of them. She was thinking. Lilly was a sniveler, said very little to anyone, and Marian was always drinking and never worked.

Marian splashed cold water in the sink. She cupped her hands and sluiced water on her face, making small sounds and shaking her head. Bruno was standing by the refrigerator, smoking a cigarette and smiling with amusement at Marian growling and splashing.

Erin left the kitchen. She was glad now that Riley hadn't come in for a drink. She wouldn't want him to see anything as embarrassing as the girls in their present mood. She went and sat on the bed, waiting for Marian to go to her room. Ten minutes later it was quiet. Bruno returned and shut the door after her.

"What's the matter, honey?"

"Nothing."

"You mad about my kicking your boy friend out?"

"No. And he's not my boy friend."

"Okay. Riley's a nice guy. But I still don't want him here."

"He won't come here."

"So, how's your grandmother?"

The question was unexpected. Erin thought a minute. "She's not very well. She has a bad heart—real bad."

Bruno smiled at that. "With all her dough, why doesn't she buy a new one?"

"She takes medicine for it. And my visits help her out. I guess she doesn't have much to live for."

"That's right. When you get that old the only thing waiting for you is death. You live all your life just to die. She's going to die because she's all through with her life."

"Let's not talk about it," Erin said.

"All right. It's a gruesome subject anyway."

CHAPTER FIVE

The next morning Erin stood by the window, looking out. She was holding a cup of coffee. Bruno was sitting, a pair of shell-rimmed glasses perched on her nose. She was working with a folder of papers, checking them with a silver automatic pencil.

Erin yawned and shivered. She hadn't had much sleep during the night and Bruno had awakened her with the offer of fresh coffee. She was still tired and the brightness of the morning seemed a bit unreal. "Do you know that I don't care what day this is?" she muttered. "I don't know what day it is; I really don't care."

"It's a good day, man; who cares?"

Erin nodded and picked up the coffee cups, brought them back to the kitchen and rinsed them out. Marian and Lilly were still asleep and the sink and stove were clean. There were a few eggs left in the refrigerator. A banana was rotting on the shelf and the refrigerator smelled like banana and cucumber. Erin didn't know how the odor of cucumber came to be there.

Under the sink there were two solid rows of empty wine and whisky bottles. On the back porch there were two cardboard cases of beer tins and a Chinese bamboo plant. The morning sun glinted from the empty bottles. The house was quiet.

Back in her room, Bruno had set the papers to one side, covering the top sheets with a notebook binding.

"Do you want more coffee?"

"No," Bruno said softly.

Erin lay back and watched the sun fall across her legs.

Bruno said, "Did you know that I used to live in LA?"

"No, I didn't know that. When was it?"

"Not too long ago, really." Bruno's voice was thoughtful. She was in a remembering mood.

"Do you know how I got the scratch for the Sedge-Hammer?"

"I've never thought about it. I suppose I just thought of you as always having it. The same with the garage here; I just never thought about where, or how, you got it."

"I hustled," Bruno said softly, not looking at Erin. "Does that surprise you?"

Erin looked up at the ceiling, feeling a weight in her chest. "Yes, it does."

"I hustled for every goddam penny of it. Before I came to San Francisco I was in Vegas, on my own. I was there for eight months. Before Vegas it was New York."

"In New York, did you...."

"Sure, same thing. And before New York it was LA." She paused. "That's where I started, in LA. I was kind of stupid at first, I hung out in bars and tried to make my pile from swizzle-stick commissions. I don't know how much crème de menthe I drank in LA before I got wise—it must have been tons. In New York I was a call girl."

A little brown bird with a rust breast landed on the window sill. It cocked its head at Erin, winked, then flew away. Erin looked back to the ceiling. She said, "I didn't know anything about you. I didn't know any of this."

"No one knows it. I'm not ashamed of it, though. It was an easy thing to do in the beginning. I was only nineteen years old then."

Bruno was silent then.

Erin lit a cigarette and handed it to her. Bruno inhaled deeply, nervously, then passed it back. She said, "When I finally pulled out of New York I had some money saved. Not very much, but enough. In Vegas I held my own, saving pennies and stashing it in a bank here in SF. The last mark I hit was better than any year in a clip joint in LA." Bruno paused and smiled wryly. "I had a bartender in Vegas, steering for me. It was a nice deal all around."

Erin shivered.

Bruno said, "It cost this guy fifteen hundred at the end of our association." She stopped, put on her shell-rimmed glasses, then continued in a matter-of-fact voice. "After that I called it quits and came up here to open the gallery. That was a year ago, and now for the first time in my life I have a sense of real security. I feel that if all my plans go just right I'll have it made—forever, without ever having to skin my tail for a buck."

It was quiet.

Erin felt better now, despite the sordid images that followed in the wake of Bruno's tale. She looked at the other's profile.

"It's a tough racket, Erin," Bruno said. "But I wanted the buck. I fought for it all my life and even now I'd do anything for the holy dollar. Anything. I realize it's not a very chic pursuit these days, but that's the way it's always been with me. The buck means security with a big S; the buck means life. It separates me from the hogs and lets me do as I goddam well want."

They remained seated for more than an hour. Marian and Lilly were moving noisily in the kitchen. Erin sat with her eyes closed, thinking over what Bruno had said to her, listening to every word being repeated in her mind. And strangely enough, she didn't feel hurt by it.

Bruno returned to her work. The pencil scratched. Erin closed her thoughts and finally dozed.

When she opened her eyes again she saw that she was alone and that the sun had crept from her legs and was now burning straight into the alley. The glare reflected on the ceiling, seeming to make the room larger and cleaner. She remembered what Bruno had told her of her life, and she felt that Bruno's struggle to attain something was somewhat like her own— at least she preferred to think of it that way—and she felt more kindly towards Bruno for sharing her secret; but at the same time just as removed. Why should she always feel out of things? Surely she hadn't envied Bruno her past. If anything, she feared it, believing that it made Bruno all the more right, the stronger for having had the courage of her convictions.

There was no one in the kitchen now. Egg-stained dishes were piled in the sink, evidence of Marian and Lilly. All the doors in the hall were closed except for Marian's.

Marian was lying on her stomach, sprawled on the bed working a crossword puzzle, one foot raised behind her, her chin cupped in her hand. She looked up when Erin came into the room.

"Where's Lilly?"

Marian twisted her body and looked over her shoulder. "She's gone to San Jose to see her brother. He was threatening to come up here to see her, so she went down there. It's a family thing. If she doesn't see her brother now and then, he starts to worry."

Marian looked cruel, always looked cruel, even when smiling or laughing.

"Who was Seth's son?" Marian asked. "It's a four-letter word."

Erin shrugged. "I know a lot of four-letter words, but I've never heard of Seth's son."

Marian moved again.

"Did Bruno go to work yet?"

"She's not going to work. At least she asked me if I'd take her place at Sedge-Hammer tonight."

"She downstairs?"

Marian nodded, returning to her crossword puzzle. "What's a three-letter word for 'before'?"

"Ere."

"Thanks, baby."

Erin found Bruno downstairs. Canvases were stacked in two piles and Bruno stood in the midst of them, writing in one of her notebooks. She passed her hand through her hair and rubbed the pencil along her faded jeans. She had changed clothes. She stopped working when Erin came down the staircase. She closed her notebook and removed her glasses.

"I fell asleep," Erin said.

"I guess you needed it."

Bruno lit a cigarette and held it between her teeth. "Do you want to go to Sausalito?"

"Are you going?"

"Yes."

"What's happening in Sausalito?"

"I'll show you when we get there. It's a surprise—you might get a bang out of it. We'll take the car. Marian's going to work Sedge-Hammer for me, so I've got the day and night off."

Bruno picked up her sweater and glasses and Erin followed her out to the car. Bruno put the notebooks into the glove compartment. The car was a late-model green Plymouth with a battered fender and badly worn upholstery. They pulled back the tattered top and struggled to tuck it behind the rear seat and button the covering over it.

Bruno drove, Erin sitting next to her, letting the clean warm air whip the untied mass of her hair and force her to squint her eyes. The weather was perfect, boats on the bay, the sky still cloudless. It was windy crossing the Golden Gate Bridge, but later, in Sausalito, it was calm and hot. Bruno parked the car on the north waterfront, where the land was practically at bay level, and they looked out over the flat blue water to Belvedere. A row of low buildings was set on pilings over the water, a boat yard directly before them. Next to that, going north, were dilapidated light-industry buildings and more boat yards. Between the highway and the pier buildings was a rusted train track overgrown with weeds. A black dog was sleeping in the lavender shade of a boat pulled up on the way.

"This is it," Bruno said.

"What is it?"

"The area.... What do you think of it? Look at that crazy red brick building. The tall thin one next to the boat yard."

The building was entirely of brick, the color of burnt cinnamon, the upstairs windows almost hidden under a sheet of drying ivy. The walls were chipped and scarred, the windows broken. A rusted light shade hung over a tall doorway. It looked as though it had once been a fire house.

Bruno took out her notebooks and spread the sheets on her knees, laying them out for Erin. The first sheet was covered with floor dimensions and areas marked Living Quarters, Walls, Bath, Gallery Proper. There were rough estimates listed for plastering, painting, plumbing, and rewiring. A price column was on the second sheet.

Erin looked at them, then shook her head. "What's it all about?"

"It's an idea I've had for some time. I'm thinking of expanding... getting more. Maybe it sounds silly—because I'm in debt up to my ears—but I still want to move ahead... no matter *what* it costs. I think I can swing it *if* everything breaks just the way I want it."

They crossed the weed-grown tracks and Bruno opened the door to the old building with a key she carried in her pocket. "Watch out for dust. It doesn't look like much but it will once the joint's fixed up. It'll look jazzy when it's fixed the right way."

It was dark and cool inside, dust had settled everywhere, and Erin could see that the wiring was exposed and held in place by hooks and electrical tape. The walls were cracked and entire sections were missing. A small spiral staircase in the rear led to the second floor. The only ground-floor windows were at the rear, overlooking the bay.

"Once these walls are replastered they'll look fine. See this first wall? This's only makeshift, put here after the place was built. I can knock it out with no trouble at all, and that'll give the ground floor twice the space." She felt the wall with her hand, studying it as if she intended to tear it down right then. "There won't be anything to the fixing up. I've got all the details in my notebooks."

Erin stood by the door in the makeshift wall. "What's back there?"

"More space. That's why I'll have the wall torn out. There's a balcony out there. And that's one of the wildest things about this place. Goes right out over the water like the deck of a houseboat. The railing's kind of rotted but the pilings are good and the floor is solid."

Out on the balcony the breeze was warm, salt-smelling, coming in off the bay and barely rippling the water. The rear of the boat yards swung out on the right, the pier extending a small distance. On the left was the rear of a pier shed, the wide loading doors open and revealing a gloomy empty interior. Gulls were sitting on top of the shed.

"It's a fine place," Erin said, "but I still don't get it. What's the idea you have?"

Bruno winked, spread out her books on a table by the balcony door. "I'm going to open a second gallery. Going to call it Sedge-Hammer Two." She lit a cigarette and winked again, looking pleased by her own announcement. "The lease on this old place expired two years ago and it hasn't had a permanent pick-up since then. One guy, some little fag who thought he was a promoter, took an option on it seven months ago, thinking he could raise enough capital for a charming beer-wine joint. He couldn't get a nickel, so I picked up the option once he dropped out."

"How much longer do you have left?"

"A month."

"Have you been able to get the money together?"

Bruno hesitated, and a troubled look passed across her face. "Well... not exactly. As a matter of fact—no. I hocked Sedge-Hammer and I still owe on the garage. I guess I'm cutting myself up pretty thin, but once this place gets on its feet it'll pay for itself in two or three months. I'm not worried— I'll get the money."

Erin was puzzled by it all.

Bruno said, "I know it sounds screwy, honey, but the more I expand the bigger and better I feel. I've come this far with it and I'm not going to let it go."

"How will you get the loot? You're not going to sell the gallery, are you?"

"I wouldn't get enough out of it. I need about two thousand more."

"How much do you have now?"

"About two thousand. Actually, I need more than that to do it right, but I can squeeze by on less."

They left the balcony and Bruno stood by the staircase, looking at her figures and frowning. There was a streak of perspiration on the side of her face. She said, "I think I can swing it if... I know damn well it's what I *want* to do anyway.... I'm going to take in a partner, honey."

"Who?"

"You."

"But I haven't any money. You know that."

"Your grandmother has it."

"I couldn't ask her for a cent."

"So, why not?"

"Well, it's not her so much, it's Hibbert. If he ever found out why I wanted the money he'd talk my grandmother out of it. Hibbert has a real big influence on her. He's her eyes and ears, practically. She listens to everything he tells her."

"He wouldn't have to know about it. You wouldn't have to tell him."

"No, she'd talk it over with him. He's her advisor. Or else she'd talk it over with Mr. Shelby, the family lawyer, and old Shelby would speak to Hibbert.... No, he'd only get curious and nose around until he found out.... Then kaput."

"What's the old bastard got against it? I've never looked cross-eyed at him. I only saw him that one time."

"It's not really you, Bruno. It's everything. I guess he's against everything. It's me more than anything else."

"What's he got against you?"

"I'm his little girl, or so he thinks. I guess it's gone to his head. He's disappointed in me."

"Why? Because you didn't come back from LA all shiny-eyed and married with a big red rose in your teeth?"

Erin smiled. "That's probably it—at least partly."

"He sounds like a screwball."

"He's not a bad guy. He's just old-fashioned. He thinks I'm walking the long and bumpy road to hell."

"If he's such buddies with your grannie then what does she think about you? Is she against you too?"

"No. He's never told her anything. I suppose if he got drunk enough he would, but he'd only tell her enough to let her know that he disapproves of my life. He'd never tell her why; he'd just say that I'm on my way to damnation and he doesn't like it. That would be enough. My grandmother swears by him."

Bruno looked thoughtful; her eyes were glittering again. She knocked her cigarette ashes on the floor and looked carefully at Erin. "That's too bad," she said. "I suppose you love your grandmother, though."

"Sure, I guess I do. She's the only family I have." Erin touched Bruno's arm. "I hope you weren't counting too much on me, Bruno."

"In a way I was."

"I suppose I could ask her anyway. All she could say is `no'. But I can't promise anything."

"Forget it. I don't want you to get into any trouble with your folks. We'll think of something."

"A second gallery is a crazy idea," Erin said.

"Sure it is." Bruno brightened and looked around at the cracked walls and littered floors. "I've only told you half of the scheme. I already have some contacts lined up. I know this kid and his sister who make real snob neckties. We'll sell through here on commission. All kinds of stupid junk can go through this place. Not only paintings, but LP records, pocketbooks, plaster busts of Beethoven and Schweitzer, Atlas, Nefertiti... anything. It'll *all* go in this place." She smiled reassuringly. "And don't worry about a thing, we'll get the bread somehow before the month is out and we'll still be partners. I can't work this dump alone, so I'll let you work for your share of the partnership. In a year you'll be a full partner. And don't worry about living costs—I can carry you. I'll rent the garage and we'll shack up here."

"It sounds damn good...."

"It should. It is good. It's a great idea and I'll *make* it work...."

They went upstairs and looked at the proposed living quarters. It seemed perfect to Erin. The back windows looked out over the water. The tide was low, and refuse could be seen lodged in the muck by the balcony pilings. Birds waded along the graveled edge and kicked over small stones.

"We'll think of something," Bruno said after a minute.

Erin looked down at the water. She felt there was something here worthwhile to hold onto, something solid and meaningful. She smiled down into the water, the sun reflecting from it and moving gently in her eyes.

Already, Erin felt a queer sense of pride and ownership in the old building. She closed her eyes and stood for a few minutes in the quiet.

"Something will come up," Erin said.

Bruno smiled, her eyes glittering strangely. "Well... I'm glad you see it my way."

Bruno flipped her cigarette out the window and they returned to the ground floor.

CHAPTER SIX

Bruno parked the Plymouth in front of the iron gate that opened to the grounds around Howard House. She looked at it for a long minute. Erin followed her gaze. Bruno didn't take her eyes from the house.

"I remember this house now," she said. "I've passed it plenty of times and I've always wondered what kind of people lived in it."

"I lived in it until I was seventeen," Erin answered.

"You're not exactly the type of person I had in mind when I was imagining who lived in it. I was thinking more along the lines of that old cat Hibbert. He's more the type to go with an old place like this."

They sat and watched the house.

What difference would it make what Hibbert would say if they went inside? After all, it was more Erin's house than it was his. She was the only heir to Howard House—not Hibbert. She reminded herself again that he was, after all, only a family employee. She had every right to invite Bruno in to see the house. Hibbert had nothing to say.

"Do you want to go inside and look around?"

Bruno broke into a grin. "Hell yes. It'd be kicks. I dig old houses. I'd like to live in one myself. Wouldn't it be crazy to live in something like this? Think of the racket we could make."

They entered through the gate and stopped by the old tree. Erin felt a brief stir inside. She had been a miserable little girl, she decided. She was glad that it was all over.

Bruno was saying, "When I was a kid I used to make all the haunted house flicks. Every one that came out, I'd eat it up. I saw *The Cat and the Canary* three times straight through, and my old man had to come in and drag me from the theatre." She chuckled. "He whipped me good, said I shouldn't see spooky things. He said it'd make me a midget."

"You're not a midget. He was wrong."

"He was wrong about a whole lot of things," Bruno answered.

Two huge Victorian vases were on either side of the front porch, spiky ferns spilling out of their mouths. The door was carved dark wood, the glass colored.

"This house isn't haunted," Erin said.

Bruno nodded. "Maybe not. Maybe it isn't."

Hibbert answered the doorbell, smiling brightly at Erin when he swung the door open. Then, when he saw Bruno, the smile faded and he lowered his eyes.

"Hibbert, this is Bruno."

Hibbert nodded glumly and shuffled back a few steps. "We've met," he muttered sulkily. "We've met once before."

Bruno pushed out her hand to the old man, grinning as though it were all a great game and she was enjoying herself immensely. "Sure, we've met, Mr. Hibbert. You came to my place once. Erin's told me quite a bit about you—said you're like an uncle to her."

Hibbert regarded her suspiciously, then grudgingly shook her hand. He asked them both to wait while he went upstairs to see if his mistress was still napping.

Bruno wandered past the velvet curtains to look into the main room. Erin stood at her side. The room was dark, the shades being drawn, and the walls seemed to be almost black. The carpeting was soft and thick under their steps. The books along the glassed-in shelves cast off a sour yellow smell. Over the fireplace were two portraits, both formal pictures of a woman before a dark curtain. The first one, Erin's grandmother, showed the old woman when she was still in her twenties; her hair was piled high on her head, little curls spitted about the temples. Her grey eyes were alive and staring, the shapely lips unsmiling. She was holding a small bunch of flowers with a satin ribbon attached.

The second portrait was of Erin's mother, looking amazingly like Erin, sitting rather primly and holding flowers, before a curtain that was almost black, with wine-colored highlights. The woman was beautiful; her hair was thick and long, like Erin's and the mouth was shaped the same.

Erin turned away. She didn't like to see the pictures.

Even as a child the somber formality of them had frightened her.

Bruno pointed to one of the portraits. "Is that you?"

"Where?"

"The picture. The one in the red dress."

Erin didn't have to look at it. "No. It's my mother."

"They're pretty corny pictures."

"I suppose they are."

Bruno chuckled and sat on a high-backed chair. She lit a cigarette and looked around for an ash tray. There was none.

"Throw the match on the floor," Erin said. She felt pleased to say that. She looked at the match on the carpet and wondered what Hibbert would say or think when he found it there.

Although the house was hardly a shrine, Erin felt that it needed dese-crating to right whatever wrong she believed it had inflicted on her. She wished that she could play a monstrous joke on the house—on her own childhood. Perhaps it was because she felt her childhood had played a joke on her; she wasn't sure. But the match on the floor—and now the ashes from Bruno's cigarette—amused her and helped the need for desecration. Perhaps it was desecration of all ideas, of all people who upheld the ideas that seemed to hold her back from the freedom and security she felt had been stolen from her.... She wondered what had actually been stolen.

She looked around the room, the hallway. Hibbert was sure taking his time.

"You ought to have your picture put up there when you get this old house."

"Maybe I should."

"How about that one Merlin painted of you? That'd be a helluva laugh, wouldn't it?"

Erin smiled. It was an idea. She'd like to have a picture there. But it wouldn't be Merlin's. Whose, then? Riley's? She tried to imagine a paint-ing by the wild Riley hanging beside her mother and her grandmother's stuffy oils. The thought amused her.

"Yeah." Bruno sighed. "This's quite a dump."

"I don't like it."

"That's because for you it's haunted. It's not haunted for me."

Erin didn't answer. She stood by the hall curtain and watched the grand staircase, the shadow of the chandelier falling across the carpeting. Bruno was right. The house was haunted for her.

Hibbert finally returned from the second floor and nodded a brusque okay to Erin, then, without a word, shuffled off to his place in the kitchen.

Erin led the way to the second floor. The old woman's door was open and Erin could see her propped up against the pillows, waiting, listening for their footsteps, looking fragile and pale, like a flower lying on the bed.

"Hello, Grandmother. Did Hibbert tell you that I brought a friend?"

"Yes, Erin," the old lady answered. "Come in. Come in."

"She's right here with me. Grandmother, this is Miss Snider."

"Hello, Miss Snider," she answered brightly. She was staring at the cen-ter of the room, her eyes revealing nothing, her expression a blank. She held out her hands and grasped Erin's for a quick greeting, then moved them towards Bruno. "Ah, you have very strong hands, Miss Snider. Very strong. Erin, come sit here by me. Miss Snider, bring Hibbert's chair from the window." She reached out and touched Erin's face, as though receiving a message from it. "You've been out in the sunshine, dear. I can feel it on your skin. It's warm and fresh.... Have you two girls been out in the sun?"

"Yes, ma'am," Bruno answered. "We drove to Sausalito."

"You have a machine?"

"Yes."

"Well, I do hope you drive carefully. Hibbert reads me everything in the morning papers, and there seems to be more automobile crashes on the bridges every day." She clucked her tongue slowly and stroked Erin's hand. "I can remember when San Francisco didn't have any bridges. We only had the ferry boats. I think they were much nicer than the bridges. But what with all the machines nowadays I suppose the bridges are necessary."

The old woman's mood was a good sign to Erin. The tray of pills and medicines didn't seem as ominous as they had the day before.

"What do you do, Miss Snider? Do you work at the same office as Erin?"

Erin threw Bruno a warning glance. Bruno winked. "No, ma'am. I own a shop. An art gallery."

"That must be interesting work."

"Yes, it is."

"Where is the shop? Is it in Sausalito?"

"No, it's in North Beach."

The old woman nodded her head. "There's been quite a bit of trouble there lately, according to the papers. The artists had trouble with the police. Hibbert was reading to me about the Beatniks."

"No trouble has come my way," Bruno answered.

"Of course not. I didn't think there had been any trouble." She cocked her head toward Bruno's chair. "Do you and Erin share an apartment?"

"I'm Erin's landlady. She rents from me."

"I see. Hibbert mentioned you, Miss Snider."

Erin looked away. She could imagine what Hibbert had been saying to her. Something stupid. Why didn't he mind his own business? After all, he was only an employee.

"I've met Hibbert once before," Bruno was saying. "He seems to be a very nice gentleman. I know that Erin feels very strongly about him. He's like an uncle to her."

"Yes, that's quite true."

Bruno continued, "He came to see Erin once and she wasn't at home. I was there working over my stock and that's how I met him." She paused. "He seemed rather angry that afternoon."

"Angry? Hibbert?"

"Yes."

"I can't imagine Hibbert being angry. Although he did say that Erin's living quarters left much to be desired. I believe he also said it would be better for Erin to live up here with us."

"I like it right where I am," Erin said.

"Of course, dear. That's what I said to Hibbert. I told him that you were young and a young girl has a mind of her own."

"I know it's not much of a place," Bruno said. "That's why we're thinking of moving."

"Moving, you say?"

"Yes, to Sausalito."

"Is this true, Erin? Are you going to move to Sausalito?"

"Yes, Grandmother, I think so. Miss Snider's going to open a new shop there and I think she wants me to help her run it."

"You... a businesswoman, Erin?"

"Why not?"

The old woman smiled. "Well, I hope you have a better head for figures than I had. If I didn't have Mr. Shelby to handle my affairs I don't know what I'd do. I never was very good with business matters. Your grandfather of course was a regular whiz. Perhaps you take after him."

Bruno nudged Erin and winked, then made a face. To the old woman she said, "I think Erin'll be very good at her job, ma'am. She'll do much better than at the office where she is now."

"That would be nice. It's always good to advance." She lifted the covers higher on her chest and turned her face to Erin. "Would you like some tea, dear? I think Hibbert's making some. Why don't you see if it's ready? You can help carry the things." She smiled. "That's a good dear."

Erin glanced significantly at Bruno, shaking her head, then left the room. She found Hibbert in the kitchen. The tea things were ready. He looked up when she came in. He was wearing his house slippers and he seemed smaller than ever. He didn't look very dignified in his baggy trousers and shirt garters, but his expression was proud and self-assured.

"I don't think it was a very good idea to bring that woman to see your grandmother. She's blind, of course, but it still doesn't seem right."

"What's wrong with it? Bruno's a friend of mine, and I happen to have more say-so about who I bring here than you do. I'm sick of all this crap, Hibbert. There's not a damn thing wrong with my bringing Bruno here. I don't want to hear another crumby word about it."

He drew himself up and pinched his lips together, glaring at her and tilting his chin in a gesture of defiance. "You don't see what's wrong with it? Then I feel terribly sorry for you. I may be an old man, and certainly I'm only a servant in this house, but I still think I should have some say. I helped raise you. When your father passed on I was the only man for you to come to. And when your stepfather came here I was *still* the only man to come to...."

"What do you mean by that?"

"You know what I mean. Your stepfather wasn't a man. He only thought he was. He was a weak, effeminate being who only married your mother for her money. Surely you knew that."

Yes, she had known it, and she remembered how she had felt when her stepfather had been around her. She had always wondered if he had been trying to prove to her that he was a man.... She remembered it. She said, "I'm sorry, Hibbert."

"Don't be sorry. I don't think you know who, or what, to be sorry for. You say that because you feel you have to say something. Sorrow is wasted, coming from you."

She shook her head. She was sick and tired of fighting with everything. The hell with it all. She didn't want any more of it. She was sick of being pushed into corners, of being criticized. She said, "I suppose you're right, Hibbert. Or at least you honestly believe you're right—and maybe that amounts to the same thing. But I don't feel I can live the way I want to, and I feel too screwed up to have to live the way *you* want me to."

"You don't know *how* you want to live. You never knew. You ran away from here when you were seventeen, you ran away from your stepfather... and from me. You ran away from your grandmother and Howard House. And I can imagine why you came back. You left all the threads hanging out and you expected to find all the answers here. You left too much here."

"I don't know what the hell you're talking about. I didn't leave anything here."

"Yes, you did. You left four years here. You were in Los Angeles for four years. You're still seventeen and you don't know how to live like an adult."

"That's a stinkingly pat answer." She lit a cigarette, tossing the match in the sink, regaining her composure. "You've been reading, Hibbert. Maybe you've been reading too goddam much. It's made you pious."

"I don't like the tone of your voice."

"Don't you? Why don't you like it, Hibbert?"

He picked up the tray and started for the door. "You sound too much like your friend Bruno."

Erin turned pale and angrily pinched her cigarette. "You once said that I could talk to you, that you were still old Hibbert."

"Yes."

"What was it we were supposed to talk about?"

"Whatever is on your mind, Erin."

"And what if nothing's on my mind?"

"Then we have nothing to talk about... do we?"

"No, we have nothing to talk about. And meanwhile, I'd appreciate it if you don't bother my grandmother with any little stories you wish to dream up."

"Like what?"

"Like about my 'living quarters leaving much to be desired.'"

"Should I lie to her for you?"

"No. It'd be easier just to say nothing about it. Wouldn't it?"

"If you say so, Erin."

"I say so."

He pushed the kitchen door open with his back, carrying the tray, and the door swung shut after him. Erin followed. Hibbert's stooped little figure was moving slowly up the stairs. She realized that only a minute ago she had believed he had no dignity about him. That wasn't true. Despite his shabby clothes and house slippers he seemed dignified to her.

She wondered about Hibbert.

He turned at the first landing and looked down at her. "Before I forget. You had a telephone call this morning. I said I'd give you a message."

"Who was it?"

"Mrs. Ferrara."

Erin frowned. "I don't know anyone by that name."

"She asked for you."

"I still don't know her. I don't know anyone named that."

Hibbert shrugged. "She said she was in town and that she lived on Hyde Street. You can get the address from telephone information. She's not in the book yet."

Erin was puzzled. She followed him up the stairs, watching his back, his shoulders, and she remembered once when she was a little girl she had had a sliver jammed tightly under her fingernail, and had run to Hibbert. Had he been so old then? No, she remembered his hair had been not quite so white. His eyes had been more alive. He had told her to watch the top of his head, and he had pulled the sliver with a fast sure motion. She had felt no pain.

She returned to her grandmother's bed.

"We've been having a chat," her grandmother said. "Miss Snider is a very amusing person."

"Yes, she is," Erin answered absently.

For the next twenty minutes, while they talked, Erin tried to remember who Mrs. Ferrara was. She had heard the name before—and recently—but she couldn't quite place it.

Then she remembered, and she looked up from her cup of tea with a startled expression.

Of course. Mrs. Ferrara was Bunny. Erin's one-time closest friend had married a man named Ferrara.

CHAPTER SEVEN

On Saturday morning when Erin went into the kitchen she found only a note scrawled on a grocery bag and propped up against the empty butter tray. It said something about Bruno's going to work early and taking Lilly with her, and that they would all meet later on in the evening. Perhaps at Vortigern's. And if not there, then at the garage for a drink after eleven o'clock.

Marian wasn't home. The house was dead, eerie in its silence.

Erin couldn't find anything to eat for breakfast, so she made a pot of coffee and drank a cupful as she stood in the center of her room. She was wearing only pajamas and Japanese sandals, and she shivered suddenly.

She was hungry, wanted to eat out, but she had spent the last of her art school money the day before. She would have to wait until later to eat.

The weather was gloomy, and there were no reassuring shouts from the children that usually played in the alley below her window. The ceiling of the sky was low and grey and birds moved restlessly. The room seemed stuffy. The coffee was hot but tasted sour and greasy.

She thought of Bunny, now "Mrs. Ken Ferrara." She should call her, if only to prove to Bunny and herself that there were no hard feelings. But she had nothing to say to her, let alone to her husband.

A picture of Bunny rose before her. She was wearing the carhop's outfit of matching green slacks and blouse and uniform jacket, standing under the neon lights of the drive-in restaurant in Los Angeles. Christmas carols were being piped to the open car-parking area by the long-play record machine in the drive-in's office, the music floating in the air, the voices singing of snowy hills and icy lakes, of Christmastime and Santa Claus. The voices carried gently over the hot Southern California night, with the palm trees swaying and hissing in the smoggy in-shore breezes from the western mountains and desert.

It was a Christmas, if one could call it that, that Erin would never forget, and would never remember without a bitter feeling.

Christmas in Los Angeles was a joke, like wearing a pith helmet to the North Pole, or taking a minstrel show to Nigeria—it just wasn't done. Santa Claus drove a butterfly Mercedes, and the wintry snows were a mixture of cornflakes and glue. The department stores were crowded and in the elevators people said "Merry Christmas."

The drive-in where Erin and Bunny worked had put up tinfoil icicles and sprayed snow on the picture windows. A Santa was perched on the roof, floodlit, looking like a soda-pop advertisement, poised and about to descend the restaurant air-conditioner that had been bricked up to resemble a New England chimney.

The pick-up room was between the parking area and the kitchen. The girls got their orders there, pulling the loaded trays along the tin board of the kitchen opening, and threw cubes in drinks from the ice bin that was fixed into the wall. The room was used as a smoke-break area as well. It was against the rules to smoke in front of the customers. It was considered undignified.

That Christmas Eve Bunny avoided Erin. She hadn't stopped for a cigarette in the pick-up room all evening, but had stood out on the ramp and watched her cars. Erin hadn't spoken to her since the night before. Bunny had passed Erin several times during the course of the shift but had said nothing. Finally, during the ten o'clock hill, Erin stopped her by the restroom ramp.

"You haven't had a smoke break all evening."

"No," Bunny answered. "It's been a busy night."

"How're your tips?"

Bunny shrugged her shoulders. "It's Christmas Eve. About what I expected."

Erin took a drag from Bunny's freshly lit cigarette. "I don't see how people can spend Christmas Eve all by themselves. Especially if they've got enough bread to eat in a dump like this and drive a car around. I don't get it. I hate to be alone myself."

Bunny shrugged again. "They can do what they want...." She looked deliberately over her shoulder at her cars. "Everybody should do whatever they want to. I have to run, Erin. Meet me here first chance you get. I have something to tell you."

It was eleven o'clock before they had a chance to be alone at the restroom ramp. The traffic had slowed and a few of the other girls were in the pick-up room. Bunny and Erin stood behind the telephone booths. An Elvis Presley record was being piped over the loudspeakers. The breeze was somewhat heavier, still warm and still carrying the odor of the mountains and the smell of gasoline fumes.

Bunny spoke quickly, as if afraid Erin would interrupt her.

"Congratulate me, Erin. I'm going to get married. His name is Ken Ferrara. I want you to meet him. We're going to get married next week."

Erin felt her cigarette burning close to her fingers and she dropped it on the ramp. She knew that she had no right to feel betrayed, but she did. Bunny was her only friend. Bunny knew that.

One of the headlights in Bunny's section winked and Bunny turned and looked at the car, irritation crossing her face. She bit her underlip and adjusted the angle of her drive-in cap. She said, "I'm sorry, but I have to scram now."

Erin turned and walked past the booths to the washroom. She smoked a cigarette, washed her face several times, and studied her expression in the mirror. She could hear her customers honking their horns impatiently. She could hear the door being tried by women who wanted to use the room.

Finally the hop captain came with the pass key and Erin left the room and walked slowly, deliberately, to the employees' dressing-room. Without a word she changed into her street clothes, took her tips, and walked off her job. She knew that she would never return to it. Her only thought was to get drunk and get away from the phony Santa on the roof and the Christmas carols over the loudspeakers....

Later, almost one o'clock, a full hour after Christmas Day had begun, she found herself walking slowly along Wilshire, watching the traffic stream pass and looking at an occasional pedestrian. She didn't stop walking until she came to a slope of green lawn. She sat on a stone retaining wall and looked at the warm night and the palm trees overhead. She was slightly drunk, having stopped at every bar along the way and having allowed Christmas-happy barflys to buy her drinks. Now she felt warm and woozy, lonely, exhausted from her long walk.

She hummed a tune to herself and thought back to her childhood and the playground she used to go to every Saturday. Mother would put up a lunch for her to eat on the knitting benches by the metal slides. She thought of the redwood bark chips the city supplied for the play area grounds. The caretaker hosed the bark down in the morning and the steam would rise from it and linger in the air every Saturday morning until the sun came out and dried the bark to a light cinnamon color. She thought now that she could smell the bark, but it was only the palm trees on the grassy slope.

She saw that there was a man sitting on the slope not too far from her, and for a moment she was startled. He hadn't moved or made a sound, but had sat with his back to a palm tree, watching her.

He was thin and rundown, his sunburnt face unshaven and his cheap suit rumpled. He wore no necktie, and she saw the dark hair on his chest.

She became self-conscious of his unmoving eyes, and she muttered a snappish, defensive, "Merry Christmas." The man grinned for a moment, then lifted a wax carton of chocolate milk, as though toasting her, and swallowed briefly.

"Merry Christmas?" the man asked softly, settling back against the palm tree. "Lady, they don't have no Christmas in Los Angeles...."

She sipped the greasy coffee and watched the dull gloom of Saturday morning become the dull gloom of Saturday afternoon. She was surprised that she could recall the incidents of that final week in Los Angeles so clearly. She had never tried to remember before.

She returned to the kitchen, saw the grocery bag note, and thought that this was another thing.... Bruno had seemed strange, tense, the night before, as if something was bothering her and she was making an effort not to let it show. Yesterday, Erin had stayed sober and Bruno had returned from the gallery early. Erin had noticed the change then. Bruno had been jumpy and snappish, although she had said nothing aimed directly at Erin. But Erin had felt the tension between them. She had said nothing about it.

Bruno was probably worried about the Sausalito deal. They hadn't talked of it since they had crossed the bay to look at the property, but Erin knew that it was still on Bruno's mind. The lease would be up soon and Bruno had to have the money before that. She could probably pay for a lease extension, but that wouldn't do any good unless she had the money to start on the building repairs. It would be a shame to lose the chance. The night before, Bruno had stayed up past three in the morning, working on her bank statements and notebooks.

Erin finished the coffee and then showered. The water made her feel a little better. She stood in her room, watching her figure in the closet mirror. She pressed her hand flat on her stomach.

She dressed quickly, not bothering with a bra, pulling a loose dress over her head and stepping into her scuffed low shoes.

She was thinking of food again when the doorbell chimes woke her out of it. She went to the staircase, leaned over the shaky railing, and called out for whoever it was to come in.

It was Riley. He opened the door and peeked in, looking suspiciously along the walls of the garage, squinting at the paintings, then up to the staircase and Erin. He grinned and closed the door behind him.

He was wearing an expensive topcoat with the collar pulled up to his neck, his shaggy hair hanging over the edge. He seemed pleasantly drunk as he walked the length of the room, and for a brief, haunting moment he reminded Erin of the man against the palm tree in Los Angeles with the carton of chocolate milk.

"Howdy."

"What the hell are you doing here, Riley?"

He held up his hand, the one with the twisted thumb, and lifted his eyebrows in mock surprise. "Please, no profanity."

"What the *heck* are you doing here?"

"I'm a spy. I'm Cicero Riley. I was on Grant Avenue when I spotted Lepke Buchalter with some mousy blonde chick, so I figured you'd be here and I raced right up."

"You shouldn't be here," Erin said from the staircase.

Riley ignored that. He brushed an imaginary speck from the topcoat. "You dig the new coat?"

"I can't talk to you, Riley. I'm busy."

He ignored that as well. "Don't you dig the new coat?"

"Yes," she answered impatiently. "It's fine."

"It's a good fit." He grinned. "It's Merlin's—he just bought it."

"Will you please get the hell out of here, Riley?"

"Gimme a cup of coffee. I can smell it."

"Then will you leave?"

"Sure. I'm Honest Riley."

In the kitchen, Erin showed him to the table and lit the gas ring under the pot. Riley smelled like sweet wine, and he seemed happy. Erin poured the coffee as though she wanted to get it over with as quickly as possible. She was conscious of being watched, of the uncombed hair falling carelessly on her shoulders. But when she looked, Riley didn't have his eyes on her. She felt uncomfortable, her guard momentarily down. She pushed the filled cup at him, slopping a bit of it on the table, and dropped a spoon beside it.

"Do you use cream?"

"Sure."

"We don't have any. How about sugar?"

"Sure."

"We don't have any sugar."

"We're going to get along just fine today," he said. He sipped the coffee.

"This stuff tastes horrible. Did you put tobacco in it?"

"No, just coffee."

She poured a cup for herself and sat opposite him. She waited a minute in silence, then asked, "What've you been doing with yourself?"

"Painting."

"Do you still want to paint me?"

"Yeah."

She thought of the portraits on her grandmother's wall. She said, "Maybe one of these days, if you're still around, I'll let you do a portrait for me."

"Of who?"

"Me, of course."

"Sounds like it might be kicks."

She watched him for a minute. "What made you come here today?"

"I didn't have anything else to do. It's too gloomy to paint. I need north light and there isn't any coming in where I paint. I need sunshine."

"You should move to Arizona."

Riley shook his head. "Have you eaten yet?"

"What makes you ask?"

"Merlin slipped me five. I was going to put some food in me to absorb some of the wine."

"And you want me to eat with you?"

"Yeah."

"You're out of your mind."

"Yeah. Now let's go get something to eat. How about Chinatown?"

"How did you know I haven't eaten?"

"I'm a spy."

She thought about it, then went to her room to pick up her canvas jacket. She had to wait for Riley to finish his coffee. "If we're going to eat, then let's get the holy hell out of here. Every time I see you I end up getting into trouble."

"Who? Me?"

The telephone rang and she looked startled, then frowned. "You see what I mean?"

It rang again, insistently, and Riley shrugged. "You'd better jump to it."

She stopped the phone at the fourth ring. She caught her breath at the sound of the phone voice. It wasn't Bruno, as she had expected; it was Bunny. She knew the voice from all others and there was no mistaking it.

"I've been trying to find you," Bunny said cheerfully. "Didn't you get my message? I talked to some guy, I think it was Hibbert, and I told him you should call information."

"Yes, I got the message."

"Then how come you didn't call? Or come over to see us?"

"I don't know...."

"Hey, are you mad or something?"

"No, Bunny."

"Can you come out here today? Ken isn't working, he's on some kind of strike, and we have two full bottles of tequila left. Can you make it today?"

"I don't know," Erin answered.

Bunny sighed loudly. "Why can't you talk? Is someone there with you? Someone listening?"

"Yes."

"Well, bring them along then, old pal. We have enough tequila to go around. I'd like to see you, Erin. You owe it to me because you didn't come to the wedding. And I want you to come by today while Ken is celebrating the strike. He's in a real gassy mood and says he wants to meet you."

Erin thought it over, then said, "All right. I'll come by."

"Are you sure you're okay?"

"Sure. Why not?"

"Well, jeez, you sound kind of beat. Not like the old Erin."

"I feel fine."

"Good. Come right by and bring your friend, whoever he is."

Erin hung up and looked at the phone, then at the African mask on the wall. Bunny had assumed her friend was a man. And she had sounded fiercely cheerful. Perhaps Erin had expected, or hoped, that she would sound miserable.

Riley said, "You okay, man? You look kinda bugged. Was that Lepke?"

"No, it was an old pal of mine." She forced cheer into her voice. "Do you like tequila, Riley?"

"Sure. I'm Pancho Riley."

"Then how about drinking tequila for breakfast? We'll skip eating."

"I'm with you, man. Let's go drink tequila. I'm Tequila Riley, the Scourge of South of the Border."

"How much have you had to drink already?"

"I'm Wino Riley."

"I figured that. You looked drunk when you walked through the door."

Riley followed her down the stairs, whistling through his teeth and his cigarette. Out in the street, the greyness made his face seem pale. He shivered and stood by while Erin locked the door.

"I always get good and drunk when there isn't any north light," Riley said. "Werewolves flip out when the full moon is full, but old Riley he flips out when he sees no north light. I'm Rembrandt Riley—Scourge of South of the Border."

They stopped by the alley and Erin asked, "Do you know who we're going to see?"

"Tequila."

"That's right. But we're going to see a friend of mine—someone that I haven't seen for some time. Someone I once knew in LA." She studied his face. "So don't go goofing off or anything."

"Hell no. I'll just drink breakfast and say nothing."

She felt the profound gloom of the day cover her like a blanket, and she was determined not to allow it to affect her. She would let the day play its own tune. She was glad now that Riley had showed up. She would use him in a subtle way. She needed Riley. It was the same feeling as with Bruno, needing someone to create an impression for her. Erin wanted to prove to Bunny that she hadn't been hurt by the incident in Los Angeles. And with Riley along, even if he was half crazy and somewhat ragged—in spite of Merlin's new topcoat—she felt that the situation would be easier.

"Where we going now?" Riley asked.

"To the bus stop."

"We don't have to take the bus. I've got wheels."

"What'd you do? Steal a car?"

"No, just Merlin's shiny new scooter."

"What did you leave Merlin?"

"I left him his girl." He chuckled. "What more does the old bastard want? He's my best buddy, man."

They entered the alley and piled onto Merlin's scooter. Riley drove and Erin sat sidesaddle on the rear cushion. She was reluctant at first to put her arms around Riley's waist, but she almost fell off when they rounded the first corner.

Riley drove slowly, following Erin's directions to the Hyde Street address, and he tooted the scooter's horn at each intersection.

CHAPTER EIGHT

Bunny's apartment was first a small hallway that separated a kitchenette and a washroom, with the living-room to the left and the bedroom to the right. A cheap Oriental mat was on the floor, the pale blue walls were decorated with popular art reproductions, the furniture was imitation Danish. There was a desperate lived-in atmosphere about the rooms. Raw wood blinds held back the gloom of the afternoon, and everywhere there were the curiously mingled odors of fresh laundry and liquor.

Bunny met them at the door, wearing a Hawaiian-style Mother Hubbard loose over her figure, the pale blonde hair shorter than it had been in Los Angeles. She seemed to have put on weight, and the effect was startling. She wore no make-up and her features had a freshly scrubbed look.

Ken Ferrara turned out to be a tall man, thin and wiry, in his late thirties, with an eager baby mouth, a blond pompadour, and tattoos on his arms and wrists. His dark blue eyes seemed suspicious and dreamy. He acknowledged Bunny's introduction with a hesitant smile and a cheerful wink. He was fairly drunk, his movements unsteady.

Bunny looked at Riley with obvious curiosity.

"Say hello, Riley," Erin said.

Riley nodded. "Hello."

Ken Ferrara stepped forward, expelling a powerful beer breath, introduced himself to Riley and shook his hand, "Well, how about a drink? Bunny told me not to touch the last two bottles of tequila until you folks arrived, so I've been having beer." He paused. "Bunny's not drinking, so we have the rest of the tequila to ourselves."

In the living room, Ken performed various host-like motions, indicating sitting positions and fumbling with the cap of the first bottle. He displayed the label and announced that the tequila was *anejo*, which he pronounced with the hard *j*, then announced in conspiratorial tones that *anejo* was translated "aged" and he recommended it very highly—being an old hand at drinking tequila.

Riley sat, watched the bottle, and made no comment. Erin stood by the kitchenette with Bunny. The change that marriage had produced in Bunny was still in Erin's thoughts.

Bunny said, "You look good, Erin. I half expected you to look as tired as you sounded on the phone. But you look good."

"Thanks. How come you're in SF?"

"Ken," she said, casting an amused glance at her husband, affecting the attitude of the dutiful and patient housewife. "He quit his job in LA to work up here for his brother, who owns a trucking outfit. But right now they're on strike; went out the day before yesterday." She grinned. "We've been celebrating for two days now. The tequila was around the house, so Ken decided it was high time to start getting rid of it."

Erin said nothing. It had been a mistake to come. Bunny married wasn't the same, and the change had been too great. Erin felt as if she were talking to a stranger.

"I guess I look pretty different to you," Bunny said.

"You look good to me," Erin lied.

"I should." Bunny lowered her blue eyes for a brief moment. "I've been taking lots of vitamins and milk and crap. No booze. Just health junk."

Erin knew what Bunny was going to say, so she said nothing.

"I'm pregnant."

Erin managed the proper smile. "Congratulations."

They were both quiet. What could they say now? It was all so ridiculous. They avoided each other's eyes. What was Erin supposed to do, talk about babies and curtains? It was obvious that Bunny wasn't going to ask, "What have you been doing with yourself?" There was just nothing to say.

"Did you say you're pregnant?" Riley called out. He was holding a tumbler full of tequila. "Great! That's just great. Did you know that if all the Chinese walked four abreast in a single line they'd cover the world? The Great Wall of China can keep them from spilling over." He swallowed from his drink. "By God, you're pregnant!"

Bunny looked puzzled. She turned to Erin. "Where'd you find *him*?"

Erin was irritated now. Riley was her only defense. She didn't feel like abandoning him. And besides, whatever Bunny thought, she decided Bunny was wrong. Completely wrong. She said, "Riley? He's a very good friend of mine." She went to the imitation Danish couch and Ken graciously poured her a drink.

Ken looked at his wife. The tattoo on his right wrist was of a dragon. The one on his left wrist was a girl in a blue bathing suit. He said, "Would you like a drink, honey? There's still some cola in the refrigerator."

"No. I'm full of cola now. I'll be all right."

"Did you take your pill yet?" Ken asked.

"No."

"You should take it," he said seriously.

"I'll take one later. I don't really have to take them yet."

Ken said to Erin and Riley, "You know, Bunny has to take these pills...."

"Really?" Riley said.

"Sure. And one of the neighbors told us... well, first, you see, the pills are that gelatine kind, half blue and half pink... anyway, this neighbor said that if you swallow the pill down with the blue side first it'll be a boy. The pink side first and it's a girl."

Riley widened his eyes. "Really? Is that what the neighbor said?"

Ken nodded. "Yeah. Isn't that a riot?"

"It sure is," Riley said. "I think that's a riot, all right. Blue and it's a boy?"

"Sure."

Erin nudged Riley. She knew that she had stopped him from carrying on with it until both Bunny and Ken caught on. As it was, they had another drink and began to talk of something else. Riley started to needle the situation again, in the midst of the talk, and Erin interrupted him. Not that she disapproved—she thought it was an excellent idea—but she didn't feel that the time was exactly right for it.

"Riley?" she asked. "Are you a friend of mine?"

"Sure. Erin's the beautiful princess and I'm the court painter."

Ken said, "What kind of work do you do, Riley?"

"Work? I don't work. I used to work, years ago; I think it was in an orange juice stand. No, it wasn't an orange juice stand. It was a hot dog stand. I sold hot dogs. So I guess I could be called an unemployed hot dog seller."

Ken Ferrara was silent.

"The boss used to count the hot dogs. If I dropped one by accident on the floor the boss made me put it into the Dropped Hot Dog Bin. Then he'd count the missing ones and count the dropped ones, then count the money in the till. It was impossible to steal from him."

"So what did you do?" Erin asked.

"I worked a week, then opened the till and took all the money and closed the store. I was working under a phony name in the first place."

Only Erin appreciated the story.

They had a few more drinks. The coffee table became cluttered with cigarette stubs and the surface was ringed wet from the tumblers. The circulation in the room was poor and the smoke hung in blue layers.

Riley turned to Ken after a while. He said, "Actually, Ken. I'm a painter. I'm an unemployed painter."

"I see," Ken said thickly. His eyes were bleary now and the lids were blinking in slow motion, his movements clumsy. They had finished half of the first bottle of tequila.

"Let's have some more tequila," Erin said. "Have you ever been in Mexico, Ken?"

Bunny said, "We just came back from there. Before we came up here we took a trip as far as Guadalajara. We were gone for almost three weeks."

"Is that where you bought the tequila?"

"Yes."

They poured drinks. Erin felt the need to compete with Bunny grow even stronger now. She wanted either to leave the apartment or to force Bunny into an equal feeling of embarrassment. However, she realized that she didn't have to make any effort to do this personally; Riley was doing it for her. Riley was obviously enjoying some private joke at Ken Ferrara's expense, but Erin wasn't quite sure what it was. She wasn't even sure if Riley himself knew what it was. But anyway, this joke was producing results in Erin. She found that she was completely relaxed, having a good time at last.

She had feared, when she entered the apartment, that it would be impossible for her to enjoy herself. But not so now. Ken was unaware that Riley was pulling his leg. Bunny was sitting stiffly, hands folded neatly on her lap and exposing the swell of her Mother Hubbard, not looking at Erin or Riley. She seemed genuinely puzzled about the undercurrent in the room. She also seemed to be as disappointed in Erin as Erin was in her.

Riley talked about Mexico, explaining something to Ken. A few more drinks, a half hour later, and Erin began to feel the effects of drinking on an empty stomach. Riley was definitely more drunk, and Ken Ferrara was on the dangerous edge of becoming stupid.

"Mexico is a great country."

"I agree with you, Ken. You got it right. I'm glad you said that. It's very keen of you to see that."

"Mexico is a great country."

Outside, the Hyde Street cable car passed with a slow rumbling sound and the floor of the apartment house shuddered. The first bottle was empty. Bunny went into the kitchenette and cut some meat for sandwiches. She set them out on the coffee table.

"I thought you might be hungry."

"Ah, the inner man," Riley said thickly.

Ken staggered to a portable record player and set on a stack of bad records. Erin saw that Riley took no notice that the music was bad. He was busy stuffing a meat sandwich into his mouth and washing it down with tremendous gulps of tequila. He had removed Merlin's topcoat and was wearing a white shirt and the Canadian GI trousers.

"Were you in the Army?" Ken asked.

"No."

"I thought you might have been."

"I'm 4-F. I'm a psycho."

Ken said nothing. Only Erin and Riley were drinking now.

"Are you working?" Bunny asked Erin.

"She's a psycho," Riley said.

"No, I'm not working," Erin answered.

Ken turned drunkenly to Riley. "My wife and Erin were the best of friends in LA. They haven't seen each other for a long time."

"That's what I hear," Riley said.

Erin, wanting to change the subject, but not particularly the mood, asked, "Ken, Bunny tells me you're out on strike."

"That's right."

"Strike?" Riley said. His eyes widened and he sprinkled salt on his thumb. He swallowed tequila. "That's the right idea, Ken, my friend. Strike. Throw off those shackles of Capitalist domination. Show the front office who the boss is: the working class. Man, you strike and you better the working class and make it a better world for the little man." He poured another drink.

Ken's expression became puzzled, then hard, and he thrust his jaw towards Riley. "It's not quite like that, fella. It's not a Commy thing."

"Who said it was?"

"You, fella. You sounded just like a goddam Commy."

"What's a Commy sound like?"

"The way you sounded."

Riley smiled. "Why are you striking?"

"Because the union tells me to, that's why."

"Are you a union member?"

Ken glowered. "You're goddam right I am. I'm a Teamster."

"Why does your union want a strike?"

"To get us more loot!"

"Who're you striking against?"

"I don't know, for God's sake.... The guys who pay us."

Riley sipped from his drink and shrugged. "Who pays you?"

"The bosses." Ken Ferrara narrowed his eyes. "What're you driving at, fella?"

"Nothing. Not a gaddam thing. All I said was that you should strike against capital and get a better deal. Then you called me a Commy."

"You sure sound like one."

"*I'm* not striking against the bosses for better wages. *I'm* not a member of a union that's telling me to strike for a better wage or working contract. If you say that's Communism, then *I'm* not a Commy...."

"You're twisting everything around, fella." Ken stood up, swaying drunkenly, and glared down at Riley, then at Erin. "I don't know who you are, Riley. You come in here and drink my liquor and call *me* a Commy. I didn't ask you to come here. You're my wife's guest. Just remember that."

"I didn't come in here and call you a Commy, Ken," Riley soothed. "You called me a Commy. Remember?"

Ken thought a minute. "Yeah, that's right." He sat down again and glared into his empty glass. "But if you don't like it here you should go back to Russia."

Bunny, who was sober, shook her head. "Honey, forget it. I'm sure he didn't mean anything. He didn't call you a Commy. He only said—"

"I heard what he said," Ken muttered darkly. "He's a Beatnik Commy."

Riley and Erin burst into uncontrollable laughter. Riley's shoulders shook and his face became red. "That's the funniest line I ever heard, man. You're a great cat. `He's a Beatnik Commy.' That's priceless!" He looked at Erin who was trying to balance her drink and laugh at the same time. "Princess, don't you think that's the greatest line you ever heard?"

"That's great," Erin said between her laughter. She was proud of Riley. Riley was all right. He was half crazy, but he was all right. She felt drunk now, the tequila sat very easily in her and her stomach didn't grumble. The taste was superior to bourbon or sweet wine. She must remember to drink only tequila from now on. She said, "Riley, you're funny. I'm drunk and I think you're funny."

"I ought to be. I'm a Beatnik Commy. When my mother had me she took the pills and swallowed the red end first."

They both laughed again. Riley whooped. Ken sat stewing, thrusting puzzled glances at his wife. Bunny was desperately trying to ignore Erin and Riley.

Riley stood up and proposed a toast. Ken staggered up and held on to Riley for support. Everyone stood except Bunny.

"A toast to the Great Wall of China."

"That's a Commy country," Ken said seriously.

Erin couldn't contain herself then. She went out into the hallway and laughed, practically wheezing. She laughed until she wondered what was so terribly funny. Then she laughed again. She went into the washroom and washed her face in cold water. She could hear Ken Ferrara in the other room, playing more corny records and talking with Riley.

Erin combed her hair and clipped it in place with her comb ring. She returned to the living room, feeling gay and woozy. The afternoon had been a success. The Ferraras were embarrassed—and Erin wasn't.

It was a grand feeling.

The second bottle was better than half gone. Riley was demonstrating to Ken the proper way to drink. Ken was splattering salt and adding to the confusion on the coffee table. Riley seemed to be having the time of his life.

"I'd like to talk to you a minute," Bunny said.

"Sure," Erin said. "Go ahead."

"In the kitchen."

They went into the kitchenette. Bunny looked worried. "I'm glad that *you* came by, Erin, but Riley's getting under Ken's skin. I know they look friendly right now, but that's Just Ken's way. I can tell when he's really mad."

"Are you asking me to leave?"

"I don't mean it to sound that way, Erin. I only wanted to tell you about it. Riley's a nice guy, don't get me wrong, but Ken's a bit drunk right now and I don't think he's appreciating him, that's all."

"You've changed," Erin said.

"I suppose I have."

"You used to be different. Riley's in there pulling your old man's leg and you don't even know it. The way you used to be, you would've seen it."

"I saw it, Erin," Bunny said rather coldly. "But Ken didn't. And Ken's a nice guy...."

"Then let's forget it."

A cable car passed and the floor shuddered again. It sounded late outside. Cars honked their horns and street signals clanged a hollow lonesome sound. It must be getting late, Erin thought.

"How long have you known Riley?" Bunny asked.

"Not too long. Why?"

"I don't know. He's a nice-looking guy."

Erin thought about that. "I hadn't noticed, but I suppose he is."

"Does he really paint?"

"What're you fishing for, Bunny?"

"Nothing."

"Sure he paints. He says he's a good painter."

Back in the living room, Ken looked at them, his eyes bleary and his face flushed. His golden pompadour had collapsed, and he had removed his shirt. He was showing Riley the tattoo on his chest, an enormous eagle with small flowers surrounding it.

"Hey, Princess, look at this guy. Look at that eagle. Isn't that something? He's a regular *Pictures at an Exhibition*."

"A what?" Ken asked with a slur.

"It's a piece of music. Written by a cat named Moussorgsky."

Erin said, "He's a Russian."

Ken ignored that. He showed a bluebird on his calf. "I had that one done in San Diego when I was in the Navy."

"The Navy's a good outfit," Riley said.

"Goddam right it is," Ken said.

"Ships and all that," Riley said.

"What?"

"I said the Navy has ships and things like that."

"That's right," Ken said.

"Do you have any more tattoos, Ken?"

"No."

Later, Bunny happily announced that the tequila was finished. Erin suggested they leave. Ken made no protest. Riley found his topcoat and finished his drink. Everyone shook hands. Erin was staggering. She was at that stage of drunkenness where she was wondering if she would remember this very moment the next day, and if she did she was wondering what she would think of herself. She shook hands with Ken and smiled broadly at Bunny.

Ken's eyes had a feverish glitter in them, and he was grinning, showing his teeth. He shook hands with Riley at the door, the smile on his face cold and false. "Well," Ken said heartily. "We had a good time. And, Riley, even if we don't see eye to eye on a few things, I think we got along just swell."

"Sure," Riley answered. "Just grand. I think you're a real brick, Ken."

They continued to shake hands.

Erin tensed. She saw the frozen grin on Ken's face. She was about to warn Riley, when the punch was telegraphed. Riley saw it in time and stepped back. Ken was still grinning. He looked crazy. Riley dropped his topcoat to free his hands, and when Ken lunged again he chopped him easily in the face. Ken staggered back into his hallway and slammed heavily against the wall.

Bunny screamed.

Riley retrieved his coat and Erin followed him down the staircase that led to the street level. Doors in the hallway opened and people asked about the screaming. Erin heard Ken Ferrara shouting in a high drunken voice.

"You dirty Beatnik Commy bastard!"

Out in the street, they laughed again and piled on the scooter. Neon signs blinked farther down the block, and a cable car passed, bell ringing, tracks rattling. There was no moon and the air was cold and misty. There was a taste of salt seeping up from the bay. Riley looked over his shoulder at Erin. "Do you want me to tell you that I liked all of your friends?"

"No. Forget about it." She was still grinning from her laughing seizure.

"The things I do for a free drink." He shook his head sadly. "Goddam, the things I do." He drove down Hyde Street, honking the horn. "Where to now?"

Erin had to shout back. "Riley, let's you and me get some more tequila."

CHAPTER NINE

Erin stood by the marble fireplace in the main room of Howard House, her eyes riveted on the portrait of her grandmother. She barely moved. The sun was held back by the tightly drawn curtains and there was barely enough light for her to see by. She looked pale and drawn; her skin was splotched and dark under the eyes. She felt sick and dizzy. She hadn't eaten yet, and her eyes felt as if they were capable of vomiting.

She had seen her reflection in a darkened shop window when she had walked up the hill that afternoon to the old house, and she had felt ashamed of her appearance. Her hair was disheveled, she wore no lipstick, and her showy shoes had split at one toe. The shoe looked like an alligator with its mouth yawning open. She was going rapidly downhill in appearance, and curiously enough, she didn't mind it at all. Perhaps, after all, that was how it was supposed to be. When she had seen herself in the shop window she had had to look twice to make sure that it was herself.

Now it didn't matter.

No one had spoken to her yet, but she suspected the worst. It was as if she could smell it in the house, as if it had seeped down from the upper rooms to the ground floor.

The house was very still.

Mr. Shelby, the old woman's lawyer, was still at the telephone, taking notes, or perhaps doodling, and talking in low whispers. He had acknowledged Erin's entrance with a businesslike nod of his head. Erin had waited in the main room.

She tried to remember all that had happened the night before. It had been so strange and confusing. But, when she considered the useless turn her life had recently taken, it didn't seem strange. Still, everything was confused. Even the buildings and the automobiles and the ships that travelled the seas were terribly detached and unreal, almost frightening. Everything was pointless.

Was that why her wild night with Riley had been so agreeable?

She listened to Shelby's whispering. She tried hard not to think of what was upstairs. She thought of the night before....

After leaving Bunny they had driven crazily, drunkenly, on the scooter, tooting the horn, weaving over the hills. She hadn't remembered when they had stopped at a store, but they must have because Riley had another bottle of tequila and two limes.

They drank straight from the bottle and sucked on the limes, making sour faces. Across from the church steps, where they had been, the park had seemed dark and forbidding. The wind had become bitter cold and the streets deserted.

Riley had sat with his back to the church, holding the bottle in his hand—and again Erin had been reminded of the man in Los Angeles with the chocolate milk sitting at the palm tree on the grassy slope of hill.

Later, at Vortigern's, they had had soda water spiked with tequila, and had listened to the jazz group. She didn't know when it had been that she had returned to the garage. She hadn't seen Bruno; she had even avoided the Sedge-Hammer during the night.

That afternoon, when Shelby had phoned, Bruno had already left for work and Erin hadn't seen her. Shelby had called at two o'clock. She had left the garage at two-fifteen.

She looked up at the portrait of her grandmother and felt no bitterness or remorse. She felt hollow and tired.

Shelby hung up the phone and came briskly into the darkened room. He looked like an ageing athlete. He was a large man, probably in his late fifties, with a bronzed moon face and snowy white teeth. The crown of his head was bald, and a horseshoe of white hair grew around his temples. The hair looked like a victory wreath. His blue eyes sparkled. A masonic ring flashed on his hand. He wore an expensive dark suit and a white silk necktie. He looked like the Hollywood ideal of a successful lawyer.

His voice was powerful, trained, direct. His smile was the equivalent of a hearty handshake. His tone was somber at the moment.

"I'm terribly sorry, Erin. I've been tied up on your telephone." He tried to look solemn. "It's been quite a while since we've met... I hate to have us meet again under these circumstances."

Erin nodded, quietly suffering her hangover and dreading what she knew the remainder of the day would be like. The room smelled stuffy and sour. She felt dizzy and sick again.

Shelby's voice tried to adjust itself to the weight of his words, but he was far too jovial to assume anything as foreign as another's tragedy. He said, "I'm sorry about your grandmother, Erin. I called as quickly as I could. I didn't have your number, so I had to look about the house.... I found it in Hibbert's room."

"When did it happen?"

He looked surprised. "You know?"

"It wasn't hard to guess."

"No, of course not. It happened last night. Or early this morning."

"It was her heart?"

"Yes. Dr. Hayward's up there with... is in her room at the moment. He can tell you more about it."

She sat down in a high-backed chair of carved lions, flowers, and sour velvet trim. She wondered if she would cry.

Shelby paced the room with pent-up energy, snapping his fingers. "Dr. Hayward called me as soon as he could. He didn't know what else to do, who else to contact." He looked at her, as if to estimate the depth of her grief. "It was expected... this was expected," he said quietly.

"Yes."

"And still it comes as a terrible blow to me. I knew your grandmother very well. In fact, it was your grandfather who gave me my start."

Erin nodded. She said, rather uselessly, "She spoke very highly of you, Mr. Shelby."

A few minutes later Dr. Hayward entered the room and joined them. He was a tall man, taller than Shelby, with a drawn face and a drooping right eyelid. He looked loftily about the room, wrinkling his brow. "Hello, Erin," he said softly. "I don't suppose you remember me."

"Of course I do."

"I suppose Mr. Shelby here has told you about...."

"Yes. We were expecting this to happen."

Hayward's drooping eyelid lifted slightly. "Really? Yes, of course.... The first attack weakened her considerably. She became stronger when you returned, but the severity of last night's attack must have been too great for her...." He paused, seemed almost ashamed. "I'm terribly sorry that it happened, Erin."

She shook her head. She didn't know how she felt. The final living link had passed on and she had no urging toward remorse. She knew that she was firmly attached to many things in her past, but she realized now that none of it had been with her grandmother. She regretted this—but she felt no remorse.

She looked about the room, half expecting to see Hibbert lurking in some musty corner. She wondered how the old man was taking it.

Dr. Hayward's nurse waited in the hallway, a beige coat thrown over her arm, a bored expression on her face. Her thin legs looked hairy under the white stockings.

"The ambulance should be here any minute now."

Erin nodded absently. Everyone seemed tense and uncomfortable, as if they were waiting for her to weep. Didn't they know that she had loved the old woman, but that she wanted nothing to do with her death? Didn't they know she wasn't going to cry? Why did they stand there waiting for her to ease their tensions by showing her emotions for their benefit? She didn't need tears. She needed a drink. She didn't need tears to prove that she had loved her grandmother.

She thought of the money that was now hers. She could do plenty with the Howard money. And the big house—it was hers now. She didn't like to think like that, but it was there and she couldn't avoid it. She had just inherited a fortune.

Shelby put his hand on her shoulder. "I'll make all the arrangements, if you wish, Erin. You won't have to worry about a thing."

"Thank you, Mr. Shelby."

Hayward went to the hallway and talked with his nurse. Shelby said, "Would you like to go into the kitchen while the ambulance men are here? Or would you rather go to her room for a minute?"

"No—the kitchen will be fine."

She stopped and said good-bye to Hayward. She avoided the disapproving look in the nurse's eye. In the kitchen, she was grateful for the opportunity to make coffee and set out cups. She was embarrassed with her inability to feel sad, and, aside from that, Shelby's self-assurance upset her.

He sat at the table, holding a gold fountain pen in his hands.

"I want her to be cremated," Erin said. "When you make the arrangements I want you to see that it's understood. She always wanted it that way."

"I didn't know that, but I'll see that it's done...."

"Yes, you take care of it."

She poured the coffee. She was thinking of the cremation. It would be much easier that way. She didn't want to face another cemetery scene. She could imagine herself, older now, reflected in the polished surfaces of a chauffeur's sunglasses.

"I want to get the whole thing over as quickly as possible."

Shelby nodded.

"She had no other relatives?"

Shelby looked surprised. She wondered if he thought she was being irreverent. It amused her to think that he did. "No, no other relatives. You're the only heir."

"I hadn't meant it like that. What I meant was, is there anyone else that I should notify?"

"Any friends?"

"Yes. She was well-liked by—"

"Forget all that. I want the cremation to be closed services. Or whatever it is they call it."

"Of course." He sounded disappointed.

"I want it done quickly." She paused and looked moodily into her coffee cup. "I hate death," she said.

He nodded again. A film of perspiration was on the crown of his head. His French cuffs were thrust out on his wrists, showing the huge, aggressive cuff links. His Masonic ring sparkled. When he glanced at her, Erin lowered her eyes.

"You knew my mother...."

"Yes. I can understand how you must feel."

"Thank you."

He sounded as if he wanted to know how irreverent she wished to be. He said tentatively, not shrewdly, but prying, "There are other matters...."

"Do you want to talk about them?"

"If *you* wish."

She listened as the ambulance men came into the house and walked heavily up the stairs. Shelby followed the sound with his eyes, looking at the kitchen ceiling. "There's the matter of the will," he said. "It was revised after your mother's death. Your grandmother wanted it done at that time because she feared for her own health."

She was almost enjoying this. Shelby was uncomfortable, choosing his words carefully. If he knew how she hated death and its complications and how she had loved her grandmother, then perhaps he would understand. But he didn't know. He saw her with a hangover, reeking of tequila from the night before, saw the alligator mouth of her shoe. What else could he think?

"She provided for Hibbert."

"To what extent?"

"Twenty-five thousand dollars."

She pursed her lips when he named the sum.

"Of course that's only a fraction of what you'll receive," Shelby said with distaste.

"I hadn't asked that. Do you think I'm being irreverent?"

"Yes... you're acting very callous."

"I don't want to seem that way. I wanted to bug you."

"Why?"

"Because you look righteous and pompous. You've always looked that way. When I was a little girl I used to puff out my chest and imitate the way you'd walk into the house. I guess I wanted to get even with you.... No, that's not the real reason."

The ambulance men descended the staircase.

"They're taking her away," Erin said softly.

Shelby was silent.

"I loved her," she said. "But she's dead and I don't feel up to humoring the dead." She glanced nervously across the table. "Will you remain as my lawyer?"

"If you wish."

"I wish. I want you to understand me, Mr. Shelby. A lawyer should have confidence in his clients. You understood my grandmother?"

"Yes, I did."

"Will you volunteer to remain as my lawyer?"

"Yes, I'll volunteer."

"Thanks. I didn't do that to see if you'd crawl, Mr. Shelby. But I need the confidence the same as you do."

He looked thoughtful for a minute. "You're very honest, Erin. I'm surprised."

"No, I'm not honest. I only pretend that I am because it makes everything easier."

"Either way, it achieves the same result. You're honest with others even if you're not with yourself."

"That's a clever thing to say."

"I hadn't intended it to sound clever."

"Are you shocked by my irreverence?"

"Not deeply. You're probably acting the way most people would like to be able to act after a death."

"Is it refreshing?"

"Not especially. I've seen it before. But only in Mexico."

She smiled warmly at him. "Would you like some more coffee, Mr. Shelby?"

"Thank you." He smiled back at her, and wiped the top of his head with a large white handkerchief. "I suppose the matter of the will—"

"What about it?"

"It should be handled as quickly as possible?"

"Yes."

"Any time?"

"As soon as you can."

"Then you'll bring Hibbert around to my offices?"

"I'll bring him in."

"Do you know where he is?"

"What?"

"Do you know where Hibbert is?"

"Isn't he here?"

"No."

"Didn't he call the doctor?"

"No. Today was Dr. Hayward's regular visiting day. There wasn't any answer and the door was unlocked. She was dead when he arrived. There was no sign of Hibbert. Hayward imagined he had taken a holiday."

"Then Hayward called you?"

"He called his nurse first. She and I were the witnesses."

"And Hibbert wasn't here?"

"No. I thought you might know where he would be."

She shook her head, puzzled. She had pictured Hibbert upstairs with his head in his hands, his eyes pink from crying.

"Does he have a day off?" he asked.

"No. Even if he were given one he wouldn't take it."

"Do you have any idea where he might have gone? Does he have any relatives?"

"No."

"It's damn peculiar, his not being here. That means he doesn't know about Mrs. Howard, then...."

"I guess I'll have to tell him." She looked at him seriously. "You don't think there's anything wrong, do you?"

"I'll admit it looks suspicious, but I don't think there's anything wrong. Dr. Hayward is positive it was her heart."

"What're you thinking?"

"I'm only keeping an open mind. I'd hate to have an investigation. And if Hibbert doesn't show up, or explain his absence, then it could lead to one. It's a possibility."

Erin nodded.

Shelby stood up and slipped his gold fountain pen into his pocket. "Is that all for now?"

"Yes. Would you like more coffee?"

"No, thank you." He started for the door, Erin going with him. "I'll be at my offices. I'll make the arrangements and get in touch with you later."

Erin nodded.

"Are you sure you'll be all right?"

"Yes."

"Do you have friends you can be with? Or do you feel that's necessary?"

"I'm going to get drunk."

He frowned. "Then I'll call you later, either this evening or first thing in the morning." He paused. "I'll have to notify the newspapers."

"I don't want anyone coming here."

"I'll see to it. When Hibbert gets here have him call me."

"I'll do that, Mr. Shelby."

They shook hands and Erin stood at the door until his big Chrysler pulled away from the curb and disappeared around the corner.

The house was quiet.

She wondered why Hibbert had left. He couldn't have had anything to do with the old woman's death. That was ridiculous. But, of course, it was correct of Shelby to consider the possibility. Erin didn't believe he had anything to do with the death; Hibbert was too good a person. She had known him all her life. She pictured him now, shuffling along the streets, lost, grief-stricken. She shuddered.

In her grandmother's room there was still an indentation on the bed where her grandmother's body had lain. The men from the ambulance had made the bed carelessly. There was a reflected pool of light on the ceiling where the sun glanced from the silver medicine tray. The room smelled of death to Erin and she stood there, feeling cold, waiting for some sign of emotion to show in her. Nothing came. She imagined her grandmother waking in the middle of the night. Had she known that she was going to die?

Erin went to her old room. She hadn't been in it since she left, four years ago. It had changed. The walls had been repainted and none of her things remained. There was the taste of camphor and paint in the air. She found a few unidentifiable trinkets in the drawers and a stack of her grandmother's old clothing in the closet.

Where were her old things?

She found them in the basement, neatly packed in a metal trunk, and she searched the tiny drawers sentimentally. A school photograph, pencils, a dog tag, a plastic hand mirror, an envelope filled with strips of silver foil. She closed the trunk, disappointed because she hadn't enjoyed looking at the things. She had felt saddened by them. She went upstairs and turned on the radio and poured herself a cup of lukewarm coffee.

Sitting in the kitchen, she realized that the afternoon had all the necessary requirements to bring about a sense of summer laziness and well-being. She felt none of it. The kitchen, with all its heart-warming props, seemed mysterious and unfamiliar.

The phone rang, breaking the spell, and Erin became frightened again. What if someone asked to speak to her grandmother? She hesitated before answering it.

The voice was soft, practically a whisper. "Hello, Erin...."

"Yes. Who is this?"

There was only the sound of breathing.

"Who is this? Hello...."

Silence. Then the line went dead. She hung up and stared at the dial face, terrified, her face pale. From somewhere there was a creaking sound. The basement?

The phone voice had frightened her deeply. It could have been Bruno. But it didn't sound like her. Who was it? Why had they hung up?

She quickly left the house, locking the front door. She had left her jacket behind, but she didn't return for it. She started to run down the hill.

CHAPTER TEN

"Did you call me on the phone just now?"

Bruno looked puzzled. "No, I thought that you were zonked out asleep. What's the matter? You look pretty shook up."

"I am."

"Hangover?"

"I suppose that's it. Other things. But maybe I'm hung over, too."

"I've got some beer. That's supposed to fix you right up."

The gallery was empty. Outside, the sun was pale yellow and the shadows were lengthening; a thin wind was beginning to pick up scraps of paper and whirl them in the gutters. Traffic was becoming heavy and there weren't any children playing on the sidewalks. Housewives passed the gallery window with grocery bundles in their arms.

The beer was cool and biting in Erin's throat, and her stomach rumbled. The beer settled her. She felt a false sense of well-being. Bruno's presence helped her.

She drank the beer until the rumbling in her stomach ceased. Bruno watched her intently, as if studying her, and noticed the gaping split in the toe of Erin's shoe. She asked how it had happened. Erin shrugged, answered vaguely that she had been riding a motor scooter. Then they grew silent. Bruno opened a beer for herself and continued to study Erin. Erin paced the gallery floor, wanting to hear noise, wanting to escape from herself. Anything. She finished her beer, opened another. She continued pacing, thinking, biting her underlip. She had been foolish to be so frightened as to leave her coat behind. She should have returned for it.

She paused, stood in the center of the room. She had to tell Bruno what had happened. She had to tell someone, anyone. She said, simply and unemotionally, "My grandmother's dead."

"What?"

"Dead. You know, like dead. I'm having her cremated."

"You're kidding."

"No, I'm not. My lawyer, Shelby, called the garage after you left for work. He didn't say anything on the phone, but I knew she was dead the moment I walked into the house. It was gruesome. I wouldn't even look at the... at the body."

Bruno looked serious. She shook her head and pulled her lips tightly across her teeth. "How do you feel about it, Erin?"

"Busted. Nothing. Not a goddam thing. I was angry at myself at first because I couldn't feel anything, but now I'm not."

Bruno looked thoughtful, pursing her lips and staring at Erin's feet.

"You didn't call me at the house?"

"Hell no. If you were at your grandmother's, how could I call you? I don't even know her phone number."

"Sure, that's right."

"You don't seem to be very broken up about her."

"That's the hell of it. I can't get broken up about it."

Bruno smiled softly. "Have you been doing much drinking?"

"No. This's my second beer today."

"What's all this about a phone call?"

"Nothing. It was probably my lawyer. But he didn't say anything."

"I suppose you'll be going to the services. Do you want me to go along with you, kind of hold you up?"

"There won't be any services. They make me sick. Actually sick. I get frightened at funerals."

"Then you're going to forget the whole thing—" Bruno snapped her fingers— "just like that?"

"Just like that. I'm not even going to think about it."

"Then I guess I won't bother telling you how sorry I am and all that goody-goody jazz."

"Fine. I don't want to hear it."

"You want another drink? I can go to the store if you do."

"If you'll make it tequila."

Bruno shrugged. "Okay, you watch the stand for a minute."

Bruno left for the liquor store and Erin sat behind the desk and sipped at her beer. She thought again of her fear of the house. There was nothing to fear. Everyone was dead, all of them, so why had she been frightened? There wasn't anyone left. Her mother, father, stepfather, and now her grandmother, were all dead. Of course, there was old Hibbert left, and she had to include him in the list because he had helped raise her. But she doubted if she was afraid of Hibbert. She considered him harmless.

She didn't even believe that he could have had anything to do with the old woman's death. It seemed ridiculous. Hayward had said that she had died of a heart attack. It was only Shelby, with his prying mind, who had become suspicious of Hibbert because of his absence. And even Shelby had played down his suspicions. He didn't want an investigation. An investigation would only make his job harder, and, naturally, he didn't want that. So Hibbert was probably off the hook, even if he had done anything—which Erin refused to believe. Hibbert was just a harmless old idealist. Just a fool.

She walked around the gallery, forcing her mind away from centering on herself. She looked at the paintings and the prints on the walls, but she didn't enjoy it; the portrait of her grandmother was still in her mind. She sat at the desk again and studied the painting of herself. Then she picked up the telephone directory and found Shelby's number. She dialed. A secretary answered; then, a few seconds later, Shelby himself; his voice booming pleasantly.

"Shelby speaking—"

"This is Erin Howard."

He lowered his voice considerably. "Of course. I was just about to call you. Everything is arranged with—"

"That's not why I called you. I want to ask you something."

"Go right ahead."

"First, did you call me earlier? At the house?"

"No."

"You're my lawyer and you understand me. Right?"

"I believe so...."

"Am I rich, Mr. Shelby?"

"I beg your pardon?"

"I asked you if I am rich."

A pause. "You have been well provided for."

"I want to have my portrait painted. Could I do that?"

"I don't see why not."

"I'm broke."

"I see...."

"Do you? Good. Can you get me some money?"

"How soon?"

"Now."

A pause. "Have you been drinking?"

Erin smiled. "I'm glad that you understand me, Mr. Shelby. Can you get me the money right away?"

"How much?"

"Two hundred."

"That's quite a bit."

"You're getting paid."

"Well, I suppose I could let you have it. But it will have to be a loan. I'll have to take it from my own pocket."

They settled on two hundred out of Shelby's pocket and arranged to have it delivered to Vortigern's Bar by messenger before six o'clock. Erin hung up just as Bruno returned from the liquor store. She felt better after her talk with Shelby. She felt that death had passed her by without touching her. It was a good feeling. She could do whatever she wished now, as she had just done by deciding to have her portrait painted. She would hang it beside her mother's and her grandmother's. It would be the final, proper, irreverent, comic touch. Two stiff old-fashioned portraits, and one by.... She decided that the painter would be Riley. The decision amused her. It was Riley she had had in mind all the time. He was the only one she felt could do it. She even looked forward to the time of sitting for him. She knew she would enjoy it. So far, there hadn't been any time with him that had been bad. She had been able to honestly relax with him. There had even been... a feeling of security.

"You look like the cat that swallowed," Bruno said.

"I feel like it."

"Have you eaten yet?"

"No."

"You'd better eat, man. This stuff's murder on an empty stomach."

"No it isn't. I didn't eat yesterday."

"You'll get skinny."

"Big deal."

She opened the bottle and nervously poured two drinks into wax cups, handing one to Bruno and forcing a brave smile onto her face. It felt as if it were pasted there. She gulped at the liquor eagerly, wanting to beat her own nerves into senselessness. She finished the drink in a single gulp, then poured another drink.

"Are you going to live it up, Erin?"

"Dance on the grave?"

"That's right."

The gallery was becoming dark and they sat in the corner by the desk and drank in silence. Erin wanted to see Riley, to tell him of his forthcoming commission.

She didn't owe Riley anything. She had to remind herself that Riley was, after all, just a nice, crazy character who amused her, took her for a ride on a borrowed scooter and offered her a chance to get away from her troubles. There was nothing real about Riley. He was just a drunk, a penniless artist who asked nothing of life and gave it nothing in return.

"Have you been thinking about what you're going to do?"

Erin shook her head, almost sadly. "No."

"Do you remember what we talked about?"

She thought a bit, looking at the tequila bottle on the desk. What *had* they talked about? Sausalito? Yes, of course. Bruno was the more realistic of the two. She realized that Erin was rich, and, as was only natural, she wanted to move ahead with their plans. Their plans.... She said, "You mean Sausalito? I remember. Of course I do. Don't you worry about it. I'll take care of everything for us."

Bruno didn't say anything then.

There was still no word from Hibbert. She had called the house twice and there was no answer, then she called the garage, and after Lilly reported no word from anyone, she was tied up for five minutes explaining her grandmother's death to Lilly. Lilly was properly sympathetic—or was she too sympathetic?

Erin finished the phone calls and waited at the bar for the arrival of the messenger. It was almost six o'clock, the neon sign over Vortigern's doorway was sputtering to life, smoke was filling the large room. She asked the bartender for a drink explaining that she would pay him in a few minutes. Then, when the messenger arrived, she paid the bartender with a twenty-dollar bill.

"Don't you have anything smaller than that?"

"No."

He gave her change in one-dollar bills and a pile of silver. Since she had no pockets in her blouse and skirt, she stuffed the wads of money back into the thick envelope and left it on the bar top. The bartender shook his head in disgust and narrowed his eyes at the envelope.

"That's a lousy way to haul money, man."

"I don't have any pockets."

"Yeah, but it's still a lousy way, man."

Marian and Lilly arrived at seven o'clock. Lilly avoided Erin's greeting and walked to the table with her head bowed and her lips tightly closed.

"I'm damn sorry to hear about your granny," Marian said. "Lilly told me about it right after you called. That's a tough break."

Erin looked away and said that she didn't want to hear about it, that it was all over, and, as far as she was concerned, it was done with. Completely.

She didn't want to hear about it.

They had a bottle of sherry at the table. The wine tasted hard and sweet and it gagged Erin, but only the first drink. The second one was better. And, a second later, the third was even better.

Although it was fairly early, Vortigern's was packed, the tables crowded and people standing two deep at the bar. Beer handles thumped in the background, beer barrels were emptied with a loud whining hiss, tobacco smoke rose to the ceiling and clung there. An unwashed man with a straw hat was sitting at the table next to Erin's, practically jammed into her seat, and he was listening to everything that was being said. With the straw-hatted man was a dumpy greying woman, and, at the end of the table, a young fellow. The straw-hatted man tipped back his hat and poured beer from a community pitcher. The greying woman picked at the wax table candle, scraping it with her nails. No one spoke. No one seemed capable of speaking.

Finally, the straw-hatted man asked, "You want some beer?"

"No," Erin answered. "Do you want some wine?"

The straw-hatted man nudged the young fellow on his right. "How about it, Abe? You want some wine?"

Abe nodded.

"My name's Orcutt," the straw-hatted man said. "I'm a lawyer."

He was drunk.

"Have some wine, Mr. Orcutt."

"Not Mister. Just Orcutt. That's spelled with two t's."

Erin bought another bottle of sherry and poured for the three glasses on Orcutt's table, which, since it was so close to Erin's, was practically an extension of her own table. Orcutt seemed pleased with the arrangement. The greying woman said nothing. Abe, the young fellow, gulped his wine and stared intensely at the musicians in the corner. Marian looked disgusted and became sullen. Lilly still didn't say anything.

"Where'd you get the bread?" Marian whispered angrily.

"Dead man's gold," Erin said. "I'm going to have my portrait painted."

The greying woman asked who was going to paint the portrait.

"A friend."

"Who?"

Erin shifted uncomfortably under her blank stare. She said, "His name's Riley...."

The woman nodded with a smug smile.

"Do you know him?" Erin asked.

"I should. I'm his mother."

Erin didn't know what to answer to that. The woman was obviously lying, so Erin didn't make any comment. The greying woman waited, looking at her with burning, half-lidded eyes, then looked sourly at Abe when
Erin refused to talk to her. Marian had watched this going on and she asked
Erin if she really intended to have her portrait done. Erin shrugged. Marian snarled, looking dark and bitter, tilted her cigarette holder to an FDR
angle and nervously fingered her silver crucifix.

"Have you seen Bruno?"

"I just left her," Erin said. "We were drinking tequila."

"Does she know about—"

"She knows."

"What'd *she* say?"

"Nothing. Why should she say anything? Look, Marian, I said let's forget about everything for right now. Let's have a party. I want to drink and
have a ball. Okay?"

"Whatever you say, honey. It's your play."

Abe said, "Hey, man, let's have some more of that juice over here."

Orcutt did the honors before Erin could reach for the bottle.

Erin asked Lilly what the matter was. Lilly was saying nothing, acting
like some kind of ostrich. Was Lilly angry?

"No, Erin. I feel fine."

"You don't seem to be having much of a ball...."

Orcutt kept pouring the sherry until the bottle was empty; then another
bottle was brought and Erin paid for it from her envelope. By nine o'clock
the bar was too smoke-filled to see clearly. Figures stood in the corners
looking like people in a heavy fog. The music became louder. Riley and
Merlin arrived at nine o'clock. They came directly to the table.

"How's my tequila-drinking buddy?"

Erin smiled. "Hello, Riley."

Merlin sat between Orcutt and Abe. "Hello, friend Orcutt. What're we
drinking?"

"Sherry," the lawyer answered.

Merlin drank from Orcutt's glass.

Erin excused herself from Marian, and asked Riley to talk with her for
a minute. Riley asked, what about? She didn't answer him and he followed
her through the crowded room and out into the street.

A flatbed truck was parked at the curb by a coffee shop on the next block,
and white-jumpered workmen were hanging colored-paper streamers

from lamp post to lamp post. Three cops were standing before the coffee house, watching the workmen put up the decorations.

"What's this all about?" Erin asked.

"They're getting ready for the Street Fair."

"Are you going to exhibit?"

"No. Merlin's going to show some junk he's done." They were standing in a darkened doorway. Riley looked at her. "Is that why you asked me out here?"

"No. I want you to paint my picture. A portrait."

"Sure."

"How much do you want?"

"For what?"

"The picture."

"I thought it was the other way around. I thought *you* got paid for posing."

"I'm commissioning you."

"I've never been commissioned before. I wouldn't know how much to charge."

"Think about it."

"Okay. You pay me for the material cost and supply me with a sandwich and lots of beer while I paint and we'll call it even. But I don't know if it'll look like you. It might, and then again, it might not. I've never painted a portrait before."

Erin dug into her envelope and handed him a hundred dollars. "If you want more I can get it for you."

He didn't look at the money in his hand. "Where'd you get it?"

Erin shook her head. "It's a long story, Riley."

"I've got a long ear."

She told him then and he listened, leaning against the door. She told of her grandmother, about Shelby and the money, even about old Hibbert and his disappearance. She added the phone call and how she had become frightened. When she finished he only shrugged indifferently and folded the money into his pocket.

Erin took ten dollars from the envelope and handed the remainder to him. He was the only person she trusted right now. She wasn't afraid for Riley to hold her money, because if he ran off with it then Bruno was right; if not... then Erin was right. She had to know, so in a way she was testing him. But she already knew that he wouldn't take the money. It was such a small point to begin with, but it mattered deeply to her. She said, "I don't have any pockets. You hold onto this for me."

He shrugged again and pocketed the money.

They returned to the table in the bar. Marian noticed immediately that the envelope was missing, but she said nothing about it and only stared suspiciously at Riley, then cautiously at Erin.

The greying woman made room for Riley at the table. Orcutt was in the middle of an involved story, but only Abe seemed to be listening.

"Hello, Riley," the greying woman said.

"Howdy, Mother."

"Is this your mother?" Erin asked.

"No. She supported me once in New Orleans."

"That's right," Mother said. "You're doing okay now?"

"Yeah," Riley answered. "I'm doing fine."

Mother nodded, peeling at the candle. "I thought you'd be dead... somewhere in New Mexico."

"No. I'd never die in New Mexico."

"That's right. You'd find a New Mexican to support you."

"Why be bitter?"

"I'm not bitter, Riley. It's just that you're a bum."

"That's true. I agree with you there."

The greying woman sneered drunkenly, then looked intensely at Erin. "I used to be married to a political cartoonist in Florida."

Erin didn't answer her.

By eleven o'clock the joined tables were overflowing with empty bottles. Orcutt was leaning in a puddle of beer. Riley was half drunk, drinking sherry from a beer mug, and he watched Abe mix beer and wine like a chemist. Abe was drinking with silent desperation. His eyes were blurred and his long black hair was hanging in his thin face.

Riley said, "What're you doing these days, Abe? I haven't seen you in a helluva long time."

"I'm a writer," Abe said.

"A writer now? That's fine."

"A poet," Abe corrected.

Riley narrowed his eyes and looked at Abe as if he were weighing him in his thoughts. "How do you like being a poet?"

Abe shrugged. "It's all right."

Orcutt said thickly, "Looky, I was a lawyer for six years. Sure. Then... I quit. Just like that. I couldn't take it. Today I don't know if it's legal to spit with your eyes closed. I even had a dog. I forget its name. But I remember it ate up two lousy cans of food when it was growing. What happened to that dog? I'll tell you. He drowned. I don't remember how he drowned, but he sure as hell drowned. I think he fell in the bathtub. Or maybe I killed it. I don't remember. I was a lousy lawyer anyway."

"What kind of lawyer were you, Orcutt?" Riley asked.

"Corporation. But I was lousy at it."

"And your doggie died?"

"There's no connection," Orcutt said. "I was a lousy lawyer because I drank too much. I went downhill, used to go to the clinics and get B-1 shots and pamphlets. I couldn't whip the alcoholics, so I finally joined them."

Bruno arrived at eleven-thirty, still carrying the grocery bag with the tequila bottle outlined against it. She took an extra chair and glanced around the table, frowning when she noticed Riley, then smiled broadly at him. She set the bottle on the floor under the table.

Erin touched Bruno's foot with her own, a message meaning not to be belligerent with anyone. But Bruno didn't seem angry at all; in fact she smiled at Riley and Erin and seemed to be in bright spirits. Merlin gave a big drunken hello to Bruno and Bruno grinned.

"Have you been drinking all this time?" she asked.

Erin nodded, and the movement brought a second of weakness in her. She hadn't eaten. She touched the tequila bottle with her foot and asked if there was very much left. Bruno said no, she had been drinking steadily ever since five-thirty.

"Hell," Erin said softly, "people drink a lot."

Orcutt poked Bruno's side with his elbow. "Statistics, man. Honest-to-god statistics. San Francisco has more booze than any other city in the country, more alcoholics, more bars per capita, more insanity, and more suicides. That's statistics. It's true, too."

"Who the hell are you?" Bruno asked pleasantly.

"Don't you know me? My name's Oscar Orcutt. I'm a dog trainer. I train them to jump into bathtubs from incredible heights."

Riley laughed and Bruno turned to him. She asked, "What're you doing with yourself, Riley?"

"I've been commissioned."

"You having a party?"

"It's my party," Erin said. "My lawyer sent me money to commission Riley. He's going to do my portrait."

"To hang on the wall like we were talking about?"

"That's right."

"It's a grand idea," Bruno said. She winked. "I'm sure that Riley'll do a bang-up job. If Merlin says he's a good man, then I'll take old Merlin's word for it."

Erin liked Bruno when she was in this rare mood.

More wine was brought to the table and the night wore on towards one o'clock. The jazz became more aggressive, bursting into colored little bits and showering the smoke-filled room. Riley's face became a blur in Erin's vision. Bruno's face was also a blur. She wondered about them both, but she couldn't piece anything together. She was happily drunk, completely surrendered to her condition. She didn't want the night ever to end. She wanted to sit there forever, drinking, talking, then drinking some more. She discovered that sherry and tequila made one helluva combination.

At one o'clock Merlin's girl friend, Mac, arrived to pick him up. She stood by Riley and cursed him when she saw the condition Merlin was in. "Didn't you realize, stupid, that this old fool has to make the Street Fair in the morning? How the hell can he do that now? He can hardly walk."

"Sorry, Mac," Riley muttered. "Not my fault."

"Whose fault is it?"

Merlin raised his bleary eyes and jabbed his thick forefinger in the air, looking righteously outraged. He glared at Mac. "It's *my* fault, Mac. Sit down and have a drink.... We're having a goddam party here and don't louse it up."

Mac sighed and joined them. She didn't have anything to drink. She refused when Orcutt held out the bottle to her.

Merlin explained, "Riley's having a party, nitwit. He's been commissioned and he's going to pay us some rent pretty soon."

"Is that true?" Mac asked.

"Yeah," Riley said.

"Then I'll have a drink." She looked at Erin and smiled.

Erin was too drunk to catch it all. She felt like a human island of drunkenness, isolated from them all, completely secure by herself, not reaching them.... The clock on the wall behind the bar said one-thirty. She closed her eyes. How did it get to be so late? She opened her eyes. The clock said a quarter to two. She shook her head and poured another drink.

The party rose as one and staggered slowly out the door, weaving, lurching, leaning on one another, and they moved towards Bruno's parked car in a single, drunken knot.

CHAPTER ELEVEN

Why had she asked the party to continue at Howard House? It was senseless. Erin couldn't remember asking herself about it. She had been completely oblivious to everything except the pleasant sensation of cold air rushing against her face. That had been the ride in Bruno's old Plymouth. How had they all managed to squeeze into the car? She didn't remember. But somehow they had—they must have, because they were all in the house now, in the main room, still drinking.

Erin sat in the kitchen and rubbed an ice cube against her face and neck. The sounds of the party were muffled by the closed door. She heard the radio being played, voices, glasses clinking against bottles.

Bruno came through the door with a full glass of vodka. "What're you doing in here?"

"Ice. I wanted ice. I feel hot and sticky." Erin stared dumbly at the offered glass of vodka. She accepted it half-heartedly. "I don't remember riding in the car...."

"You passed out in the car. I had to wake you up."

The kitchen seemed proper enough, but Erin was disturbed by it when she looked around her. Something seemed to be out of place. It wasn't anything she could notice right away. She only felt it at first. She tried to concentrate, but she was too drunk, and nothing came. Her eyes felt like hot peeled grapes and her brain churned like glue. It was something that had to do with.... Then she remembered.

"The cups," she said softly. "The cups're gone. Shelby's cup and my cup. They were right here on the table."

"*What's* gone?" Bruno asked.

"Goddammit," Erin muttered darkly, "the cups. They're not where they're supposed to be."

"What cups're you talking about? You feel in the cups?"

Erin found the cups in the sink, washed and dry, the spoons put away and the sugar and cream pitchers gone.

Hibbert must have done it. She bit her underlip and wearily closed her eyes. She should have left a note for him, saying where she would be.... But she had thought only of herself and her desire to escape the death completely. She had been too anxious to save her own skin from the touch of death. Now she had missed Hibbert and her thoughts of him were still uneasy.

"What about the cups?" Bruno asked.

The door swung open and Orcutt pushed his flushed face into the kitchen. "Where.... Oh, where's the head?"

Erin pointed towards the hall, and the door closed after him.

Erin said, "I don't know why I asked them up here. I don't even remember doing it. Maybe I wanted to prove something."

"What could it prove?"

"I don't know. I'm drunk, dead dead drunk, stinko, blinded by liquor. I'm in a spin, loving the spin, Lord I'm drunk. I feel a helluva lot drunker than I look and I must look pretty damn drunk to feel like I do.... You following me?"

Bruno smiled. "You look like a clock about to run out of time, honey, bust a spring, start ringing. You better sleep. It'll be different in the morning. You'll see these creeps all over your floor, guys like Orcutt and Abe... even Riley, and you'll wish you'd never asked them here. They won't be a very jolly sight in the morning."

"You're right, Bruno.... At least, I *think* you're right."

"Sure I'm right. This's a great pad. I wouldn't trust no guys like that if it were my pad."

"Ha! That's you. I don't give a good goddam if they steal this place blind blind blind. I don't like this place."

"Well, chick, *I* do. You're just not looking at it in the right light. The place is all paid for and it's *all* yours. Every goddam room in it is yours. No more rent to pay. No people telling you what to do and what not to do. It's all yours. You can have a ball here, do whatever you damn well want to do. Just look at it in the right light. You don't see the good deal we've got with this place."

Erin nodded. The vodka tasted like witch hazel. "Would you really like to live here? Would you like to save rent, or payments, even in this dump?"

Bruno's eyes glittered. "Yes. It's a great pad. Are you thinking about it?"

"I owe it to you, Bruno. You once asked me to come in with you to save rent, so now I'm asking you. I get a kick out of being able to ask you."

"You wouldn't mind if we all moved up here?"

"I don't care what you do. I care about me."

"We're going to swing, Erin. Coasting from here on. We got it made and everything's going to be all right."

Erin's grey eyes widened then and glittered feverishly. "I want another drink," she said. "I guess I do. I'm drunk but I want more drink. It's vodka, isn't it?"

"Yes. Your friend Riley bought tons of it. The cheapest they had."

"My friend Riley. Are you angry with me because I talk to him now and then?"

Bruno looked surprised and she shook her head. "Me? Hell no. Riley's an all-right guy. I'm not mad at him. Not at all...."

Erin felt good then. She liked Bruno's mood.

Bruno said, "About Sausalito... I'm going to see those people tomorrow. Do you want to come with me? Or should I see them myself?"

Erin shook her head. She had almost forgotten about Sausalito and their plans, but she knew it was a burning question with Bruno. "Of course. But I can't go."

"I can't go over empty handed...."

Erin thought of that. Of course not. She'll have to call Shelby in the morning and ask him for the money. "How much will you need?"

"*We* need, honey. It's *us*."

"That's right."

"About five thousand."

"I'll get it," Erin said positively. "Don't you worry."

They returned to the front room. Riley was sprawled on the floor by the couch, holding a bottle and smoking a cigar, the smoke hanging in the room like blue cobwebs. Only one small light was on and the room was dim. The drapes were parted and the moon was an opal shine on the front lawn and the old tree.

Everyone was unreal in the shadows of the room. The Victorian atmosphere was a tricky stage setting. Their mannerisms took on a nervous jerkiness and they talked their stories, of past parties and mutual friends, reassuring themselves of an unspoken secret cult of which they were members. The past was offered without enthusiasm, the present with humor. The room became a mass confessional, and the late hour was the audience.

Abe drank with quiet intensity, without talking or listening, adding nothing and taking nothing, only drinking and showing interest in drinking. The greying woman, whose name was Iris, sat with Abe, ignoring him, and talked with Riley.

Riley smoked his cigar, talked, used his hands, allowed his gestures to emphasize a point without raising his voice. Erin sat with Bruno and listened to them, feeling better now after her ice-cube rubdown.

"Where'd Marian go?" Bruno asked.

"Home," Merlin answered heavily. "She said she was going home. Wherever that is."

The circle of faces watched in the darkness, listening, talking without confusion, drunk without boisterousness or gaiety. The party settled down to a smooth, even tempo, a rhythm of nothingness, more sound than silence.

"Abe's too drunk to talk," Iris said tiredly. "Abe's a poet turned alcoholic, or an alcoholic turned poet. I'm not sure which way it goes."

"I knew Abe before," Riley said.

"Before what?"

"I don't know. Just before."

Abe finally fell forward from the couch and Mac caught him before he hit the floor. He had passed out cold. Iris set him out on the couch and pulled his shoes off. She tied the laces together and hooked them around his neck, somewhat like a scarf, and the shoes rested on his chest. "He even has me do this when we're alone," she explained. "It's a throwback from his Salvation Army days. They used to steal his shoes."

By four o'clock Erin had finally pieced Iris's story together. The idea of cult and confession had penetrated into Erin's consciousness and she began to think of the story as having great importance. Later, she talked of her own past, telling it to Mac and Merlin, who had asked her questions about herself.

"God, I should never go back to New Orleans," Iris said wearily. "The gig I had was utterly. Half the time I was sick. Really sick. Know what I mean? God, it's a sick town. I don't know why anyone'd want to live there. Abe and me, we slept on a balcony for six goddam nights once. There were roaches as big as mice. Abe damn near died."

A bird sounded just outside the window and Erin looked in that direction. Why didn't the birds go to sleep? Where did birds sleep? Did birds sleep?

Iris talked.

She had, as she had said to Erin before, been married to a political cartoonist in Florida, and, after years of life in Coral Gables, she had left him to live with a tobacco salesman from New Iberia, Louisiana. When she met Riley, she was stranded in New Orleans with a suicidal banjo player. The banjo player had finally heard the Great Message and had seen the Great Light and he had leaped fifteen stories to get a better look. Riley was jobless then, as he always was, and Iris had supported him. She seemed to have a passion for artists, and when Riley left after three months she took up with Abe. She followed Abe to San Francisco, where the Renaissance offered more for poets than New Orleans did. Abe, Iris said, was sick, a better drunk than poet, and she was about fed up with him. It seemed she wanted a sculptor, but they were hard to find.

Riley said, "Yeah, Mother, a sculptor is tough. See, they have to have more visible talent than painters and poets. Most times a poet can fake it because there's enough idiots who'll listen to anything. Painters can argue their work. But I see sculptors like I see musicians. Eyes and ears, objective kick. So, sculptors are out."

"Why do I cling to Abe? He's a sick kid. There's nothing more miserable than misery recognizing misery."

Riley shrugged. "The Abes are easier to find and more difficult to contradict. Who's to say Abe isn't a genius, or even a poet? I'm not. You're not. Who really gives a goddam? If you care enough about Abe you'd save him a couple shots of vodka for the morning. He'll need it then."

"I never did like you, Riley," Iris said bitterly.

"I guess not. It doesn't matter."

Mac tried to waken Merlin then. She said, "How am I going to get old Rubens here up in a few hours?" She shook him again. "You'd better wake up, stupid. Midnight Flyer come rolling in the dawning."

"You could put him to bed," Erin suggested.

Mac protested at first, but Erin insisted. She was drunker now, much drunker, but her mind was clear enough. She showed Mac to her old room at the top of the stairs, then went into the kitchen while Orcutt, Mac, and Riley carried Merlin up to bed.

In the kitchen, Erin rubbed more ice on her face, then drank more vodka. She found a slice of cantaloupe and ate it greedily, the juice running on the front of her blouse.

Riley came into the kitchen, looking at the room as if he were inspecting the building. "Great pad. Fabulous."

"I'm hungry."

"Go ahead and eat. I'm just looking at the pad."

"Go right ahead and look. It's got plenty of rooms. Rooms all over the place. In every room you look there's a room. It even has a basement. That's downstairs."

"A weird place to put a basement."

"Did you look at the two portraits? Do mine any way you like, but make it that size. I want to put it up there to prove to everybody how irreverent I am."

He looked at her. "I'll bet you don't last another hour. I'll bet you blow a fuse."

She felt his eyes on her and she shook her head. "I'm not going to give myself that chance. I'm going to go to bed." Then she glared at him, deliberately. He came into focus and she felt an uncommon roiling in her when she looked at him, as if she suddenly suspected that he was holding a secret from her, and the effect was like a quick and sudden tourniquet applied to her throat. She had to look away then, angry and ashamed of herself. Riley definitely upset her, and it wasn't an unpleasant feeling. But she cursed herself then. Riley was a pig, she told herself, just like all the other goddam pigs.... She was lying to herself, but she insisted that he was a pig.

Suddenly she wanted to hurt him for making her feel unsure of herself with his undemanding attitude. She glared at him again. He was watching her with an amused look, a Riley look.

"And I'm going to bed," she said. She was whispering tensely. "You're a pig, Riley."

She turned away and stood by the sink, grabbing onto the drainboard for support. Riley didn't move from where he stood.

Lord, she was drunk, monstrously, hideously drunk. She couldn't control her crazy thoughts or her speech. She was thinking and saying things she knew she would regret later. But she didn't give a wild damn about it. She was deliriously and uncontrollably drunk. She turned and looked bleary-eyed at Riley.

"Are you trying to hurt me, Erin?"

"Yes. You pig!"

"What makes you think I give a goddam if you want to hurt me or not?"

"Are you stupid? You think I'm stupid? I *know*, Riley. I know it in here. I know because I'm not stupid. I can feel it all over you. But you're more clever than any other normal Grade-A pig. You're a sneaky pig!"

He looked at her with anger in his eyes and stepped slowly towards her. She moved back. Then, with a release of breath, he relaxed and shrugged indifferently. "You'll feel better in the morning, Erin. I'll see you then."

He left the kitchen and she bit her underlip as she watched the door swing shut. The pig! Oink oink. She would have loved to have him slug her; then she could hate his guts. But she couldn't hate him. Riley was a good guy. He was a crazy bum, a bum, a screwball who sang goddam cowboy songs. A maniac, that's what he was. A lousy, stinking, mooching maniac.

She left the kitchen, barely able to walk under her own power, and Bruno met her in the hall.

"I'm going... to bed—beddy-bed," Erin said.

"You look pale as a ghost," Bruno said. Her dark eyes narrowed and she ran her hand through her hair. "Are you all right? Someone take a poke at you, or something?"

"I'm fine," Erin lied. "I'm sleepy's all."

The phone rang.

"Answer the phone," Iris called out.

Erin reached for the receiver. Her voice was small. "Hello?"

Silence.

"Did... did you call me once before? Did you?"

Silence.

Erin's hand shook and she gripped the curling black cord to gain control of herself; she held her breath, turned her back to Bruno. "Did you call me before? This afternoon?"

"Yes," the voice said.

"Who is this?"

A sound.

"What did you say? What?"

"I said: why did you kill your grandmother?"

"I didn't kill anyone...."

A cracking sob. "You murdered her," the voice said.

"Who is this? Is this Hibbert?"

"Yes."

Erin sighed her relief, the tension oozed slowly out of her, and she felt gratefully limp. "Why do you talk like that, Hibbert? Where are you? Why don't you come home?"

A gurgling, clanking sound, then one word—"Pizarro."

"Where? Hibbert?"

The line went dead and she hung up. She looked around for Bruno, but there was no one in the hallway. Bruno had gone to the front room. She went upstairs then and closed the door behind her. Nothing completely penetrated. She tried to etch the call in her mind so she could remember it in the morning. But it slipped away and she knew she wouldn't remember all of it. Her legs felt heavy and she sat on the bed.

Was Hibbert crazy? He had sounded drunk, and that wasn't like him at all. She couldn't imagine him drinking.

She *had* to find him.

She undressed in the dark. There was the beginning of false dawn now, an eerie stillness settling in the room. The window was open, but there was no breeze. The curtains didn't stir.

She lit a cigarette and rubbed her eyes. Why had she exploded with Riley like that? It was a lousy thing to do. She recalled the conversation with shame. She had baited him hard. She had said some pretty rotten things. She blushed and closed her eyes. She wished that it hadn't happened.

Her eyes were heavy and she opened them. She was under the covers. Outside, a bird sounded. Don't birds ever go to sleep?

Didn't humans ever sleep? In gardens, without nests, chirping, peeping, talking good-bye. A breeze began and at last the curtain fluttered, and Erin finally fell asleep.

CHAPTER TWELVE

She called Shelby first thing in the morning, and his usually hearty voice became argumentative and sour when she explained the reason for the call. Erin pictured him dubiously watching a growing file that represented Howard money being loaned out.

She wasn't sure how much money she had, and she didn't particularly care, but she knew it to be considerable and she knew that her request wasn't altogether unreasonable, but she soft-pedaled it at first because she didn't want to get on the wrong side of Shelby. For some unaccountable reason she feared that if he disapproved of her he could somehow interfere with her inheritance. But that was senseless. The money was hers. Why shouldn't she be able to ask for any amount and receive it? How could Shelby possibly interfere? Her fears were groundless, as she knew, but they were there, nonetheless.

Yesterday she had found it much easier to talk with Shelby, perhaps because she had been confident of her charms, but in the morning this wasn't so. She didn't feel as sure of herself. There was a certain parental note, authority perhaps, in Shelby's attitude. Was Shelby a Daddy? Did she see him as Authority?

Shelby had buffaloed her on the phone, in spite of Erin's minor success at the finish.

"No."

"Why not, Mr. Shelby? It's *my* money."

"Because it's not your money yet. You've got to realize that. A *small* loan is quite all right, but the amount that you now ask for is out of the question. What business proposition is this? I've always advised the Howards on investments in the past, and I feel that my judgment has proven its worth. Of course, if you *must* press it. I can't very well refuse. Not very easily, at least. But I strongly advise my looking into the matter before I start handing out any cash."

"It's an art shop."

"Art?"

"You know, like art. Painting. Neckties. Junk jewelry with modern design. That kind of stuff. Art."

"I see...."

"No you don't. I don't like your attitude."

"What would you do if you didn't have my attitude to make you look twice at your whims?"

"Is that why you act the way you do?"

"Perhaps."

"I dig you, Shelby, but I still want the money. It's for a friend. I'm investing in a business that this friend and I...."

"You've told me that."

"Then send it to me."

Shelby sighed. Didn't Erin realize that the money wasn't hers to spend yet? Didn't she know that any amount of cash advanced to her must come from Shelby himself, and that in order to make it proper there were certain papers to sign so Shelby could claim his money from the estate when it finally came due? Didn't Erin realize this?

Of course.

Then Shelby would have to look into the matter. If the money was going to come from his pocket, then he had every right to protect the investment for himself as well as his client. If it was a cut-and-dried matter of handing over Erin's own money, Shelby could hardly argue about it, but it wasn't as simple as that. Five thousand dollars, in spite of all one hears about inflation and astronomical salaries of certain celebrities and politicians, was still a great deal of money.

"Yes or no?"

"As I say, I'll look into the matter."

"Right away."

"You're a headache, Erin. Tomorrow you'll buy the Golden Gate Bridge from a `friend.'"

That was how it had gone, bantering back and forth, Erin hung over and unconvincingly aggressive, Shelby cautious and stern, fatherly, tolerant. And they had finished with Shelby's having the final say. He would look into the proposed investment, would come directly to the house to speak with Miss Snider and study her idea, hinting that perhaps other motives were behind his decision to come to Howard House, that perhaps he would capitalize on his "fatherly" upper hand and try to talk sense into Erin.

Erin hoped not. She didn't want any Daddy crap to come between what camaraderie they had established so far.

Bruno didn't care either way.

"So, who's Shelby?" she asked with an indifferent shrug. "It's your loot, not his. Your estate's probably his best account and the old bastard wouldn't want to lose it. So you can do whatever you want and he'll eat bird-seed off the end of your toes if you want him to." She stretched out on the bed and yawned. "If he comes here to play adviser, let him. He's harmless. I'll show him the plans, the books from Sedge-Hammer, and maybe I'll even run him over to Sausalito to see the property. If he wants to play adviser I'll humor him...."

The sun was over the eastern rooftops and the air was bright and clear. A beautiful summer day. From the window Erin could see the long green lawn and the old tree that reminded her of her lost childhood, or merely forsaken childhood. The spiderwebbed curtain fluttered in a warm breeze and touched the post of the bed. Erin sat by the telephone and smoked a cigarette.

"I'm starved," she said.

"That's a good sign," Bruno answered. "It shows you're still young, still got bounce. When you get older you won't even be able to crawl out of the sack after a night like last night."

"*You* still feel good."

"I didn't drink as much as you did. Lush is a bad kick; I've told you that before. I smoked at the gallery, in the rear by the little window. The smell goes right up the airshaft."

They dressed and went downstairs, and right away Erin was struck with the stuffy odors of liquor, stale cigar smoke, and dirty feet. She opened the front door to let in fresh air.

Riley was wide awake, his eyes red-rimmed, an empty bottle lying at his feet. "Good morning to you, and howdy."

"Are you *still* awake?" Bruno asked.

"I slept some. But that goddam Orcutt snored so bad I kept waking up. I held his nose twice, but he didn't even care. He snores on his back, his side, his rump, and even on his gut. The guy just snores."

Erin looked around the room. Orcutt wasn't anywhere in sight. Only Abe and Iris, both curled up on the sofa.

"He's sleeping in the hall," Riley explained. "I dragged him down there, hoping he'd be quieter. But the hall acted like an amplifier. Like sleeping in the Hollywood Bowl."

In the kitchen they found two tins of meat, and Erin made sandwiches and reheated the coffee she had made the day before. They had finished eating before Shelby arrived.

The lawyer didn't ring the bell or rap on the doorframe. He walked directly into the hall and looked at the wild scene in the living-room. He wrinkled his nose, then fixed an eye on Erin, who was standing in the kitchen doorway.

"We had a little party," Erin explained weakly.

"So I see." He cocked his bronzed head like a huge bird and passed a hand over his bald head, the Masonic ring flashing. His black shoes glistened and he shot out his white cuffs. He rocked on his heels and glared.

Orcutt pulled himself slowly up from the hallway floor, his straw hat bent on the side where he had slept on it. Erin asked Shelby if he would like a cup of coffee. "It's no bother. Honest."

He went into the kitchen. Erin followed him, feeling that so far the affair was going very badly—did Shelby think that they had danced on her grandmother's grave waving the spoils of inheritance?—and she wondered why she should care if it did go badly. She poured coffee for Shelby and introduced him to Riley and Bruno.

Was Riley the young chap commissioned to do the portrait? Indeed? Shelby shook hands all around and regained his composure, as if he had slipped under a shockproof robe, sat down at the table without formality and nodded cautiously to Bruno. They began to bite around the edges of the investment.

Riley looked pleased with himself as he sat apart from Shelby and Bruno, who were engaged in talking over the Sausalito details. He looked at the ceiling with a knowing smile, then at Erin, watching her with his thoughtful, red-rimmed eyes.

Erin poured herself more coffee and tried to follow Shelby's questions and Bruno's answers, but she felt Riley watching her and she couldn't concentrate on the conversation. She stood next to Shelby and self-consciously tried to look a part of it, but when she did follow them for a few minutes she immediately lost interest. Riley upset her. Almost the same as he had the night before.

Orcutt came into the kitchen and put his head into the sink, turning on the cold water onto his neck and splashing vigorously, slapping with his hands and wobbling his head. He didn't bother to remove his straw hat. The running water left a dark damp streak on his shirt. He finished, babbling sounds and drinking from the cup of his hand, then turned slowly and faced the table. He looked directly at Shelby and smiled. He said, "Hello, Sam...."

Shelby looked startled, and he regarded the shabby figure of Orcutt with suspicion. Then recognition and astonishment crossed his face. His mouth hung open and a dumbfounded smile tugged at the corners. "By Jumbo!

Jim Orcutt! Well, how are you, boy? What're you doing here?"

"Just having a ball, Sam," Orcutt said.

"By Jumbo! I wondered where you'd disappeared to." He thrust out the palm of his hand and shook Orcutt's hand. "You look... good, Jim."

"Nuts."

Shelby laughed uncomfortably. "Same old Jim Orcutt. By Jumbo. Never thought I'd see *you* again." He looked around the room. "Knew Jim here years ago. Practically a classmate of mine."

Erin was surprised at that, and she looked at Orcutt carefully for the first time. It seemed that he actually had been a lawyer. When Erin looked at him she saw that he looked old and seedy, where before she had thought of him as being young and seedy. But he was old, the sagging lines carefully concealed by the diversion of his outlandish dress. It was easy now to believe that he had been "practically a classmate" of Shelby's.

Orcutt was embarrassed and attempted to cover it with a few lame jokes. Then he hastily slipped from the room, saying that he was going to check the front room. A few minutes later Erin heard the front door close and she went to open it again. Orcutt had left, taking Iris and young Abe with him.

Back in the kitchen, Shelby was expressing his desire to see the Sedge-Hammer books and the Sausalito property. Everything seemed to be in order so far, but he wasn't about to make any premature decisions or promises.

Shelby left the house and Bruno followed him. Riley stayed behind. At the door, Bruno stopped and whispered to Erin.

"I'll be back later. Don't worry about a thing. I'm going to have Marian open Sedge-Hammer because the Street Fair's a big day for me and I don't want to miss a dime of it. Every penny counts. Especially when you got scars on your butt to get where you are. You don't want to backslide, you just want to move on. Not back. So don't worry about a thing."

"I won't worry. You sell Shelby and do a bang-up job. You know how to handle him."

"Sure, I'll take care of it. If you get a chance, meet me at the gallery and we'll look the Fair over together. It'll be kicks." She winked happily, more happily than Erin had ever seen her. "Don't worry about Sausalito. We'll make a mint."

"I'm not worried," Erin answered. How could she be? She didn't really care about making a mint. It was Bruno's idea. It was Bruno's desire for possession, success, that was pushing Erin into the deal. Of course, she didn't mind it; in fact, it pleased her to be able to do it.

Bruno left the house, half skipping along the pavement, and Erin returned to the kitchen. Merlin and Mac were there, having coffee.

Would the stream of faces never end? The house was becoming a bus depot. She should post a time schedule for the arriving and departing guests.

Merlin looked as if he were in a daze. His face was grey and his hair was uncombed. He looked sick. "I slept like a log," he whispered hoarsely. He sounded shot, liquor-scratched.

"That used to be my bed," Erin said.

"It's a good bed."

Riley whistled softly through his teeth, smiling again.

Erin shot him a look. He still upset her. She said, "What's the matter with *you*, Riley? You've been giving me funny looks all morning."

"Guilt, man."

"What?"

"You must feel guilty."

"Don't analyze me. Just paint me. But don't analyze me."

Riley looked at her, solemnly, tiredly. "You're a good subject to paint...."

"Don't flatter me."

"I wasn't. Not really."

"Then don't say that tripe to me. Not this early."

"You're buying in with Bruno?"

"You know that."

"Good idea."

"You don't have to sound so goddam caustic about it, Riley. You get on my nerves. You're a sneaky sonofabitch."

"You're being touchy. Last night I was a sneaky pig."

She closed her mouth. "Okay. I'm sorry, Riley. I'm being touchy. That's true."

Merlin looked at Mac, frowned, rubbed his jaw, and stirred his coffee with his thumb.

"Where'd everyone go? They cut out already?"

"They went to the Street Fair, nitwit. And we're going—"

"Hey! Street Fair!" He looked frantically around the room. "Today's the day I make my dough. What'm I doing here?"

Mac smiled sweetly and cupped her chin in her hand. "Now you're getting it, Rubens. It's coming to you."

"No no, I'm atmospheric."

"You're hilarious this morning. Good old jolly Merlin."

Merlin nodded absently. As they were leaving, he looked back to Erin and Riley and said, "Did you know that my mother named me after a wizard?"

When they left, Erin looked sadly at the breakfast mess—the meat tin with gelatin oozing out onto the table, the bread scraps, cold coffee cups with cream rings, and piles of cigarette stubs. It was a depressing sight. She felt tired and let down. She felt Riley watching her again but she didn't look at him.

Hibbert should be here to clean up. Erin didn't want to do it. As far as she was concerned the mess could sit here and gather dust until another wild night added to it, doubled it, tripled it—she didn't give a damn. It was too much to demand of her to clean a house that she didn't have any feeling for. She had the feelings, actually, but she refused to acknowledge them. She let everything sit where it was. Don't kick over anything and nothing will crawl out from underneath.

"Hibbert called me last night. Do you remember the call I told you about? It was him."

Riley didn't answer and she didn't look to see what his expression might be. "What's eating you, Riley?"

"Nothing. You said that Hibbert called you."

"He told me I'd murdered my grandmother."

"You can remember what he said? You were pretty drunk last night."

"I remember. He said that I'd murdered my grandmother."

Riley saw that she was speaking seriously. He leaned forward in his chair. "What else did he say?"

"Just that, really. Oh, and he said 'Pizarro.' I'd asked him where he was and he said 'Pizarro.' I think maybe he was drunk. He doesn't drink, I'm sure of that, but he sounded drunk to me. Riley, I'm worried about him. Maybe he's lost a few marbles. Maybe he's gone crazy or something."

"Pizarro? He's the guy that conquered Peru. Maybe he meant a hotel. Did you look it up in the phone book?"

"No."

"Do you want to see him?"

"Yes. He has twenty-five thousand dollars coming to him."

Riley whistled appreciatively. "That's a lot of bread. What did he do? Did he inherit everything?"

"No, just a small part. I get most of it."

"Then you're a bona-fide rich chick?"

"That's right."

"If you want to see Hibbert, why don't you look him up? He probably thinks you drove your granny to death by the goofy way you've been acting."

"Maybe. Come to think of it, that's probably it. It sounds like the kind of thing he'd dream up."

"Maybe he's right. You ever think of it that way?"

"You're just like him."

"How so?"

"The Daddy routine. You look at me as if you knew me and I didn't know myself. You look at me as if my fly was unbuttoned and you're not going to tell me about it."

"Even if it was I wouldn't look at you that way."

"No, I suppose you wouldn't. Why're you such a bum, Riley?"

"You just say that because you've got a few beans in the bank."

"No I don't," she said softly.

"I'm not a bum."

"I suppose you're a knight of the open road. A travelling man."

"That's me. I'm a travelling man."

"You don't like me, do you, Riley?"

"Sure I do. But you don't want to hear about it."

"What makes you so sarcastic this morning?"

"I'd never seen you in action before last night. But that was last night. Right now I don't know what you think you are."

"I must have said lots of silly things."

He looked at her and smiled. "Not so silly."

She stood up from the table. "Forget it, Riley. About last night, I mean. I know it was a lousy thing to do, but I won't say I'm sorry."

He grinned at her. "Good morning."

"Okay. Good morning."

She stood there thinking of Bunny, then of Bruno; she thought of Christmas in Los Angeles and summer in San Francisco. She thought about how fine it was to have a good hangover and not have to think anything out to a pat conclusion. Hangovers were the best diversion in the world. She closed her eyes then. Daddy. Yes, Daddy. No, Daddy. Sure, it's all right. Don't turn off the light. She wished she hadn't drunk the cheap vodka.

"I have a hangover."

"I wouldn't be surprised."

"Don't you preach to me."

"So who's preaching? I'm agreeing. Did something I say get stuck in your back?"

"No. Maybe it was something that *I* said."

"Last night, for instance?"

"Shut up, Riley."

"I think you'd better find Hibbert and give him his dough. It might help ease your mind. It'll make you feel better."

"You're a kangaroo, Riley. What's your first name?"

"Didn't I tell you?"

"No. You once said it was Pancho Riley. Then you said it was Wino Riley. I don't know which one is your real name."

"It's Homer."

"Like in Winslow?"

"Sure. Homer Matthew Riley. Matthew's from the Bible. Homer stands for home run."

Erin found her jacket and slipped it on. Without a word, Riley handed her the envelope with the remainder of her money.

She was surprised to see it, and for some reason she blushed. She remembered how she had thought of him the night before. She had forgotten about the money as well as how she had thought of him. They both came back to her now.

Outside, the sun was glaring bright and hot and she felt pale and worn out. The big tree in the yard looked beat. "I like that tree," Riley said.

"I'm glad you like it, Homer."

He frowned. "I should never have told you."

The traffic was heavy, most likely because of the Street Fair on Upper Grant Avenue. A church bell rang, slowly, counting time, echoing. An old man with a drooping moustache was sitting on his porch with a yellow cat in his lap. He winked and nodded when Erin walked past with Riley. She returned the wink.

When she looked up at the cloudless sky she realized, with a sudden, painful wrench, that her grandmother was dead and that she wouldn't feel the sun on her hands any more. She was lying in a box about to be cooked. It was a horrible thought. Erin felt her throat tighten. She didn't feel irreverent now. She felt bad because it was such a beautiful day.

CHAPTER THIRTEEN

The Pizarro Hotel was an ancient four-story building on Leavenworth Street, a grey-windowed, camel-colored affair. A canvas awning over the sidewalk had a fading pennant that read, *Under New Management*. To the right of the lobby, visible through the dirt-streaked front window, was a "waiting room"; a few pieces of overstuffed furniture the color of dirty eggplant set in a semicircle around a seventeen-inch TV set with a plastic magnifying device attached to the screen. A pay telephone was on the left. An accordion steam heater clanked and gurgled. The lighting was poor, the carpet threadbare, and a tattered rubber rainmat cut a dirty licorice path to the cubbyhole desk. There was a braided iron elevator cage near a narrow staircase, and next to that a potted palm pot minus the palm. The walls were yellow and everywhere there was the cold jailhouse smell of lysol.

The desk clerk was a baby-faced old man with a green celluloid eyeshade and a dark green shirt, a red plaid necktie vibrating against the shirt. He looked suspiciously at Erin and Riley, then pretended to sort a pile of letters in front of him. He peeped up through the eyeshade when they stopped at the desk.

His sunken mouth was set in a tight line. He looked as though he had been pushed around quite a bit, and when he saw Riley's poor clothes and long hair he sneered and cocked an eyebrow to emphasize his comparative respectability. His voice squeaked like a rocking chair. "Anything I can do for you?"

"We're looking for someone," Erin said.

"That so?"

"Do you happen to have a Gerald Hibbert registered here?"

The man lowered his eyes and shook his head.

"I think he phoned me from here."

"So? Lots of folks use that phone. It's public."

"Maybe he checked in when you weren't on duty."

"There's no one here by that name."

"Maybe he used a different name," Riley suggested.

The baby-faced man pulled himself up straight and glared at them. "Look here, you two, I told you he's not here."

"I *know* he is," Riley snapped.

The man lowered his eyes again and put his hand flat across the registry book. "If he *was* here... what would you want to see him about?"

"This girl's his daughter. I'm his son-in-law."

"I... don't want no trouble."

"Just give me his room number."

"Three-twenty."

The elevator didn't work, so they walked. Three-twenty was towards the rear of the building, next to a fire-escape sign. A single light burned in an orange milky bowl and the hallway was the color of nicotine. Erin knocked on the door, waited, then knocked again. The door opened and Hibbert stood there in his battered slippers and undershirt, his suspenders hanging from his hips and his trousers bagging at the knees. He looked sour and disappointed when he saw that it was Erin. He didn't bother to look at Riley. He returned to his narrow bed and sat down.

The room was bare. The only decoration was a snapshot of Erin stuck in the bureau mirror edge. The one window looked out to a rain-streaked airshaft.

"What do you want?"

"You phoned me," Erin said. "You told me you were here."

"Yes, I suppose I did. Who is this fellow?"

"A friend of mine. His name's Riley."

Hibbert and Riley shook hands. Hibbert smiled at Riley, then blinked uncertainly at Erin. "Do you want to talk to me?"

"Yes, of course. That's why I looked for you."

He shook his head. "I don't think it's wise right now."

"I've already told Riley what you said to me over the phone, if that's what you mean. You can talk about it all you want. I think it was a rotten thing to say to me."

"I didn't want to say anything at all. I called once before but I didn't say anything. I'd been... drinking. I'm not very used to drink. I don't know why I did it. It's just that I felt very... very bad about everything. Very bad."

"How do you feel now?"

"Not too bad. I had a good breakfast this morning."

"Why did you say that I killed Grandmother?"

Hibbert took his time selecting a shirt from the drawer. When he finally had it on and was hooking up his suspenders he looked at Erin with a sad face, his eyes dull, his hand shaking at the collar button. "Because you did, Erin. You knew that I knew about it. So there's no reason for us to talk about it now. I sat here and drank dinner wine and I tried to think about it, tried to arrive at the right answer. I guess I knew what it was before I even sat on this bed. I wasn't going to say anything about it. I'm still not going to. I don't even want to talk about it. The whole thing's unnecessary now."

"What's unnecessary? You phoned me twice. The first time you scared me half to death, and the second time you accuse me of killing Grandmother. I think it's plenty necessary. I don't even know what you're talking about." She waited for his answer. Then, "Well... what *are* you talking about?"

"The night you came to the house," Hibbert answered wearily.

"I didn't go to the house *any* night."

Riley said, "Tell her what happened, Mr. Hibbert."

"She already knows."

"She says she doesn't know. So tell her."

Hibbert sat on the bed and looked unconvinced. He spoke tiredly, as if he wanted to get it over with. "When you came to the house, that's what I'm talking about. You were probably drunk if you say you don't remember. You saw me and I saw you."

"Did you let me into the house?"

"You're serious, Erin? You don't remember anything?"

"Not a thing."

"No, you didn't come by the front door," he said slowly. "I must have left the kitchen door open. You came through there and you stumbled on something, probably the table, and that woke me up. I remember the time. It was one o'clock. My clock has luminous dials and figures, and that's the first thing I noticed when I opened my eyes."

"Go on."

"Well, I thought at first that it was your grandmother, that maybe she was calling for me. I put on my robe and went out into the hall. You were standing on the staircase landing, near the top. I thought you might be wanting to sleep there, so I went back to bed."

Erin looked at him, wide-eyed, incredulous. "How could you tell it was me? I don't remember any of this. I... I was drunk that night, with Riley." She looked frantically at Riley. "What time was it that you took me to the garage?"

"I don't remember. It might have been one o'clock. Maybe later. We were both pretty drunk from that tequila."

Hibbert nodded. "It was you, all right. I could see your jacket, the canvas one with that hood, the same one you have on now."

"It was dark? Didn't you turn on the lights?"

"I didn't see any reason to turn them on. I went right back to bed, then about a half hour later I heard you running from the house. I went upstairs and found your grandmother's door wide open. I went in and found her on the floor by the window, where the tray was supposed to be."

"And the tray? Where was it? It was supposed to be next to the window by the bed."

"It was pulled away from the bed, nearer the corner and out of her reach."

Erin pictured it. She said nothing for a long moment. Hibbert watched her. For some reason she felt guilty of all that he accused her of. She knew she hadn't been at the house, but she still felt guilty. She said, "Why did you run away?"

Hibbert shook his head again. "Because I saw that she was dead, and I became frightened. I left the house and was going to find you, but I didn't. I saw that the lights were out at the place where you live, so I went down to the saloons on Grant Avenue. There were plenty of people there with beards, shouting and singing, drinking. I went back to the house and thought of phoning you, but I didn't."

"You should have. I was home, and believe me, I was too drunk to get out of bed. I couldn't have walked up that hill to the house."

Hibbert nodded uncertainly. "I don't know. Maybe so."

"Did you put Grandmother back in bed?"

"Yes, when I returned to the house. I even put the tray back where it was supposed to be. I knew it was Dr. Hayward's day to visit, so I left the house and didn't lock the front door. I took my money and came here, downtown, and bought some dinner wine. I got drunk, and for some reason I didn't stop drinking." He frowned. "I'm broke now. I spent my last change for my breakfast this morning. I had two hundred dollars and it's all gone."

Riley looked surprised. "Did you spend all that bread on wine?"

"No. I must have lost it, or some of it, when I was out last night. I remember having it on top of a bar next to my glass. Maybe someone stole it. I don't remember very well."

Riley looked satisfied with that.

Erin asked, "Did you return to the house and wash those cups?"

"Why, yes. I'd called you during the day. I didn't mean to scare you, but I must have been too drunk to talk. I thought you'd still be there, so I took a cab to the house. I was even going to phone for the police... but I didn't." He looked at Erin sorrowfully. "I didn't want to get you into any trouble. I knew she was going to die. I knew that. So I said nothing. What difference would it make? She was going to die anyway. I tried to think like that... and it made some sense. But I called you last night anyway. I had to know...."

"I didn't kill her," Erin said softly.

"You must have said something to her to excite her, or disturb her. She was afraid of the dark. She knew when it was night. She said that she could smell and feel the night in the air. You must have said something in the darkness that frightened her... and killed her."

"I said nothing to her," she insisted. "I wasn't here. You must have dreamed that you saw me."

"I didn't dream it," Hibbert answered.

Erin couldn't talk of it any more. She was ready to believe anything about herself. Yes, she could have done it. Maybe she had. But yet.... She knew that she'd done nothing. But the fear that she might have done it terrified her and warned her away from thinking of it. She no longer trusted herself. She was capable of believing anything.

She said, "Mr. Shelby wants to see you. There's the inheritance that's coming to you."

"I don't want it. I don't want any money."

"He has to offer it to you, at least. He wants to see you anyway. He asked me to find you and tell you that."

"I don't want to see anyone."

"I want you to know, Hibbert, that I didn't go to Howard House that night. I swear to it."

He didn't answer. She took fifty dollars from her envelope and set it on the bureau. She felt sorry for him. He didn't belong in a cheap downtown hotel. Howard House was his home. It was more his than it was Erin's. She realized that now. It had never belonged to her. It belonged to Hibbert. He was the last link to anything resembling a family. The old man truly loved her and he honestly believed he was shielding her from the police. She said, "Hibbert, did you know that Dr. Hayward said it was definitely a heart attack?"

"Then you must have frightened her by saying something...." He sagged back on the bed and covered his eyes with the palms of his hands. He seemed to be on the verge of silent weeping. His thin chest moved quickly. Erin watched him, her brow furrowed, her grey eyes wide. She was unsure of how she felt. She didn't know what to say.

Riley said, "When did you miss the money, Mr. Hibbert?"

The voice from the bed was mechanical, almost dreamy. Hibbert either hadn't paid any attention to the question or he placed little importance on it.

"Your money," Riley repeated, "when did you miss it?"

"This morning."

"Were you pretty drunk last night?"

"Yes."

"What kind of bills were they?"

"Three twenties."

Riley turned to Erin and nodded an okay. Then he left the room and walked slowly down the hallway. Riley said, "He's a nice little guy."

"Yes."

He stopped her and held her with his hand. His unshaven face was pale in the deep gloom of the stairwell. "Did you go to the house, Erin?"

"No, I didn't."

He nodded and said nothing. She knew that he believed her. His expression softened and his eyes didn't sink deeper in his face, as she had expected them to.

Downstairs, the desk clerk turned the pages of a detective magazine and didn't look up until Riley had planted himself in front of the desk and gave an impression of not intending to leave. The clerk's hands trembled on the pages and there was a look of guilt on his face.

Riley tapped the marble top of the desk. "Put three twenties on the desk or I'll stomp your face in."

The clerk looked startled, his forehead glowing an eerie green from the eyeshade, his thin lips jerking at the corners. "What? Look here, you—"

"You wouldn't reach the phone. I'm telling you to put up the money or I'll kick in your face. It's that simple."

"Get out of here!" The clerk gritted his teeth with rage and stepped back a pace. "You must be crazy—"

"You heard me once. Put Hibbert's dough on the desk and we'll forget about everything."

"I don't know what you're talking about."

"The wallet. Take your wallet out."

The clerk was weakening visibly. "I'll... call the cops."

"I'd break your neck first. They'll toss you into the tin for rolling drunks in your own hotel."

He started to protest again, but Riley threatened a movement towards the desk opening. The clerk held up a thin hand to stop him. Riley waited. The accordion heater gurgled behind them. The clerk looked sheepishly at Erin, then fearfully at Riley. Riley tapped the marble again with his bent thumb. When the wallet appeared he took the three twenties from it and sealed them into an envelope that he picked up from the desk top.

"Thanks."

The clerk was pale with hate and he didn't answer. Erin said, "You're a two-bit bandit, to roll an old man. You ought to be ashamed of yourself."

"Get out of here! Beat it!"

Outside, Riley gave the envelope to Erin. "When you see Hibbert again, give it back to him. Tell him to watch his dough from now on."

She stared unbelievingly at him for a minute. She didn't know what to say or think. She thanked him with her smile, and as they walked, she felt a definite pride in him. Not because he was self-assured or proud, but because it was obvious that he had already completely forgotten the incident. He expected no thanks from her. She found she was glad that she had Riley at her side. The people on the street stared at both of them, Riley because he was indifferent and unconventional, Erin because she was beautiful and carelessly dressed. And she found she couldn't give a damn about their staring eyes. Riley's presence did that for her. It was easy for her to carry herself without guilt, with Riley. He had been decent with her in every respect, and she realized that she accepted him as easily and as honestly as he accepted her.

She smiled secretly to herself, deep in her thoughts, and unconsciously put her arm through Riley's. He didn't seem to notice any difference. They walked slowly through the Stockton Street tunnel, heading back towards North Beach.

CHAPTER FOURTEEN

It was impossible to tell where the pavement ended and the street began. There were too many people. The hot narrow street was roped off at both ends of a single block on Upper Grant Avenue, the Street Fair being held in the stifling confines between the ropes. A squad car was stationed at the south end, two policemen standing by, sweltering in the heat, watching the milling crowd that was packed in the narrow block. All traffic was rerouted, detour signs were posted at the ropes.

It was three o'clock. The heat was intense. Colored ribbons, banners, and streamers were hung over the street, the technicolored crisscross sagging like a monstrous spiderweb. A loudspeaker blared over the milling heads of the crowd, while bearded poets shouted from a platform into a tin-voiced microphone.

It was a carnival. There were exhibition stalls and stands on the pavements, with barely enough room to squeeze between them and the buildings; apartment windows on both sides of the street were open and people with cans of beer and comical hats were shouting down at the crowd. A policeman watched a *Punch and Judy* show over the heads of a mob of children.

Riley and Erin squeezed into the crowd and were swallowed. They walked sideways, going north. Erin was jostled, pushed, pinched, greeted. There was the fat odious smell of perspiration clashing with the gagging sweetness of cologne, rising suddenly to fill the already choking air, to mingle with the odors of beer, mustard, and carnival canvas. Paintings were exhibited on both sides. There were leather workers, weavers, jewelers, photographers, woodcutters, ceramists, poets. But nowhere did they see any sign of Merlin. They continued through the crowd. Beer cans littered the street, men carried their young children high over the crowd on their shoulders.

They went through it until they finally found Merlin's display stand near the north end of the block.

"It's a goddam crush," Merlin said. "I wouldn't walk through that for a dime. Want a beer?"

The smell of the beer was strong and pleasant and the cans squirted foam as they were punched open. Merlin's stand was a simple plywood frame, hinged in the center, and set against the curb. The paintings were on the board as well as stacked in a wire frame near Merlin's card table and canvas chairs.

Merlin looked old and bleached in the sun and his large hands shook on the can of warm beer. Mac was nowhere in sight.

"She's gone up to the pad to bring the beach umbrella for the sun. I can't take much more of this. I'm getting old."

"You didn't get arrested?" Riley asked.

"Not yet. A young cop came by earlier and gave my stuff the fish eye. The day's still young, though. Anything can happen."

"Have you sold anything?"

Merlin managed a grin. "One painting. That one there."

He pointed to a girl in a forest setting. The detail of the figure left nothing to the imagination. Merlin said, "I got two hundred mother beans for it. Ordinarily I'd ask for two-fifty, but this sale doesn't go through an agent or a gallery, so it's pure gravy for me—wine money, Riley. I'm keeping every cent of it for myself. A guy came up to me, some kind of a fat guy, and says he wants it. He gave me the down payment on it, and his address card. So I've been drinking on the down payment. Want another beer?"

A baby carriage passed the stand, the father a ghostly figure with thin beard and sandals, sick-looking in the sun. Women jostled past with low-cut blouses and tight trousers, housedresses, cocktail dresses; beads clicking, cologne gagging the air.

Riley said that Merlin was doing pretty well, and, if he was fortunate enough to be arrested, there would be even more sales later on.

"That's right," Merlin said. "You should've heard the poetry. Some of it's okay."

"I heard some of it already," Erin said.

"No, not the junk they've got now. That's Berkeley trash, just little poets with hand-me-down ideals and experience. Let me tell you, Erin old girl, there's nothing more embarrassing than a young man protesting against the state of the world. And there's no one more naive than a tyro dedicated hipster. But you should have been here earlier. They had some pretty erotic stuff."

Erin said, "Why do you want to get busted, Merlin? I don't understand it."

"Sure you do. If I get busted, then I get my name in all the papers as a suppressed Beatnik-artist, a victim of the narrow-minded Gestapo and all that crap. Whether it's true or not. I really don't give a damn. I get my name in the papers, maybe even my picture, a good mention that I paint beautiful girls in the high name of art, and then creeps and art lovers from all over the city come knocking at my door. Hell, I wouldn't be able to knock out as much as I could sell. I'd have to beat them off with a club."

A few minutes later, restless and curious to see the rest of the Fair, Erin left them and forced her way back down the street. She spotted Orcutt and Iris in the crowd but didn't stop to talk to them. She saw the show, looked at the ceramists, then finally bought four hot dogs from a walking vendor. When she returned to the stand Mac was there with the beach umbrella and another six-pack of beer. The umbrella was a huge orange affair with a metal stand and a fringe around the edge.

They ate hot dogs, drank cold beer, and sat under the umbrella. The sun glowed through the canvas and their faces were pink and orange. People came by and peeked curiously under the fringe to see what they were doing.

"Go away. I'm busy," Merlin said.

Riley said, "You want to buy a painting?"

"I might," a young man said.

"Come under here then. Get out of the sun."

The man squatted under the umbrella, smiling uncertainly, and leaned on the card table. He was wearing an expensive silk summer suit, Italian cut, a pink shirt and a slim necktie.

"It's not really cooler under here," Erin said.

"I'm sweating," Mac answered.

"You want to buy a painting?"

The man looked at Riley. "Are these yours?"

"No. But for right now I'm representing the artist. The painter himself is too drunk and too old to talk. You'd have to talk to him when he was much younger."

"They're very good paintings," the man offered.

Merlin looked at him, a puckish gleam in his eyes. "What exactly *were* you thinking of? Are you the fuzz?"

"I beg your pardon?"

"A cop."

"No."

"Then you don't want to buy a *painting*. If you're serious-minded and want to buy a *painting* then you'd better talk to Riley here, or go to some other stall. But if you want to buy a *picture*, then I'll sell you one. There's a big difference between a *picture* and a *painting*. My *pictures* are better than

windmills and creeks, and even watercolors of the Golden Gate Bridge."
He pointed to a small canvas, a study of a female and her lover, lying on
a flowery couch, arms locked, expressions bored. "Take this one, for example. This is called *In Partibus Infidelium – Number Thirty-One*. That
means, *In the Land of the Infidels*. I've done thirty-one pictures exactly like
that. You like it? I've sold every one of them to art lovers all over the United
States and Canada. Each picture is like this, only with different colors and
faces. Pretty nifty, huh?"

The man looked embarrassed by all this. "I was thinking of the one
mostly done in reds. The large one right out there."

"Oh, you were thinking of *that* one. I suppose it matches the color scheme
in your living-room. Is that right?"

The perspiration shone on the man's forehead. His necktie looked as
though it were strangling him. "Well, as a matter of fact it's the bedroom.
Does that matter?"

"Not at all. If you buy it you can cut it up for cocktail coasters if you want."
Merlin swallowed more beer, finishing the can, and motioned for Mac to
open him another. "I've sold one painting already, so I'm ahead of the game.
That's why I talk to you the way I do."

"Are you sure you're the artist?"

They argued on. Merlin pointed out that he wasn't the *artist*, that he was
the *painter*. He quoted the painting in question at a hundred fifty, offering to match the frame with the decor in the man's bedroom. They finally
shook hands on a promise to think about it, and the man started to leave.

"Just a minute," Merlin said. "If you go to the nearest cop and lodge an
indignant citizen's complaint against my pictures I'll toss the frame in for
nothing and only ask for one twenty-five."

When the man had left Mac narrowed her eyes and looked disappointed. "You shouldn't have talked to him like that. He might have
bought the goddam thing."

"He'll be back," Merlin said. "My painting matches his bedroom."

"Merlin's a carnival barker," Riley said. "He should be selling bearded
ladies, crocodile people, and two-headed snakes."

The festive excitement of the Fair seemed to increase, the noise of the
crowd grew louder; music poured through the loudspeakers. Teenage
hoodlums roamed through the crowd. People started to move into the bars.

An hour later Erin and Riley left Merlin and Mac and walked down
Grant two blocks to Vortigern's Bar. The window had a whitewash sign
on it welcoming the Street Fair crowds. The bar was fairly crowded. Erin

saw Lilly sitting by herself at a rear table, looking thin and drawn, her eyes enlarged by the dark accent of lashes and night rings. She was drinking soda water.

"What's up, Lilly? Aren't you going to get out into the sun?"

"No."

"Okay if we sit? It's hotter'n holy hell outside." They sat at Lilly's table and Erin asked where Marian was.

"At the gallery. Bruno went to Sausalito with your lawyer, that Shelby character. Marian's working because Bruno expects a big day from the crowds." She looked fearfully at Erin, then looked away. She spoke haltingly. "Did you know that Bruno has a fanatic, a morbid, love of money?"

Erin bought a pitcher of beer and Orcutt came over to their table, having materialized from somewhere near the jukebox. Without a word, he poured himself a glass of beer from Erin's pitcher.

"Where's Abe and Iris?" Riley asked.

"Up the street," Orcutt answered. "I left them with a sculptor that Iris found. She's finally found one."

Erin had no further interest in the Fair. Just before they left Merlin, the man with the silk suit had returned and paid Merlin the down payment for the red picture. Merlin seemed to be enjoying a good day, in spite of his inability to become arrested.

Orcutt and Riley were busy telling each other jokes. Erin spoke to Lilly in a low voice. Lilly answered, saying that nothing was the matter with her, she was just feeling a bit lousy. Last night, too. She hasn't been feeling very well for a couple of days.

She offered Lilly a drink.

"I don't want a drink. I'm not going to get drunk."

"Who said anything about getting you drunk? I didn't ask you to get soused with me. I only asked if you wanted a drink."

"No... I'll stick to soda." Lilly straightened her position in her chair and looked frankly at Erin. She said she wanted to talk to Erin. It was *very* important; something that had been on her mind, that she'd been trying to ignore but couldn't. No, not there at the table; somewhere else. The washroom. Would Erin go to the washroom?

"Sure. What's up?"

"I can't talk about it here."

They went into the washroom and Lilly shot the bolt behind them. Erin looked questioningly at her, suddenly irritated by the atmosphere of petty mystery, washroom secrecy; she despised this sort of thing as high-school tricks. Lilly ran cold water on a paper towel and gently applied it to her cheek. She watched Erin in the small dirty mirror.

"I'm really kind of gutless, Erin. I wasn't going to tell you because Marian told me not to say anything. And I know how mean she can get when she wants to.... She'd been smoking pot all morning and she was pretty mean by then. That was right after you phoned from the bar here. It was about five-thirty."

Erin, by this time, was impatient and exasperated. "Okay. I don't get it, but I'll bite. What's it all about?"

Lilly was taken off guard. "Why... about Bruno."

"What about her?"

Lilly went back to the tap water and the towel. The splashing in the yellow-ringed bowl was the only sound. She said, "The other night... Bruno killed your grandmother...."

CHAPTER FIFTEEN

Erin turned off the tap. She wasn't bitter, or even angry; her emotions were uncommonly neutral. It was almost as if she had known it all along and had been keeping the truth from herself all this time. She felt free now. She knew that it was over.

Lilly didn't look steadily at her. She kept shifting her eyes. "I'm... sorry, Erin. Honest. In a way I even feel sorry that I told you about it. I don't like to see any trouble. But, like I said, I *had* to tell you about it. It was eating inside me."

"How did you find out about it? Were you there?"

"Who, me? No, of course not. I found out about it by accident. I over-heard Bruno telling Marian, after she had done it. Even Marian was surprised, but she didn't say anything to me about it."

"Did she say how she did it?"

"Yes. She said she went there in the middle of the night and deliberately frightened your grandmother to death, knowing she had a bad heart. She also knew that you were a cinch to inherit. And, I guess, she figured she'd cash in herself."

"I was passed out when all this was going on?"

"That's right. I remember that when we got to the garage we tried to wake you because Marian wanted to party it up, but we couldn't even get you to mumble. It was like trying to wake the dead."

"When was that? I mean, what time, about?"

"About one-thirty. At least that's when Bruno came in. I was in my room and in bed. I felt sick, so I passed out as soon as we got there. That's when I heard Bruno come in. I looked down the hall and I saw her, big as life, all red in the face from that weird excitement she gets, and togged out in your jacket. I thought she was doing some kind of drag act for Marian's benefit. That's when I heard her say that she had scared your grandmother to death. Later, I guess about ten minutes after, Marian came in and asked me if I'd heard. I said yes. Then she told me not to say anything."

"You called the house next evening. But Bruno had called about twenty minutes before you. She said she was in a liquor store buying some tequila. She's the one who told us to come down to Vortigern's last night. We were supposed to keep our eye on you."

Erin simply nodded. She remembered how Bruno had drunk the tequila and how she had started to lay the foundations for the Sausalito deal. Erin wasn't shocked. Nothing shocked her now.

And Bruno had been worried yesterday. Why not? Hibbert had seen her on the landing that night, or at least he had seen someone who he believed was Erin. That was the hurting part: that Bruno had tried to have the crime shifted to Erin. That was the filthy trick that did it.

Erin said, softly, mechanically, "I can guess why she did it."

Lilly looked sympathetic. "I know. I heard her mention to Marian that she had just solved all of her problems. I remember that part of it."

Erin frowned.

"Are you going to tell the cops?"

"No I'm not."

Lilly looked surprised. "Why not? I sure would."

"You're not me. Something'll come up."

"Well, aren't you even teed off?"

"Of course I am. I'll take care of it." Erin slid back the bolt on the door. "We'd better get back to our table now."

"Not me. I'd better run right back to the gallery."

"Whatever you say, Lilly. And thanks for telling me."

"Like I say, Erin, I *had* to."

"Thanks anyway."

Lilly smiled. Her face had regained some of its color and her eyes were more steady.

They stepped out into the tiny hallway outside the washroom.

"You'd better hustle back now. I may be up later."

"I'll see you then. And, Erin, don't say anything about this."

"I won't say a word. Don't worry about it."

Lilly left the bar and Erin returned to her table, feeling drained and shaky. She poured herself a drink, knowing that she wasn't going to get drunk. Outside, the sun was setting and it was becoming dark. Erin sat with her back against the wall, absorbed with her thoughts. Now that she knew about Bruno she was surprised to find that again she felt nothing. Her grandmother was dead and this fact held no further impact for her; it was relatively unimportant now because it was past and the sadness had been buried, even if the body had not.

It was how, and why, she died that hurt Erin.

Hibbert had said that her grandmother had been able to feel the darkness in the air. Erin shuddered. Could it have been darker than blindness?

It was over with Bruno, completely and irrevocably over; nothing could bring back a liking for her, even if it were worth bringing back. Erin felt cheapened. The bitter confusion of her life became magnified and it seemed to melt into a solid lump of nothingness. Why should she think about it? Life was wretched and disgusting. It was meant for the stupid idiots who could swallow its lies and shadowy promises. Only fools lived in peace. She thought of the cemetery where her mother was buried. Give and take, old ashes to even older ashes... have another drink and the hell with it. One negated the other.

"You look kind of white in the face," Riley said.

"It's just the light."

"There's not much light in here."

Erin nodded. "That's what I mean."

Riley poured himself a beer, finishing the second pitcher, and swallowed carefully, draining half the glass. Erin stood up from the table and asked him to come outside. She had something to tell him. She wanted him to walk with her.

The street was like an oven, but a wind was starting and the rush of warm air smelled of salt and fish. They walked north on Grant to the Street Fair area. The crowds had thinned out considerably. Artists were packing their paintings and exhibits. Merlin had left long ago and only limp shreds of ribbon and pages of poetry were left. Sad paper dunes in the lamp-lit gutters.

They stood in a shop doorway and watched the street. A small light was lit in the shop window; a miniature lighthouse that winked first red, then yellow light. A boy with a stoneware dinosaur in his hand stood by an old Chevrolet parked at the curb. There was a printed sign on a box on top of the car that read, *La Pace*. A man with thick grey hair was packing bowls into boxes while a woman stood beside him with a straw bonnet and a wax cup of red wine.

Papers moved in windy whirlpools. Only the bars and cafés were open now. Farther on, the Sedge-Hammer sign swung in the wind.

Erin told Riley about the conversation with Lilly in the washroom. When she had finished, he shrugged, and finally he said that it was a bad thing. He added, "Everyone goofs somehow, but Bruno really screwed it up for you. Have you talked to the guy in the hotel yet? Did you phone him?"

"No."

"He's going to be glad to hear about it."

"What am I supposed to do meanwhile?"

"About what?"

"About Bruno?"

Riley shrugged. "I don't know. I'm not a cop."

"But she killed my grandmother...."

"Maybe. Maybe she went there to hit her up for a loan and the old lady died during the conversation. Real innocent like."

"That's ridiculous," Erin snapped.

"Of course it is. But that's what she'll tell the fuzz if they try to pin it on her." He lit a cigarette and appeared thoughtful. "Look, if you want an eye for an eye and that sort of thing, why don't you get a club and go clobber Bruno over the head with it? That'd solve everything."

"That's stupid, Riley."

"Then go tell the fuzz."

"I can't do that."

"Well, if you don't, then Hibbert will. Because as soon as you tell him you didn't do it, that it was Bruno, he'll call in the cops. And you're going to have to tell him, to get yourself off the emotional hook."

Erin nodded wearily. "I suppose you're right."

"Maybe you should see Jim Orcutt."

"Why?"

"He's a lawyer. Find out what can be legally done."

"I don't care about that. I don't give a damn about the legal end of it."

"Aren't you kind of sorry that the old lady got it?"

"Yes, of course I am. It's a rotten thing... but I remembered what Hibbert said this afternoon. She was going to die anyway. So she died. That's all I feel about it now. Nothing more. She's dead. The rest of it's bad."

"It's all bad," Riley answered. "I'll tell you a little something about myself, if you want to hear it. See, I've got one of these very simple minds. The good guy wears a big white hat and the bad guy wears a black one. I like my entertainment real simple."

"Is this entertainment for you, Riley?"

"Sure. I'm entertained. If I didn't want to be entertained I'd move out of this Beat Disneyland and get a job, or maybe draw dames like old Merlin. But I don't. For me this's a big joke, like living in a TV tube. It's one of the few ways I can live and be entertained, because I keep everything on a simple basis. The cops wear black hats and I wear a big white hat on my soul. In my life I'm one of the good guys. I head them off at the pass and wear butterfly boots. When I win the girl I kiss my sunset and go riding off into my horse. It's a nice arrangement. But... there's always some bastard like

Bruno who wants the wrong waterhole...."

"Do I want the wrong things, Riley?"

"Yeah. Someone should throw you down a well."

She smiled. "Are you going to help me with this mess?"

He shrugged. "Yeah, I'll help you."

"And then what? I mean after you help me, what happens? Do you really believe that the man in the white hat will gun down the guy in the black hat, and then you can live happily ever after? Do you believe that?"

"I do. If I didn't, I'd go and join the bad guys."

"What do you expect out of it? I mean, if you help me."

"I'm not expecting a damn thing. I'm only doing this because I'm sick."

Erin studied him for a minute. "Are you going to kill Bruno?"

"Do you want me to?"

"No, of course not."

"What do you want me to do? How am I supposed to help you? Shall I just find her and call her nasty names?"

"You confuse it, Riley."

"No, you confuse it. Think about it, man. You want me to help you, but you don't want her clobbered with a club or thrown to the cops, you don't want me to call her nasty names, and you don't want me to call her nice names. Bruno killed the old chick and you want me to do something about it, but you don't know what." He shrugged indifferently. "Okay, you lead the way and I'll follow."

"Something will come up," Erin said.

"Sure, something'll come up."

The lighthouse blinked red, and when they left the doorway, the *La Pace* Chevrolet pulled away from the curb and rounded the north corner. Riley pointed absently to the car. "I know the guy in that car. His name's David."

"Why didn't you talk to him?"

"I couldn't, because I'm not really here. I'm not even me, and besides he was busy packing his stuff in the box. I feel like telling him something."

"What?"

"That I've got a job."

"What's that?"

"You're paying me, aren't you?"

"I suppose so, if you want to put it that way."

"Then I've got a job. I'm doing this for money, as well as because I'm sick."

They returned to Vortigern's. The air inside was a brassy green and fuzzy with smoke. Riley stepped to the bar and bought two beers. They stood by the door, apart from the tables, and drank slowly, watching the warm wind toss papers down the street.

"I've just decided," Erin said in a low voice, "that I hate Bruno. I hate her very much."

CHAPTER SIXTEEN

It wasn't until later that they decided to try Howard House. They had been to several spots earlier, looking for Bruno, but they hadn't had any luck. The garage was locked. Erin had called the gallery twice and Marian had reported no word from Bruno. They finally decided to try the house. It was late when they arrived and there were no lights showing. The front door was unlocked and they went right in. The main-room curtains were drawn tightly over the windows to close out the light from the chandelier. Erin and Riley stood in the hall and looked at the room. It had been cleaned. The bottles and glasses were gone and the ash trays had been emptied into the fireplace.

"Someone's been here," Erin said.

Riley looked around him and shrugged. "Maybe somebody ate your mush and sat in your chair."

"Shut up," Erin said. "You're drunk."

"Probably."

The kitchen door was propped open with a garden brick. There were thudding sounds coming from the garden. Erin held Riley's arm and listened. The sounds were steady, soft, like a wooden pole beating on a rug. Erin stepped out onto the porch and peered into the darkness. She couldn't see a thing beyond the splash of light from the kitchen.

"Hibbert? Is that you?"

"No."

She looked in the direction of the voice, to the far corner of the garden, and saw a tiny red cigarette glow. The thumping sounds continued. Riley stood at her side and cupped his hands to his eyes to cut the kitchen light.

Erin said, "Is that you, Bruno?"

"Sure is, honeychile," Bruno said. "Who's that with you? Is it Riley?"

"That's right," Riley answered. "How you doing, Bruno?"

"I'm fine and dandy, Riley. This night routine is a gasser. Come on outside, you two. Join me."

Erin turned to Riley. She spoke in a low voice. "I don't know if I can, Riley. I'm afraid that I might spit on her...."

"Forget it. Just don't talk if you feel the hate too much."

"I told you how I feel...."

"I know. I'll do the talking. We'll think of something."

They moved from the porch and groped their way along the wide stone path to the beacon of Bruno's cigarette. They could barely see. Erin waited until her eyes adjusted to the darkness before she stepped from the stones. Then she saw Bruno sitting on top of a large packing crate, or what seemed to be a crate; her legs were swinging and the heels of her shoes were kicking the side of the box. Then Erin saw that it wasn't a box; it was a compost bin, with a chicken-wire opening on one side.

There were the mingled odors of dirt and flowers. The garden was sheltered from the wind, but everywhere else it was blowing wildly, whipping trees and bending the heads of the plants, dancing ghosts of paper in the streets, hissing through the telephone wiring. It was a warm wind, like the blast from a furnace, and an offshore smell of ocean came with it. And there was another odor: the harsh stink from Bruno's cigarette.

"Join me, friends. I'm communing with nature."

"What're you smoking?" Riley asked.

"Bliss. Pure bliss." Bruno laughed deep in her throat. "Come join me on this big rabbit hutch."

Erin said, "It's a compost bin."

"Is it? I thought it was a rabbit hutch. I was wondering where all the rabbits had gone to."

"I saw a rabbit," Riley said. "Had a weskit and railroad watch...."

They sat on the compost bin and waited for something to happen. The wind lifted the ends of Erin's hair and moved it to her shoulders like a fur piece. Her lips felt dry. She could taste the hot salt of hate in her throat. She was tense. She sat silently, hating Bruno and wanting to even the score for all the lies that she had lived.

Would this mess ever straighten itself out? Erin didn't want to go to the police. The police would only punish Bruno for her crime against Erin's grandmother—if it could be proven. But what of her other crimes? Bruno had used her for personal gain, had tried to implicate her in the old woman's death. Who was going to punish her for those things? What court judged such matters?

"You know," Bruno said, "if I were a gunner and had me a gun I could have picked off both of you real easy like when you were standing in the doorway. A perfect shot. Squeeze, bang! Nothing to it. That's what you both looked like—targets."

"That's a pleasant thought," Riley said.

"It's the wind that makes you think like that," Bruno said. "Do you know that? Did you know about the wind and what it does? Somebody once said that the wind could talk. I forget who said it. Hell, maybe nobody ever did. They should have, because I believe it. The wind and I, we've been having quite a conversation. I told the wind to tell me where it's from. And do you know what the wind said to me? The old wind said: I just came in from Kansas City."

"It's an offshore wind," Erin said. "This wind comes from the west."

"How do you know? It told me it was from Kansas City. What do you think of that?"

Erin didn't answer her. She sat, nursing her hatred, and wished that she had had enough sense to stay in Los Angeles. She could have found somebody else to keep her company, someone more like Bunny, someone normal and safe.

Bruno finished her cigarette. Riley pushed himself from the bin and stood among the flowers. He looked at the frame of light that was the kitchen door. He said he knew where there was some vodka left over from the night before. Bruno asked where, and Riley told her. It was in the room that Merlin had used. Orcutt had told Riley about it.

"Why don't you go get it?"

He shook his head. "Let's all go get it."

Bruno growled and flicked her tongue angrily against her lips. "What're you being so snotty about, big shot?"

Riley answered, "Don't get me wrong, Bruno. I'm your buddy."

"Okay," Bruno said grudgingly. "Just don't try to get tough with me. Because I don't dig the big-man route." She sneered contemptuously. "I hate your guts, Riley, but you can hang around. But only because Erin here, for some weird reason, seems to get a kick out of watching you step on your tongue while you walk after her."

Erin felt that if she opened her mouth she would scream. The tension she felt was almost painful. Bruno's self-assurance was too much for Erin to bear. And yet she didn't leave the garden. She stayed, waiting, hoping that a solution would offer itself. She was depending on Riley.

Bruno smiled and turned to Riley. "See, Riley? Cut off their tails with a carving knife...." She began to sing.

> Three blind mice. Three blind mice.
> See how they run. See how they run.
> Three blind MIIIIICE....

"You sing real fine," Riley said.

"I ought to cut your tail off."

"I guess you got it all figured."

"That's right, Mac, I've got it all figured. I can see right through you."

"Well, let's not fight about it, Bruno. Let's let bygones be bygones and go get that jug of vodka."

Erin said, "I'd like a drink."

"Do you? Okay, if you want one we'll go get one. But if you'd rather stay out here with my Kansas City buddies, then we'll stay out here. Whatever you say, Erin."

"I would like a drink."

Bruno agreed. They went back into the house. Bruno was walking heavily, her shoulders hunched forward. She wore a heavy coat with a sheepskin collar. Erin figured that it was a new coat. Probably a celebration present.... She asked Bruno how well it had gone with Shelby that afternoon. Bruno looked thoughtful, as if she couldn't remember. Then she smiled and said that it had gone perfectly. Shelby had agreed to everything. Erin was supposed to call Shelby first thing in the morning.

Riley brought the bottle from Erin's old room and joined them in the hallway of the second floor. He broke the seal of the bottle. "Is there a roof to this place? Let's all go have a nice quiet drink and watch the lights."

"There's some stairs," Erin said. She pointed towards the end of the hallway.

"You'll have to lead the way," Bruno said happily. "I don't know my way around this place very well...."

Erin stiffened.

Riley took a long hard drink and smacked his lips. He recapped the bottle.

They went to the roof. The wind was stronger. The heavy roof door slammed after them. The gravel gritted under their feet. The wind was like hot silk.

It was all unreal to Erin. Directly below her was her grandmother's room, and she pictured the old woman lying in her bed, listening to the frightening sounds Bruno must have made. It was horrible. And yet, here was Bruno, drinking with them, laughing, quite capable of looking Erin straight in the eye. It all seemed impossible. Even Riley. Riley looked as indifferent as he usually did. He was even cracking jokes with Bruno, offering her the bottle.

Riley swallowed from the bottle again and Bruno made a windmill of her arms, saying that she was a free and lovely bird with a sharp beak and long long claws. *"I'm just a biiird in a gilded cage...."* She unzipped her new jacket and pulled her shirt free from her jeans. "What a night. What a weird and goofy night. I told you about Shelby, didn't I? Well, he thinks I'm real fine people." She gestured with the flat of her hand. "He's weird. They're *all* weird...."

Erin accepted the bottle from Riley and turned her back on Bruno. She couldn't stand to look at her any more. She wanted a drink. A long one. She threw back her head and closed her eyes. The vodka swirled into her mouth and rushed down her throat, burning and scraping. She drank again. Then, finally, she shuddered and lowered the bottle. She could hear Bruno laughing behind her. Laughing and shouting.

"Hear me, wind? You hear me...."

Erin took another drink and joined Riley. He was sitting by the stone chimney near the edge of the roof. The lights of the city ended at the bottom of the hill far below them, at the edge of the bay, and the water was an enormous black pool reflecting the bridge lights. Alcatraz Island flashed its tower light. The wind gusted against them. Riley took the bottle from Erin and swallowed a short drink. He smiled to himself and looked out over the city.

What a dumb thing, Erin thought. Sitting on a roof and drinking vodka.

She looked around her at the sudden silence. "Where's Bruno?"

Riley lifted his eyebrows, looking momentarily surprised. "Bruno?"

"Yes. She was here just a second ago. Where did she go?"

He looked thoughtful, then said, quite simply, "She fell."

"What the hell do you mean, 'she fell'?"

"Sure, that's right. While you were drinking she fell over the side of the building."

Erin saw that Riley was serious. She sat very still. She didn't know whether to laugh or to scream. Either one would do. But she did nothing. Instead, she went to the side of the chimney and peered over the edge at Bruno's crumpled figure, which looked like a sack of old clothes on the wide stone walkway of the garden directly below them. Bruno had obviously landed head first.

"Did you push her, Riley?"

"No. She fell. Maybe she jumped. Maybe she was so full of joy that she thought she'd go visit Kansas City with her buddies. I don't know. She just fell."

"You didn't push her?"

"Me?" He looked surprised again. "Hell no. Why should I push Bruno anywhere? That chick needed no pushing."

Erin took another drink. She needed it. She ran her hand through her hair and rubbed her cheeks where the liquor made them tingle. She was breathing faster and she could feel the pulse beat in her temples. All the early tension was gone now. She felt strangely relaxed. She said nothing. They were quiet for a long time, sitting close to one another with their backs resting against the rough brick of the old chimney. She had another drink, a small one, and watched the bridge lights reflect on the wet blackness of the bay. A few minutes later she turned to Riley. "I guess it's just one of those things that I'll never find out about."

"Seems that way," he said.

"You won't tell me?"

"I already did, Erin. I didn't touch her. Do I look like that kind of guy?"

"No."

They had a few more drinks from the bottle, not talking, then they returned to the main floor of the house. Riley went to the kitchen and closed the door. On his way back to the hall he turned out the lights. Erin stopped by the telephone stand and waited. She didn't know what to do now. She didn't want Riley to leave. But she knew that he wouldn't want to be there when the police arrived to investigate the accident. She wondered if he would return, if he left now. He hadn't said anything. She said, "I have to make several calls. Someone has to be notified about the accident."

He stood close by her. "I guess so."

"And I don't suppose you'll want to be here when the police come out?"

"No, I don't think so."

She looked at him as he stood in the dim hallway light. "That wasn't true, Riley—what Bruno said. I mean about my getting a weird kick out of watching you follow me. That wasn't true."

"I know it."

"I just wanted to tell you.... And the other night—I'm sorry I called you those names. I was baiting you. I shouldn't have done that."

"Forget it."

"I'm not very easy to get along with." She looked at him. Her breathing was faster. She felt confused. "I don't get along very well with people. I'm anti-social. I mean, most people don't like me...."

"Most people don't like me, either," he said.

"I used you the night we went to Bunny's. I wanted you to make them feel uncomfortable. I wanted to compete with Bunny."

"Sure, I know that."

"You're going to paint my portrait?"

"That's right." He was smiling now. "I'll be by here first thing in the morning. I'll bring up what paints I own. They're all I have to carry with me. I don't have anything else."

She didn't say anything. She picked up the phone and held it, the dial tone buzzing against her breast. Riley bent down and kissed her gently on the cheek. It was a nice kiss, soft, softer than she had expected, and she looked away from him. She started to dial the operator. Riley stood by the front door, smiled once more at her, then closed the door softly after him. She knew that he would be back in the morning. She knew how it would be, and it was the way she wanted it. She listened to his footsteps going down the path to the street. She could hear him whistling softly to himself.

She finished dialing the operator and wondered who she was supposed to notify first.

THE END

The Last Great Pulp Fiction Writer
By Ki Longfellow

Before I met Zekial Marko, I met one of his books. I was fifteen and poking around in a Marin County five & dime when there it was, a little beauty in a spinning metal book rack. The title? *North Beach Girl*.

For someone in a black turtleneck sweater, black tights, straight black hair, and stuck between the Beats and the Hippies, that was my book. Trouble was, no quarter.

The writer's name was John Trinian. Never heard of him. But I didn't forget it.

Before I met John Trinian I met Zekial Marko. Marko still dances like a busker on my streets, words wheezing out like a hurdy-gurdy. Anger, fear and genius turn the crank.

Zekial wasn't his given name, but then neither was Marko. Marvin Smucker or Schmucker (or whatever he once told me his real name was) called himself Zekial Marko because he believed in the voodoo of names. He said: "If you're called a thing, you become it." He found Zekial by sticking a pin in the Old Testament, Marko because he claimed to be a gypsy. Both beat Marvin all hollow for warding off demons, many of whom Marko knew personally. He was twenty-eight when we met and scared shitless, suffering from apocalyptic torments, a migraine of the soul.

He found me at a party on a houseboat moored in Gate 5, once the crème de la clot of Sausalito's waterfront. Damn, but Gate 5 used to be arty. Artists lived everywhere, secreted away in the riot of highly personal architecture and rotting hulks, all squatting on the stinking black ooze of the Frisco bay bottom… when the tide was out. When it was in, oily gray water slopped over boardwalks like the lost decks of the *Marie Celeste*. This roiling maze of what I imagined were the haunts of wild-eyed, wild-haired, wild-hearted writers and poets and painters, was all I thought I wanted.

Raked at a force ten slant, its bottom stuck fast in the mud, the houseboat was home to Sausalito's very own Zorba the Greek, a painter named Varda. Varda spent most of his time oozing Life! serving up Pasta! uncorking bottles of cheap red Wine! and seducing girls even younger than me, girls who called the old rogue Yanko—dat's Grek for uncle, he said in his high excited voice.

I passed a natty little chap with a goatee who wrote books about Zen. Or bopped around the country giving college talks about Zen. Or emoting over radios about Zen. When Alan Watts wasn't doing any of these Zen things he'd sit and booze on his own deck above Varda's deck shooting real bullets from a real high-powered rifle over his fellow transmogrifier's heads.

To reach Varda's I hiked miles of creaking swaying boardwalks with missing planks and unexpected junctions, these leading off to other adventures, or altitude changes, or alternate realities. Littered with rusty iron booby-traps, picked-over garbage, and dog crap.

By the time I got there, the party was in its prime. I'd arrived just about the time some were sliding down walls, Watts was shooting off a few rounds, and some were puking in the bay.

I wandered in with my sullen hipshot date. Who threw himself down like a snake falling out of an apple tree, took a guitar off someone already playing it, and began thrumming *I'm A Hog For You, Baby*.

What happened next, happened fast. A hand gripped my upper arm and yanked me out onto the slippery sloping deck. The owner of the grip said, "Needa frail. Jack, the dumbfuckin' cluck, says I can't get on the fuckin' boat with outta frail. It's not even his fuckin' boat."

I was the "frail" and the boat was a motor boat, one with a big wooden wheel.

There were two guys in it. One was at the wheel swaying more than the boat was. The other was the one who threw me in. The three of us were rapidly pulling away from the sinking party, barely missing the houseboat itself but giving the end of the dock a good whack. "You see that, ol' Marko, you ol' ass'ole! Fuck fucking Twain, me! I'm the bes' goddamn riverboat pilot on th'ole Mississississip."

Marko was drunker than that. He hallooed out into the dark wet wind. "Wheyhey! It's down to the salt in sea, Jack! A boat, a broad, and a star to stir her by! Here kid, have a slug of this."

Marko was talking like Bogart. I thought he always talked like Bogart. Turned out he had a grab-bag of accents which he could put on or take off like wigs.

Grabbing the bottle back, he wiped the rim with the sleeve of his unraveling sweater, his wrists as fine as a boy's. "This'll grow hair on your chest." He leaned forward and stared at me. "By the way, kid. You gotta chest?"

He had me there. I had the usual two, but they still had a lot of growing to do. I'd seen the movie. I knew how to talk to Bogie. "What makes you think I'd show you?"

Jack at the wheel, the whole boat suddenly keeled over, throwing me and Marko against its side. Falling, Marko said, "What makes you think I'd look?"

We both shut up as we chopped our way out towards the Pacific in frozen darkness, a darkness lit only by the Golden Gate Bridge. No running lights. Captain Jack, who looked—from what I could see of him—like a young man wearing an old man's mask, wasn't talking. He was swaying away at the front of the boat, communing only with himself and the bridge.

I was looking at the sea, at my hands, at first one face then the other. Marko's looked mostly dark, hairy, drunk, and cold. But his nose was wonderful. A pugnacious Slavic nose over a Pancho Villa moustache, it started out flat and fairly straight, but turned bulbous and bent abruptly to the left. A well-connected uppercut? A wall?

Marko was looking at me. He said, "Alright, kid, how the hell old are you?"

His question surprised me enough to answer it. "Seventeen."

That got him.

I really scared him by adding, "Almost."

"Jack? What's the rap for kidnapping?"

"You forget, we are subject only to the law of the sea."

"We haven't made it to the bridge."

"I admit, you're on to something there." Jack stuck his head forward, shaded his eyes, and peered out into inky nothing. The fog had not come in on little poet-yellow cat's paws, it had stomped over us in sloppy wellies. "Marko! I think I might've gone blind. Bridge's gone, so where's the fuckin' foghorn?"

Marko said, "What foghorn?"

Jack said, "No foghorn?"

Marko said, "How would I know? This was your idea."

Captain Jack bellowed out over the mournful sea, "Waaaaahaaa!"

In a little black party frock, black tights with a new hole in one knee, and goose-bumps between me and the wet chilly fog, I shivered from the spray of stinking seafoam and the salty wind. Marko was huddled into himself hogging the port. Jack swaggered at the wheel, foghorning away, and steering with his pinkie. I'd glanced back once at our wake. It lay on the choppy black waters in great troughed wallows. A series of seasick S's.

From out the depths of my chilled brain came the dumbest thing I could have said. "What do you do?"

Marko lunged at me. "Only a runty flat-chested goddamn piece of almost jailbait would ask a question like that." His face now a foot away, his breath heady waves of port. "You hear the bint, Jack? What do you do?" He edged the words out the side of his mouth, squeezing them flat, making me wish to Christ I hadn't told him how old I really was. Why not twenty? Or even eighteen? But I finally saw his face. It was as full and shining and mad as the missing moon.

"What *do* you *do*? *What* do *you* do?" Marko said it a few more times, trying out his selection of voices.

It was around then Marko said he wrote crap. He said it as if he were saying he jerked sodas, or drove a bus—like it was nothing.

Jack'd been listening. Letting go of the wheel, he yelled, "Crap? Your fucking crap isn't crap. *My* fucking stuff is crap."

Marko's desperado moustache quivered. "Don't tell me who writes fuckin' crap, Jack. You write pretentious lying shit. I write real crap."

Was I in heaven, or what! I'd been kidnapped by a writer. Two writers. Artists!

Even at seventeen—almost—I knew a little about cool. I didn't tell them how I felt, that I wanted to write, that I'd always wanted to be a writer. I knew what they'd make of that. In a word, hash.

I don't remember what happened after that. Marko must have told me about his name. And I must have given him my phone number. Somewhere in there he'd switched from Bogart to Behan. On the subject of writing his Behan said: "The trick is to dazzle the sonsabitches. Blind 'em with sass and dash and flash, glut 'em with raw red talent, create yourself right before their goosegreen eyes. And keep moving. You stop, they'll eat you with magazine knives."

"Amen," said our captain.

Marko looked up at Jack. "There's a fellow who oughta know."

"Been shat out by the worst," said Jack.

How long we bumped about out there, beats me. But Jack did the steering, what there was of it, and Jack and I did the listening. Marko did all the talking, as he was to do throughout our entire irritating, noisome, once-in-a-lifetime head-on collision. Who cared? Compared to what I would have said, what he said was something to listen to. I don't know about Jack, but for me, I thought Zekial Marko knew the way to my promised land. And he did. All I had to do was watch him run the other way. It was a long time, though, before I turned round and looked back.

I can still hear the sound of Marko's voice. Like pebbles in a sock. Amused with itself, and so at ease with words. Long words, fat words, funny words, exploding words, words like boulders, words like jackals, like floods, like dark alleys, like diving bells, like soup, like come, like stars. When I finally read a book he'd written, I knew he wasn't a great writer, but he sure was a writer. Lean and tough and funny. But I knew way before that he was a genius, and his genius lived on his tongue.

He told us stories. He lied. But then, what is talk but lies? I learned that the hard way. I once fervently *passionately* reverently believed that in all those words the truth lie in waiting, ready to make a quick grab and wring my neck. And oh, the lies, *his* lies, as I leaned close, falling down Marko's tunnel of words to the Land of Fabulous Fibs.

So young, I said as much.

He said, "It's truth you're wanting? Look at this." He stuck a finger in his mouth, pulled back his moustachio'd upper lip and exposed hard pink gums. His two front teeth were missing. "Troof itha goddith in cleaths." He let his lip go. "The bitch also wears brass knuckles. Forget truth and stick with art, kid. That way nobody but fairies hit you."

I loved him. A drunken toothless kidnapping lying pinwheeling writer. What more could any girl want?

And so it went. Sitting here now, writing on a sailboat in a high wind, I can't recall a thing Marko said. I can't remember finding the Golden Gate Bridge or Sausalito or the party on the houseboat. I can't remember what happened to Captain Jack.

Hold on. There's one thing Marko really said to me that night, just as we were climbing out of the boat. "You see this hand? This hand has a grip of steel."

"And the other?"

"Fake, but a goddamn work of art. You won't be getting rid of me."

That's how I met Zekial Marko and Jack Kerouac.

Zekial Marko phoned me the very next day. I wasn't home. What was I doing? Who knows? Probably lurking in a bookstore trying to liberate something by Nabokov.

My roommate said, "That creep phoned."

Creep? Which creep? Every lady on the loose knows more than a few creeps.

"*That* creep, you know, the one you said had no teeth on top."

Aha! She meant Marko, the writer. My heart flopped over. "Well? What did he say?"

"Don't know."

"What do you mean, you don't know?"

"Who can understand somebody who talks like that and with no teeth? I thought it was Cagney with a lisp."

"Bogart."

"Cagney."

"OK, Cagney. He probably does Cagney. Listen, didn't you get one fucking word?"

"Yeah, I got a few fucking words."

"What! What!"

"Something about he wants you to meet him."

"Where? When?"

"Now, I think."

"Shit!"

"He'll call back."

"What if he doesn't?"

"Don't be an ass, you ass. Creeps always call back."

I glared at her, speechless. An ax, a crossbow, prussic acid.

"He said something about *City Lights*. Maybe."

City Lights was *the* bookstore back then and maybe it still is. I had my cat fur covered sailor's pea coat back on in seconds and was out the door.

Turned out Marko had mentioned *City Lights* but only to say he was using their phone.

Marko didn't phone back. I found him by accident a week or so later, this time in Mike's Pool Hall… an invigorating hole back then: ill-lit, sleazy, smoky, and deafening. I was hanging out in the early noontime wearing a black turtleneck sweater, blue jeans and tennies. Aside from the footwear, who wasn't? Sitting at a back table with a cup of cold coffee, a pack of Pall Malls, a book of matches from Enrico's, and *Notes from the Underground*.

When Marko showed up, I almost knocked my little round table over trying to get to him.

Zekial Marko walked like he had his suspicions which turned out to be right. He kept his eyes moving and his head down. He wasn't more than five feet eight, and even then, already gone to seed. From the lack of any physical effort, an overdose of booze, dope, cigarettes, yelling, panic attacks, and late nights. Never fat, soft pasty white skin hung off his slender bones like sighs. And his hair, wispy and brown, stood up in places on his scalp like something enormous and loving had licked the hell out of it. I never once saw it combed. Up close, it had a smell to it like old paperbacks. I watched him walk over to a bunch of guys posing by a pool table. Vic Morrow always looked like he was in a movie.

Marko, turning away from Morrow, turned into me.

"Hello," I said. "Remember me?"

Marko, squinting at my eager face, said, "No." The squint was caused by his ciggie. Marko always spoke with a butt in his mouth where it jerked up and down under the moustache, the smoke traveling straight up into his watering green eyes. Behind the smokescreen, the green of his eye was heartbreakingly beautiful. Like a new leaf in the rain.

"The girl on the boat, the one from the party on the boat with you and Jack, remember?"

"Nope." The cigarette pointed at Mike's ceiling and stayed there.

I buzzed with anxiety. This was a well-stocked North Beach watering hole with a Hollywood actor and everything and I was standing in the middle of it, getting the brush-off.

Out of the smoky blue, he grabbed my arm—he was forever grabbing me—and hauled me out of Mike's. Lickety-split, I was dragged up Broadway.

"Where we going?"

"To see a friend. He likes dark frails."

Frails? No one said frails, except between the pages of pulp fiction. John Trinian's.

The friend turned out to be another writer. Seems when you meet one, you meet them all.

This one lived on the top floor of a five story walk-up overlooking Washington Square with its milk white church. If his windows had been clean you could have seen the square and the church through them, and if you had seen the square you would also see a statue of Benjamin Franklin. But the windows weren't clean. They were millimeters deep under greasy noseprints and flyblows. The room Marko rushed me into, all out of breath him more than me, was furnished with ass-worn dusty chairs, empty wine bottles, tattered paperbacks, dirty clothes, one round dining room table buried beneath pounds of used paper, hundreds of books, a smell that weighed more than me, lights shaded by brown paper bags, an old typewriter, and the writer himself. He was hands-down the most notable piece of furniture in the room.

The writer took up one whole corner. Waving his arms and snorting.

Hop, skip and jumping to his typewriter to peck out a word, cocking his sea otter face to get a good look at it, laughing with pleasure at the way the word looked with all the other words, hopping back, licking at wine dripping from his moustache. A golden moustache so heavy, so full of food-stuffs, I expected him to fall over face first. What held him up was en-thusiasm.

Nothing had changed because Marko and I stumbled in. Except that now he had an audience.

The writer handed us used Dixie cups slopping over with red wine, wagged his whiskers at me, winked at Marko, rolled up his white-walled eyes, cleared the phlegm from his throat, and began to read. This aloud from some papers he'd snatched from the table. Marko was deep into one of the dumpy hump-backed chairs, puffing out clouds of smoke and scattering ash.

"*Trout Fishing in America*," read the happy writer, "by Richard Brautigan."

"Who else?" belched Marko.

"We get the flavor of the piece better that way." Richard flung back his thin blond hair. Now that I think of it, he was a dead-ringer for Custer.

"Ah," said Marko, "you are practicing for literary success?"

"That, Marko, is what I am doing."

"Good thinking."

"It is, isn't it?"

"Get in a few good blows before they sink their teeth into you, bedad!" Marko was Brendan Behan again. As far as I knew, Richard was playing Richard Brautigan.

What I was doing was thinking. Like this: *Trout Fishing in America*?

Richard read on. "Half a block from Broadway and Columbus is Hotel Trout Fishing in America, a cheap hotel. It is very old and run by some Chinese. They are young and ambitious Chinese and the lobby is filled with the smell of Lysol."

A woman walked in. She was as tall and as stooped as Richard, her stringy hair just as yellow. Stuffed under one of her arms wriggled a red-faced baby. On the end of the other arm a large raw hand held a frying pan. The pan made spitting noises. She stood and gave Marko and me the once-over. From the sour look on her face, I could tell she'd had dealings with Marko before.

She said, "We feeding them too?"

I hoped not. Art was swell. No matter how bad it was, you didn't have to eat it—but food?

Richard turned his back. Marko farted. Reasonable results from the gifted. Well, it made sense to me at the time. Now? If I was that woman, I'd dump whatever was cooking in both their laps.

"It is the only furniture I have ever seen in my life," Richard read, "that looks like baby food."

"Because we haven't got enough frigging food and I'll be frigged if I go out to the frigging store." The woman was gone, taking her skillet and her babe and her army surplus hiking boots.

Marko and I listened for who knows how much longer, as Richard's wheezy whimsical voice piped up and down through *Trout Fishing*. While the weak sun traveled down the smudged windows and winked out behind the church spire over in Washington Square.

Marko interrupted only once. "You stole that! You lifted that right out of *The Savage Breast*. Admit it, you egregious fuck!"

Richard's mild eyes mildly blinked. "First you tell me what egregious means."

"It means cutting my line. It stinks."

Richard droned on.

We smoked. Constantly. Cancer? Artists don't die of cancer. They get swept out to sea like Shelley, or fall into pits of despair like Poe, or get chewed on by rats like Dorothy Parker, or walk into the River Ouse like Virginia Woolf, or blow out their brains like Hemingway. (And much much later, like Richard Brautigan. Few die as Morrow did, decapitated by a helicopter.) Most of them die when their art dies.

At some point, Marko reached out and pulled my hair. It brought my face close to his. He said, "You gotta face like an ice age, kid."

That near, Zekial Marko shone like one of Brautigan's homemade lamps. Like a five hundred watt bulb in a brown paper bag.

Did Marko love me? He wanted me. Most men'll fuck most anything, and back then I wasn't just anything. Like Tracy said of Hepburn in *Pat and Mike*, I was cherce. For certain tastes, that is. Mostly madmen and artists, which, for the most part, are the same thing. But did he love me? You know, I think he did. He must have had some reason to ask me three times to marry him.

I still love him. Is it too late to send him this? A mash note from the future.

Marko actually writing was a thing of rare… let's leave it at rare. He'd get mail from his paperback publishers, rip the envelope open and out would fall a single sheet of paper. On the paper was a list of book titles and the comment: "Pick one. Write about it. Three month deadline. Check's in the mail on accepted ms."

We'd look over the list, Marko with his ciggie, me with mine, and talk about it. What could anyone make of *Girls, Guns, and Hop*? Or my particular favorite: *Legs in the Night*.

After we stopped laughing, I'd be off doing whatever I did and Marko would hole up writing.

I never saw him read a book. I never saw him write one. I did show up at his Gate 5 digs late one night just in time to watch him throw his typewriter into the black bay mud.

Now and then, Marko would pick me up after high school in some beater he had. No one blinked. I was Redwood High School's one and only Beatnik, the evolving Hippy, the girl in black, the one who read philosophy and the classics in public, the girl who drove a white 1955 Thunderbird around Marin County until—with deep regret for the loss of the car but not for the guy who owned it—it was gone and replaced by Zekial Marko.

A garden of my gorgeous girlfriends drove down the coast to Big Sur. We found a small motel hanging off a cliff and piled into a room which included, how I can't recall, Marko. I think I told them when he talked he was better than the Beatles. No one was crazed on demon weed. (Except Simone who'd decided the walls were transparent and wandered off through one.) Those of us still in the left half of our minds were sprawled on the bed or propped cross-legged on the floor, wide-eyed slack-jawed privileged children listening to Marko tell us stories.

(By weed, I mean grass. We were too savvy for acid, too happy for horse, too confident for coke, too mellow for downers, too slender for booze, us little girls got high on Reefer Madness. Kerouac called marijuana *tea* and Marko called it *boo* and I called it *de debbil* and ran like hell. Another story for another time and another place.)

Using his Orson Welles voice, Marko told us a tale that went mostly like this: "Zedic Kosma, surrounded by his black-robed converts—a clutch of clucking Hollywood matrons with more money than brains, all rolling their painted aging eyes behind hideous homemade masks, all suckered into believing that the sacrifice of a beautiful young virgin would restore their lost youth—hissed and moaned as Kosma, evil sorcerer, part-time

Messiah and round-the-clock con-man, was just about to plunge a pike between the two heaving bazumas of Anne Woodbridge. Lovely Anne lay naked and bound atop an altar dripping with hot red wax, when suddenly!" (All gasp.) "From behind a rock arose Paul Berko, second-rate actor, third-rate poet, but first-rate leading man looker, dressed in an entire jar of vaseline and the Lizard Man costume he'd borrowed from his latest movie: *Spawn of the Killer Squid Meets Lizard Man*." (More gasps.) "Berko thumped his scaly chest, roared like a monumentally pissed-off flesh-eating dinosaur, and scared the fucking shit out of absolutely everybody. Zedic Kosma, mad genius, took one look at the Lizard Man and jumped over a Topanga Canyon cliff he'd forgotten was there while the moaning matrons flapped off every which way squawking like Edgar Allan Poe crows. Paul untied Anne, but left the black silk gag in her mouth, and together they walked away into the sunset, Paul in his rubber suit and Anne in her gratitude."

Marko smiled a secret smile. Under the Mexican moustache, teeth flashed (where had the teeth come from?) as he reached into the pocket of his short-sleeved summery shirt. "And now, gather round, my lovelies." (An aside to me earlier in the day: "Kid, you know some sweet gash.") "Here in my hand I hold a small yellow pill. Innocent. Pure. Like a tiny egg. And like the egg, capable of becoming anything at all, from a flightless prehistoric bird to a shooting star at the end of the endless universe to the mind of God erupting from a spinning Black Hole in the top of your head."

He sounded like Orson Welles playing Harry Lime, but he looked like Ernie Kovacs. But then, whoever he *sounded* like, he *always* looked like Ernie Kovacs.

My beautiful friends practically conked foreheads trying to see the yellow pill.

Marko closed his hand.

Everybody went, "Ohhh no!"

And opened it again. In his palm, not one yellow pill but many. Magic. Everybody went, "Ohhh yes!"

"Who wants one?"

Cacophony. Pandemonium. Bedlam. Me! Me! Me! Me! Me! One of those mindless "me's" was mine.

"Each of you close your eyes and hold out your hand."

We all did.

"One for you," he said, "and one for you and one for you... " and so on and so forth until he came to me. Into my palm came nothing, nothing at all.

Crushed. Wounded. Dumbfounded. Flushed with pain and shame. Left out. Put down. HUMILIATED.

I watched my happy friends wait for lift-off.

Fifteen minutes later they were totally completely massively and loudly asleep. Except me. And Marko.

Said he, "Hearts of Nembutal. Bomber downers. Like guiltless babes, they'll all sleep for hours."

"And you?"

"Didn't take one."

"Why?"

"Only way to get you alone."

Exhaled a truly mollified me, "Wow."

We piled the happy bodies on the floor and climbed into bed. And Marko told me stories. I told him a few. Without touching, we loved each other for a few hours before I grew up and away and lost him. (Though, in truth, he lost himself first.)

Simone came back with the sun. With her was some fella she'd found. They both looked transubstantiated. Marko and I were watching the light change over the ocean.

"Christ," said Marko, "it's Gary. Even in Nirvana, Snyder finds nooky."

"Ah," said Gary, his face rising with the sun, "my friend, the novelist."

Marko winced. "I don't write novels. I write pulp fiction."

Zedic Kosma found his way into the *House of Evil*, one of Marko's one hundred and eighty page paperbacks. I was Anne. He was Paul. He was also probably Zedic Kosma. To the tune of *Beautiful Dreamer*, he'd sing: *Take me to Heaven, Make me Divine, Call Zedic Kosma, It costs but a dime.*

(Marko has a second-lead in *China Blues*, my first published book. For his gift of the gab, I made him Irish, for irony I called him "Fearless O'Flooty," for truth I let him talk as he talked. The book's still in print and Marko's still in it, as fearless as ever.)

In the middle of a tight bright white afternoon, Marko was dragging me from North Beach to Sausalito, from Mill Valley to Russian Hill, from Chinatown to Market Street. Hell if I can remember why.

We found a plain brown door along a plain brown hallway in a plain brown building on Columbus Avenue. Marko stood outside and yelled,

"Hey you!" Out popped a head with a hat on it. The head was stuck on the end of a long bendable neck like one of those gooseneck lamps and the hat was like Wyatt Earp's hat, black felt, with a wide brim and a Winchester crown. The face on the front of the hatted head was big-nosed, cherub-chinned with tired eyes blinking behind horn-rimmed glasses at the sight of Marko and me filling up his open door. I looked down. Sure enough, cowboy boots.

"Who are you?" asked Marko. The guy in the hat said, "I write. I'm writing a book in here."

I beamed at Marko, saying without saying: *a writer, gee whizz and golly gosh! can we go in and watch him write? can we, ok? can we?* Marko ignored me.

Marko's standup comic's voice boomed up and down the brown corridor. "Another dope-fiend, another thief, another bullshit artist. What's it about, this book?"

"Texas," said the head. "I call it *Horseman, Pass By* and it's about Texas."

"In that case, you've come to a good place to work. Frisco's a lot like Texas, especially at milking time. For that matter, it's a lot like a fast trout stream."

And then he walked in, sat down, and talked.

The cowboy listened, pencil poised.

Walking out hours later, I turned back when I felt a tap on my shoulder. Who else but the writer from Texas?

He said, "Who *is* he?"

"A writer."

The Texan who was writing a book that'd become a movie called *Hud* and go on to write *Lonesome Dove*, said, "Figures."

Meanwhile, out in the unreal world, events were unfolding that would take Zekial Marko not only to Los Angeles, but to Hollywood.

The French took the books of John Trinian seriously. In France, a paperback writer was a real writer because in France, all books were paperback books. Not only that, each Trinian was a *roman noir*, a little comic book of crime. If there's something close to a Frenchman's heart, it's crime with style.

They'd already made a movie out of Trinian's *The Big Grab*, calling it *Mélodie en sou-sol* (US: *Any Number Can Win*). It starred the very big deal Jean Gabin and the not-yet very big deal Alain Delon, a small-time street thief turned actor. Alain was as sleek as an oil slick on a puddle in a Marseille gutter and as pretty as most of my girlfriends.

After the success of John Paul Belmondo in *Breathless*, France and Hollywood were sure American women would die for Delon. And if his first American movie should pair him up with Hollywood's hottest female box office draw? That year it was Ann-Margret, all wiggly and giggly and fresh from *Viva Las Vegas* with E. Presley. And if, on-screen, he was bookended by veteran Hollywood character actors: Van Heflin and Jack Palance? And if the cinematographer had just wrapped Hitchcock's *The Birds*?

They couldn't lose.

Now all they needed was a script.

When Marko and I were living with Alain in Francis X. Bushman's Beverly Hills house, Alain leaned across the dining room table to say it was he who'd said, "Zut alors, mes amis! The brain storm, it strikes! Nothing less than brilliance, nothing less than the great American genius, John Trinian, will do!"

And so it came to pass. Hollywood bought Trinian's *Scratch a Thief* for Alain Delon and Alain insisted Marko write the screenplay. Someone renamed it *Once a Thief*.

Marko wrote a part for himself in it and one for me. I was a smart-ass strung-out motor-mouth junkie and he was a poor old pusherman who got pushed around, got thrown in the slammer, maybe even knifed. Out of luck and out of teeth.

I had to audition to get the role. Ralph Nelson, fresh off directing *Lilies of the Field*, sat in his hotel room in the Jack Tar Hotel (Herb Caen over at the San Francisco Chronicle had a lot to say about the Jack Tar, printable but not nice), and listened to my unsteady gush, then gave me my own part.

Lying around in those huge trailers actors lie around in, Jack Palance and I agreed. Acting was no job for a real artist.

Marko meant to make me a movie star. I meant to make me a writer.

Once Hollywood called, Zekial Marko had some money.

About Marko and money. When he was little kid growing up near John Steinbeck and not yet completely terrified, he read every hard-boiled writer going: Hammett and Chandler, Cain and McCoy and Woolrich. He saw every hard-boiled flick. Starring Bogart. Or Cagney. Or Raft. Or Robinson. Or all of them all together. But John Garfield was the man for him. Marko thought he looked like Garfield. He didn't, he looked like Ernie Kovacs. But he sure as hell sounded like Garfield. Kerouac said things like *go, man, go!*

and even *daddy-o* which made Marko squirm, but Marko said *frail* and *gunsel* and *scratch.*

"Kid," he'd say, when yet another Hollywood check came in the mail, "Let's go and blow this scratch all in one place."

If I close my eyes, I can still see a tiny bar on the Embarcadero where the lights were blue, the air green with fluttering ten dollar bills, and the floor pink and brown and black with human hands as the humans themselves crawled for the cash. I remember it so well because it hurt so much. Marko thought he saw it as devil-may-care, as flamboyance. I saw it as something in him that couldn't accept praise, never achieved a sense of success.

"My stuff is crap," he said. "I don't write novels, I write pulp fiction," he said. "Another thief," he said, "another bullshit artist."

Still, he had the money (for about three minutes and forty two seconds), so there you go.

Marko loved Sausalito's No Name Bar and the No Name Bar loved him. He'd sit with Sterling Hayden and swap tales of writers and writing. Neither one talked about Hollywood. I'd listen as long as I could before I got caught and tossed out. I'd sneak back in. Sterling called me Lolita and used his size to hide me before I got thrown out again. Marko loved the *City Lights* bookstore. He knew the Beats and they knew him, but he had no patience for Ginsberg. "Pretentious cluck," he said. What he liked was the bulletin board by the stairs. He'd leave messages there or get messages, a good thing because Marko was not always easy to find. Marko loved the Beatles. He took me to see *A Hard Day's Night.* I hadn't given them a moment's thought before that. After, I loved the Beatles too. Marko loved Frisco's *hungry i* because he loved jazz. The last time I saw Marko's friend, Dizzy Gillespie, I was sitting in his lap laughing at his string of dirty jokes. The last time I saw Richard Brautigan he was falling down drunk at the Buena Vista Café. I'll never forget his kiss, one I couldn't duck. It was like kissing the mop used to clean up a shoot-out in a brewery.

One of the last times I saw Marko he'd followed me to New York City. Where a lot more happened. With so many more people. Some of it innocently illegal.

Is Marko as I remember him? Was he ever? Was his vision of himself anything like mine? I saw him with such young eyes. Would I see him now as I saw him then? Was Zekial Marko really so goddamned terrific?

You bet he was.
He was an artist and he lived an artist's life.
What could be more terrific than that?

—January 2014
Puget Sound, WA

Ki Longfellow is the author of several noir mysteries including *Shadow Roll*, *Good Dog, Bad Dog*, and *The Girl in the Next Room*, all featuring P.I. Sam Russo. She has lived in Marin County (California), Hawaii, New York, Europe and Vermont, and is the widow of Vivian Stanshall, founding member of the Bonzo Dog Band. She currently travels and writes.

Scandal on the Sand

By John Trinian

For Bernard Robert Cohn

ONE

In the deep, in cold darkness, a hundred feet below the rocky cliffs and half-hidden among the fan fronds and greenly-waving fields of sea grass, the great gray whale hovered, his tail fins moving now and then to maintain his depth. Silvery flecks of fish darted past, quick as a wink. There was no light from the surface yet. Slowly, moving almost without an angle, the whale rose to the roof of the sea. When he broke, exhaling loudly and spewing gauzy veils of pocket water from his blowholes, he saw that it would soon be light. Already the stars were losing brilliance. A narrow band of mottled pearl was growing on the eastern horizon. The dark swells were slowly rolling inshore. Moving heavily, gracefully, the whale heaved about the wind-ruffled surface, parting the waters, shallow-diving, then rising and exhaling. The whale made quick playful twists, occasionally thrusting himself clear of the water and flopping back with a terrific smash. Then, suddenly, he again dove to the bottom, to the silent canyons and dark grottoes.

With half a mind he wondered where the rest of the herd had gone. It had been quite a while since he had seen another whale. Somewhere during the night, migrating south along the coast from their last headland guide point, he had become separated. However, he wasn't too concerned. He felt safe. He had traveled the Arctic-Baja run many times before and he knew what landmarks to watch for. So, once again feeling playful, he wallowed and whisked from the surface to the deep, establishing an even four-minute diving rhythm, his huge back glistening as the black-green waters broke and roiled and foamed in his wake. He was moving, almost unmindfully, closer toward shore. He could feel the powerful surge of the tide and the deep vibrations of the combers as they crashed and thundered on the not too-distant beach. Half curiously and gathering speed in his frolic, the whale suddenly, impulsively, swerved inshore. Then, before he had a chance to check his course a second time, an unusually strong tidal channel caught and pushed him, adding to his speed, and he felt his belly hiss roughly on the sand. This was something unusual. The whale plunged, attempting a quick turn, wanting to regain deeper water, but was pushed still closer. The surf raged about him, phosphorescent white and salty clouds of spume. The tide was hitting the high mark. Behind the whale the heavy swells rolled and crested and broke and thrust him deeper, jamming his tremendous weight to the shore. He thrashed his flukes and heaved his body. He turned and faced the sea, ready to plunge. But one final wave, poised high and white-browed, raced toward him like a huge green wall and crashed and tumbled before him and he was helplessly forced aground.

As he landed, slightly dazed from the impact of the wave, beached and facing the sea with wistful eyes, the high waters seethed round him in great hissing foam fans—then, went slowly away, sucked back to sea. Salty cobwebs clung to the slick sands. The whale struggled briefly, awkwardly, without panic, swaying his great flukes and burrowing his head in the sand to gouge a return track. But the more he struggled the deeper he sank. The tide retreated and the wind died. The surf gradually grew calm. The eastern line of gray was brighter now, a thickening band of pale milk and blue and rose. Gulls wheeled overhead, cawing, watching. Exhausted now, and still a bit stunned from the force of his grounding, the whale's great body shuddered and relaxed. He felt safe. The stretch of beach was deserted and the dawn was quiet. Soon the surf was a short distance before him and his body was buried a good two feet in the shoreline. Sand fleas swarmed from black tangles of seaweed and hopped on the whale's hide. Birds tapped little piecrust marks on the shiny comber line, chasing the outsurge of foamy water, black scraps against the white, then retreating, racing about the beach, feeding, following the watery hem, pecking, dancing. Behind the whale, further along the beach, thick tufts of beach grass and patches of ice plant could be seen. The whale gave a massive sigh, exhaling loudly, and his flukes wriggled halfheartedly in the sand. His eyes blinked slowly, watching the dawn and the calming waters. One gull settled a few feet from the whale, clacked his orange beak and watched. The whale gave a deep sigh, closed his eyes and slept.

The dawn was coming.

The tiny golden-fingered clock set in the green lizard case ticked quietly on the motel bedstand. Against the pale square of beachward window Karen Fornier could see gently waving outlines of banana leaves and chain fern and young palms. She could hear the faint hiss and crush of the surf.

For a long moment, lying on her side and not moving, Karen had no idea where she was.

The wall-to-wall carpet was dark blue, the crumpled spread deep gold with little yellow flowers. On one wall there was a bad watercolor of a tiger set in a plastic bamboo frame. The room smelled of cigarette smoke and furniture polish.

Karen rose on one elbow and looked at the broad muscular back outlined against the sheets beside her. Bits and pieces of the night before came back to her. She remembered drinking and dancing with Hobart in a bar in Laguna Beach. And their long, almost passionate embraces in his leathery-smelling Continental. And watching the surf in the moonlight from the window of the motel.

Had Karen suggested they drive along the beach? Or had Hobart? Everything was fuzzy in her mind. She couldn't remember if they were heading for Tijuana or just going to Laguna Beach. She did remember however that sometime just before they had returned north toward Santa Monica they had eaten in some sort of Polynesian joint. She remembered that the waiters had worn bright red monkey jackets and that kerosene lamps had been burning among the palms that had bordered the parking lot.

She rubbed her eyes and again looked at Hobart's back, thinking that whatever the story was it didn't matter now. There had been the iced champagne in the car and the green lizard clock and the latex Trojan. So everything it seemed had been carefully arranged.

She rose from the bed, stubbing her toe on an empty champagne bottle. She stood before the window, rubbing her toe, and watched Hobart while he slept, snoring, his head buried under the pillow.

A big, weak-looking handsome man sleeping like a well-fed dragon. Or better—a lizard. Like his damned clock. Ticking away. Snoring. His head chopped off by a pillow.

"Good morning, lover," Karen whispered. "Sleep little baby and know you're clean. Always wash after you've had a woman, Hobart. If you don't it'll rot and fall off. And we can't have that happening, can we...."

Hobart's shoulders rose and fell with his breathing.

"The hell with you...."

The surf thumped on the beach. The dawn lit the quivering fans of the palms. Karen, naked, leaned on the sill; she was a beautiful woman in her late twenties with large fern-colored eyes, yawning and smoking a mentholated cigarette and finger-coiling her long ash-blonde hair.

The sky was pink and gray now. A slice of salmon. Tuesday morning. Winter. Another hot day. Like tomorrow and yesterday. The sun in Los Angeles in the afternoon on the golden manicured beaches and the jet planes scratching thin white lines in the sky and to right now, this quiet moment, with Karen staring glumly at the beach.

According to Hobart's damned lizard clock it was only a little past eight.

Karen watched a pair of gulls hovering over the water.

"One of them is me," she whispered against the pane. "The very white one. And I'm looking for sea-gull food—whatever it is that sea gulls eat—and I'm free and happy, covered with feathers, flying in the breeze with my friend. Gloria Gull and Gary Gull. Hung in the sky."

The pair of gulls caught a sky tide and were pulled out of sight.

From where Karen stood, at the far north end of the beach, at the edge of the small town at the foot of the cliffs just off the highway, she could see the entire length of the beach, some three miles, wide and empty. The sea was calm, the color of lead.

She could remember more of the night before.

The waves had been wild, exploding pale green lights as the plankton had swept the sand. And while Hobart had stood behind her, drunkenly nuzzling her neck and unzipping her skirt, Karen had sipped cold champagne and had watched the water.

Karen now wondered why she had bothered making it with Hobart. She had known all along that he would seduce her sooner or later, and she had known also that he would be a disappointment.

She turned and looked at Hobart.

She had known him for nearly two years. Hobart's father, an ex-film producer of quickie "B" westerns, and Karen's father, a successful plastic manufacturer, had formed a company for experimental film projects, and, more recently, for financing independent productions. The Fornier-Richardson partnership had done very well. And since the beginning both families, Hobart's and Karen's, had made it obvious that they thought it would be a fine idea if Hobart and Karen would become engaged.

Hobart, naturally, still sponging from his father and not wanting to offend the keeper of the coin, had liked the idea immensely. But Karen had not. She had gone out with him a few times but nothing had ever developed from their dates. Until now.

She whispered, "You're a lizard."

She gathered her clothes and carried them into the shower room where she set them on a chromium rack. She stepped into the pebbled glass stall and soaped herself under a lukewarm spray (thinking of a story she had heard about a girl who had been sprayed with whipped cream, and after her lover had licked it off he had run a cello bow over her damp breasts). She gargled and soaped again, all contact with Hobart whirl-pooling down the little metal grill at her feet.

While she toweled and dressed she could hear Hobart clumping about the bedroom and whistling "I Left My Heart in San Francisco."

She returned to the bedroom, ignoring Hobart's cheery and suggestive "good morning." The sky was blue and pink now. The light in the room made everything look cheap. The champagne bottles had been picked up and were standing beside a small tin basket in one corner. Karen brushed her hair before the vanity mirror, counting the strokes. Her eyes looked secretive.

Hobart watched her while he stuffed the tail ends of his shirt into his trousers and zipped his fly.

Karen turned, tying her hair back with a short white scarf. She was wearing thonged sandals, a blue denim skirt, and a striped blouse. She was wearing no bra, having stuffed it into her skirt pocket. Her lips were slightly pursed, her expression thoughtful, her temple hair still damp from the shower.

"Good morning."

Hobart winked and grinned. "I was wondering when you'd get around to saying something."

Karen's expression didn't change. Slowly, still watching him, she undid the center button of her blouse. She opened the blouse until the swell of her left breast was completely exposed.

Hobart looked puzzled, hesitating with his smile.

"Do you know about Cleopatra?" Karen asked quietly. "She used to stick pins into the breasts of her slave girls." She closed and buttoned the blouse. "It's true. It's an historical fact. What do you think of it, Hobart?"

Hobart's mouth was solemn, but his eyes were shining.

"That's a funny thing to say," he answered.

Karen shrugged and said nothing.

Hobart turned to the window, changing the subject, finger-combing his short brown hair.

He was a tall man with a cleft chin and dark spaniel eyes. He was dressed in black silk slacks, white linen jacket, and black loafers with tassels on them. And he still smelled, Karen had noticed, of Surf-rider cologne.

"Looks like it's going to be another nice day," Hobart said to the window. Then, turning and looking about the room, he frowned. "That business about Cleopatra. That was a funny thing to say."

"Really? Why is that?"

Hobart wasn't really sure why. He fumbled with his expression. "Well," he said cautiously, "it sounds as if you were accusing me of something."

Karen lost interest. "I always say funny things in the morning," she said. "That's one of my things."

Hobart moved closer, his voice lowering. "I'll tell you another of your things," he said. "You look beautiful. Real beautiful. And deep. Deep and beautiful."

Karen grabbed her sweater from the back of a chair.

"Don't forget to take your clock, Hobart."

"What? Don't forget what? Wait a minute. Where're you off to so early? We're paid here until—"

"For a walk on the beach."

"A walk on the beach? At this hour? But—"

She opened the doorway and looked out at the row of bungalows leading to the highway.

Hobart's Continental was parked opposite the small liver-shaped pool. Leaves were floating in the pool. Birds were sounding in the nearby bushes. Now and then, from the highway, a passing car could be heard. The air smelled clean and sweet. Damp earth and grass.

"I want to walk and think and look at the waves," Karen said. "Maybe I'll throw a few seashells at the waves. That is, if they still put seashells on beaches."

Hobart grabbed his lizard clock and his pack of cigarettes.

"But aren't you hungry, honey?" He pointed at the drive-in restaurant sign at the head of the motel. "The restaurant should be open by now. How do ham and eggs and hot coffee sound?"

"Terrible. I'm not hungry."

She didn't wait for further argument. She followed the gravel path to the rear of the bungalow and stood poised at the rim of a steep dune. Then, sucking in a deep breath, she hung in balance and fell forward (Gloria Gull), jumping and running down the slope to the beach where the sandpipers scattered and the air was damp and tangy with salt spray.

While she walked she realized that she felt good for the first time in days. Her cheeks glowed. Her hangover was completely gone, and she was surprised to discover how strong she felt.

"Cleopatra and Hobart Richardson would have made a handsome couple...."

When Hobart finally caught up with her she saw that he was breathing somewhat raggedly, and that he had tucked his damned lizard clock into the hip pocket of his slacks.

They walked in silence while Hobart brought his breathing back to normal.

"You know," he finally said, "you're an awfully strange girl."

"Girl?" Karen asked. "Why not an awfully strange human being?" She walked around a jellyfish. "Perhaps I am. I don't know. But right now it's the sea."

"What is?"

"Everything. I just saw a jellyfish. It's been years since I've seen a jellyfish."

"Well, I'm here too, you know. Doesn't that mean anything?"

Karen didn't reply.

Hobart tried to take her arm in his but she moved away. She noticed, now that the sky was lighter, a few lumpy clouds far out to sea, on the horizon, like cauliflower blooming from blue earth.

"Right now I feel like the sea. Sea animals and green water and islands. I once wanted to be Dorothy Lamour."

"Dorothy La—"

"Do you like my father, Hobart?"

"Your father?"

"I wish you'd stop repeating everything that I say. Do you like my father?"

"He's a fine man. I admire—"

"I'll tell you what he is. Not who he is. But what he is. I don't know who he is anymore. He used to be a who, but now he's a what. He's Mr. Abercrombie & Fitch. Pleats in his trousers. That's what he is. Russian Leather. Bridge. Dunhill. Prokofiev. New York in November and Medico cigarette holders. I don't think very much about my father. My real father—the same man, but he was a who then and not a what—could make me laugh, imitating Babar, the elephant. He's become quite vague since then."

Hobart asked, after a moment, "How about me?"

"You wouldn't want to hear it," Karen said. "You probably think you're hard to figure. But you're not. You're actually very easy. And if I told you what I thought about you you'd get angry with yourself and me because you'd be embarrassed to see just how easy you really are. I don't want to talk about you, Hobart. It wouldn't be fun. So let's just walk. Quietly."

Hobart nodded, pretending to shrug the idea away, but he was gritting his teeth and thinking what a lousy stinking bitch Karen Fornier was. He wondered how it was that she always managed to put him on the defensive.

The dirty bitch.

He began to plot imaginary conversation gambits to turn the tables on her. Her jibes, he felt, were terribly unfair. Especially now, considering how he had mastered her during the night.

And Karen, removing her scarf and shaking out her hair, smiled to herself, knowing exactly what Hobart was thinking....

Just as the engine began to sputter, Joe Bonniano wheeled the cream-colored Cadillac convertible to a stop before a cocktail lounge on Fourth Street just off Santa Monica Boulevard. He switched off the ignition and stared at the dashboard. Ever since he had left the San Diego Freeway the gas needle had been sitting on the empty mark.

"Goddam gas gobbler," Joe Bonniano muttered. "Stupid gold brocade piece of junk."

Joe slammed the wheel with the palm of his hand, then, sighing, settled back and knuckled his eyes. He told himself that no matter what the game was it always ended the same. The curse of Joe Bonniano. Dice, roulette, poker, the horses. It didn't matter. Everything always ended with a bust-out.

Leaning on the wheel, his thick forearms folded against his chest, Joe stared at a large photo-poster set in a glass case near the padlocked entrance of the bar. The picture showed a bleached-blonde woman seated behind a white piano, smiling, pushing her bulgy breasts over the top of her white evening gown.

"That's right," Joe said softly. "You just keep right on smiling. You dumb cluck. Smile. You got no worries. No worries at all."

Joe Bonniano slid halfway across the seat and snapped open the glove compartment. He took out a small bottle of Sperine tranquilizers and a Colt .45 automatic with one bullet fired. He swallowed three of the tablets and dropped the gun into the inside pocket of his suit jacket.

Still seated in the center of the car, Joe flipped the rearview mirror and studied his reflection. He made sour faces at himself, rubbing the bluish grit of a single night's growth. He looked tense and pale, a big man in his early forties, dressed in an expensive silk suit, pale green shirt and matching tie. His eyes were dark and heavy-lidded and bloodshot. He put on a pair of sunglasses and knocked the mirror to one side.

"I look like a goddam hood."

He lit a cigar from the dashboard lighter and sat puffing, surrounding himself with clouds of smoke. The morning sun reflected off the store windows. The shadows on the other side of the street looked cold. In the distance a line of palms swayed gently in the breeze.

What to do now?

Joe had to get in touch with someone who could help him, someone who owed him a good turn, such as Little Isaac or that bastard Perrini or good old Willie C. But it was too early to be calling anyone. They were all probably busy, either in hiding until the heat cooled down or else they were scrambling like a bunch of goddam vultures for Betseka's old power lines.

It was too early for Joe to be walking the streets—there weren't enough people around to cover him. And he couldn't sit in the car all morning—the cops would have a make on it by now.

Either way, he couldn't afford to drive it.

In his wallet Joe had only four singles. And in his pants pocket he had less than a buck in silver.

For doing last night's job, Joe was due to receive ten thousand dollars. But he wouldn't see a cent of it for eight more days. And the meet had been set for the lobby of the Sheraton-Palace Hotel in San Francisco.

He sat, puffing on his cigar, his false teeth noisily grinding, watching the street for the first signs of the heat, and wondering what he could do now. Right now. It was a cinch he couldn't sit in the car—and it wouldn't be wise to walk around Santa Monica all day either.

"What the hell. Live fast, die young, and have an ugly corpse...."

He stepped from the Cadillac, locked it, walked one block south to Broadway and stood on the corner. He felt conspicuous. He rattled the coins in his pocket and mopped his brow with a linen handkerchief.

A young girl with a lush figure and blue cross-eyes walked past carrying a white paper bag, smelling of sweet perfume and warm doughnuts. A newspaper truck rumbled by. A group of smiling young executives emerged from a taxicab nearby. Joe Bonniano turned and walked two blocks to Ocean Avenue, then across to Palisades Beach road. He felt safer being in the open, under the palm trees and near the beach.

He stopped before a newspaper rack and after taking a quick look around, he pretended to insert a coin in the slot and he stole a morning paper. Tucking the paper under his arm, he strolled along the path and watched the boats bobbing on the dirty water near the Santa Monica Pier. The air smelled of grass and seaweed and rotting wood. Gulls were circling overhead. The beach below the promenade was empty.

The tranquilizers seemed to be taking effect. Joe felt nearly relaxed. Standing in the shade of a palm he now wondered if it was too early to make his calls. After all, it made little difference if he called now or later. If any of the boys were going to come through they would do it now, at this early hour, as well as later on in the day.

He opened the paper and glanced at a very poor photograph of himself on the front page. He saw the word "Manhunt"....

"So I finally make page one. Big deal. I should send a copy to my sainted mother...."

A tall thin man with a mustache, wearing bopshades and a pair of Harold Teen trousers, carrying a plastic crocodile guitar case and a portmanteau, strolled past. When he had moved down the path and out of sight, Joe again opened the paper and looked at his picture. Scowling he tossed his cigar over the beach railing and moved toward a wooden bench under the palms.

Two old ladies wearing print dresses and straw hats were standing beside the bench. One woman, wearing a blue dress, looked a little like a pelican. She was watching the ocean through a pair of binoculars. The second woman, wearing a pink dress, looked like a thin white canary. She was holding a camera.

As Joe approached, the woman that looked like a pelican lowered her binoculars and smiled.

"Good morning. I just saw a boat through my glasses. A big one. Way far out. Near those little clouds."

Joe nodded, folding and hiding his newspaper.

"These are very powerful binoculars," the first woman said. "They're made in Germany."

"Yeah," Joe said uneasily. "The Germans are good at making things like that."

The second woman, the canary, held her umbrella in one hand and with the other gently pressed what remained of her right breast. She looked at Joe as though she recognized him.

"Excuse me," the woman said. "But aren't you the man who plays Perry Mason on the television?"

"No, Ma'am, I'm not."

Had they flashed his mug shot on TV?

"I'm sorry," the canary said. "It's just that you look a little bit like Perry Mason."

From the corner of his eye Joe spotted a cruising police car as it turned from Colorado onto Ocean Avenue. His back muscles twitched and he moved closer to the two old ladies. His hand casually reached into his jacket, his fingers touching the checkered butt of the gun.

"Ah—do you ladies like Perry Mason? I mean, are you fans of his?"

The police car had stopped directly across the street. One of the two cops had stepped from the car and was now looking at the license plate of a red Thunderbird parked at the curb.

Joe could hear the scratchy sound of the dispatcher's voice coming from the police car.

The pelican lady was saying, "Oh yes, we watch him all the time. We've missed only three shows. I've even read some of his books." She peered closer at Joe. "You know, you do look a little like him. Perry Mason, I mean."

Joe tried to smile. He had to force himself to stand still. The effect of the pills seemed to have vanished.

"I suppose you ladies are just visiting here...."

The second woman nodded. "Yes. We're from New York. Albany. We've been here five days now."

Both cops were now on the sidewalk, looking at the Thunderbird. Joe could feel the sweat gathering under his arms and prickling his brow. The gun felt heavy in his jacket.

"Been seeing the sights, huh?"

"Yes," the pelican lady said. "Last night we went to Hollywood and saw the 'Steve Allen Show.' We had to write for tickets more than a month ago."

"We hoped that Steve would have picked our card from the studio audience," the canary said. "But he didn't. Do you know what we said? We said that two ladies can talk like Steve. You know, 'fern' and 'clyde' and 'smock-smock.' But we weren't picked."

Joe looked at them as though they were insane. He had no idea what they were talking about.

"We practiced how to say 'smock-smock' in our hotel room."

Joe nodded. "That's nice. I guess."

"We're going to see Lawrence Welk this week."

Both cops had returned to their car and were now pulling away. Joe watched until the car turned right onto Santa Monica. Then he turned back to the pelican and the canary and, after a minute of listening to more of their weird chatter, he wished them a nice visit to California and walked quickly away, the paper folded tightly under his arm.

He went out onto the pier, past the merry-go-round. A few fishermen, mostly Chinese, were leaning on the railing, studying the water. The place smelled strongly of oil and fish and hotdogs.

Joe found an empty phone booth and slid the door shut after him. He wiped his face with his handkerchief. The scare with the cops had passed and again he felt relaxed, almost dulled. His brain was clicking wildly, but his nerves were calm. What with the pills and his lack of sleep he felt unreal inside himself.

He dropped a coin into the slot and dialed Little Isaac's number in Pacific Palisades. After waiting ten rings he hung up. He tried that bastard Perrini's number in Beverly Hills, and again, after ten rings, he hung up.

"Dirty bastards. Both of them. Crumbs."

That left only Willie C.

"Yeah, and Willie owes me plenty of favors...."

He swallowed two more Sperine tablets.

"Bunch of chicken-shits."

He opened the paper and for the first time read through the accompanying article.

It was the usual crap.

Joseph "Joe Banana" Bonniano was being sought in one of the greatest manhunts in the history of Southern California for last night's brutal "gang-style" slaying of Herbert Betseka, well-known bookmaker and kingpin of local crime, etc., etc., etc. Then there was a follow-up about Mickey Cohen, organized crime in Los Angeles, Cosa Nostra, and a cheap rehash of "Joe Banana's" police record. There was one picture buried on the inside page—two cops standing near Betseka's body, one cop pointing to the bullet hole in the head and the other grinning ghoulishly into the camera.

Joe folded the paper and shoved it into his jacket pocket.

"Always the same kinda crap."

For one thing, one bullet in the head could hardly describe a typical "gang-style" slaying, and for another, if Herb Betseka had been such a well-known bookmaker and kingpin of local crime, then why hadn't the Los Angeles fuzz busted him long ago?

"Yeah. Tell me that."

And, also, and more important to Joe, he had never been called "Joe Banana" in his life and he wondered where the newsboys, or the cops, got those lousy nicknames....

A fat old woman wearing an Hawaiian muu-muu was rapping on the glass door.

"Hey! You using that phone? Or're you readin' the goddam paper?"

"I'm using the phone."

And to prove it he dropped another coin into the slot.

He dialed Willie's number and waited for the mechanical burr, chanting, "Be Home Willie, Be Home Willie, Be Home—"

"Hello."

It was Willie's voice, soft and cunning. Joe leaned closer to the mouth-piece.

"Willie? That you, kid?"

"Yes."

"Listen, Willie, this is—"

"I know. Go ahead and talk. I'm okay here."

"I need help. Real bad."

"It's early, Joe."

"I know. But I'm in a bad fix. I've never screwed you, Willie. Never. We've always been tight and straight with each other. Right? And now I'm in a bad way. I need help."

"Go on."

"Okay. You know what happened? About last night?"

"I heard. Everyone knows about it."

"Okay. Now listen. I'm busted. Cleaned out. Understand? I can't get back to my hotel room, or to the hotel safe. The place is probably crawling with heat."

"I hear you, Joe."

Joe's false teeth were uncomfortable against his gums. He mopped his face again and shoved his sunglasses atop his head.

"You've got to come through for me, Willie. No one else wants to touch me. I think everyone's running."

"If you're tapped, then what happened to the big roll Herb was supposed to be carrying? It was on the television this morning."

"Willie, believe me, that's either newspaper bullshit, or else the cops stole it and they're pinning it on me. What the hell—would I be calling you now if I wasn't in an honest-to-God bind? Would I?"

"Okay, Joe. When do you get paid?"

"Frisco. In eight days."

"Okay. Relax. I'll come through."

"I need it now. Right away."

"Where are you?"

"Santa Monica. On the pier. I could meet you at the place in Pacific Ocean Park. I can take the tramcar and be there in a few minutes."

"No go," Willie said. "That's a bad place for now. You remember that spot on the beach where we talked with the chiseler?"

"Yeah, sure."

"Okay. Meet me there. At the south end, far south end. There's never anyone around there. It's always empty."

"All right. What time? When can we meet? It'll have to be soon."

"You'll have to wait there," Willie said. "Don't go wandering off nowhere.
I'll be there sometime before five this evening. Meanwhile I'll scuffle
around and try and get what you're needing. That's about all I can promise. Sometime before five I'll show. It might be an hour from now, it might
be around noon, it might be four—but I'll show. So take it easy. Relax. And
remember, I'll come by *once* and only *once*. Don't hang me up by straying
off. So you be sure and be right there—waiting."

"Thanks, Willie."

"Don't thank me. This squares us for good—that's all."

The line went dead.

Out on the pier, Joe lit another cigar and sighed. He knew that Willie
would never fail him. In a few hours Joe would have plenty of money, more
than enough to tide him over in San Francisco until the meet. The three
or four bucks in his pocket no longer bothered him. He would sit on the
beach and take the sun and wait for good old Willie C.

A few minutes later, having found a cruising taxicab, Joe told the driver
which beach to head for and he sank back on the chilled plastic seat. He
rolled down the side window, closed his tired bloodshot eyes and puffed
on his expensive cigar.

Hobart and Karen paused at the water's edge. The force of the waves
seemed to have lessened. They rose sluggishly, curling and plopping on the
sand. The sky was bright blue now, reflecting on the shore slick. The beach
was still deserted. Far to their left, beyond the high slopes of sand and
patches of beach grass, they could hear the faint whine of passing traffic
on the highway.

"What're you thinking about?" Hobart asked.

"Nothing," Karen answered.

"People just don't walk around thinking nothing. Surely you were
thinking of *some*thing."

Karen glanced at him, wondering what he expected of her.

Was she supposed to act shy, avert her eyes, slip her hand into his?

After a long moment, she said, "I was thinking about clocks."

"Oh. Clocks...."

Why should she bother to say more? Hobart wouldn't understand how
she had felt when she had seen the lizard clock on the motel bedstand.

Why didn't she simply tell him that her period had started that morning and she was feeling a bit down?

Had Hobart carried that clock to awaken himself for another round? Or to time himself?

She imagined it ticking on his hip now. Probably in the same pocket with the Trojans.

"Don't you feel like talking, honey?"

"No." She shook her head, not wanting to be thawed—or baited. "I'm not in a very talkative mood."

Hobart's voice grew intimate. "I think I know what you're thinking about...."

Her voice was more harsh than she had intended. She looked at him sharply. "Do you, Hobart?"

He broke his stride.

"Now wait a minute, Karen. You sound bitter about something."

"Do I?"

He wet his lips. His eyes tried to read past hers, to see how much of her act was real, but all he could see were the eyes, large and green. They stared at each other for a long moment, then Hobart blinked and looked away. He tried to console his anger and confusion by remembering how she had been with him during the night, champagne mouth, under him, making love to him. But he couldn't. Not completely. He had drunk too much wine before hitting the sack. Everything was vague in his mind and he felt cheated for not having been able to recall the memory.

"Yes," he said, "you sound bitter." He looked back into her eyes, trying a bluff. "What's the matter, Karen? Did I do or say anything wrong last night? If I did then I'm sorry. What more do you want me to say?"

"Nothing. You didn't do anything wrong." She removed her sweater and tied it around her waist. "Either way, I don't feel up to discussing it right now." She started walking, slowly. "Maybe not ever. You can walk with me if you want. But please let's not talk." She looked at him, not unkindly. "I mean that, Hobart."

Hobart followed in silence, glaring down at his loafers as they sank into the sand.

Karen hadn't meant to be abrupt with him. But she didn't want to encourage him. How could she tell him what she thought of him?

Could she tell him that, indeed, she had enjoyed having had sex, having had a release, as she always did, but that he had meant next to nothing to her before the sex and even less to her now? Was that what he wanted to hear? Could she tell him that he was a bore, and that he had been, for herself, a lousy lay and that she had been grateful for the loan of his body and nothing more? And that she couldn't now, or ever, bring herself to play up to him and act the movie-lover bit so damned early in the morning when she felt a terrible need to search for something, anything, inside or outside herself that would help erase the idiotic outcome of the night before? And that she didn't want a ride home but wanted to stay alone on the beach with the sand dollars, and that she knew, even now, exactly what he was thinking—that he had seduced her like some old smoothie with his lizard clock and iced wine, and when he had finished with her and thought her asleep he had crept off to the motel john to wash himself as if she had been some cheap whore he had to watch out for? Could she tell him that everything was crowding her and that it was disgusting the way he had wanted to marry her because his father had wanted it, and disgusting, too, that since father was footing the bills, Hobart had stocked his Continental with expensive booze and rubbers and a lizard timer as if she had been a three-minute egg?

"I know you don't want to talk right now," Hobart said. "So I'll say just one more thing before we shut up."

"All right. Say it."

Hobart's eyes shined with hate, but his voice was a gentle purr. "About last night," he said. "It was, for me, a very important and very wonderful thing."

"Okay. You've said it."

Karen fished in her skirt pocket and found a pack of cigarettes under her folded bra. She lit one and continued walking.

She could see that the south end of the beach was empty. But here, at a point halfway from the town, a few people were arriving. She could see two or three cars parked at the top of the slopes just off the highway.

A lone sunbather came down the well-beaten path leading from the car park. He stopped near the surf, dropped his bundle of beach junk, and watched as Karen and Hobart strolled slowly past. When they were yards from him the sunbather stripped to his bathing suit, looked at the sun with a frown, then started to oil his body.

The second person to arrive was the lifeguard. He had been at the beach for more than an hour, but had been sitting in his car listening to radio music and half dozing. His name was Alex. He was a short dark man with a bald head and a tin whistle strung round his thick neck on a silver chain. He had been drinking straight shots with beer chasers at Hermosa Beach the night before and was now terribly hung over.

A bit past the halfway point of the beach another figure was walking. A beachcomber, dragging his wired coin scoop behind him. When he came to the volleyball area, where the trash cans were padlocked to wooden poles, he pulled his scooper through the sand from the path to the poles. He found four pennies, a broken tooth, a nickel, and seven bottle caps. When he rested, sitting cross-legged with his back to a trash can, he carefully rolled a cigarette from sniped butts and watched with narrowed eyes as Hobart and Karen passed before him. With a snarl the beachcomber scraped a match stick on his shoe and lit his cigarette.

At the surf line, Karen picked up shells and stones and tossed them to the waves. At her side, Hobart watched with barely concealed impatience and jealousy. When Karen found a shell that interested her she dropped it into her blouse pocket. Hobart snickered smugly. Karen held back a smile, watching him from the corner of her eye.

They strolled past dark piles of cabbage-like seaweed and charred boards in wet bonfire pits. The sun came over the rim of the cliffs on the far side of the highway. Behind them, toward town, a few more people were arriving. Before them, the remaining mile or so of beach was wide and empty.

After a long quiet time, Karen suddenly stopped and squinted ahead, cupping her hands to her eyes.

A great dark mass was near the surf at the far end of the beach.

She asked, "What's that?"

"What's what?"

Karen pointed. "Down there. Can you see it? Directly ahead of us. There's something on the beach."

Hobart took advantage of the moment and moved closer to Karen. "I don't know," he said. "It's probably a big rock."

Karen moved away from him.

Hobart glared.

Karen said, "It's too big to be something washed up. And I don't remember a rock being there."

"Well what's so damned important about it?"

"Nothing," Karen answered. "It's not important at all."

"Whatever it is, it's pretty damned big. If it's not a rock, then it's probably a shipwrecked boat. Like a fishing boat, or something."

Karen fingered the shell in her blouse pocket. The dark shape ahead was just a thing. But she continued to finger her shell and squint and wonder.

"It's important," she decided, "because I think it is."

Walking once again, drawing closer to the end of the beach, Karen saw, to her surprise, that the great dark hulk was a whale lying on its belly, facing the surf several yards before it. Karen caught her breath.

"It's a whale," she whispered. "Hobart. Look. It's a whale."

"So it is."

Karen hadn't heard him. "An enormous whale," she said.

A moment later they were alongside. Karen stopped and stood perfectly still, not knowing whether the thing was alive or dead. For a minute she did nothing. Finally, when she spoke, her voice was a bare whisper.

"I wonder how he got here."

"How would I know?" Hobart was whispering also. "He probably died and floated here. When they die they bloat and get just like great big corks."

Karen gave him a dirty look.

Hobart grinned back.

The whale appeared to be about fifty feet in length. As big as a boxcar. The tail fins were more than ten feet across and were covered with a thin film of dried sand. On the high back a ridge showed, and, following that, a series of knuckles down to the flukes. All about the upper sides and back there were large patches of grayish discolorations.

Moving to the head of the whale and bending closer, Karen could see white streaks of dried salt, like marble veins. A solid mass of barnacles covered the upper jaw like stone porridge. Slowly, gently, Karen reached out and stroked the whale's hide. Sand fleas hopped from her touch. The whale suddenly shivered and exhaled and inhaled, the blowholes whooshing.

Karen leapt back.

"He's alive!"

Hobart had jumped back the same instant as Karen. "Yeah," he whispered. He looked a bit frightened now. "He's sure a big sonofabitch, isn't he? I always thought they exaggerated the size of whales." He made a small sweep of his hands. "I'll bet he weighs plenty. Maybe he's the kind that has ambergris in him. The stuff the perfume manufacturers pay plenty for...."

Karen hadn't been listening.

"What'll we do?" she asked.

"Do? What do you mean, what'll we do? What the hell can we do? Grab him from behind and start pushing? This thing is as big as a goddam house."

"We have to do something," Karen insisted. "We simply can't walk away and leave him here."

"And why not?"

"Because... just because, that's why." She watched the whale for a minute; then, suddenly, turned and pointed to the steep slope which protected the beach from the highway. Still whispering, she said, "Hobart, why don't you go up to the road and find someone. Find a policeman—or something. I'll wait here."

"Look," Hobart argued, "somebody's probably already called for someone. And besides, they have ways of handling whales that get beached. You read about it in the papers all the time. They shoot them or something. Then they cut them up and make cat food out of them."

"They can't do that," Karen said. "That's monstrous."

Hobart looked smug. "Nothing monstrous about it at all. They do it all the time. I've read about it in the papers. That's what they do. Shoot them and make cat food out of them."

Hobart was grinning broadly now, pleased with the look on Karen's face. He straightened his shoulders and looked at the whale as though he would be more than glad to do the shooting himself.

Karen felt disgusted, reading his thoughts.

"Hobart, go up to the road and find someone. A policeman. And I don't give a damn what you say about shooting and cat food. I don't think they'll do anything as cruel as that. So you go up there, and I'll wait right here."

Hobart started to argue. But he saw how stubborn and intent she was. He muttered something under his breath, then turned and angrily plodded across the beach toward the dunes.

Karen watched him until he had climbed the hill and disappeared into the tall beach grass. Then, seating herself beside the sleeping whale, she fondled the seashell in the palm of her hand. She began to hum softly to herself.

The whale exhaled and inhaled again.

"Don't worry, Mr. Whale," Karen said. "I'll take care of you...."

TWO

Ten o'clock. More cars arrived at the north and midway points of the beach, parking on the hard-packed areas at the head of the slopes. A young couple came carrying a plaid blanket and several six-packs of beer. A group of surfers spread out tatami mats and set down radios and put the sharp prow ends of their lacquered boards in the sand, forming a row, like technicolored gravestones. A Toonerville Trolley lunch wagon parked on the beach near the lifeguard's high chair and the volleyball area. The freckled red-faced proprietor swung open and propped the glass-paned sides of the wagon. The popcorn machine began to pop and watery orangeade swished in a big plastic ball. And the first transistor radio of the day began to play rock 'n' roll from the downtown Los Angeles station.

More people arrived. A leathery blonde woman wearing a red bikini waved hello to Alex, the hung over lifeguard who was drinking a bottle of Calso while slumped on his perch under a canvas parasol. A pudgy man wearing Bermuda shorts and Dayglo socks sat on a spread newspaper; he set his shoes on Joe Bonniano's picture. Several groups of young girls wearing tight suits and new breasts arrived bearing more radios and magazines and squeeze bottles of sun lotion. *Sea & Ski. Coppertone, Motion Picture. Bronzetan.* And rock 'n' roll music thumped and twanged and the sun glittered from the sweeping crowns of the long rolling combers. Young men wearing clamdigger shorts started tossing a football. The odors of frying meat and mustard and popcorn wafted from the chimney of the little lunch wagon.

At the south end of the beach, Hobart Richardson stood undecided on the path alongside the highway. Below him, through the reeds, he could see Karen and the whale, like toys. Hobart's face was shiny with perspiration, his white linen jacket under his arm.

"Go find a cop," he muttered. "Sure. Just walk up to the road and find a cop. Just like that! Who the hell does she think she is?"

He walked to some shade bushes and spread his coat on the sand. He sat and wiped his brow with the back of his hand. A fly landed on his knee and he scooped it into his cupped hand. But when he uncurled his fist, finger by finger, the fly zipped out. He sat there, cursing, sweating, looking around him for another fly.

Across the road, on the northbound lane, a taxicab pulled to a stop and a big dark-haired man wearing sunglasses and a flashy silk suit stepped out. Hobart watched as the man handed the driver a few bills and fished in his pockets for change. Then the big man crossed the road and stood on the path, chewing on an unlit cigar and slowly looking around.

Joe Bonniano noticed Hobart sitting in the shade of the bush. He started toward him with slow steps, his right hand close to his inside jacket pocket.

"Good morning," Hobart said.

"Did Willie C. send you?"

"What? I beg your pardon—"

"Willie C. Did he send you?"

Hobart looked puzzled.

Joe Bonniano studied Hobart for a long moment. Then he relaxed and lowered his hand to his side.

"Forget it," he said.

"Sure," Hobart said.

Joe Bonniano glanced at his wristwatch; then, mopping his face with his handkerchief, he stepped through the reeds to the edge of the slope. When he saw the whale and the figure of the woman he looked troubled for a moment. Then he wiped his brow, glanced again at his watch, and started down the slope.

Hobart watched Joe Bonniano until he was out of sight. Then, alone once more, he settled back and lit a cigarette. He figured that he would remain for a while in the shade, then return to the beach and tell Karen that he hadn't been able to find a policeman, that he had looked everywhere.

Hobart had no intention of walking back toward town just to find a cop and have to walk all the way back again. He didn't want to become involved with the stupid whale. It was none of his affair. Let the authorities shoot the goddam thing and cut it up for cat food.

The hell with Karen and her stupid whale.

Again he tried to picture how Karen had been with him the night before. And again he couldn't.

A sexy girl. Damn strange girl. Of course, she was crazy about him. Especially after last night. But her attitude this morning still puzzled him. She had acted as if they had done something wrong. And that, of course, was ridiculous. For one thing she certainly hadn't been a virgin. And for another, they were practically engaged. Their families had wanted it that way. And so had Hobart. But now....

What had that business about Cleopatra and her slave girls' breasts been about?

Hobart remembered how he had felt when she had told him about it. His fingers had curled and his heart had lurched pleasantly in his breast.

What had she meant by it? Why had she exposed her breast like that? Had it been some sort of cue for him? Was that the reason she was acting so abrasive? Because he hadn't followed through on her suggestion?

The thought almost excited him.

Proudly, Hobart reminded himself that he had aroused her the night before. Of course, he wasn't absolutely certain. But he imagined how she must have been. He did remember, however, that after she had gone to sleep he had staggered into the john to wash himself.

Sun stripes fell across his shoulders, burned on his neck. The cigarette hung from his lips, smoke curling in his narrowed eyes.

Fantasy. Some more bits about Cleopatra and her slave girls flirted with his thoughts. Karen Fornier standing before a golden idol, or perhaps an altar (an altar would be better, more fun). Hobart the High Priest with a gleaming dagger in his fist. Dark naked women dancing and chanting in the background. Karen cringing in fear....

Then he thought of the whale lying on the beach, and how mysteriously bitchy Karen had been acting all morning, and in spite of himself he again felt confused and angry.

When he finished his third cigarette he pushed himself to his feet. He gathered his jacket, brushed the sand off, and stepped away from the bush.

A voice called.

"Hey, you...."

Hobart looked up to see a mounted policeman who had halted his horse on the path and obviously had been watching him.

Hobart raised his hand in greeting. "Well—I've been looking for you."

The cop shifted in his saddle, unsmiling.

"Have you?" the cop asked. "Do you always go looking for cops under bushes?"

"Well—no, of course not. You see, officer—"

"Yeah, I see." The cop was suddenly brusque. "Okay, chief, you stay right where you are. And don't move."

The cop slid from the saddle, spurs jingling. He brought the reins overhead and took a few paces forward. He stood with his legs spread apart, watching Hobart through black Air-Force sunglasses.

He was taller than Hobart by at least two inches, a lean hard-looking man with wide shoulders. His mouth was wide and thin, his nose beaky. He was dressed in black from his gleaming riding boots to his hat. A pearl-handled revolver was slung on his hip, gunfighter style.

As he approached Hobart he tugged at the wrists of his black leather gloves.

Hobart's mouth was dry.

The cop said, "Okay, chief, now suppose you tell me what you were doing under that bush."

"I wasn't under it. I was just sitting near it. That's all."

"Helluva place to go to the john, chief."

"I wasn't going to the john," Hobart said stiffly.

"We'll see about that," the cop said. "Stand back. About three steps. Over there. And don't make any sudden moves."

Hobart did as he was ordered and the cop looked the ground over. When he finished he returned to his horse. He removed his black leather jacket and tied it to his saddle. Then, drawing a notebook from his shirt pocket, he turned to Hobart.

"This is awfully silly," Hobart said, trying a friendly approach.

The cop's black glasses stared coldly at him. "No one asked you what you think, chief," he said.

The horse whickered; his flanks shivered and he pawed the dirt. The cop rested a gloved hand on the butt of his revolver. The black gunbelt squeaked and his handcuffs clicked and winked in the sun.

"Let's have your full name, chief."

"Now, look, officer. I came up here looking for you. I've told you that. I want to report—"

"Your name," the cop snapped.

Hobart made a little show of being patient in the face of such stubborn ignorance.

The cop's jaw muscles tightened.

Hobart said, "It's Richardson. Hobart Richardson. My father is—"

"Never mind about your father, Richardson. It's you I'm interested in."

Hobart rolled his eyes in exasperation. "Will you or will you not allow me to make a citizen's report? I came here looking for you but I couldn't find you. So I sat under the bush to wait. So when I find you, you start giving me a hard time."

"You found me, chief."

"Yes. Well, you see, my fiancée and I were walking along the beach and we found a whale. It's right down there at the end of the beach. If you'll

just step through the bushes to the top of the hill and take a look I'm sure
you'll—"

"You want to report a what?"

"A whale. W-h-a—"

"I can spell."

The cop went through the high grass and stood at the edge of the slope.
When he saw the whale his lips spread in a thin smile. Behind his glasses
his eyes glittered. Slowly, without thinking, he made a fist with one hand
and punched it into the other. When he returned to the path he asked Hobart if the whale was dead or alive.

"It's alive."

The cop nodded, looking pleased.

"Okay, Richardson, you've reported the whale." He opened his notebook
again. "Now, let's have your full name and present address. If you have a
driver's license or any acceptable identification pass it to me."

Hobart handed the cop his wallet. The cop removed the driver's license,
which had been sealed in clear plastic. After comparing the photograph
on the license with Hobart, the cop wrote in his notebook and returned
the wallet.

"You'd better get yourself another license, chief."

"But mine doesn't expire until—"

"I'm not talking about the date of expiration," the cop said. "I'm talking
about your license. It's been encased in plastic. Drivers' licenses are property of the state. Encasing your license in plastic constitutes mutilation of
state property. And that's a crime, Richardson. Remember that. So if I were
you I'd get my license in proper condition."

The cop strode back to his horse and swung into the saddle. He leaned
on the pommel, hand over hand.

"Okay, chief. You can go back down there and get your girl friend.
There's no reason for you two to hang around anymore. I'm riding on to
my call box, but I'll be coming right back." The cop's black glass eyes flashed
in the sun. "Meanwhile, don't go fooling around that whale. Whales are
dangerous... especially killer whales."

The cop spurred his horse. Hobart remained on the path until the cop
and horse had disappeared around a bend.

When he returned to the beach, Hobart saw that the big man in the silk
suit had settled on an open sports page about thirty yards from the surf.
He was watching the whale, the sea, and his wristwatch.

Hobart went to the whale and sat down beside Karen.

"Well," Karen said, "who did you find?"

"A mounted cop," Hobart answered. He was still feeling surly from the shabby, offhanded way the cop had treated him. His voice was edgy. "Naturally I had to walk about two goddam miles before I finally found him."

"Thank you," Karen said. She didn't believe him. "That was nice of you, Hobart."

Hobart nodded. "He told me that I should gather you up and that we should leave."

"Why?"

"He said that the whale's dangerous."

"How?"

"He said that it was a killer whale."

Karen raised her brow. "Really? He doesn't look like a killer whale to me."

"Well, I'd think that the cop would know more about these things than we would."

"Maybe."

"Well, look, are we or aren't we going to do like the cop said?"

"You can do whatever you want. I'm going to wait right here until the whale gets back to sea."

Hobart didn't bother to argue further. His stomach ached from having missed breakfast, and, curiously, he didn't mind staying on the beach. For one thing, he didn't relish the idea of having to walk clear back to the motel right now. And for another, he hoped that something would happen to the whale, something that would knock Karen off her high horse.

Gazing at the hideously blotched hide of the whale, the barnacled prow and thick ridge and flukes, Hobart decided that never before had he seen anything quite so ugly. A killer whale. He could believe it. Anything as ugly as the monster before him had to be a killer.

Hobart's stomach rumbled under his rib cage. His lips felt raw from too much smoking. He jerked off his shoes and shook sand from them. There was sand inside his socks. He could feel it grating between his toes. On his hip he was aware of the faint tick of his clock.

All this, Hobart reflected miserably, just for a piece of ass.

He sat and stared at the big smelly killer whale, feeling hot and tired and disgusted.

Karen, meanwhile, was feeling very much at her ease. The one jarring note in her mind was what Hobart had said about the authorities shooting the whale. Other than that she was enjoying herself. She was hardly aware of Hobart's muttered curses, or the silent watching figure of the big man in the silk suit and sunglasses.

Karen wondered what the whale was going to do once he was awakened. How would he get back to sea? She refused to believe they would shoot him. It seemed too cruel, too unnecessary. The few accounts she had read about beached whales, she remembered, the whales had always been dead when discovered.

But this whale was very much alive.

What was going to happen to this one?

The mounted cop pulled in at his call box near the volleyball area. He dismounted, unlocked the door and lifted the phone.

"This is Mulford. Eight-four-one-eight. Charley? Yeah, I know, Charley. I'll be checking in late. No. I've got something down here but I can handle it okay.... No, nothing like that. It's a grounded whale. A civilian found it a few minutes ago. Down at the far south end. No, no crowds—it's empty as usual. I haven't talked with the lifeguard yet—but I will. A tow truck? Yeah, Charley.... What's that?"

Mulford's hand dropped to his revolver.

"Yeah, Charley. The whale's dead. It's been dead all night as far as I could tell. Sure, I'll hold on down here and wait for the tow. No, I can handle it okay. I'll have the lifeguard guard with me. Right. See you later, Charley."

Mulford relocked the box and walked down the beach.

Alex had seen Mulford coming his way and had crawled from his perch. He was standing in the shade of the chair, wearing a white helmet and nervously fingering his chain and whistle.

Alex had disliked Mulford since the first day they had met, more than three months ago. He didn't like the cold look in Mulford's eyes. He reminded Alex of an officer he had served under in Korea, a real mean sonofabitch who eventually had been murdered by one of his own men during a night battle.

"Morning, Mr. Mulford," Alex said, putting on a peon smile.

Mulford nodded. "How're you, Alex?"

Alex shrugged. "You really want to know? Well, I feel like hell. Fuzzy all over. Like I'm wearing a fur coat under my skin. I was drinking last night. Hermosa Beach. Some kind of ding-a-ling party."

Mulford smiled and laid his hand on Alex's shoulder. "You ought to know better than that, chief."

"Yeah. Maybe so. I'm not used to drinking." He moved from under Mulford's hand, feeling uncomfortable. "I've been drinking Calso all morning."

Alex turned and watched a group of kids playing near the surf. All around the area there were sunbathers and noisy radios. Nearby, a portable television set was playing. Alex blew his whistle at the kids, warning them back from the waves. Then, almost reluctantly, he turned back to face Mulford.

"So what's new with you, Mr. Mulford?"

Mulford's voice was casual. "I've got a grounded whale," he said. "At the south end."

"A whale? Really?"

"Yeah."

"Is it—dead?"

"Yeah, it's dead. Been dead all night as far as I can tell."

Alex could see his own smiling nervous face reflected in Mulford's sunglasses. But he couldn't see Mulford's eyes.

"So listen, chief, don't go spreading the word around. I don't want a mob collecting down there."

Alex nodded, but he sensed something else behind Mulford's words. He said nothing, wanting to keep his nose clean, wanting to have as little as possible to do with Mulford.

He said, "Do you think I should—call in?"

Mulford's lips twitched. "No, that's not necessary. I've already called in to the station. Everything's already been set up. I've got a tow truck coming."

"You think a tow can handle it okay?"

"They won't send a small one. They'll send one of their big rigs."

Alex's hangover seemed somehow worse.

He said, speaking slowly, as if he were trying to read the rules and regulations in the sand at his feet, "What we're supposed to do is get a bulldozer down here and dig a real deep trench. Then we push the whale in and cover it up." He looked up as a teen-age girl walked by. "Of course, I've never had a beached whale before. But that's what they told me to do in case of one."

"That's one way of handling it," Mulford said. "But in this case I'm having it towed up to the foot of the dunes. Then, later, a county rig with a crane will pick it up and haul it off to a tallow works, or someplace. See, we can't leave it near the water. It has to be towed away in case the tide rises. A dead whale, if it's bloated, can be a helluva hazard to the fishing and pleasure boats. So I don't think we'd better call for a bulldozer. This way," Mulford went on smoothly, "you won't have to worry about a thing. I've taken care of everything for you. All you have to do is sit up there on your perch and make sure the kids don't drown."

Alex nodded, feeling uneasily relieved. He had been working as lifeguard for only three months and he didn't want to become involved in anything that could possibly become complicated and turn wrong. And besides, he was too hung over to want the extra responsibility.

"Okay," he said. "If you say so, Mr. Mulford. I'll keep it quiet like you say." "Good boy."

A little girl came up to Alex and asked him where the potty was. Mulford said good-bye and left Alex with the little girl. He crossed the beach, went to the lunch wagon and ordered a cup of coffee.

The red-faced proprietor set out a cardboard cup and filled it from a dirty looking urn.

"Coffee's on the house today, Mr. Mulford."

Mulford grunted.

"Helluva nice day, ain't it?"

Mulford nodded, watching the clouds on the horizon. They looked a bit larger. When he blew into his coffee, steam fogged his sunglasses. Western music was blaring from the lunch wagon's radio.

"And how's the crime business these days?"

"It's okay, Nick," Mulford replied.

Leaning on the dirty counter-top, Mulford sipped his coffee and studied the sunbathers. Several yards away, not far from the volleyball area, Mulford spotted a young man in clamdigger shorts lying on a blanket with a young Negro girl. Mulford's coffee suddenly tasted greasy.

"Smart-assed bitch," he muttered.

Nick, the proprietor, grinned and leaned forward.

"You say something, Mr. Mulford?"

"Yeah. That nigger over there. What the hell would a little roll of tar paper like that be doing taking a sun-bath." He chuckled. "You think she needs any more color on her, Nick?"

Nick's smile faded to an uncomfortable grimace. He busied himself at the grill, pretending to scrape a stain with his spatula.

"What do you think, Nick?"

"I dunno. I guess things like that don't bother me. Hell, they're just kids. Can't be more'n sixteen."

Mulford snorted. "Yeah? And she'll probably grow up to be a goddam Black Muslim. Ella Mae X." Mulford nodded knowingly. "Ella Mae X and her straight razor."

Mulford tossed his coffee cup to the sand and returned to the call box.

A group of kids had gathered near his horse. They were stroking the warm velvety nostrils. Mulford barked at them, telling them to get away, that the horse might kick them, that horses were dangerous. Reluctantly, the kids stepped back and watched as Mulford swung into the saddle and, just like a TV cowboy, spur-kicked and turned the horse and thundered down the path, heading south.

Mulford was elated. Alex had been easier to handle than he had thought. Everything was going perfectly. Mulford's hatchet face was grim, his eyes squinting.

The whale....

Vague thoughts, little flashes popping in his brain. Giant squids under the sea. Evil, dark things. Crushing submarines. The vicious killer whale closing in, fangs dripping blood. That one-legged sea captain in that movie, being dragged to a watery grave by the mad white whale. Great flukes thrusting from the deep, thrashing wildly, breaking wooden boats like so much matchwood. The evil of the world. Officer William R. Mulford, a smoking .45 in his gloved fist. Childish thoughts, pages torn from horror comic books, read long ago, flapping in his rapturous brain as the chestnut horse trotted easily along the path.

As he rode, Mulford's hand rested on the butt of his gun.

Children shrieked at the waves, plunging close, splashing. Mothers sat nearby, drinking beer from pull-top cans and Dixie cups, gossiping under colored shade umbrellas. A game of volleyball was in heated progress. The ball thumped over the net and the teams shifted on the sand, their eyes on the ball.

Alex sat brooding, half slumped in his chair. Since his talk with Mulford he had been feeling uneasy of mind. But he wasn't probing too deeply to find out why. He was content to let everything slide past him. He didn't want to think about it. But the tiny snag remained in his thoughts and it wasn't helping his throbbing head one bit.

He opened another bottle of Calso from his cooler bag and settled back to watch the sunbathers.

For the past few minutes he had had his eyes on a pair of teen-age girls who were listening to their radios and talking. The nearest one, a cute blonde lying on her stomach, had untied the back of her halter and her companion, a skinny brownette, was rubbing lotion on her back.

Leaning a bit to one side, Alex watched from under the wide brim of his helmet. The blonde's breasts were large and pale, pressing against the cheap straw mat beneath her, bulging away from her rib cage. Alex sighed and shifted his weight.

Watching the blonde, he found himself thinking of the girl he had met at the Hermosa Beach party. A lovely young thing with slightly bucked teeth and hair the color of Burgundy wine. Alex had damn near nailed her on the back lawn but the host had staggered out with a bottle of Scotch and had interrupted them.

The blonde had raised herself on her elbows and was now reaching for a pack of cigarettes. Her shoulder wings glistened with oil. The breasts were swaying under her, almost free of the halter cups. Alex held his breath, watching intently, waiting to see if one of the breasts would accidentally work free.

"I must be getting horny," he muttered. "I thought lifeguards were supposed to score all the time...."

The blonde lit her cigarette and sank back to the mat. Her breasts returned into the halter cups.

"Lousy little bitch. She probably knew exactly what was happening. Jail bait. Turn me into a sex fiend."

The sun turned the sea into a sheet of crinkled blue tinfoil. A jet plane whistled overhead. The nearby television set was tuned to a quiz show. Alex could hear studio applause and brassy music for the prizewinner.

In the distance, against the golden haze of the beach, he could make out the small dark lump of the whale.

When Joe Bonniano saw the cop coming down the slope and making directly toward him, his first thought was to make a run for it. Then, remembering the presence of the whale and realizing the cop's mission, he quickly transferred his gun to his hip pocket and settled back on the sports page. The rest of the newspaper was still folded in his jacket pocket.

When Mulford passed. Joe couldn't resist making a remark, teasing the comedy of the situation.

"Good morning, officer."

Mulford nodded.

"Looks like you got yourself a whale, huh?"

"Yeah."

Joe Bonniano grinned and locked his thick arms round his knees.

Mulford stopped at the tail fins. The whale was bigger than he had imagined. His stomach turned with excitement. He removed his gloves, tucked them into his gunbelt, and walked around to the other side where Hobart and Karen were sitting.

Mulford's tone was almost friendly.

"Still here, Richardson?"

"Yes, sir. We thought...."

"Sure. Well, everything's under control now. There's nothing more for you to see around here."

Neither Karen nor Hobart answered him. Karen continued to sit, but Hobart rose and stood at her side, looking undecided.

No one moved.

From his distance, Joe Bonniano watched and listened. He was still too drugged and tired to fully appreciate the danger of his position. He wasn't too worried about the cop—he had dismissed him as being a hot-shot cluck. He watched the cop and the woman, wondering which one would back down.

Mulford was still waiting, watching Karen closely, knowing that her will was holding Richardson there.

Karen continued to ignore Mulford. She watched the whale with a strange stubbornness.

Mulford hooked his thumbs in his belt and glanced at the head of the whale. It looked ugly to him. Giant squids. Lurking monsters. A smoking .45 and Officer William R. Mulford....

Karen finally rose and brushed sand from the rear of her skirt.

"I'm going to stay," she said.

Mulford's expression hardened.

"Now look, lady—"

"No," Karen said calmly. "This is a public beach. So I'm going to stay. I found the whale and I intend waiting right here to see what's going to happen to him."

Twenty yards away, Joe Bonniano chuckled softly to himself.

"What *is* going to happen?" Karen asked Mulford.

"I've called for a tow truck. It'll tow it up to the foot of the dunes. Away from the tide."

"And then what happens?"

"Then the county disposal people will most likely cut it up and take it elsewhere. Probably to a tallow works."

Karen turned to Hobart, her eyes flashing. "I suppose you didn't bother to tell him that the whale is still alive!" Hobart blinked.

Mulford said, "He told me."

Karen gestured to the whale. "But if he isn't dead, then why bother to drag him up to the road? If the whale's still alive then why doesn't someone try and get him back into the water? I don't understand...."

Hobart took her arm. His voice was gentle, but not sympathetic. "Now look, honey," he said. "I've already told you once. This is a killer whale. And when they get stranded like this there's nothing anyone can do about it. It's just like I told you. They shoot them and—"

"And cut them up for cat food!" Karen hissed. "I know. You've told me. About ten times!" She jerked her arm free and faced Mulford, who pretended to be bored with the argument. "Is that right?" she demanded. "Is that what they do?"

"That's right, lady." He still looked bored. "Look here, let's not have any trouble about this. Richardson's right. I've got my orders. So why don't you two just run along and let me get on with my job here."

Hobart broke in. "The officer's right, Karen. Let's walk back to that drive-in and get some breakfast. You'll feel a helluva lot better once you—"

"Breakfast!" Karen's hands curled into fists, knuckles white. "Hobart, did anyone ever tell you what a thickheaded, selfish, insensitive bastard you are? Did they?"

Hobart pretended, with an effort, to let her remarks slide past him. He managed a ghastly little smile. Looking past Karen, he winked a male-to-male wink at Mulford. Mulford's expression didn't change.

Karen insisted. "Well, did they?"

"Don't push this," Hobart whispered. "Don't you think you're taking all this a bit too seriously? After all, whales get stranded everyday. You read about them in the papers all the time—"

"No, I don't!"

"Well, maybe not *all* the time. But you know what I mean. It's not exactly what you'd call an uncommon occurrence. It happens now and then. And the authorities have their own ways of taking care of them."

"How delicately you put it," Karen said acidly. "They have ways of taking care of them! Bang-bang. That's how they have ways of taking care of them. Hobart, can't you get it through your thick head that the whale is still alive? Alive and breathing, just like you, and the policeman, and that man sitting over there—all of us. Doesn't that mean anything to you? He's still alive, and he's only a few feet from the water."

"You're getting awfully hopped up about this thing, Karen. You're tired and upset. And—" his voice dropped to a bare whisper, "—after last night you're probably—"

"Believe me, I feel no different after last night than I ever have. I don't give a damn what you think you accomplished last—"

"Now listen to me, Karen! I—"

She pulled away from him, glaring. Then, gradually, her fists uncurled and the fever faded from her eyes.

"Don't say another word," she said quietly. "I don't want to hear any more of it."

Karen sank back on the sand, crossing her legs and planting her elbows on her knees. Everything seemed hopeless. She felt, right now, very much the same as she had when, as a teen-age girl, she had gone to Mexico with her language teacher and three other girls from her class—as if she were again in some strange land, unable to communicate with the natives. No one seemed to understand what she was trying to tell them. No one seemed to care. Hobart was a timid sadist. The cop was more honest, more brutal about it. Even that big clumsy-looking oaf sitting on his newspaper seemed not to be giving a damn—he looked like Central Casting's idea of a small-time mobster.

Karen was surrounded by foreigners.

Insensitive bastards. Everyone of them.

She looked at Mulford. No one moved. When she spoke, her voice sounded unnatural, even to herself. "Are you—going to shoot this whale yourself?"

"That's right, lady," Mulford answered. "I'm just doing what I'm supposed to do. Just following my orders."

Karen started to argue, then made a resigned gesture. She cupped her chin in her hand and said nothing more. The whale exhaled and sucked in a great breath and his flukes swished lazily in the sand.

THREE

It was nearly noon.

At the head of the beach, before the drive-in restaurant and motel, Homer Riley braked the heavy-duty tow truck, squinted through his sunglasses, and carefully wiped the oil and dirt from his hands with a red waste rag. An oil-stained cigarette hung, Bogart-fashion, from his lips.

The truck Riley was driving was one of the largest in the Hercules fleet, a big International Harvester, three-axle diesel with a one-inch cable on a new Tulsa winch, a shiny black and white muscle-bound truck with chromium horns and a Christmas tree of red and amber lights. Painted on the motor cowling was a cartoon of Hercules towing the world, and a jagged pair of lightning bolts which framed the words "Radio Dispatched." The smoke throbbing from the stack hung in the warm still air. Country music was blaring from the drive-in loudspeakers.

Dragging from his cigarette, Riley leaned on the big wheel and gazed tiredly at the sunbathers far down on the beach. They looked like confetti. The country music ended and it was very quiet. Riley swung open the cab door and unbuttoned the top of his dirty coveralls. Birds sounded in the nearby bushes.

A purple Jaguar sports car zipped past the drive-in and the driver, a brunette wearing lavender glasses, honked her musical horn and waved at Riley.

Riley lifted his arm in a return wave.

"And I love you, too, dollink. Whoever you may be...."

He picked up the two-way mike from the dash board hook and thumbed the sender button.

"Come in, Hercules. This is Twenty-three calling. Come in, Jack. Twenty-three to Hercules."

The receiver box hummed under the glove compartment. The dispatcher's voice came in weak and tinny.

"Hercules to Twenty-three. I hear you good, Riley. Where've you been?"

"I tried to tell you," Riley said. "I've been in a dead area. I could barely hear you the last time. You sounded a hundred miles away."

"Okay, Riley. What was wrong with the truck in Santa Monica?"

"It had a broken axle. I finished with it about ten minutes ago."

"Where did you drop it?"

"North from here. Pacific Coast Highway."

"Where's here? Where're you now?"

"In front of Nero's Nifty Drive-In. North end of the beach here. I heard that much of it before you faded out. So I came down here to check in."

"Good. Then you're right in line. We've got a county tow for you. There's a cop there—out on the beach. You'll find him okay. He'll probably be looking for you. He's a mounted cop."

"He's a what?"

"A mounted cop," the dispatcher repeated. "The cop has a horse. Look for a horse."

"Okay. What's the tow?"

"A whale. So get to it, Riley. Then knock off and come on in. Take your time if you want. It's on the county, and I've already got Jimmy out in the other big truck."

Riley tossed his cigarette out. He scratched the back of his neck. "What did you say, Jack? Will you repeat the tow?"

"A whale."

"You mean a whale-type whale?"

"Roger."

Riley shrugged, thumbed the sender button. "Okay, Jack. Where's it supposed to be located?"

"It's about three miles south from the drive-in. It's on the beach."

Good old Jack. Where the hell else would a whale be?

"You got that, Riley?"

"Yeah, I got it. The whale's on the beach. Twenty-three to Hercules. Over and out."

"Hercules to Twenty-three. Over and out."

Riley hung up the mike. He sat for a long moment, rubbing his eyes behind his sunglasses and watching the ocean. What he needed was a cup of black coffee—several cups of coffee. He had been working most of the night. His back and shoulders felt cramped and for the past two hours he had been half dozing at the wheel.

He stepped from the truck. He yawned and stretched and wriggled his bare toes in his heavy engineer boots. He removed his glasses, ran his hand over his rough brown hair, and entered the restaurant.

It was cool and quiet inside. The big windows facing the beach were tinted blue. The plants in the booth dividers were real. Farmy odors of bacon and coffee hung in the air. Riley slid onto a plastic stool at the counter and when the waitress came he ordered three cups of coffee.

"Three cups?"

The waitress was a shade on the plump side, with short brown hair and a cute dimpled smile. She smelled of starched fresh linen. The signature plate over her left breast read "Joanne."

"You can pour them in the same cup if you want," Riley said. "One right after the other. I need coffee."

"I guess you do."

Besides the waitress and Riley there was only the cook. He was sitting at the far end of the counter, looking bored and leafing through a girlie magazine.

The waitress brought a cup and left the Silex pot on the counter.

"Help yourself."

Riley sipped the coffee, then settled back for it to cool.

"Business looks slow," he said.

The waitress shrugged. "It's not *my* restaurant."

Riley gulped coffee and refilled the cup.

"Tired?"

Riley nodded.

"Been up all night?"

"Just about," Riley said. He pointed to her nameplate. "Is that your real name?"

The waitress nodded. She pointed to Riley's left breast.

"Is that yours?"

The red-stitched lettering on the coveralls read "Dave."

Riley shook his head. "No. These coveralls belonged to a guy named Dave at one time. Or David." He swallowed more coffee. "Does that sound logical?"

"It sounds very logical. And you're not Dave. Or David."

"No. What do you think I am?"

"I don't know."

"Sure you do," Riley said. "Everyone looks like something. My father looked like a Rufus. Do you know what a Rufus looks like? He wears fedora hats and Arrow shirts. With little blue stripes. A Rufus works as a mechanic for a Pierce-Arrow agency. You look like a Linda, or a Laura, or perhaps an Eve. But you're Joanne. And you look like that, too."

"Thank you."

"My boss looks just like an Edmund. But his name is really Jack. What would you say I looked like?"

"Like a tired tow-truck driver." She refilled his cup and looked thoughtful. "Actually, though, you could be—a Sam? Max? Either way I'll lay odds it's something exotic and sexy. And if it isn't, then I'll lay odds again that you've changed it to something exotic and sexy."

Riley grinned. "I could change it right now. But I won't. My name is Homer."

"Now I think you're kidding me."

"No I'm not. My name is Homer Riley. And did you know there's a whale lying on the beach?"

"You look like a Riley," the waitress said. "And how do you know there's a whale on the beach?"

"Because I'm supposed to tow it." He put a half-dollar on the counter. "When you think about a whale, what's the first thing that you think about?"

"Moby Dick."

Riley stood and put on his sunglasses.

"Was that the right answer?"

"Sure. Most people probably would have said Jonah, or Pinnochio." He lifted his sunglasses and looked at her for a moment. "Shall Riley come by here again? Would it be worth Riley's while?"

The waitress smiled, almost seriously. "If Riley doesn't, then Joanne will be awfully disappointed."

Riley returned to the truck. He sat behind the wheel, the motor idling, wishing now that he had a good stiff drink. The coffee and flirtation had made him feel like a new man.

"What the hell. It's never too early for a drink...."

He drove two blocks back into town, found a liquor shop and double-parked. He entered the shop and bought a half-pint bottle of Johnny Walker Red Label. Back in the truck he took a big swig of Scotch, corked the bottle, and with his red boom light flashing, made a tight U-turn and blended into the southbound traffic.

As Riley drove, feeling the Scotch steal deep inside him, he began to sing a badly garbled version of an old T. Texas Tyler number.

On the beach, not far from the volleyball area, in a little secluded valley between two high dunes, Fredric Langfield and his current wife, Becky, sat on a dark green car blanket. At their feet lay several empty beer cans and a large straw basket.

Fredric was seated on a low wicker stool, leaning on his cane and idly watching the sunbathers beyond his little valley.

Beside him, Becky sat cross-legged on the blanket, smoking a Mexican cigarette. She was wearing a pink two-piece bathing suit. Her face was pale, without makeup or expression. Her great dark eyes were staring, unblinkingly, at the empty beer cans.

Fredric Langfield still had the look of the Thirties about him; the rakish Barrymore hat, the malacca cane, the dandy clothes, the Sherlock Holmes cape lying across his long thin legs. He was in his late fifties. His face was craggy and pale, ravaged, deeply lined. His eyes were black and piercing, his voice rich and deep. An orange scarf was knotted loosely around his long turkey neck.

"Is there any beer left, Becky?"

"No. But I can get some more. There's a lunch wagon not far from here."

Fredric shook his head. "Don't bother. It was just a passing thought, my dear. Therapy. I just wanted something to do with my hands. I wanted to use a can opener."

"How do you feel?"

"Lousy."

"Would you like to go home?"

"No."

"Would you care for something to eat? I can get us some hamburgers."

"I detest hamburgers."

Becky held up her pack of Delicados. "Would you like a cigarette?"

"I would like a marijuana cigarette."

Becky dropped the pack at her feet and returned her gaze to the empty beer cans.

Fredric had once been a near-star in motion pictures. Before entering films in the early Thirties, he had been a successful Shakespearean actor on Broadway. But Hollywood had elected to cast him in one villainous role after another—buying him, draining him, abusing his talent, pushing him from costumes to westerns to horror movies.

And now, semi-retired and barely clinging to the doubtful reality of his surroundings, Fredric was living entirely on a small income from property and television residuals for guest shots and a series of wine commercials he had made some two and three years ago.

Becky, his sixth wife, was in her early twenties, a beautiful girl with brooding brown eyes, sullen lips, thin nervous hands and perfect white teeth. A high-fashion type slightly out of focus. At her feet lay a black skirt and sweater, and a Greenwich Village amulet fashioned from what appeared to be a falcon's claw and a few mashed two-bit pieces.

Becky Langfield pitied her husband. She feared him, loved him, hated him, and was indifferent to him. Since marrying him two years ago, she had become suspended in the limbo of his occasional residual checks, his fading prominence, in the day-to-day play of his ego which sometimes seemed to be breaking up, like now, while at other times it seemed to be gathering greater strength....

"Perhaps one beer," Fredric murmured.

"I'll get it."

She left the valley and went to the lunch wagon, ignoring the soft whistles from the young men in the clamdigger shorts. She bought a can of beer and carried it back to her husband.

Fredric took his time opening it. He seemed to enjoy using the can opener. He drank slowly, his Adam's apple bobbing.

"Thank you, my dear."

Becky nodded and again sat beside him.

She had long since ceased to question her motives for marrying him. True, Fredric had been a movie star of sorts, and Becky had been flat broke when she first met him at his oldest son's apartment in the Village, where she had been living on a cot set up in the kitchen. She had married Fredric almost on impulse, telling herself that she had nothing better to do. She had moved with him from New York to Hollywood, and had set up her tarot cards and her pocket novels in a run-down apartment-motel called the Arabian Nights just outside Beverly Hills.

A strange life, attending Fredric's long affair with narcotics, going to séances, watching old movies in cheap flea houses, and jotting down an occasional note about Fredric's career in the Thirties.

While Fredric talked now, she watched him, detached, listening to his timing, the expert way he played his voice.

"This," Fredric was saying, "must come to an end. All of it. I've got to quit, Becky. Quit it completely. Do you understand that?"

"Yes."

"I've really got to quit this time."

And again, she said, "Yes."

But Becky knew that he would never quit. Not now. And, curiously, she didn't really care one way or another. Whether Fredric quit or not wasn't important. Becky was hung up, completely, neither caring nor uncaring.

So far, her life with Fredric had a certain reassuring consistency. Each day seemed to blend with the last, to predict the next. At one time, she remembered, she had cared. But now, drifting aimlessly in the wake of Fredric's troubled ego, in the comfortably drugged days and nights, she felt nothing one way or the other. It was always the same, inevitably, fatefully, and Becky had long ceased to think about it, to question it.

Every day was ritual. In the early hours Fredric would announce his intention to kick his habit. Then, as the hours grew to midday, he would begin to change his mind. "Just a little taste," he would say. And Becky had to play the role of his conscience. She would have to refuse him, hide the morphine from him, knowing all the while that the rules of the game invariably dictated her giving in to him. And Fredric would take his taste and he would enter his own sly world, a world denied her, and again, the next morning, she would have him back and the game would start anew.

And still, she didn't care. Everything blended. Magically. Full circle. As she had always known it would.

Every morning started the same way with them. Neither Fredric nor Becky would move from their bed until the tarot had been read, the horoscope consulted. Then, munching crackers and drinking coffee milkshakes and smoking a bit of dope in the curved clay pipe, they would lay back on the crumb-freckled sheets and watch the morning quiz shows, "Art Linkletter," "Queen for a Day," an old film. Then they would rise and smoke a few more pipes and listen to Vaughn Williams or Carl Orff, depending entirely on the weather, and dress and go out to the beach, or to a neighborhood movie, or visit a few of Fredric's spooky old chums from his career days.

All in all, it was, for Becky, pretty much what she had learned to expect. It had been in her cards years ago....

"I realize," Fredric was saying, "that I've been talking about quitting for some time now. But today, right now, this very minute, I *know* that I must." His great knuckled hands quivered on the scrolled silver head of his cane. "Little sorceress, right now it's like containing an ant colony. Ready to break down. Do you understand?"

"Would you like another Librium? Or a Nembutal?"

"No," Fredric answered. "I haven't started my slide yet." He smiled, his face crinkling like a thin white walnut. "If I don't start laying off I'll end up screeching in some cheap clinic. I'll lose more weight, and the bastards will run a 'Then and Now' photograph of me in the newspapers. I'll be cast with Wally Reid and Bela Lugosi.... I can feel it creeping up on me, Becky. Dark. In waves.... 'Being your slave what should I do but tend—upon the

hours and times of your desire?—I have no precious time at all to spend—
nor services to do... till you require.'" He sighed deeply. "Those are nice lines,
aren't they? Compact and clean and shiny. Like a needle. Do you know,
Becky, I've often asked myself if Shakespeare wasn't a junkie...."

"Do you want a pill now?"

Smiling still, he fixed her with his dark shiny eyes. His voice turned sly.
"I could use a small taste of Morpheus right about now. That is, of course,
if you're holding." He squinted, cobwebbing wrinkles. "*Are* you holding,
my dear?"

"No."

Fredric looked resigned. "Ah, well. 'What is your substance, whereof are
you made—that millions of strange shadows on you tend?'... Dammit, girl,
did you bring any shit with you?"

"No," Becky answered. "But I think you've got your fit hidden in your
cape."

Fredric chuckled. "You *are* a sly one, ducky. What you say is quite true.
I stashed my cape just in case you had the sagacity, and the sympathy, to
impress a few ampules in your bathing costume. Perhaps in the wired bra?
Rubbing against your little pink nipples?"

"I only brought the Libriums and the goofers and the beer."

Fredric made a face. "I suppose right now you're cursing me, aren't you?
You resent me."

"No. I don't resent you. You're an Aries."

"*And* Marlon Brando, *and* Van Gogh. I'm terribly sorry. But the relevance
of the stars means so little at a time like this. It's the ants that I'm concerned
with. They're beginning to break from the colony within. Traveling
through my ancient limbs, red antennae wriggling, freckled little feet
tramping about my blood-smeared veins." He cocked his head and smiled.
"You know, in a moment like this, caught in the spotlight of my own fancy
bullshit, I realize, in all honesty, that I was once a great actor."

Becky gave him a tired smile. "Quit fishing," she said. "You're still a great
actor."

"But when I'm high? How am I then?"

"You're a terrible ham."

Fredric sighed. "I was afraid of that."

"You're all right on pills."

"Yes, I know. I've got some Artanes in my vest pocket. But nothing really seems enough. I'm a dope hog."

Becky lit another cigarette and lazily plowed her bare toes in the warm sand. She felt as if she were acting out a scene she had rehearsed many years ago.

Fredric passed a gnarled hand across his eyes. He swallowed dryly.

"Becky do you think that if I can manage it on pills today, pills alone, without anything else, that I'll still be all right by this evening?"

Becky nodded, thinking of the coming night, vaguely hoping that he could.

Fredric, not having seen her nod, asked again if she thought he could pull through the day.

Becky said she was sure he could. She placed her hand on his knee, being kind to him, but still not really giving a damn whether he made it or not, knowing in her heart that he wouldn't. She felt remote from the scene even now while she was feeling and witnessing the first little dip in his self-sliding.

"It's terribly important," Fredric said. His voice contained a curious confessional note. "It's more important to me than you think, my dear. More important, in fact, than I care to admit to myself."

"I know it is."

He looked at her, traveling, for a split second, into her eyes and seeing her naked brain. He said, quite softly, "Yes, I suppose you do know...."

He had to tell himself that it *was* important. Very important. He had to hold on. He couldn't shoot himself out of one more chance.

His agent had gone to a great deal of trouble to arrange a meeting between Fredric and the TV producer August Losada, who was, according to the agent, seriously considering Fredric for second lead in a ninety-minute drama spec. The role was that of an evil magician. And it was important to Fredric. Very important. He had to chant it to himself. It was important. Don't blow it. Don't shoot it.

But still, nagging him all the while, Fredric knew that Becky had, as always, stashed the shit somewhere, and that sooner or later she would have to surrender it to him and let him sneak off to the john.

Because, in spite of the importance of the night's forthcoming meeting, the reality, it was, after all, just one more wicked twist to the game....

"Becky, if I lose this one like I've lost all the others, then there will be no sense whatsoever in my remaining in this house."

Becky said nothing.

She gazed with strange longing past the beach to the bright clean glitter of the sea. The clouds had grown beyond the horizon, rising like slow explosions from the hem of the sky. Atop the nearest dune, blackbirds hopped in and out of the spiky tufts of beach grass.

Becky stroked her left breast, feeling the two little ampules pressing against her nipple, suddenly hating the necessity of their being there. Slowly, with thumb and forefinger, she rolled the morphine against her breast and wondered how long her husband would be able to tough it out.

Earle Kavanaugh stood on the path and watched as Homer Riley slowly backed the big diesel truck through the high reeds to the edge of the slope.

Leaving the motor running, Riley jumped from the cab and kicked wooden chocks under the rear wheels. He engaged the power-takeoff gearbox, setting the gear in neutral and releasing the cable drum. He pulled the lead chain and hook from the drum until a few feet of cable hung over the rear of the truck. Then he killed the motor and walked back to the slope edge. He leaned against his truck, looking down toward the beach, at the figures gathered around the whale.

Earle Kavanaugh stepped through the reeds. When he came to Riley's side he tipped his alpine hat in greeting. He was a sunny-faced little man with snow-white hair and gleaming false teeth.

Riley nodded hello.

Kavanaugh said amiably, "Hey, for a minute there I thought you might be backing right on top of my girls."

Riley lit a cigarette and adjusted his sunglasses. He waited for Kavanaugh to continue.

"I have two girls," Kavanaugh said. "Norma and notso-norma. Hee-hee. A little joke. Norma and Wanda, actually. One blonde and one brunette. For contrast. They're lovely girls." He held his hands over his thin chest. "Great big jams. Absolutely lovely girls."

"That's fine," Riley said. He figured the little man to be one more Los Angeles screwball. Better to humor the guy. "But I guess I was lucky, huh? I didn't run over a one."

"I'm not a nut," Kavanaugh said. "I saw the look in your eyes. I really do have two girls with me. And their names are Norma and Wanda." He pointed over his shoulder to the reeds. "They went off into the bushes to change their clothes. But I'm not sure which bushes they went into. That's why I said I thought you might be backing on top of them."

"I see," Riley said. But he didn't see. "Anyway, I'm glad they weren't changing where I was parking."

Kavanaugh grinned. "You're still patronizing me. Well, who can blame you? So it was a lousy way to start a little chat with you. So who's perfect?"

"I guess no one."

Earle Kavanaugh tilted his hat to the back of his head and drew a toothpick from his flowery silk vest. A camera equipment bag was slung on one shoulder, a camera on the other. A tripod and camera and tinfoil sun reflector were standing on the path.

Riley returned to the truck cab and took a heavy swig from his bottle of Scotch.

There was something damned familiar about the little man. But Riley couldn't quite place him.

When he corked the bottle he turned and saw that the man was standing behind him, leaning on the left front fender and chewing on his toothpick.

Earle Kavanaugh held out a well-worn business card. "There I am," he said. "That's me. 'Earle C. Kavanaugh. Representative of Talent.'"

Riley nodded and handed back the card. He held up the bottle.

"Want a drink?"

"No, none for me, thanks. I've got a lousy liver. Hepatitis. The whole bit. Booze and me—we're no more."

"Sorry to hear that."

Riley drank again.

"You see, young man, I do publicity work. Sometimes I do good; sometimes I don't. Beer one day, champagne the next. Up and down, and down and up. That's life."

Right now he was obviously in beer. Looking closer at Kavanaugh's clothes, Riley saw the mending marks. And, he noticed, the man's snowy hair needed trimming around the ears and neck.

"I'll be honest," Kavanaugh was saying. "I specialize these days in nudes for men's magazines, newspaper publicity whenever I can get it, stills and such."

"You free-lance," Riley said.

Kavanaugh searched Riley's face for a quick moment. Then, smiling somewhat sadly, he slowly nodded his head.

"You're a sharp guy, Dave."

"The name's Riley. These coveralls belonged to another guy."

"Okay, Riley. You're still a sharp guy. Yeah. I free-lance." He shrugged. "But it wasn't always this way. I used to have my own business. Legit. I was big in the cheesecake crap. I've had my ups and downs."

"You know," Riley said, "I was just thinking that you looked familiar."

Kavanaugh's false teeth flashed. "You've seen me? Sure. You know, I'll bet

I used to be in one magazine or another just about every month. Of course in those days I used to have a piece of the action in a lot of those old rags. Burlesque magazines. Remember them?"

"Yeah. And I remember now where I saw you." Riley sat on the running board, still holding the bottle. "About fifteen years ago, I was bumming around, much the same as now. And I got busted in San Antonio. I remember your picture was on the wall in the day tank. Someone had torn it from a magazine because of the chick. Whoever she was. A blonde with a tight pair of Levis cut off at her crotch...."

Kavanaugh's smile grew dreamy. "It's funny you should remember."

"I've got a good memory. I stared at that blonde for twenty days."

"I used to be the nitwit painter, or paperhanger, or plumber, who went around the house trying to do his job while the well-stacked mistress of the house stood around half undressed and watched. The harassed little man—that was me. A corny routine, but it never failed. 'Pete the Painter and the Blonde Bombshell.' 'Roland the Rug-layer and the Red-hot Redhead.' Good clean burlesque for fifteen cents."

"They still have them," Riley said. "But now it's all in the movies."

"That's right. It came back big. A million-buck business. 'Mr. Teas.' That's the film that really did it. And there was Hank Henry's film 'Not Tonight Henry'.... That's where the real dough is."

"How come you didn't get into it?"

"Are you kidding? I'm broke. It sticks out all over me." He adjusted his camera-case strap and looked down at the scuffed toes of his shoes. "For a thing like that a guy needs a good stake...."

Riley corked the bottle and stood.

"Sorry," Kavanaugh said. "I get carried away with my ills. The reason I talked to you is that I happened to notice that you've got yourself a whale down there." He walked to the rear of the truck and squinted down toward the beach. "That *is* a whale, isn't it?"

"It's a whale."

"Well, I was wondering if before you do whatever it is you're going to do with it, you'd let me take a couple of shots first. I'd like to get the whale for background. My girls posing around it. You get the idea?"

Riley nodded.

"Good. I won't take more than ten minutes or so. Now get this caption. It's right off the top of my head, you understand. We've got this lovely little twist in a bikini, big jams, smiling teeth. The whale right behind her. And the caption reads—'Wanda Is a Whale of a Girl, Whadda You Fellas

Think?'... Now how does that grab you, Riley?"

"It sounds good."

"Is it okay by you then?"

"Sure. It's okay by me."

"I'll use Wanda. That's my brunette." He tapped Riley's arm and winked. "And listen, Riley, if you want to meet either of the girls, just give me the look. I'll give you a good intro. Okay?"

Earle Kavanaugh left, whistling gaily. Riley went around to the other side of the truck. Two women, obviously Norma and Wanda, were coming down the path toward Kavanaugh. They were wearing skimpy bikinis and carrying their street clothes in big straw baskets.

Norma was the blonde, with a puffy hairdo the color of mercury. Wanda, the brunette, was smaller and rounder than her companion.

"Okay, girls," Kavanaugh cried out. "We're all set. Wanda, you're going to be the whale of a girl."

The girls looked bored. They didn't bother answering him. They picked up the tripod and reflector and followed Kavanaugh down the slope to the whale site.

Homer Riley remained at the rear of the truck. He set his bottle of Scotch on the truck's bed and covered it with the battery booster cables.

He leaned against the bed and watched Kavanaugh and the two girls crossing the beach. The girls were walking tiptoed on the hot sand.

Seeing and remembering Earle Kavanaugh from that photograph had put Riley in a pleasantly melancholy mood.

It had been years since he had thought about that jail in San Antonio. It came back to him now. He could remember vividly how the photograph had looked, taped to the day tank wall.

The photograph showed a busty blonde model and the little man, dressed in an artist's smock and floppy bow tie. The little man was trying to paint a farm scene. But the country blonde in the Daisy Mae shorts was kibitzing over his shoulder, her blouse threatening to split open.

Riley had been just a kid then, hardworking and naïve. But a lot had happened since. He had served a hard year in the Colorado State Prison for severely beating two cops during a bar fight. And he had been married for one semi-glorious year in Montreal, Canada.

The marriage had been doomed from the start.

Both incorrigible romantics, Riley and his bride had expected more from each other than just being together. By the time they both suspected that the final reel had come, when, traditionally, they were supposed to ride off into the sunset and the everlasting happy fade-out, they had discovered that they weren't quite prepared for it. They had resented the fact that their movie was complete, that they knew one another too well. Neither one of them was ready to face the truth about himself. Then time began to drag on them. One anticlimax followed another until they started to hate each other. To liven up their lives they took to drinking and screaming and punching each other. And when that happened, it was all over but Riley's packing his bag and heading back to the border.

Since then there had been hundreds of women. But nothing seemed quite to match what they once had. And that, for Riley, seemed to be the sum of it—they had "had" something.

The traffic on the highway was heavier now. Riley could see the flash of the cars through the reeds. It was hot and he was sweating again.

Down on the beach, the group of people and the whale looked like something from a surrealist dream.

Riley pulled the bottle from under the cables. He took a quick drink, stashed the bottle, and yawned until his ears popped. He turned and looked at the truck with a sigh of boredom.

How much longer could he continue driving the damn thing? A month? A week? He wasn't sure. But he had known when he had left his little beach cottage in Seal Beach the night before that he wouldn't be able to last much longer.

Riley had never held a job for more than six months at a time. And he knew that this one wasn't going to be an exception.

He was going to quit, and damn soon. He wanted to pack up and move on. He was tired of working, of being in Southern California, of living in modern society.

Over the years, Riley had managed to save a bit of money. He had an idea of moving north, into the Sierras, someplace near Downeyville, on the north fork of the Yuba River. He wanted to buy a dog and a piece of land and settle down for a long spell.

He wanted to get back into the sort of country he had come from, back to mountains and snow and pine and big quiet rivers.

And maybe he could find himself another woman like his crazy ex-wife....

A buzzing crackling noise interrupted his thoughts. It was Jack, the Hercules dispatcher. Riley walked back to the cab and lifted the mike from the dash hook.

"This is Twenty-three. Over."

"Hey, Riley, have you finished with that tow yet?"

"I haven't even started," Riley said. "I just now found the cop's horse. It was staked in the bushes."

"Okay, Riley. Call in when you're finished. Remember, take your time if you want. It's on county time. Over and out."

Riley acknowledged the call and hung up.

For a long moment, he stared at the black receiver box fixed under the glove compartment. Then, shaking his head, he spoke under his breath.

"No, Jack. It's not on county time. This one's on Riley's time. Because I just quit your lousy job about one minute ago...."

FOUR

The horizon clouds still appeared like a great wall rising over the sea. But a few had mushroomed and were now almost in the center of the sky. Occasionally, a cloud tip would briefly pass before the sun and the landscape would suddenly darken. There were more gulls in the sky, cawing and sweeping restlessly on the air currents. The day was still bright and hot and the spirit of the beach hadn't changed.

At the edge of the sand, a group of kids were busy working on a sand city. Turrets and towers and scalloped walls rose from the sand. And as the tide swept to the edge of the city, the foamy waters entered a prepared channel and filled, for a few magic moments, the moat surrounding the walls.

Fredric Langfield could see Becky's shadow just outside the open doorway of the rest-room building. It was cool and dark inside. The cinderblock walls were painted pale green. The floor was dirty white tile, the row of toilet stalls dark gray enamel. The room smelled of piss and saltwater.

Fredric urinated in the standing bowl, splashing the water guard and disinfected brick. At the washstand he bathed his face and gazed for a long minute at himself in the dirty mirror.

"I was once a very handsome man...."

His eyes looked haunted now. His mouth was drawn, his cheeks sunken. He removed his hat and ran a comb through his dyed hair. Then, glancing quickly toward the doorway and seeing Becky's waiting shadow, and hearing no warning whistle, he stepped into a corner stall and slid the bolt.

In a matter of seconds he had his outfit in his hand. He unwrapped the first ampule, removed the sterile sleeve from the point, and plunged the needle through the stopper. He drew the morphine into the spike's body. He waited, listening, breathing very slowly. Then he slipped free of his cape and jacket and shot up the load. He dropped the amp into the toilet bowl. Then he geezed up the second amp and sat on the plastic seat.

Minutes later, Fredric stepped back into the bright sunshine to join his wife. He looked very much like his old self, completely relaxed, contained, and smiling.

Without a word, Becky reached into the straw basket, under her bathing suit and the green blanket, and handed Fredric his sunglasses.

"Thank you, my dear."

He bowed gallantly and they proceeded up the beach. They paused near the water while Fredric watched a group of kids who were frantically re-building a fallen section of their sand city.

"Shall we stroll, my dear?"

All around Fredric there were noises—radios, shouting, waves, gulls—but he no longer minded. Indeed, he found himself isolating each sound and savoring it, allowing his thoughts to trip all around the meaning of the sound.

There was something significant about the beach now. The sun was a warming, soothing thing. The odors of the sea were no longer harsh and unpleasant. Fredric could barely feel his feet crunching on the damp sand.

"Becky, look at those clouds." He pointed with his cane. "They've been growing all morning. Great masses now, all rimmed with silver and gold."

"How do you feel?" Becky asked.

"I feel fine. Very good. There are no more ants. But look at those clouds. They're beautiful. They make dark puddles on the water."

As they walked, a scrap of paper danced before them.

Fredric smiled, thinking about ghosts and a time when, in the movies, he had been killed by a tomahawk crushed into his blood-bursting scalp and how later, when he had attended the premiere, he had been stoned out of his mind on marijuana and bennies, and he had watched, completely detached, a bunch of screaming Indians (Mexicans, actually) drag him to the ground and kill him, and he had smiled knowingly in the safe dark-ness of the theatre, hearing the audience gasp at the reality of his death. How great it had been to be able to sit back and watch yourself being pun-ished on the screen but actually feeling nothing, just smiling and listen-ing to the terrible war whoops of the Indians and his own death rattle.

It was a helluva life.

From his vest pocket he drew the five Artane tablets and swallowed them without water.

"Did you just take the Artanes?"

"Yes, my dear. We're clean now. Everything we're holding now we have a prescription for. We are no longer bustable."

Becky shrugged and said nothing more. She walked a few paces behind him, lugging the heavy basket and thinking no thoughts which required a description to herself. They were simply Becky thoughts.

Fredric was completely enchanted, under the spell. He could think of nothing that could truly harm him. He was aware of the vulnerability of his body, but all immediate fears had crept into some secret corner of himself. The Langfield Theater. Warmth and safety and truth.

Everything was going to be fine. He was no longer worried about his meeting with August Losada. Fredric felt all-powerful, able to cope with all situations. The pills were making him higher.

They paused while Fredric watched a young couple lying on a large terry-cloth blanket decorated with a Confederate flag.

And again he tripped to twenty-two years ago in the San Fernando Valley shooting a Civil War Picture... and Fredric, young and handsome, wearing a bandit's mustache, astride a chestnut horse, squinting under the glare of the reflectors... no longer aware of the camera under the parasol or the boom, slowly rising, through the wisps of smoke from a burning rubber tire which resembled a flaming hayrick, or the horse jogging under him as the dispatch rider (young fag extra) thundered up the slope, swung to and handed him the change in orders from General Lee. "Colonel, sir—"

The young couple on the terry-cloth blanket rolled to one side. The young man glanced up and noticed Fredric.

As Fredric continued walking, he heard the young man take in his breath and say:

"Hey, honey! Did you see who that was? That was—"

They walked for a long while in silence. They came to the part of the beach where there were no people. When they came within a hundred yards of the whale site, Fredric paused, shook his head in disbelief, and stared at the great dark shape of the whale. Then, removing his sunglasses, he saw the small group of people, and, to his left, the big tow truck parked atop the slope.

"For a minute there, I thought...."

After a minute, Fredric gestured to Becky for his wicker chair. When she unfolded it he settled himself on the seat and leaned on the scrolled head of his cane. Smiling, he whispered under his breath:

"Leviathan...."

William R. Mulford stood glaring at the still-closed eyes of the whale. His thumbs were hooked in his cartridge belt. His face was frozen in anger and frustration. All around him, people seemed to be watching, waiting for him to make a move.

There were too damn many people—eight now besides himself.

The whale site was becoming a circus ground.

It seemed that every time Mulford tried to get one of the civilians to leave, two or three more would suddenly pop up from nowhere. Like the seedy photographer with the gaudy vest, and his two half-naked models. And there was that old man wearing the hat and cape, seated on a stool a hundred yards off, with a young girl dressed in black standing beside him.

If Mulford didn't hurry up and get his business with the whale over and done with, soon there would be a regular mob gathered around him, like it was carnival day—grinning faces, hot whale-smelling air, popcorn, peanuts, cotton candy.

He had to do it now.

Mulford looked toward the slope. He saw the figure of the driver in coveralls standing beside his truck. Mulford's hands slowly gripped his belt, fingers squeezing the row of bullets. Then he stepped aside, turning away from the whale, wondering suddenly if the military creases were still sharp on the back of his shirt, wondering why he thought it was so important.

Almost painfully, his heart lurched in his breast and he found himself turning away from Karen Fornier's stubborn determination, from Joe Bonniano's slightly mocking face, from the photographer and the two models and Hobart Richardson.

Mulford looked to the sea, to the dark clouded sky.

Where had those clouds come from?

"Billy...."

But that had been in Kansas, twenty-five years ago, in a cool dark barn that had smelled of leather and earth and animals.

"Billy, I catch you fooling around them cats once more and I'll boot the shit out of you, you hear! So come on out of there and get the goddam hell away from that there box and leave them kittens be. You hear me, Billy, I mean just what I say now...."

Helpless kittens, all warm and squirmy and clumsy, snuggled up to their drowsy self-important mother, sucking milk and mewing blindly. The sun coming through the cracks in the old boards and making thin yellow stripes across the cat box. The mother's eyes half closed and contented.

"Billy! You get the hell out of there and I mean right now—you quit teasing them cats and get out here or sure as shooting I'm going in there and stomp you a good hard one smack on your ass...."

Old Uncle Sheridan, the cripple, standing and shouting in the sunbaked courtyard, leaning on his crutch and acting tough and dragging his bent foot after him.

"Billy? What's that sound in there? What do I hear? Are you hurting that mother cat? Billy! Answer me, goddammit...."

For one quick moment, Mulford was aware that he no longer cared about the presence of the eight people or his shirt or his revolver and he frowned, as if in pain, gazing down at the shiny black points of his boots, and he heard it again....

You filthy cat! Crunchy little skull and tummy full of milk!

Uncle Sheridan dragging his foot into the barn and stopping as if he had run into a wall.

"Billy! Oh, my God...."

The tiny slip, as if there had been a hitch in himself, had pulled, and before it snapped back into place and everything began to flow smoothly again, Mulford had to pause and catch his breath. He had been deeply, terribly frightened.

Everything had happened then. In that hitch. And Mulford had been forced to turn away, to the sea, to the gathering clouds, to his boots....

"Now look, Bill, a man should have himself a wife, raise himself a family. You can't blame yourself for your first marriage going bad. It was as much Sheila's fault as it was yours. Now, you're making pretty good money on the force, so why don't you...."

The night before, Mulford had dated a girl friend of his brother and sister-in-law's.

For months, quietly, persistently, over coffee and after dinner during the TV commercials, in his brother's tract home in Alhambra, they had been nagging Mulford to meet their friend, a nice girl, they had said.

"How about it, Bill? Jenny can ask her friend over for dinner, and you can just sort of happen by. If you don't like her you don't have to take her out. Think about it, Bill."

"I don't know...."

"It can't do you any harm to look. How about it?"

"All right...."

As arranged, Mulford had met the girl at the Alhambra house, and after dinner and television he had taken her for a ride in his unpaid-for Chevy convertible.

After dancing and buying her drinks in several high-priced dives, still wearing his gun (a policeman is never off-duty), he had taken her to a secluded spot and had tried to ball her.

She had resisted him. Red-faced and gasping and angry, smelling like a church foyer. Mulford had shoved her angrily against the car door. He had half slumped behind the wheel, tight, uncoiled inside.

"You filthy cat! Crunchy little skull and tummy full of milk!"

While the girl sat there, arranging her skirt and sniffling, proud and silent, Mulford realized that there had been one moment during his wild embrace, when she might have consented.

And, as he had become aware of it, had felt the hot quickened mouth, the ever so slight arching of her buttocks and the imperceptible spread of her thighs, Mulford had known, deep inside, that he would fail, as he had many times before. He had known that he couldn't, wouldn't become completely aroused.

Coldly, deliberately, Mulford had been become more demanding, knowing that had he been more gentle with her, she would have given in. But he had become heavy-handed and clumsy, scaring her off, forcing her to go cold. He had wanted her to turn him down.

In that one moment, one he would never admit to, Mulford had felt that he could right everything by simply jerking out his revolver and shooting her in the face.

Instead, he had slumped behind the wheel and had to sit on his hands to keep them away from his gun.

He had cursed her for being a frigid woman. While inside, in the frightened dark of himself, Mulford had realized that he was no different from the thieves and punks and murderers he loved to see being punished.

He cursed the girl, hating her guts and hating his brother and old Uncle Sheridan and hating the whale before him now, staring down at the shiny points of his boots and frightened of himself and the police force and his ex-wife, Sheila, who had told her shyster attorney that he was a sadist and a homosexual... afraid of the whale, hating it now, right now, liking the good heavy feel of the gun on his hip. He turned to face the eight people who were, he noticed, not watching him after all.

The hitch was gone. It had taken less than five seconds. A black bird had flown from Mulford's shoulder. He felt strong and right, and he no longer doubted that the creases were still sharp on the back of his shirt.

Earle Kavanaugh had positioned his tripod and camera on the other side of the whale. The tinfoil reflector was propped in the sand a few yards to the right of the tripod.

Wanda stood in the path of reflected light. Waiting to one side, out of camera range, Norma sat with the clothes baskets, looking bored and only half listening to Earle's steady chatter while he explained what sort of pose he wanted from Wanda.

"You see, honey, you bend over, facing the camera. And kind of grab your knees. Like this. See? That's a breast-spilling shot. Okay, now you try it. And smile. Keep your face straight to the camera. Okay. Now when I drop my hand I want you to give me a great big smile. And suck in your tummy."

Earle held up one hand, holding the cable release with the other. He dropped his hand, paused, and pushed the shutter trigger.

"That was fine. Now let's try a few more. Let's have a bigger smile, honey. Cheese. It's great joy-time here on this lovely beach. You're just an innocent young maid clowning around a whale."

He took two more shots of Wanda. Then he excused her and brought Norma into the patch of light. He readjusted the reflector after positioning Norma on the sand, kneeling with her back to the camera.

"Okay, honey. Undo the back string of your halter. Sit right down on your calves. That's it. Now look over your shoulder at the camera. Look as if you were just caught in the act of taking off your halter."

While Earle worked, he was aware that the big guy in the silk suit and the cop were watching him. Posing models in public, before strangers, had always made Earle uncomfortable. As if he were some kind of pimp, or a carny character. He knew what people thought of him—that he was some kind of semi-pornographic Hollywood hustler.

This was partly true, but Earle still resented it. He liked to think of himself as a public relations man, a representative of talent, a wheeler-dealer.

"Good girl. Don't run away, honey. Let's get a couple of leap frog shots."

"Who leaps who, Earle?"

"Norma, you leap Wanda first. Keep your toes pointed out. I don't want a picture of the bottom of your feet."

"You kill me, Earle. You really do."

Earle smiled and busied himself behind the camera.

The trouble was that lately his luck had been bad. If he hadn't kept what few contacts he had left in the nudie magazine line, Earle had no idea how he would have managed. He was definitely on the skids, and he knew it. He was two months behind in his rent, his car had been repossessed, his wardrobe was growing thinner with each passing month, and speculation model-photography was growing tighter. There were too many good photographers around.

Like that kid, Riley, had said—the big money was in nude movies. And, for the past few years, Earle had been scheming to break into this new and lucrative angle. But that would take at least five or ten thousand dollars up front before he could hope to get any further backing. And where the hell would a guy like Earle get five or ten G's?

It was hopeless.

"Okay, girls. That about wraps it up for here."

He had taken seventeen shots in all.

"What now, Earle?"

"We'll go over by the dunes," he said, speaking low. "I'll get a couple lying down and sitting shots. Then, if we can find a nice secluded spot, I'll try and work in a few nudes. That's extra jack for the both of you."

Homer Riley crossed the beach, passing Kavanaugh and the girls along the way. When he came to the whale he stopped by the tail fins and nodded to Mulford. Mulford didn't bother to return the nod.

Looking at the whale, Riley figured that he could get the cable chain and hook under the flukes if he dug a tunnel in the sand at the narrow point near the body.

Riley walked past the fins to Mulford, who was standing near the head.

"You the driver from Hercules?"

"Yeah."

"It took you long enough to get here, chief."

"I know. I was hung up, north of here, in a dead area for my radio. And my rig was the only one they could've sent down here for a job like this." He looked up the wall of the whale's hide to the ridge along the back. "None of the other wreckers would be able to haul in a load as big as this."

Mulford didn't seem to be paying much attention. "Do you think you can get your cable down this far, chief?"

"I can get it down okay," Riley said. "But I won't be able to drag it all the way up the hill. When I get it to the foot I'll call in for a crane. Maybe they'll have to cut it into pieces before they can bring it up to the county trucks." Riley removed his sunglasses and measured the whale with his eye. "This thing probably weighs close to forty tons. Maybe more."

"Okay. Let's get on with it."

Riley took a job book from his hip pocket and flipped the pages. He inserted the carbon and found a dirty stub of pencil.

"I'm not sure how I'm supposed to write this up," he said. "I imagine they can fill it out for me back at the garage."

Mulford leaned closer, looking at the job book.

"All you'll need for now is the location and your time of arrival and departure. You can scratch out the make of vehicle and nature of accident or job and write in county tow—a whale."

"I've never towed a whale before," Riley said. "You'd better sign for it before I get started. Put your name and badge number and station house on the line printed right after the big red X. Right there on the bottom."

Mulford propped the book on his knee and started writing.

Riley lit a cigarette and looked around at the bystanders.

The cop, he decided, was a mean sonofabitch. Just another cop, like all cops. He reminded Riley of a guard he had known in the Colorado State Pen.

The rest were a weird bunch.

Joe Bonniano was still sitting on his paper, holding his handkerchief in one hand, arms locked around his knees, smiling and watching.

Hobart Richardson was standing near the head of the whale, looking sullen and suspicious. His jacket was over his shoulders, the sleeves hanging free.

Karen Fornier was still seated. She was watching Riley through narrowed eyes, mouth solemn, a cigarette burning in the sand at her feet.

In the distance, Fredric Langfield continued to sit on his wicker stool, stoned out of his mind, unmoving, leaning on his cane.

Beside him, Becky sat on the folded car blanket, the straw basket propped between her legs.

Why were they all so quiet and watchful?

It didn't seem right. It had been Riley's experience that whenever he arrived at a scene with his rig, there was always a certain interest shown by the bystanders, no matter how terrible the accident, or how small the job.

Why were they all watching him?

He had the uncomfortable feeling that he wasn't wanted, that he had interrupted them in the midst of something.

Without a word, Mulford handed back the job book.

Riley dropped it into his hip pocket and stood there, feeling foolish, waiting. No one moved or said a word. The cop was looking at him as if he wanted Riley to leave.

Riley felt like an actor who had wandered onto the wrong stage. The whale and the people looked and acted as if they had been grouped for a photograph of emotions. Like a Smirnoff ad gone wrong.

"Well... I guess I'd better be going back to the truck to get the cable...."

"I guess you'd better," Mulford said.

Riley made no move to leave.

"Anything wrong, chief?"

"No...."

"Then let's get on with it."

Riley turned and started up the beach, feeling their eyes on his back. He had walked about ten feet when he heard a swishing noise directly behind him. He glanced over his shoulder.

The whale's flukes were moving on the sand.

Joe Bonniano chuckled softly under his breath.

Mulford took off his sunglasses and returned Riley's look. His lips twitched in a faint smile.

Riley started back to the whale. He stopped a few feet from the cop, puzzled, frowning.

Just then a muffled ringing broke the silence. Everyone turned and glared at Hobart, who was frantically fumbling for the lizard clock in his hip pocket. When he pulled it out the ringing was louder, more shrill. Hobart flipped the case open and stabbed the alarm button.

Slowly, everyone returned his attention to Mulford and Riley.

Hobart stood with the now silent clock in his hands, his face flushed a deep red, his jaw thrust out defiantly to an audience that was no longer there.

After a moment, Mulford asked, quietly, "Something the matter, chief?"

"Yeah," Riley said, slowly. "The whale isn't dead."

"I know," Mulford said.

Riley glanced at the whale, saw the flukes again swaying on the sand, heard the blowholes whoosh and suck.

"Look, if you knew the whale was still alive, then why the hell did you put in a call for a tow?"

Mulford put his sunglasses back on. Moving very casually, he shifted his weight on the sand.

"Do you expect me to dig a hole under a live whale's tail and simply tow it away? Maybe the whale's got other plans. That thing probably weighs forty tons, maybe more. If I tried to drag it up to the dunes it would probably drag my truck out to sea." He shook his head. "This is the silliest thing I've ever heard of."

Karen rose from the sand and moved to Riley's side.

"The officer," she said, looking hard at Mulford, "says that it's his job to shoot it. I've tried to argue with him, but apparently the whale being alive means very little to him. Something about his duty, and the whale being a menace."

Riley looked more closely at Karen. Shadows of gulls passing overhead crossed her face and she returned his look, not backing away.

She reminded Riley of his crazy ex-wife.

In a second, suddenly aware of her, he took a sound from her eyes, and nothing within her stopped him. Riley was almost surprised by this. He smiled by not moving a muscle and he turned back to Mulford. The shadows of the gulls floated across the sand to the sea.

"What are you going to shoot it with?"

Mulford didn't answer.

"I'd like to know what you think you're going to shoot it with."

Mulford rested his hand on the butt of his gun. A significant gesture. Very cowboy. When he finally spoke, his voice was soft, with a hint of menace.

"Now look, chief, you're here under my orders. Try and remember that and we'll get along just fine. My station house put in a call to your people and you were told to come here. You tow the whale as far up the beach as you can. Just like you were told to do. And I'll do my job, just like I've been told to do. I don't want any trouble. Not from you. And not from the young lady. I won't tell you how to do your job, and you won't tell me how to do mine. That way we can get this business over and done with and we can all go home."

"The whale still isn't dead," Riley said. "And if you really think you're going to kill it with that little gun of yours you've got another think coming. You can't shoot a whale with—"

"I've already told you, chief," Mulford broke in. "And I've tried to be nice about it. I thought I was making myself clear. I don't intend to make a big production number out of this business—it's been dragging too long already. I've had just about enough arguing and bitching. From all of you." He looked at Hobart, then at Karen and Riley. "What happens to this whale and how the proper authorities intend to dispose of it while it threatens the health and safety of this public beach is none of your business. It's my business." Again, Mulford rested his hand on his gun. "Now do you read me?"

Karen caught Riley's eye. She indicated the slope with a tilt of her head. Riley turned and saw another uniformed cop standing atop the slope beside the tow truck. The cop was waving his arm.

Mulford followed their gaze and when he saw the new cop his jaw muscles tensed and his lips twitched angrily.

Riley said, "I think someone's trying to get you."

"You wait right here," Mulford ordered.

Mulford pushed past him, and Riley watched as he plodded across the beach, his spurs winking in the sun. Hobart, who had kept silent during the argument, now came to Karen's side, as if to remind her, and Riley, that she was his property.

Karen ignored the gesture. She was suddenly with Riley inside her eyes, secretly, immediately drawn to his hard farmer and thief-like character, a bit surprised to find herself there. The quick deep awareness of their first encounter wasn't repeated. She had tucked it away.

"What do you think?" Karen asked.

"About the cop?" Riley shrugged. "I don't know...."

"I don't see what the beef is," Hobart said. "I think the cop spelled it out quite plainly."

"You do?" Riley asked.

"Sure," Hobart said. He narrowed his eyes, sizing Riley. "It's the cop's business, and not ours. Karen here—" he jerked his head toward Karen, "—has been arguing with him half the morning. And she hasn't gotten anywhere. What the hell? It's just like the cop said. We don't know a damn thing about whales, and even less what to do in case one gets washed up. But the cop does. Whales get washed up fairly often and they have a routine way of handling them." Hobart nodded his head, as if that gesture ended the discussion. "I think that's pretty plain."

Karen asked, "Have you ever towed a whale before?"

"No," Riley said.

"You see," Hobart said. "Then all this hullabaloo seems pretty stupid, doesn't it? This guy's never towed a whale before. But the cop has dealt with them, probably quite a few times. I don't see why we have to try and interfere with the man's job. The cop has his orders, like he said. He's going to shoot the whale. Period. As far as I'm concerned that should end it. Why fight it?"

Riley lit a cigarette and said nothing.

Joe Bonniano had watched as Mulford had left the scene and had stalked past him. And when he had looked over his shoulder and had spotted the second cop standing atop the dunes by the truck, he had had a momentary flash of panic.

Then, shrugging, he had swallowed another tranquilizer. He was safe so far. There was no need to get jumpy. That dumb cop had no idea who he was.

Joe had no intention of leaving the scene—not yet. He couldn't afford to miss Willie when he arrived. And, considering the way matters stood, with the whale business coming to a climax, Joe's absence would only draw attention and suspicion to himself.

He unwrapped and lit another cigar, and for the hundredth time that morning he looked at his wristwatch and wondered what was keeping Willie C.

What would happen if Willie came now? Surely he would see the two cops gabbing up there. Would Willie think that Joe had been captured while waiting on the beach?

Joe had imagined the south end of the beach would be empty. Just as it always was. And what does he find when he arrives? A goddam whale, a bunch of gawkers, and a cop. How rotten can his luck get? He was afraid that the longer he stayed the worse it would be. Perhaps the cop was calling for more help. Then the place would be swarming with cops.

He was getting jumpy again. He forced his thoughts to other, more pleasant things. Fire hydrants in summer with the water whooshing out. The click of billiards. A good day at the track, with a bright sun and a private box and perfect pickings. A good-looking woman smelling of expensive perfume. One of the clubs at Lake Tahoe at one o'clock in the morning with the snow falling outside, the cocktail waitresses walking around in tight ski pants. Joe and Herb Betseka in Philly right after the war....

He remembered how it had been the night before. It was hard to believe that it had all happened less than fifteen hours ago.

Joe had been calm, almost detached, when he had parked his car two blocks from Betseka's house. He had entered through the gate and walked along the sweeping drive up to the big house. He had rung the bell, knowing that Betseka was alone in the house.

Joe had been following the bookie's routine for the past three weeks.

Herb Betseka had opened the door.

"Joe! Come on in. How's the snowstorm back East? You have a good flight? When you called me a few minutes ago I could hardly believe it was you...."

"Hello, Herb."

"Come on in. Normally I wouldn't answer the door myself. But this is one of those nights. And, knowing it was you...."

Joe had followed Betseka past the indoor pool to the private office. Once inside, with the quilted leather door closed behind them, Betseka had sat on the edge of his desk and had said:

"Well, Joe. It's been years. You look like you've put on a little weight."

"Maybe."

"But you're looking good."

"So are you, Herb."

"We both do! Look at us. When we were kids we were both skinny runts. We've come up in the world, Joe...." Betseka's smile had altered then, very slightly, sobering. "And so... what brings you out to the Coast?"

"The usual. Business. A little pleasure."

Joe had been on the Coast for a month. He had gone first to Nevada where he had conferred with his eastern bosses and reluctantly, without any other choice, had agreed to the Betseka contract.

"The heat's on back home," Joe had said. "And they're getting worried. They don't know how far it's spread. You've been quiet, Herb. They haven't heard much from you lately."

"Like you say, Joe—business. You know how it is. I've been keeping my end up. Why should anyone get worried?"

"I don't know. I just thought I'd let you know how they're thinking."

"Sure. How about a drink?"

"No. Thanks."

"On a diet?"

"Sort of."

It had taken Joe a while to learn that, as far as any important records were concerned, Betseka kept nothing in the house. All the books had been stashed in a coin-operated laundry office in Glendale. And they had been destroyed by jelly fire only a few hours before Joe's visit.

"You know, Joe, I was just telling Marge—she's out for the night, but she'll be back in about an hour—I was just telling her the other day—"

Joe had pulled the .45 and had leveled it at him. Betseka's face had blanched, then had grown hard and sly.

"Is this—some kind of joke?"

"It's no joke."

"They told you to do this?"

"Yeah."

"And you're actually going to go through with it?"

"Yeah."

Then Betseka had smiled, somewhat sadly. "You know, Joe, you always were a lousy gambler. Have you figured the odds on a thing like this?"

"I think so."

"They're not in your favor, kid. Once you pull that trigger you'll be in line for one on you. You won't even break away from the post, you dumb—"

Joe had pulled the trigger and Betseka had flopped back, dead....

Joe rose from the beach, his eyes troubled, thinking about the way Betseka had died. He picked up his sports page, folded it, shoved it into his jacket pocket.

Last night's hit would have been perfect. But just as he reached his car he had been spotted by Marge, Betseka's wife, who was returning early.

The curse of Joe Bonniano.

Perhaps Herb had been right....

Joe paced the sand, puffing on his cigar. A cloud passed before the sun and the beach darkened. A light wind ruffled the sea. Then the sun returned and the day was bright again. Joe Bonniano continued to pace, and to look now and then at his wristwatch.

When Officer Mulford reached the path just past the Hercules truck, he saw the squad car parked on the shoulder of the road. The red dome light was flashing. Mulford went around to the driver's side. Just as he had expected, Sergeant McLeod, big and beefy, white-haired and red-faced, was seated behind the wheel. His uniform jacket was unbuttoned and his necktie pulled loose. His expression showed his usual mild disdain for Mulford.

"You're late."

"I know, sir. I called in and explained."

"We don't get overtime, you know."

Mulford nodded. "I don't mind, Sergeant."

"Well, I don't give a damn what you do or don't do, Mulford. I don't like my working day interrupted by your tardiness."

Mulford's expression didn't change. He didn't care what McLeod, or his fellow officers, thought of him, just as long as they left him to himself. Mulford had never been on friendly terms with any of the men in his station house, Sergeant McLeod in particular.

"I've been expecting you back for the past hour," McLeod said. "I was just about to knock off myself, so I thought I'd better come down this way and take a look." The other side of his words said that he resented having to chase all around the countryside looking for stray officers. He went on, "I wasn't even sure where the hell you were. Until I saw the Hercules truck and your horse."

Mulford said nothing.

McLeod looked in a bad mood. He had been, most likely, swilling free beers back in town.

"Okay, Mulford, suppose you tell me why that damned thing hasn't been towed up from the surf?"

"Well, sir, there was a kind of hitch. I was a bit premature with my report."

McLeod looked up suspiciously.

"Nothing serious, Sergeant," Mulford assured him. "When I called in earlier I believed the whale to be dead. It appeared dead to me. That's why I reported it as such."

"But it isn't dead," McLeod supplied.

"It is now. No worry there. I had to put it out of its misery. I couldn't think of anything else to do, and I didn't think you'd appreciate it if I'd bothered you again."

McLeod grunted and stared blankly at the dashboard panel.

"Okay, Mulford. Let's not be at this business all the goddam day. You've still got to write up and check out. And I don't want your mount on duty any longer than necessary. I'll roll on back and let them know that everything's under control. Meanwhile, get that goddam carcass away from the water. Get it up to the foot of the hill here."

"Yes, sir."

McLeod squinted, studying Mulford's sunglasses. "Don't think I'm sanctioning this sort of thing, Mulford. You say the whale was still alive when you reported in? Okay. But I don't like it. I want you to understand that."

"Yes, sir."

McLeod gunned the car into the traffic lane south; then, with a tire yelp, he U-turned into the north lane and headed back to town.

Mulford remained on the path, watching the flashing dome light disappear into traffic. His thoughts were more easy now. His explanation to McLeod had somehow put an official stamp on his proposed action. It was a minor point that he hadn't yet shot the whale.

Officially, the whale was dead.

And, officially, it had been shot and killed by him.

FIVE

A hundred yards from the whale, Fredric Langfield turned to Becky and whispered:

"It's going to happen now. The whale doesn't stand a chance. No one can stop it. Watch very carefully...." His voice grew lower, more intense. "'Which to secure no skill of leach's art, mote him avail, but to return again to his wound's worker, that with lowly dart dinting his breast had bred his restless pain, as the wounded whale to shore flies through the maine.' Watch, Becky, watch. Read it from the air...."

Unconsciously, Becky clenched the amulet and pressed it to her breast, the talons biting.

Fredric hunched forward. He was aware of his entire being shifting. He felt he was the only one on the beach who was truly aware of what was about to happen. Becky couldn't understand. How could she? Only a junkie could know. Only a junkie can feel the sky's pulse. And the vision was real, so it seemed the more significant. It was all laid before him in absolute detail. The whale. Death. The clouds dark and fat, towering from the sullen-colored sea, shadowing the land.

Fredric sniffed the salty breath of wind. Like mad Lear. Tangled in broken sea nets and glossy flakes of shell and drug-stained dreams, Fredric's crazy high, with the pills tramping deliciously in his skull and the morphine flowing gold in his veins, floated smoothly on. And he no longer doubted the presence of the great whale before him, or the black policeman stalking across the beach to the white-garbed tow-truck driver.

"'... That with lowly dart dinting his breast had bred his restless pain, as the wounded whale to shore....'"

Fredric's dark eyes grew sad and he said nothing more.

Earle Kavanaugh and the two models stood beside the whale, arguing.

Now that the light had gone bad and their modeling session had ended, the girls were anxious to leave. Earle wanted to stay for a while. While they had been working in the dunes he had reloaded his camera and he wanted to take a few more shots of the whale. He had overheard Karen and Hobart talking about Mulford's intention to shoot the whale. And since there were no press photographers around Earle figured he might be able to peddle a picture of the shooting to one of the Los Angeles papers.

"Look," Norma was saying, "we came out here in my car, so I say let's go. If you want to stay here, Earle, you can stay. But I've got a date tonight."

Wanda said, "Relax. It'll only be a few minutes. So Earle's paying us for sunbathing."

"Sure," Earle said. "That's the way to look at it."

Joe Bonniano tossed away his cigar butt. He had decided to give Willie another fifteen minutes. Then, if no one showed by then, he would leave the beach and try another call. Standing around and doing nothing was getting on his nerves. Any minute now that cop could do a double take on Joe and make him. After all, even dumb cops aren't that dumb.

Mulford was halfway across the beach.

Karen was watching Riley.

Hobart was watching Karen.

A moment later, Mulford entered the group. Without a word or side look, he started directly for the head of the whale, determined to end the thing once and for all.

Riley looked at the whale and a sudden deep feeling whimmed him. Without quite knowing why, he stepped forward and blocked Mulford's path.

Mulford stopped.

"I think you're making a mistake," Riley said. Mulford whipped off his sunglasses. His voice was barely controlled.

"You're begging for trouble, chief! You want trouble—then just keep getting in my way, keep shooting off your mouth!" His fists closed. "Now get the hell out of my way!"

Riley didn't move.

Mulford couldn't back down. Not now. He had boasted his intentions to too many people, himself included. He was seriously considering shoving Riley aside when Hobart Richardson suddenly stepped between them, deciding to get into the act. Hobart put his hand on Riley's arm, gripping it, as if to restrain him.

"I think the officer means what he says, fella. So if I were you I'd mind my own business and—"

Riley wrenched his arm free, throwing Hobart off balance. Hobart staggered back, stumbling. He lost his footing completely and fell against the side of the whale.

Earle Kavanaugh's camera clicked.

The blowholes snorted and whooshed.

For the first time since grounding that morning, the whale opened his eyes. Seeing that he was surrounded by strange figures and noises, he sucked in a huge breath and started rocking his body.

The crowd moved back.

Sand fleas swarmed from the whale's hide. The earth trembled. The whale bucked and writhed. He was beginning to move back toward the sea.

Mulford found himself staring directly into the left eye of the whale, watching it roll and blink in its socket. Then, moving mechanically, he stepped to the head of the whale. He drew out his revolver, eased back the hammer, and, as the eye turned to watch his movements, he pressed the muzzle of the gun to the eye.

Mulford's lips flickered in a cruel smile and he squeezed the trigger.

The report echoed in the dunes.

The moment Mulford squeezed the trigger he snatched the gun away, as if to retract his action.

The left eye of the whale exploded like a sack of gelatin and gummy bits of ooze splattered Mulford's shirt front. Slime ran from the gaping socket and the whale's body shuddered. His jaw opened slowly, as if to scream, but no sound came forth.

The whale could understand none of it. Despite the blindness in one eye and the terrible pain he still tried to return to sea. He could see the waves, white and frothy, tumbling to the beach before him. He began to rock with greater urgency, panic finally gripping him. Behind him, his broad flukes whipped back and forth, splashing gusts of sand in all directions.

Joe Bonniano ran back another twenty feet, away from the threat of the flailing tail fins.

Hobart was still on his knees beside the whale. He scrambled frantically on all fours, past the stunned Riley, past Karen. White and shaken, his eyes wild with fear and excitement, Hobart pushed himself to his feet and grabbed Karen about the waist. She was crying and struggling. Hobart held her tighter.

Mulford gaped at the whale in disbelief.

Wasn't the brain directly behind the eyes?

Moving quickly, he dashed to the other side of the whale and again aimed the gun. The right eye blinked and grew wide with fear. Mulford pulled the trigger —three times in rapid succession.

The shots shattered the air, washed back from the hills, rolled out to sea.

Totally blind now, the whale again opened his jaws in a terrible silent scream.

Karen was screaming, "Stop it! Stop it! Stop it!" and Hobart was wrestling her back, his hands gripping her breasts, his grinning face pressed into her neck.

Mulford staggered back, horrified. He fired twice, emptying the gun, shooting blindly at the plunging head.

But the whale didn't die.

Mulford was frozen.

How could?—the brain was—William R. Mulford with a smoking .45 in his gloved fist.

He couldn't believe it.

During the first few seconds of the shooting, Earle Kavanaugh had been snapping one picture after another. He had started the moment Riley had upset Hobart's balance and the whale had awakened.

Earle was the only one present who still had complete control of himself. And he was thinking only of his pictures.

Before the action had started, when he had been planning to shoot only a few news shots, he had taken a new light reading and had readjusted the aperture. In the first four or five seconds since the gunshots, Earle had taken many pictures. And he knew they would be minor masterpieces— the dark boiling sky in the background, the long tumbling combers, the sun's rays spilling from behind the clouds, the cop firing pointblank into the whale's eyes....

The whale was going crazy now. Enraged and thrashing up and down, the whale rose higher with each mighty heave of his body, gaining momentum. Fifty tons of whale thundering on the earth. Then, suddenly, he rose straight up, poising momentarily on his flukes, a writhing, teetering, two-story building of whale.

Somebody shouted:

"Look Out!"

Everyone ran.

The whale balanced himself in the sky, then crashed back to earth. The whale's flukes swung around and, with almost unbelievable speed and force, caught the running Joe Bonniano and threw him high into the air.

Screaming and thrashing his arms and legs, Joe was hurled through the air and dropped to the beach more than seventy feet from the spot where he had been struck. He rolled, churning sand, stopped, tried to rise, then crumpled, unconscious.

Earle had snapped Joe being struck, and Joe in midair. He jerked the film-advance, aimed, and triggered another shot of Norma and Wanda running to Joe's aid.

Success popped in Earle's brain. A full page in *Life* magazine. No—the hell with one page—make it five pages. An incident on the beach. Big money. Text and pictures by Earle C. Kavanaugh.

Swinging back to Mulford, Earle automatically pressed the shutter when he saw another flurry of action....

Without pausing to think, Riley was scrambling across the ditch where the whale had been. Before Mulford could protect himself, before he could leap aside, Riley's fist smashed into his mouth.

Mulford staggered back, feeling the numbing bash and the hot spurt of blood from his gums. The emptied revolver flew from his hands. He tried to double up, but Riley's fists continued to hammer into his face and stomach. Mulford crumpled, doubled over, threw his forearms before his face. Blood was streaming down his jaw, splashing his shirt and dripping onto his boots.

Riley swung, hitting Mulford's skull, feeling his knuckles pop and the near pleasant shock of connection zip up his arm and jolt hard in his breast. Riley winced. He stepped back and positioned Mulford's head with his damaged right hand, and with his left he pulled back and down to come up and under the cop's guard.

But Mulford read the telegraph of the punch. Still gasping for air and shaking with pain, Mulford dropped to one side, landing on his elbow and breaking the set up. He kicked out hard at Riley's shin.

Shock ripped up Riley's thigh. For a split second he thought he had been shot. And, also, in the quick flicker of anger and pain, he imagined that he was back in that bar in Colorado, fighting with the two cops. He clutched his leg, bending, and saw Mulford's boot swing toward him again. He jumped aside and the boot grazed his ankle.

Mulford pushed himself to his feet, reeling and dizzy, spitting blood.

Riley limped in and threw his left. He caught Mulford on the side of his neck. Mulford rolled with the punch, then crouched and jumped. They wrestled a moment, staggering. Mulford's knee came up between Riley's legs and Riley sank to his knees. He rolled, trying to duck Mulford's kick. But the boot caught him in the pit of his stomach and the air gushed from his lungs. A roaring sounded in his ears. His eyes started to roll.

Mulford stood on shaky legs, breathing hoarsely, blood smearing his puffy lips. He looked down at Riley with a contemptuous sneer; then, taking careful aim, he kicked Riley on the side of his head.

Riley fell over. Before passing out, he saw his bloodied hand and he tried to laugh. Then everything swam before him, turned gray, then black, then to nothingness.

The whale flopped and rolled, trying to keep the sand from blocking his nostrils. He was dragging himself away from the water, heading at an angle toward the dunes.

Norma and Wanda had no idea what to do in cases like this, so they had taken their clothes from their baskets and had wrapped the unconscious Joe Bonniano in a pile of skirts and sweaters and bras.

Joe's breathing was shallow, his face pale, accenting the blue of his beard. A thin trickle of blood was drying on his chin and neck. The sleeve of his jacket had ruptured at the seam and a white pile of shoulder padding was peeping from the silk flaps.

While the girls fussed and tucked their clothes about him, Joe started to come to. His eyelids fluttered. Through a mist of pain he could barely make out the forms of what he imagined were two nurses hovering over him. He wondered if the operation had been successful, if the doctors had managed all right with his appendix.

He tried to move his head to one side, but the shattered collarbone sent hot flashes of pain through his chest. He clenched his false teeth, biting hard, hurting the gums. Finally, after a long moment, he remembered where he really was and what had happened to him.

"Willie...."

"Take it easy," Norma said. "You'll be all right, mister. Honest. Just don't try and move."

"I gotta...."

He had to do what? What the hell could he do? When he tried to move, the pain became too great. The fog began to close again. Half delirious, Joe remembered Willie, and he told himself that he had to get away. He had to stand up and make a run for it. But he couldn't move. Each suck of air felt like red-hot barbed wire being whipped around his lungs. He forced his eyes open and stared at a lacy bra cup.

"What—what the hell is that?"

"Please, mister. Don't move. You've been hurt. But you're going to be all right."

What about the gun in his pocket? Had they found it?

Who were those women? Nurses?

Of course, they must be nurses. They were trying to soothe him. Nurses always soothed people who were hurt.

Had the croakers searched him? Did they know who he was? Is that why they had strapped him to the operating table?

"What's on my chest?" he asked. A terrible weight seemed to be pressing on his chest. He rolled his head, fighting to stay awake. "Something's on my... chest."

"It's only a brassiere," Wanda said.

"A brassiere?"

"Yes."

It certainly was a damn heavy brassiere. That nurse must have the biggest pair of tits in the world.

What had Herb said? That Joe wouldn't even break away from the post? That the odds weren't in his favor? That was a laugh and a half. Joe had known that all along. Because that's the way it had always been. No matter what. Dice, roulette, poker, the horses. Everything always ended with a bust-out.

So go ahead, girls. You just keep right on smiling. Smile. You dumb clucks. You got no worries. No worries at all. The only way you'll ever know is by learning the secret. And the secret was to Think Shit. It was that simple. All the girls with the brassieres that weigh more than a sack of .45's with one bullet fired from each one. Think Shit.

And just before Joe fell into the pleasant darkness of his mind, he heard a woman's voice, echoing, coming as if from the far end of a long black tunnel.

"Someone better call the cops and get an ambulance down here right away...."

SIX

The clouds were now all over the sky. Thin cathedral rays of sun spilled from silver patches between the black. Mothers had been gathering their children long before the shots had been fired. Nearly everyone had heard the shots, but thought they were the first soft grumblings of thunder. The air smelled rainy. Beach umbrellas were collapsing and blankets were being rolled. The jazzy music from the remaining transistor radios sounded feeble and lonesome. The tide was sweeping up the shore line, eating footprints and sand castles. A few sun puddles lit the dark sea. Ghosty papers pranced the emptying beach and motors and horns could be heard from the parking lots at the slope heads.

Nick, the proprietor of the lunch wagon, lowered the highway side of the wagon windows. He poured himself a cup of coffee from a thermos which he kept hidden under the counter.

Alex left his perch, and Nick, seeing the lifeguard approaching the wagon, set out another cup and poured from the thermos.

"Thanks, Nick."

"How's the hangover now?"

"Okay, I guess. I'm a healthy guy. I get a lot of sun." He glanced over his shoulder, frowning. "A day like this, it's kind of spooky. And kind of pretty, too."

"It's gonna rain," Nick said. "I been watching them gulls. They're nervous, the way gulls get, cawing around. Did you hear the thunder a few minutes ago? I looked up, kind of expecting to see lightning, but there wasn't none. Just the thunder."

Alex shifted nervously. He hunched over his coffee, pretending to inhale it.

Alex had heard the shots a minute ago, and he had known them for what they were. From his high chair he had seen the whale (or what he thought was the whale) rising on its tail. And Alex was more worried now. Something had gone wrong. Very wrong. He hated to think about it, but knew that sooner or later he would have to go down and investigate.

He sipped his coffee, brooding. He had the funny feeling that Mulford might try and blame him for whatever went wrong.

"Yeah," Nick said, "it sure as hell looked nice this morning. But it's dead now. Can't make a buck this way, huh, Al?"

Alex gulped his coffee. "I'll be shoving off, Nick."

"Hey, no rush. I'm not trying to push you."

"Thanks, Nick. But I've got to go anyway."

"Take care, Al. See you tomorrow—if the sun shines."

Alex moved off and Nick watched him for a minute; then, he raised the volume on his radio, which was still tuned to the western station, switched off the orangeade and popcorn machines and started scraping down his grill.

"It sure didn't take you very long," Norma said.

Wanda knelt beside Joe, breathing a bit rapidly from her trip up and down the slope.

"Are you kidding? Dressed only in my bikini? I didn't even have to put out my thumb."

"Is someone going for an ambulance?"

Wanda nodded. "*And* the cops. I told the guy that stopped to call the ambulance people and the police station both." She bent closer to Joe. "Is he still breathing? He looks kind of dead to me."

"He's breathing," Norma said. "But he sure sounds bad. He wheezes now and then. And he said that name 'Willie' again."

"Well, the ambulance guys will know what to do...."

Riley knelt at the water's edge, bathing his hand, salt stinging the knuckles where the flesh had torn. He soaked his waste rag and limped back to the whale's ditch. He had to sit down, still woozy from the fight. The Scotch he had drunk earlier was sour in his stomach. The back of his mouth tasted like green pennies. When he lit a cigarette he noticed that his hands were still a bit shaky from his reaction.

Karen joined him, sitting on the sand beside him. "That was a nice thing you did."

Riley grunted and blew smoke. "Maybe it could have been. But it wasn't. It didn't come out quite like I'd planned. I got clobbered."

"I felt.... When I found the whale this morning I felt good. I didn't think that anything like this would happen. It's—" she shrugged. "I don't know... anyway, I'm glad that you did what you could."

"Nothing I did helped, really. The whale got his, no matter how many kicks in the gut I took." He looked around him, peering into the gloom. "Where's our gun-toting cop now?"

"He was cleaning up a minute ago. But now he's standing over there, near the whale. I think he's gone a little crazy. I mean, he's looking at the whale as if he were wondering why he hadn't obeyed orders, why he hadn't rolled over dead when he shot him."

"Is the whale dead now?"

Karen shook her head. "It's still alive. That's the bad part." Her eyes flashed. "When I think about it—I get sick all over. Did you see those eyes? The way they were—"

"Yeah. Has anyone called an ambulance for that big guy?"

"Yes. One of the photographer's models just came back. She said that she also sent for the police."

Riley looked up sharply.

"The police?"

"Yes. Don't you think that that cop should be arrested for what he did to the whale? And to you?"

Riley shook his head.

"I attacked him first," he said.

"But that shouldn't have any bearing—"

"It does. I know a little bit about how cops think."

"I'll tell them what really happened—"

"And they'll probably pigeonhole it. Assaulting cops isn't a very popular activity around here."

Karen looked worried. "You don't really think you'll get into trouble, do you?"

"It could happen," Riley said.

Hobart Richardson hovered in the background, watching them with narrowed eyes.

Riley looked at her, thoughtfully. "You're a damn quick woman, aren't you?" He worked his hand. Nothing seemed to be broken. He said, "You know for sure what you're up to?"

"Yes. I know."

Riley shrugged. "All right. What's your name?"

"Karen Fornier."

"Mine's Riley. Homer Riley."

"I thought—"

"No. These coveralls belong to another guy."

Hobart lit a cigarette, his face briefly lit over the match cupped in his hands.

"Is that your boy friend?" Riley asked.

"Not really. He's just a friend. We came out here together."

"You leaving the same way?"

"He's with the cop."

"I suppose he is."

"You know he is." Riley stood and helped her to her feet. "Let's go see how that guy in the flashy suit is."

They went over to Joe Bonniano and Riley knelt at his side, feeling under the pile of clothes for his pulse.

"It's not pumping too hard."

Wanda's eyes widened. "Is that—serious?"

"I don't know," Riley said. "I know where to find the pulse, but once I find it I really don't know what to do with it."

After wiping away most of the blood and sand from his face and straightening his uniform as best as possible, Mulford had wandered around the area, searching for the scattered ends of what he imagined had once been a whole. He had tried to act as if he were still in charge, but there was a sullen, indifferent air about him.

Now he stood, alone and puzzled, staring at the gooey, blasted eyes of the whale. The whale was breathing loudly, but no longer moving about.

Mulford knew that the brunette model had gone to get a motorist to call his station, and, halfheartedly, he tried to piece together some sort of story. But nothing came to him.

His mouth still ached from Riley's blows and he was feeling light-headed, as if he had had five or six stiff slugs of bourbon.

Without thinking about what he was doing, he reloaded his gun and slid it into his holster. Then he reached up to his breast and idly stroked his badge....

Earle Kavanaugh drew Norma and Wanda away from Joe, taking them to one side.

"You girls had better split."

Wanda looked surprised, then suspicious.

"Why?"

"You called for more cops, didn't you? And when the cops get here they'll start asking questions, won't they?"

"So what?"

"Think about it, honey. After the cops, the reporters come. Right? And then they start prying and asking questions."

"So what the hell's wrong with that? I thought you wanted us to get publicity. You said—"

"Sure, I said it. But not anything like this. A thing like this—being questioned by cops and reporters—can give you a bad name. You girls want to keep your names clean. And you never want a bad press in this town, honey. Never. And a thing like this can go bad." Earle snapped his fingers. "Just like that."

What Earle said was partly true. But mainly he didn't want the press to become interested in any angle, especially good cheesecake, in case they did show. That way it was all the more for Earle.

"Maybe you're trying to pull something...."

"With what? How?" Earle held his palms up. "Publicity's my business, honey. You'd think I'd try and screw my own scene? If I thought it'd do you any good, would I tell you to leave? What's the percentage in that?"

A few minutes later, Earle watched them go, their figures disappearing over the hill. When they were out of sight he hid his camera and equipment in some nearby tufts of beach grass. He figured that the cops would probably want to suppress Mulford's action that day. And he didn't want any cops confiscating his film. He didn't want them to think he had anything damaging in his camera....

The ambulance was the first to arrive. It stopped on the shoulder, then backed into the grass between the Hercules truck and Mulford's horse. Two attendants in police uniforms, but not wearing side arms, jumped out and swung open the rear doors.

"Where's it supposed to be?"

"Down on the beach, I guess."

As they rolled out a collapsible stretcher with leather straps and chrome wheels they heard a siren coming down the highway. A moment later, a squad car braked to a stop and bounced up onto the path, the revolving dome light flashing red.

The first cop out was the driver, a tall thin man with ginger-colored hair and a pasty complexion. He stepped into the road and started to wave on the traffic with his flashlight.

The second cop, a big bull-necked Negro with a thick guardsman's mustache, stepped from the passenger side of the car and joined the ambulance men.

"Ho' ya, Becker," the first attendant said.

Becker returned the greeting. He unbuttoned his uniform jacket and hitched his trousers. His handcuffs clattered at his thick waist.

"It's Mulford," Becker said.

"He hurt very bad?"

"Mulford's not hurt," Becker said, chuckling. "You two boys ought to know better than that. You know nothing will ever hurt a bastard like Mulford." He stroked his mustache and peered down the slope. "Another man is injured is all I know. And from what I gather, it was Mulford's fault."

"That figures," the first attendant said.

"The Captain's on his way," Becker said. "He was just pulling up when the call came in. And he's mad, Hank, boiling mad, in his own quiet way, which can sure scare the hell out of you."

"This I've got to see," Hank said. He picked up a black bag and tossed it on the stretcher. "Okay, kid, let's go pick up the pieces."

Becker followed them down the slope. When they came to Joe Bonniano, where Earle Kavanaugh was still waiting, Becker moved on, looking for Mulford.

He found him, still staring at the whale.

"Hello, Mulford."

Mulford started, blinking as if just awakening. When he saw Becker he smiled, almost sneering.

"Hello, Becker. I suppose you came down here for the guy that was hurt."

"That's right."

Mulford chuckled. "You wouldn't believe what happened. The guy got in the way, just as the whale was flopping around. I tried to tell him to stand back. But he wouldn't listen."

While he talked, Mulford's eyes began to dim. His voice grew flat. For a minute he had had a grip, but it was slipping now.

"See, Becker, the whale stood up, real high, straight up, like the tower of Pisa, and when he came down—when he came down the tail swung around and—knocked the civilian for a loop. But listen, he's not hurt bad. He's probably just faking. Who can tell? I don't know. But it was an accident. I'll write the whole thing up in my report—just as it happened. But who'd know the whale would—stand up? I didn't know whales could stand. Who ever heard of—"

Becker gripped Mulford's arm.

"Knock it off, Mulford. Get hold of yourself."

"Sure, Becker. I'm all right. Just a little groggy. Who wouldn't be? That guy from Hercules attacked me." His eyes turned sly. "Did you come in a squad car?"

Becker nodded, trying to read Mulford's eyes.

"Why do you ask?"

"Because I want you to take the Hercules guy in with you, that's why. Book him. When I get back to the station I'll prefer the charges. Interfering with an officer in the line of his duty. Assault. And so forth."

"Captain Alexander's on his way here, Mulford. So I can't be taking anybody in. I've been told to wait here for the Captain. And you, too. So if you want to make an arrest you'd better wait until after you see the Captain."

"I'm going to see that that sonofabitch gets the book."

"Okay," Becker said. "You do whatever you want—but after you talk with the Captain."

Becker turned and left Mulford with the whale. On his way back to the stretcher, Karen intercepted him and introduced herself.

"Before you hear too much of what the other officer says, I'd like to tell you what I saw. I've been here all day. I found the whale."

Becker took out his notebook.

"All right, Miss. If you'd care to give me your full name and present address...."

While Karen talked with Becker, Riley headed up the slope to his truck. He found his bottle and took a quick swig. The Scotch soothed him. He started the diesel motor and switched on the red flasher and the boom spotlight. Light sprayed down the slope, sending long thin grass shadows to the beach.

Presently, he saw Karen crossing the sand, approaching the hill. When she came to the truck he held the bottle out to her.

"Have a drink. It's early. But it looks and smells like night."

Karen thanked him and took a deep swallow. "What did the cop have to say?" Riley asked.

"Nothing. He listened to me, but he didn't say anything."

Everything had happened too fast for Hobart Richardson.

He was still angry with himself for having run away from the whale on his hands and knees. And, when he had watched the fight, he had been afraid, as if he were half expecting the truck driver to turn on him next.

And now Karen wasn't talking to him, being too busy trying to make time with that greasy trucker.

Hobart jammed his hands into his pockets and felt the lizard clock press against his hip. He drew it out and stared at it for a long moment. Then, suddenly hating the damn thing, he cursed loudly and hurled it out to sea.

There! Get rid of it! That was the end of it! That stupid bitch, Karen!

And everything had been going good until she had seen that goddam whale. It seemed like days since they had first walked the beach that morning. And days since he had eaten. He wanted to leave. He knew that Karen wasn't going to leave with him. But he remained, stubbornly, salting his wounds and liking it. The clock was gone, and that, at least, was good. Although he had no idea why.

A light patter of rain began to fall, pocking the sand. Thunder rolled in the sky. The wind hissed and the air smelled stuffy with warm sand. In the distance, the diesel motor throbbed. The collection of lights atop the slope looked like a miniature circus. The rain pattered on and the thunder passed.

"Becker!"

Hank had set the stretcher down in the ambulance.

Becker came from the squad car and leaned in the rear of the truck. Hank was squatting beside the oxygen tanks, playing his flashlight on Joe Bonniano's face. The second attendant moved aside, letting Becker get a better look.

"What's wrong? Did he die?"

"He's not dead," Hank said. "He's got a broken collarbone. We've given him a shot of morph, in case he wakes up. But you'd better take a look at this."

Becker took the .45 and turned it slowly in his hand. Then he leaned over and took a closer look at Joe.

"Goddam...."

"Yeah," Hank said. "Isn't this something? Joseph Bonniano. Captured by a whale."

"What do you mean, a whale?" Becker grinned. "He's just been captured by us. The hell with the whale. Mulford obviously knows nothing about this, so let's keep it to ourselves. As soon as the Captain gets here I'll report it to him. We'll all grab the credit."

"And Mulford?"

Becker's teeth flashed. "William Mulford can go to hell. He's had something like this coming to him for a long time." Becker chuckled. "Jesus, I can hear the Captain now. Mulford spending half the day with the most wanted man in L.A. County parading around right in front of him."

The attendants shut and locked the rear doors. Becker returned to his squad car and watched as the ambulance rolled onto the highway and headed north, the siren screaming and light flashing.

Captain Alexander was a tall, bald man with soft-suede brown eyes and five o'clock shadow. His assistant, Sergeant Haslett, was a younger man, with hazel eyes and a slightly cleft chin. Both men were dressed in civilian clothes and were hatless.

The ambulance bearing Joe Bonniano had left the scene several minutes before the Captain arrived in his unmarked sedan.

While Becker gave his report, Alexander's face showed no expression. He took no notes, didn't interrupt, merely nodded his head now and then. When Becker finished, the Captain and Sergeant Haslett moved to one side and talked in low, earnest whispers. Alexander did most of the talking, Haslett listening with his lips pursed thoughtfully. When they seemed to have reached an agreement, they returned to Becker. Haslett called the cop from the road.

Alexander said, "All right, Becker. Let's keep the Bonniano angle quiet for right now." He turned to the cop with the ginger-colored hair. "You stay on the road and keep the traffic moving. Don't let anyone stop, for any reason. I've called ahead for a man from the Zoological Society. Let him through, but no one else. His name is Gilky, or Bilky—something like that."

"Yes, sir."

"And the press. If anyone from the press happens by, let them through. I'm not expecting them, but if they do come, say nothing about Bonniano. Let me take care of that. I'll release a general statement later. Just say you don't know a thing. But don't irritate them. This business is bad enough as it is."

When the cop returned to the road, Haslett asked, "What do you think, Captain?"

"I don't know. The way it looks now... I suppose we'll have to underplay Mulford's bit. But not as far as the department is concerned."

Alexander started down the slope, following the boom light path. Becker and Haslett followed.

Riley, standing near the whale, turned to Karen.

"Here come the big boys."

The three cops stopped before them.

"Are you the man from Hercules?"

Riley nodded.

Alexander turned, looked at the whale, then back at Riley. "The officer here—" he tilted his head toward Becker—"has already told me pretty much what happened between you and Officer Mulford."

Riley said nothing.

"I don't think you have too much to worry about, Dave. No charges—"

"The name is Riley. Homer Riley. The coveralls belong to someone else."

"Sorry. Well, Homer, don't worry about any charges being brought against you. The way I understand it, your action was justifiable under the circumstances. Rash, but justifiable."

Haslett said, "Before you leave, Homer, we'd like to have your full name and present address. We may have you make a statement—for department records only. It's just a formality."

"Sure," Riley said.

Alexander turned to Becker. "Would you please ask Officer Mulford to see me now?"

Becker grinned and moved off to the whale and Mulford.

Alexander thanked Riley and again assured him that there would be no charges brought against him. Then he and Haslett walked several yards away and stopped. When Mulford joined them, Riley was able to hear their voices, hard and clear.

Alexander was saying, "... just what the hell you thought was going on here."

Mulford started a reply; then, seeing the Captain's eyes, he changed his mind. He nervously shifted his weight.

Alexander continued. "We've had you on three-wheelers, and you goofed it. We've tried you on traffic, in the booking department, and in patrol cars. But each time you managed to bully about and—"

"Sir, I—"

"Shut up," Alexander said, "I'm not finished yet." He looked disgusted. "And then, because you requested the duty, we put you on a horse. We figured that on a horse you might settle down, because that seemed to be the duty that you wanted. Now on a horse, Mulford, all one has to do is ride around and play Mountie and make sure that the tourists get correct information and see that the kiddies aren't cheated at the hot-dog stands. And what do you do, Mulford?"

"Captain, I—"

"I don't want to hear a word from you, Mulford. Not yet." Alexander's eyes narrowed and a line deepened on his forehead. "Even on a horse, on a lonely, pleasant stretch of beach, you somehow managed to get yourself into trouble again."

Mulford started to answer, and again he fell silent. A tiny vein was hammering at his temple. His temper was barely under control.

"First," Alexander went on, "you lied to your station dispatcher. Second, you lied to Sergeant McLeod when he came out here to investigate your absence. Third, you repeat this same lie to the civilians present on the beach. Fourth, you take unauthorized action by attempting to shoot and kill a sleeping whale. And fifth, to top everything off, you publicly brawl with a truck driver who had been sent here to carry out instructions which came from your own station." Alexander's face was grim. "Mulford, just what in God's name do you think you were trying to pull? Answer me that. I'm really curious to find out how your mind works."

Mulford sputtered, his eyes crazed. Unthinkingly, his hand moved to his gun.

"Captain, I think—"

Alexander interrupted with a wave of his hand.

"You've had two suspensions in the past two years, Mulford. I've overlooked quite a few of your escapades in the past, but I wish now that I hadn't. You've been uncooperative, vain, antagonistic to the public as well as to your fellow officers. And more than once you've made unjustified arrests...."

Alexander's interest seemed to trail off. He lit a cigarette and thoughtfully stared at the burning tip.

Mulford began to relax. The worst of it, he figured, was over. He knew the Captain, knew that the most he would get would be another suspension. Mulford managed to look contrite, but he was smiling slyly inside. He had managed to ride out the worst, and from here on in it would be simply a matter of time....

Then Sergeant Haslett took over. His tone was understanding, almost sympathetic.

"Officer Mulford, would you mind if I asked you a few questions?"

"No, sir."

"I'd like to know a bit more about the man who was injured."

"That was an accident, sir," Mulford said. He felt more at ease talking with Haslett. "You see, sir, the man was injured by the thrashing of the tail. The tail struck him and he—"

"What I want to know," Haslett interrupted gently, "is why you didn't go to the man's aid. As an officer—"

"At that point, sir, when the civilian was first struck by the whale, I was attacked by the driver from the Hercules Towing Company. He came charging at me and—"

"The injured man," Haslett reminded him. "I want to know if you went to his aid. That is, of course, after you'd finished brawling with the tow driver."

"Yes, sir, I did."

Sergeant Haslett smiled and nodded to himself. "And did you perform any first aid?"

"Ah—yes, sir. I did what little I could."

"You knelt at the man's side? That is, you were as close to him as you are to me?"

"Yes, sir."

"Fine. Now, Mulford, did Sergeant McLeod post the recent want sheets before you left the station?"

Mulford looked puzzled. "Yes, sir...."

"Did Sergeant McLeod make it a point, as usual, that all officers should pick up their hot sheets and check the flyers?"

Mulford nodded. He was beginning to sense a trap, but he had no idea what Haslett was driving at. He tried to think ahead, to overtake Haslett's lead and say something to put him one move ahead. The injured man had been on the want sheets—that much was obvious. But who the man was, and what he was wanted for, Mulford had no idea.

Captain Alexander said, "Mulford, does the name Bonniano suggest anything to you? Does it ring any bells? Think hard now. Bonniano. Joseph Bonniano...."

Mulford's face went dumb as the trap closed on him. He started to protest, but Haslett moved in again.

"That's right, Mulford. Joseph Bonniano. And all the while you were parading about, and wrapping yourself in a tangle of lies, Bonniano was sitting right in front of you, and carrying a loaded .45 automatic in his pocket. The very same weapon he used to murder Herbert Betseka last night."

"How does that strike you?" Alexander asked.

"Captain, I'm sorry, but—"

"Sorrow isn't enough," Alexander snapped. "Mulford, please accompany Officer Becker to his car." He turned to Becker. "Becker, relieve Mr. Mulford of his call-box key, identification card—"

"Wait a minute, Captain—"

"Consider yourself under arrest, Mr. Mulford! Officer Becker, relieve Mr. Mulford of his call-box key, identification card, badge, nightstick, handcuffs, and his weapon. Mulford, you may keep your book of rules and procedure until it's determined whether you're to remain in the department.

Officer Becker, the prisoner is in your custody."

Becker moved to put his hand on Mulford's arm, but Mulford jerked free.

Haslett reached out and lifted Mulford's weapon from his holster. He handed it to Becker, who dropped it into his hip pocket.

Mulford felt his empty holster.

Alexander and Haslett walked a few yards up the beach and looked toward the sea, their backs to Mulford.

Becker said, "Okay, Mulford, let's go."

"I can walk by myself."

"All right. Then let's go." He reached for Mulford's arm.

Mulford jumped back, his face wild. "I'm warning you, chief! You keep your filthy boogie hands to yourself!"

Becker smiled, but his eyes were cold. Without looking away, he raised his voice. "Captain? Mr. Mulford is now a civilian. Right?"

"Consider him as such," Alexnder replied. "He is under arrest and in your custody."

Becker stepped closer. "Okay now, chief, let's start marching."

"I told you to keep your black—"

Becker stepped in and swung, throwing his weight into the punch.

Mulford doubled over, gasping. Becker had hit him low. Mulford's face was purple, tears glittering in his eyes.

Becker grabbed Mulford's hands and spun him around. In a matter of seconds, Mulford was handcuffed and Becker was pushing him up the beach, prodding him with his stick, jabbing him in the small of his back.

Sergeant Haslett lit a cigarette, inhaled deeply, and shook his head sadly. He said, "You know, Captain, you'd think that a man like Mulford would know better than to try and resist arrest."

Alexander nodded. "You'd think so, wouldn't you...."

SEVEN

Dr. Robert Gilky was a big suntanned man in his late forties who looked like he was in his early thirties. His hair was black, crew-cut, and face square and rugged. He was dressed in faded blue jeans and a bright red sweater. He showed his credentials to the cop with the ginger-colored hair and bounded down the slope, a high-powered rifle slung over his shoulder.

Alexander and Haslett met Dr. Gilky near the whale. When they finished explaining the situation, Gilky loaded the rifle and the three men moved toward the whale. Gilky peered at the gaping eye sockets.

"Nasty business. Terrible."

Minutes before Gilky's arrival, Alex, the lifeguard, had approached the Captain to explain himself. Alexander referred him to Becker. When Alex reached the top of the slope he saw Mulford slumped in the rear of the squad car, cuffed to a bar on the back of the front seat.

"Who're you?" Becker asked.

"Alex Haluzar. I'm the lifeguard."

"Where were you all day, Alex?"

"Well, Mr. Mulford told me that he was—"

Becker laughed under his breath and opened his notebook to a fresh page....

On the beach, Dr. Gilky was saying. "You can't kill a whale like this, by shooting it in the eyes. To hit a vital spot you have to aim for the spine, say three to five feet behind the blowholes. The brain is far back on the skull. And it's protected by a thick bone plate." He hefted the rifle in his hands. "Sergeant, would you mind giving me a boost? I'll have to get on top of the whale."

"What if he starts flopping around again?"

"In that case, I'll have to jump for it. I'll keep the safety set until I'm ready to fire. The moment I get up there you'd better move back. If he starts to move I'll jump over the head and roll."

While Haslett prepared to hoist Gilky up, Earle Kavanaugh crept down from the dunes and aimed his camera, using the available light from the tow truck behind him. Since the girls had left, Earle had been creeping around unnoticed in the gloom, taking his pictures and fading back into the grass and the dunes.

So far, the story and pictures were, in his mind, already bought and paid for. And already, he had the money invested. A quick color nudie film. High-class. First cabin all the way. Earle's lovely girls. Girls parading in the raw—just as nature had intended. Earle Kavanaugh was going to make his million....

Dr. Gilky stood atop the whale, balancing himself, ready to jump if the whale happened to move suddenly. But the whale wasn't moving. Gilky crawled to the blowholes. He released the safety, raised the rifle, and fired five bullets in a tight pattern. He reset the safety and jumped clear.

The whale shuddered and his flukes made a slow half-swish, as if he were trying to gather strength for a final thrust. But the gesture halted in mid-air and the animal's entire body quivered. The flukes fell to the sand. Air hissed from the blowholes.

"He's dead," Gilky said.

The three men started back.

"He would have gone back by himself," Gilky said.

"How's that?"

"If your officer had just fired in the air. He would have awakened the whale and he would have gone back to the water by himself."

The last of the sirens had faded. Dr. Gilky had roared back toward town in his candied-apple-red Jaguar. No one from the press had arrived, and that, as Haslett had remarked before leaving, had been the only decent break they had had during the entire affair.

Directly after the killing of the whale, Earle had said good-bye to Riley and had left the scene, his precious film tucked safely in the inside pocket of his seedy sport coat. He walked down the path, tripod and camera slung over his shoulder, his alpine hat angled jauntily over one eye, Fred-Astaire style. For Earle Kavanaugh the day had been one of the best he had ever had.

Only the Hercules truck remained. One of the officers had ridden Mulford's horse back to the station. The towing lights lit the swaying reeds. The wind spun long sandy ribbons along the path. Briefly, as before, a light rain fell and then moved on. Jewel-like drops glittered on the cowling of the truck, quivering with the steady turning of the motor. The winch whined and growled as Riley worked the whale up the beach. The whale was moving slowly, jerkily, inch by inch. The big truck rocked on its chocks, moving back with each jerk of the cable.

Standing in the shallow trench of the whale's path, Fredric Langfield gazed up at the great yellow eye of the boom light.

Becky was waiting nearby, holding the wicker chair and straw basket.

Since arriving at the whale site, Becky had said very little. Earlier, she had felt, as usual, completely isolated from Fredric because of his high. But now, watching him, she felt, for the first time since coming to California, a gentle stirring of concern for him. She no longer felt like a partner in crime or a nursemaid.

Fredric was a sick man, incurable perhaps, but she knew that she was little better. She had to care about what was to happen to them, what was to happen during Fredric's night. She couldn't think of one legitimate stall for him not to meet his agent and August Losada. All Fredric needed was a quick shot, if he wanted it, and he would be able to swing with anything.

Becky would play the game with him all the way. Deceptive dodges and twists were unnecessary. She no longer envied Fredric his addiction, his ability to disappear at will. Because, after all, she had been trying to do the very same thing herself.

"Call me Ishmael...."

Fredric's voice rose in the wind. His cape whipped around his spare frame.

"Call me Ishmael.... Whenever I find myself growing grim about the mouth; whenever it is damp, drizzly November in my soul; whenever I find myself involuntarily pausing before coffin warehouses—'" he walked in the trench, following the slow passage of the dead whale "'—and bringing up the rear of every funeral I meet; and especially whenever my hypos get such an upper hand of me, that it requires a strong moral principle to prevent me from deliberately stepping into the—'"

"Fredric...."

The old actor turned to the soft voice, his eyes black and shining. He stepped from the trench and stood before his wife.

"You rarely call me by my name. Were you aware of that? I sounded quite good, didn't I? I wasn't hammy at all. I couldn't possibly be. All this—" his hand swept toward the whale "—is real. For once I saw a vision and I wasn't disappointed. Becky isn't your real name, is it? I forget what it is...."

"It's Beatrice."

"Beatrice. That's a lovely name. You see, I can remember all my lines save the real ones. You're very beautiful, Beatrice."

"We'd better leave," Becky said. "We don't want to be late meeting Mr. Losada."

He hesitated. "I almost forgot about that. Do you think I could pull it off—"

She put her fingertips to his lips, hushing him. "Yes," she said. "You can swing with anything now."

Riley released the lock-link and shook the hook free of the chain. He pulled the cable from under the flukes and dropped the cable on the sand. He lit a cigarette and leaned against the hide.

In the distance, dark against the white foam of the combers, he saw two figures walking north along the beach. Riley lit a cigarette and looked up at the sky, inhaling deep and relaxing. Before starting back up the slope he saw, near the water's edge, the tiny flare of a match. And for the first time since Mulford's arrest, he remembered that the girl's boy friend was still there.

Back at the truck, he pulled the winch handle, threw the gears into reverse, and rewound the cable. He picked up the chocks and climbed into the cab. He switched off the rear lights and shut off the gear. He lit two cigarettes and handed one to Karen Fornier, who was sitting quietly on the passenger side.

"We'll get a hamburger first," Riley said. "And three cups of coffee."

"How did you know—"

"I just watched your mind walk by."

When there was a break in the traffic, Riley gunned the diesel and rolled out onto the highway. As he drove, south toward Santa Monica, he began to sing, very softly, a badly garbled version of an old T. Texas Tyler number.

Hobart remained on the empty beach for a long while. He had watched the lights of the tow truck until he could see them no more. Then, smoking his last cigarette, he lifted the collar of his jacket and started walking north along the shore line, back to the motel.

Hobart chuckled softly in the dark.

Let the dumb bastard have her. She was a lousy piece of ass anyway....

The whale lay on its belly, its blasted eye sockets gazing at the distant sea. Tiny insects crawled and hopped from the bushes and swarmed over the unmoving hide. A gull wheeled overhead, silently, a winged ghost scrap, lowering, flapping, finally settling on the brow of the whale. The tide swept the sand, like frothy hissing white lace. The sandpipers came and raced the dark surf, and the gull clacked his orange beak in triumph and began to peck at the torn flesh around the eye of the whale.

THE END

Memories of My Father
By Belle Marko

Marko was born Marvin Leroy Schmoker on October 21 in Salinas 1933 and raised on a cattle ranch with his Brother, Kenn. They were both sent to St Vincent School for Boys in Marin County, California, when they were around 12 and 14, my dad being the younger. They lived down the road from Steinbeck and would hang out with him after school. This could be where they both got the writing bug. Kenn was a mystery writer and a surrealist painter.

Not sure how he ended up in North Beach, but he was probably around 19 or 20. Apparently he met my mom while he was bartending at "The Tin Angel" in Sausalito. He was working for drinks, my mom told me, and he was not even 21 yet.

I went to art school at CCAC and Michael McClure was my English teacher. He recognized my name and told some sordid tales about my dad in the Beatnik days, but all the stories were always about him doing something bad or... I don't know, not worthy or not right to share. Michael did however tell me that my dad coached Alan Ginsberg in some writing skills—they all hung around together.

Everyone knew him as Marko and at some point he decided to call himself Zekial Marko or pen name John Trinian.

At one point—I must have been around 7 or 8—he lived at the well know haven for artists, writers and outlaws, Gate 5. He was living in an abandoned school bus with no wheels for a while, then he shacked up with a girlfriend named Katrina in a gypsy boat with beaded curtains. He also lived with another gal on a tug boat tied up to the *San Rafael*, an old paddle wheel ferry. One night I was sleeping there and was awakened in the middle of the night to my dad dragging me out onto the rails on a skinny walkway to get me out of a fire. He had fallen asleep with a cigarette in his mouth and the mattress was on fire. He flung it out into the bay and I could see it still bobbing around smoldering as the sun came up on the bay.

One of the best things my dad ever did for me was to take me camping on the Yuba River. He was actually making friends with the ranger so he could live there for the summer at the camp ground. He was a scoundrel that way, always making friends with the people that he wanted something from.

Daytimes we would swim in the river and at night sometimes he would drive all the way to Reno to gamble. I was only a kid and had to find my way around and hustle for food on my own while he was in the casino till very late. Then we'd get in the old Ford Truck he called Lulu Bell Verde and drive all the way back to the campsite.

He was an amazing story teller and could mesmerize an audience at parties or he'd be a total menace and pee in the corner or make out with someone's wife.

One of my favorite stories about him concerns the MGM movie of *Once a Thief*. He plays the part of a junkie that ultimately hangs himself in his jail cell. The character's name is Luke. As he's being hauled into the LA County Jail he does a little jig and looks into the camera, playing the part so well with his shirt un-tucked.

The back story is that the scene was shot in the actual jail and my dad had begged the director to play the part. The director didn't want him to play the part as he was notorious for not showing up on set on time. Sure enough, the scene was rolling and my dad was nowhere to be found. The director was furious and had a stage hand run down the hall to find a payphone to call central casting to send another actor, and as he was passing cells, he hears: "pssst, hey! Get me outta here!" It was my dad in jail for real! He begged the jail to let him out, promising to get back in the cell after the scene was shot. So he was actually in jail for drugs and alcohol and mischief and was totally loaded in the scene, hence he was "playing the part" really well. You can see his pupils are totally pinned in the scene. Hilarious and tragic all at the same time.

He was popular and unreliable, his own worst enemy in many ways, getting in his own way with self-sabotage and isolation, depression and bouts of rage and horrible remorse. He was plagued with demons and eventually alienated his family and friends. He died a lonely man.

—San Anselmo, CA
November 2013